Praise for *Ryeport Redemption*

"Cribb writes very well, with a style reminiscent of historical novelists of a bygone era."

~ Foreword Reviews

"Thanks for taking me on a wonderful adventure, introducing me to interesting characters, allowing me to visit Ryeport and Nextwest and the Guiding Light Church, and providing me a mystery that kept me intrigued."

~ Lauretta Kraus

"Overall, this is an entertaining satisfying novel delivered by a talented storyteller."

~ Blueink Review

"Readers willing to undertake this daunting tome will be rewarded with an engaging adventurous tale."

~ Kirkus Reviews

VINEYARD
RIVER
WOODS
RIVER
POST
ERNIES COVE
CARTERS ROCK

QUARRY ROAD
EASTER VILLAGE
COACH ROAD.
COTTAGES.
CHURCH.
LANDING. — FISHING BOATS.
RIGGING DOCK.
COTTAGES
HARBOUR LIGHT
DRAGONS TAIL
ROCKENS COTTAGE.
RYEPORT

Published by
Hasmark Publishing
www.hasmarkpublishing.com

Disclaimer

This book is designed to provide information and motivation to our readers. It is sold with the understanding that the publisher is not engaged to render any type of psychological, legal, or any other kind of professional advice. The content of each article is the sole expression and opinion of its author, and not necessarily that of the publisher. No warranties or guarantees are expressed or implied by the publisher's choice to include any of the content in this volume. Neither the publisher nor the individual author(s) shall be liable for any physical, psychological, emotional, financial, or commercial damages, including, but not limited to, special, incidental, consequential or other damages. Our views and rights are the same: You are responsible for your own choices, actions, and results.

Permission should be addressed in writing to info@lescribb.com

Editor: Janet-Lynn Morrison
jjlmorrison@gmail.com

Cover & Book Design: Anne Karklins
anne@hasmarkpublishing.com

ISBN 13: 978-1-989756-63-8
ISBN 10: 1989756638

With much love and grateful hearts we dedicate this book to our parents, Les and Joyce Cribb.

This tale sprang from our Dad's ever active imagination. We watched over many years as finally with retirement, he had the time to use his gifts as a storyteller to create this wonderful, captivating adventure.

We are very proud of his achievement and delighted to see it in print despite the many challenges that were thrown into his path. But the greatest gift he left us was a legacy of love and laughter. All of his funny stories, funny hats, funny songs and funny faces that he entertained us with brought so much laughter. His love for, and fierce dedication to his family and every one of his "Papa Hugs" will be with us always. Our beautiful Mum, was right there through every celebration and every crisis. With her gentleness, eternal patience and quiet strength she was always our port in the storm and a "guiding light" to us all. We were well loved.

It is our hope in finishing this part of Dad's journey for him that the reader will have a chance to experience how wonderful it is to get lost in a good book.

Anne, Jackie, Lisa and David

TABLE OF CONTENTS

From the shore the villagers gathered to see the Seahorse off and the crew hurried to make her ready to sail. From his shop he too had been watching for her departure, but his initial enthusiasm that the arrival of the ship would mean new opportunities for he and Meg, was gone and was now replaced only with rage as he remembered the assault of the captain upon his new bride. "Good riddance", he thought, and then all went dark as the belaying pin struck him on the back of his head.

Now under cover in the bottom of the jolly boat Sailmaker was unable to move or call out as the sailors hurried to get him aboard the ship unnoticed. Slowly as he began to regain consciousness, he recognized what had happened. He had been shanghaied! He struggled to call out for help, hoping to be heard by his friends onshore but his voice was just a whisper and the ship had already moved past The Dragon's Tail.

He was now beyond help and at the mercy of the violent Captain Currie. He was also destined for a new and unexpected friendship, but one with unforeseen and terrifying power which was to change the lives of everyone he knew and loved.

Ryeport Harbour
From the author's sketchbook

CHAPTER 1

Sailmaker's friend-in-need

The intended purpose for the ships owned by 'The Friends of the Missionary Society' was to provide funds for their work and transport workers and supplies to their overseas missions. On this particular voyage, The Seahorse was to exchange two priests in Cuba. The outgoing pair, Tobias Clyde and George Wilson, were young and enthusiastic, whereas the returning priests were older men coming home to retire in England. Whilst in Havana, the ship would also deliver farming equipment and pickup supplies of mahogany, tobacco, cocoa, and rice as arranged by the society's agents at that port. Other miscellaneous cargo was sometimes carried for a fee as opportunities presented themselves. On this trip, that miscellaneous cargo had been materials for the new church in Ryeport.

The ship's last outbound port of call, on this occasion, was to be Port-au-Prince, Haiti, where they were scheduled to take on board a cargo of sugar and rum. One of the privileges enjoyed by captains of these vessels was the right to carry a limited amount of cargo for their own personal gain, free of freight charges. On this occasion, Captain Currie intended to purchase a quantity of rum. That cargo would bring him a good return on resale in London. The ship had enjoyed good weather and made good speed on the outbound voyage. The main entertainment on board was Brannigan, the fiddler. Brannigan would couch his fiddle in the crook of his left arm rather than tucked under his chin so that his raucous voice could 'sing' the words to his shanties and ribald ditties as he played.

One other break in the boredom was the frequent 'men under punishment parade' and the inevitable rigging of the grating on which the offenders were lashed. However, it seemed that the same luckless individuals were repeatedly chosen for punishment by the bullying officers, and punishment was always administered Navy fashion in the presence of the ship's company. Not all punishment was of the corporal nature; sometimes it was a reduction or loss of rations, mostly rum. Sailmaker was a frequent recipient of all forms of punishment. On the captain's instructions, he was to be punished for any offence, real or imagined. Had it not been for the presence of the missionaries, Sailmaker's punishment would have been deadly. However, much to the captain's annoyance, the reverends, Clyde and Wilson, always made their presence very obvious and not only witnessed but openly recorded all offences and the punishment meted out. The crew were, therefore, treated more leniently than they otherwise might have been.

However, the vindictive captain's intentions regarding Sailmaker hadn't changed. He had no intention of allowing him to return safely to England. He not only wanted him dead but also wanted to enjoy his death. He had thought that his best opportunity might present itself on the journey home. But now he was concerned that the two returning missionary priests might prove as obstructive as Clyde and Wilson by continuing the scrupulous recording of his punishments. So, Currie decided to change tactics. He had never allowed Sailmaker shore leave because of the risk of his jumping ship. Now though, Currie decided that it would better suit his purpose to allow him time ashore in Port-au-Prince. He summoned the cook to a quiet spot on the quarterdeck. "Cook, I intend to give Sailmaker the opportunity to jump ship," he told him. "I shall include him in the second watch ashore in Port-au-Prince. But I want you to go ashore with the first watch and hire some local thugs to kill Sailmaker. You are to remain ashore long enough to point him out to your hired thugs; then you must watch and make sure the deed is done before you pay them off. Report back to me right away. Understood?" The cook grinned, revealing an ugly assortment of teeth stained by chewing tobacco. "Sure, I understand. Good riddance to bad rubbish I say." He knuckled his forehead as he took the bag of coins from Currie.

Sailmaker was surprised but relieved when he learned he was to be allowed ashore. As the captain expected, he had every intention of allowing The Seahorse to leave Haiti without him. When The Seahorse moored alongside, she was the only ocean-going vessel in the harbour. Once ashore, Sailmaker tried to discover what other such vessels were expected there in the near future. He was hoping to sign aboard a ship returning to England as crew. However, no such ships were expected in the near future. There was always the possibility of unexpected arrivals, of course, but it looked as though he would have to survive ashore for an undetermined amount of time if The Seahorse were to leave without him. He headed away from the docks towards the centre of the town, unsure of what to do. He had very little money, and the prospect of jumping ship here was growing less attractive all the time. "Perhaps I could find work ashore," he muttered. "I'll need money for food and shelter until a berth is available."

He was suddenly aware of scuffling noises behind him. He turned and came face to face with a group of men armed with heavy sticks. Frantically, he looked for an avenue of escape, and for a moment, he thought he might get some help as he caught a glimpse of the cook peering from behind some stacked crates across the street. Then one of the thugs delivered the first blow. After that, Sailmaker, unarmed and outnumbered, was quickly knocked to the ground. His shouts for help brought no response, and his senses were reeling as he struggled to protect his head with his battered arms and hands. This, he knew, was not just a robbery. He was unlikely to survive this attack. Then just when all seemed lost, he heard a shout quickly followed by a thud and a scream of pain, and one of the thugs dropped beside him like a felled tree. Another shout and another of his attackers stumbled and fell. The remaining two, surprised and shaken, backed away.

A strong arm reached down and helped Sailmaker to his feet. That arm was attached to an imposing black man over six feet tall. "Now the odds are even!" said the owner of the helping hand as he gave Sailmaker the stick dropped by the unconscious thug. "Why don't you boys try us on now?" He stepped over the fallen thug and advanced towards the remaining pair, his heavy club poised in a threatening manner. The remaining thugs backed up, then turned tail and fled. Sailmaker's saviour turned towards him with a smile. "It seems you're not too popular around here, English." Sailmaker's rescuer was still smiling as he examined Sailmaker's injuries and tried to dust him off. "Are you alright?"

"Aye. Thanks to you! But I'll have a few more cuts and bruises to nurse for a while. Ouch! And a limp I didn't need. Many thanks. You sure know how to use that stick."

"What was that all about?"

"I honestly don't know. They jumped me for no reason," Sailmaker said, although he certainly had reason to suspect the captain may have been behind it.

One of the men felled by the newcomer's club was showing signs of recovery. Sailmaker's new friend dragged the man to his feet. "Let's find out," he said. "This fellow seemed to be their leader." He waved his club in the man's face. "I'm sure he'd be happy to tell us why they picked on you." "That bloke over there paid us," gasped the frightened thug as he pointed in the direction of the cook's hiding place. "He wanted this bloke dead," he said indicating Sailmaker with his free arm. That caused Sailmaker to remember his earlier sighting of the cook, and ignoring the pain in his right knee, he took off at a run. The cook bolted from his hiding place, but despite his limp, Sailmaker soon caught him and dragged him back to his new friend. Still, under threat of the black man's stick, the thug identified the cook as the man that hired them to kill Sailmaker. "'e's the one who paid us. 'alf down. The rest when this bloke's dead." Again, he indicated Sailmaker.

"What shall I do with this one?" Sailmaker's rescuer asked, indicating the frightened thug.

"Let him go. But let's get the blood money back first! We've got the one we need right here," responded Sailmaker pulling the cook closer. The black man took the hastily proffered cash from the thug, gave him a goodbye cuff with his club and allowed him to run off. "My name's Latour," he said. "Paul Latour. What's yours?" The two men shook hands. "Sailmaker. I'm crew on The Seahorse, the ship tied up at the dock. This here villain is our ship's cook." He turned to face his frightened captive. "Now, Cookie, I want to know why you set those thugs on me. And you'd better speak up, or you will meet with the same fate you intended for me." The cook looked petrified, but his fear of the captain was stronger. Sailmaker nodded to Latour. "May I borrow your club for a few minutes, friend? I dropped mine, chasing after this bloke." Latour smiled and threw him the club. Sailmaker deftly caught it, pushed the cook to arm's length, then swiftly rapped him in the crotch with the club. Latour winced as the cook screamed and fell to the ground holding his injured privates. "Speak up," said the grim looking Sailmaker. "I'm not prepared to wait very long. I owe you much more than one little tap for all the punishment your lies have cost me onboard. And now you were paying to have me murdered. I think I'm entitled to an explanation." However, that one 'little tap' proved to be all the persuasion that the cook needed to confess the captain's plot and his part in it. He pleaded for mercy, saying that the captain had threatened him with a hundred lashes if he failed in this assignment.

Latour listened thoughtfully to the cook's confession and then offered to have some local friends lock the cook up until after The Seahorse sailed. "I don't imagine you'd want him reporting his failure back to your captain, would you?" he asked Sailmaker. "Well, I hadn't really intended to return onboard," answered Sailmaker. "I knew the captain wanted me dead, but I'm sure he intended to have me killed on the ship. I was going to allow The Seahorse to sail without me, hoping to get a berth on another ship to get me back to England."

"Good luck!" Latour said despairingly. "I've been trying to get off this island for months. The only ships expected for the next few weeks are the ones plying local trade between the islands. Even if an ocean-going ship did arrive unexpectedly, I doubt you could get passage. The senior missionary here has been trying to get me a berth for months." An hour later, with the cook safely locked away in a warehouse cage, Latour and Sailmaker were enjoying a meal in a tavern, using some of the blood money taken from the thug and cook. Latour was explaining his desperate need for two berths to England. "I need passage for myself and my fourteen-year-old. Had it not been for that, I would avoid this area after dark. But we have to get away from Haiti. We desperately need to get to England. If it's not possible to get there directly, any European port will do. From there I would stand a better chance of getting us to London."

Sailmaker was thoughtful for a while before speaking; he said. "Just how badly do you need passage?"

"Truthfully, it's a matter of life and death."

"Are you running from the authorities?"

"What authorities?" said Latour derisively. "You carry your own authority here." He nodded towards the club he had wielded so effectively on Sailmaker's behalf. "No, we're running from the Bokors, the black magic priests. I ran afoul of them about 16 years ago after they killed my father. They set a maddened dog on me. It nearly tore me to pieces. Father Gooding, the head of the local mission, arrived just in time to kill the dog and save me. He then took me back to the mission, where he and his daughter nursed me back to health. In the months that followed, Father Gooding's daughter

Louise had spent endless days and nights caring for me although it seemed certain that I would die from the infection caused by the dog bites. I had lost a lot of blood. Later, I converted to Christianity, and I've worked at the mission ever since. Louise and I fell in love and were married 15 years ago. Our only child was born about a year later. But the Bokors that set the dog on me were determined to drive the missionaries off the island. They saw the mission as an obstacle to their plans to control the whole area. They also attacked the regular voodoo priests, the healers. My father was one of those healers that they killed. Over the past 10 years, the Bokors have got stronger and more aggressive. It was just over a year ago when my wife died from eating poisoned fruit. My wife bought that fruit for all of us at the mission, but Louise ate some on the way home. Had it not been for that, the whole mission might have been poisoned. The fruit seller was new in the area and has never been seen again." He lowered his head as he recalled the painful memory.

"Then the Bokors set two of their maddened dogs on Father Gooding. We weren't able to save him. He had lost a lot of blood, and the infections caused by his injuries did the rest. The Bokors want our child, you see. They believe that if they had the Christian child of a missionary priest and raised it in their black ways, they could create a very powerful black magic priest. But when they fail to 'turn' someone, they sacrifice them at one of their barbaric rituals.

"A few weeks before Father Gooding died, he wrote a letter to his friend, a bishop in London. He told me that letter would guarantee safety for my child and work for me. Provided I could get to the bishop that is. But each new day is dangerous for us and getting worse as the Bokors grow more daring. The Christian priests are losing ground. The young man that replaced Father Gooding is a good man but inexperienced in these matters. He won't be able to protect us as well as my wife's father did. I'm really frightened for my child."

Sailmaker fixed his eyes on Latour's. "Can you cook?"

"Can I cook? Have you not been listening?" Latour straightened up. Angrily, he asked, "Why ask me about cooking when I'm telling you I am concerned for my child's safety? My child is my only concern now."

Sailmaker raised a hand causing Latour to pause. "Latour, I was thinking: The Seahorse is going to need a cook, right?" He raised his eyebrows and one hand as he asked the question. "Your friends have their cook locked up. I believe that the best chance you have of getting away from Haiti might be as a cook aboard The Seahorse." Latour's anger faded when he realised that Sailmaker's seemingly off-topic question was really an attempt to solve his problem. "What makes you think that I'd get taken on? And don't forget my child."

"Well, The Seahorse has no spare crew. The captain's a hard man. The smaller the crew, the lower his expenses, and the lower his expenses, the more money he gets to keep from the operating costs of the ship. Usually, if the cook jumped ship or died on the voyage, the captain would assign a member of the crew to cook's duties. But we have barely enough men to work ship. If you can cook, reasonable like, I think he might sign you on."

"What about my child?"

"Cabin boy. I'm sure the cap'n would like to be waited on, especially if it doesn't cost him anything."

Latour lowered his head and sat quietly for a few seconds reflecting on the unexpected suggestion. Then he said, "I'm sure you are familiar with the fate of cabin boys on ships that have been at sea for a while. Sailors have a really bad reputation when it comes to moral values. Cabin boys are often abused by some very evil characters."

Sailmaker leaned across the table and said, "The Seahorse has an unusual advantage there. The galley is in a deckhouse. The cook's bunk is also in the galley. I'm sure you could make room for a young boy. You could even make it a condition of signing on. Don't forget if you have to, you could offer your services free in exchange for your passage. As for some rum sodden lout laying hands on your lad," Sailmaker shrugged. "You're a big man, and I've seen you handle people in a fight. They wouldn't want to upset you. Now can you cook?"

Latour looked disgruntled. "Yeah, I can cook. That became my main job at the mission once my freedom to leave the compound was restricted. My wife taught me; she was English, so she taught me English style. She also taught me to read and write. I did a lot of reading. I love books, English or French, any kind of learning actually, even recipe books." Sailmaker was quiet, obviously thinking. When he looked up again, he said, "No one must know that we are friends or that you helped me tonight. If the cap'n suspects anything like that, you won't stand a chance. In fact, your chances might be better if he thought we were enemies. Maybe I will tell him I was attacked on shore and thought you might be one of those that set about me. I've got enough bruises to prove I was in a fight." Latour was silent for a while. "Is there anybody here in this tavern from your ship?" Sailmaker looked around discretely. "No. This is farther inland than they would normally go. The only reason I'm this far inland is because you brought me here to lock up the cook. Normally the crew would stop at the closest tavern to the ship. The first place they could find drink and women."

"So, the cap'n has a real dislike for you." Latour was looking Sailmaker straight in the eye. "Why's that?" So, Sailmaker told Latour of the incident at The Harbour Light and how he was shanghaied after rescuing his young wife away from the hands of the drunken captain. "He's been trying to kill me ever since. My strongest hope lies with the two missionaries we are taking back to England. I'm hoping they will try to protect me as those on the outbound journey did. "Actually, they promised to tell the returning priests about my situation and ask them to help me. So, I'm hoping that I'll survive the natural dangers of working in the foretop, as well as his unjust punishments, and make it home to my wife and friends."

Latour was thoughtful for a while before saying: "It looks as though I'd be asking for trouble to hitch up with you. You seem like a decent man, but I don't know you. And my first concern has to be my child's safety. You've been suggesting 'cook and cabin boy.' Do you really think I could keep my child safe amongst that crew?" Latour was staring him down and looking very tense. Sailmaker, recognising the validity of his new friend's concern, said, "Keep him in the galley. Neither of you will have to sleep in the fo'c'sle. There are some good men on board. We'll all look out for the lad, and I'll help as best I can. We can watch each other's backs while we're on board."

Latour took a deep breath. "It seems that I'm caught between two evils. I know we won't be safe here for much longer. But I don't know if what you're suggesting will be much safer. Come." He stood up. "Let's get you back to the dock. Provided you've decided to go back on board, that is. Personally, I think you would be safer to lay low here and wait for a different ship. If you wish, you could take refuge at the mission with us until a suitable berth opens up." Sailmaker looked surprised. "That's a very kind offer. Thank you. But that wouldn't solve your problem, would it? You saved my life tonight, and I would like to repay that debt. Also, I'm anxious to get home as soon as possible. Right now, The Seahorse seems to be my only chance for that. Let's decide on how you should approach the captain."

. . .

It had been several months since The Seahorse had left Ryeport, and with the understandable exception of Meg, the village had finally adapted to the loss of Sailmaker. Her parents wanted her to move back into the inn, but she declined, still hoping that Sailmaker would return. When he did, she intended to be there waiting for him in the home they were building for themselves.

The Guiding Light Church was growing very well and quickly. Mason had a large and busy crew on the job, and the walls were almost at ceiling height. The frame for the giant crucifix window had already been installed in the seaward wall, and the bottom section of the cross had already been fitted with its first thick glass panels.

Westerhof attended many of the Sunday services in Ryeport. He had been so impressed by the project that he had raised some extra funds from his wealthy friends, and that money had allowed Gerry to hire extra masons to speed the work along. The fine stone, rescued from the aborted mansion outside Southampton, had been utilised just as it had been cut to frame the windows and doors for that building. That finely dressed stone had also been utilised to frame the corners of the church. Stone that had been taken from the cliff face had been shaped for the walls between the framing. A few relatively minor adjustments had been made to suit altered dimensions, and some carving had been needed to match the free stone from Southampton, but Mason had been able to keep the character and style consistent throughout the building. He was well pleased with the very attractive result, and it showed.

One fringe benefit was a surplus of both materials and money left over from the job. "There's enough money and material left over to extend and refurbish the disused cottage that we used to store Albright's lighting equipment, Roddy. It will make a very attractive 'vicarage' once we've finished with it. It's a lot closer to the new church than your present home, and I will make it comfortable enough to assure your parents that you are not living in poverty. Then, provided you don't object, my friend, I'll refurbish your present cottage. Because, Roddy, I'd like to make that my new home. Bishop West is coming around, you know; he's getting caught up in the enthusiasm. I already have his approval regarding your new vicarage and also his consent for me to occupy your old cottage. I'll pay for any alterations there myself, of course."

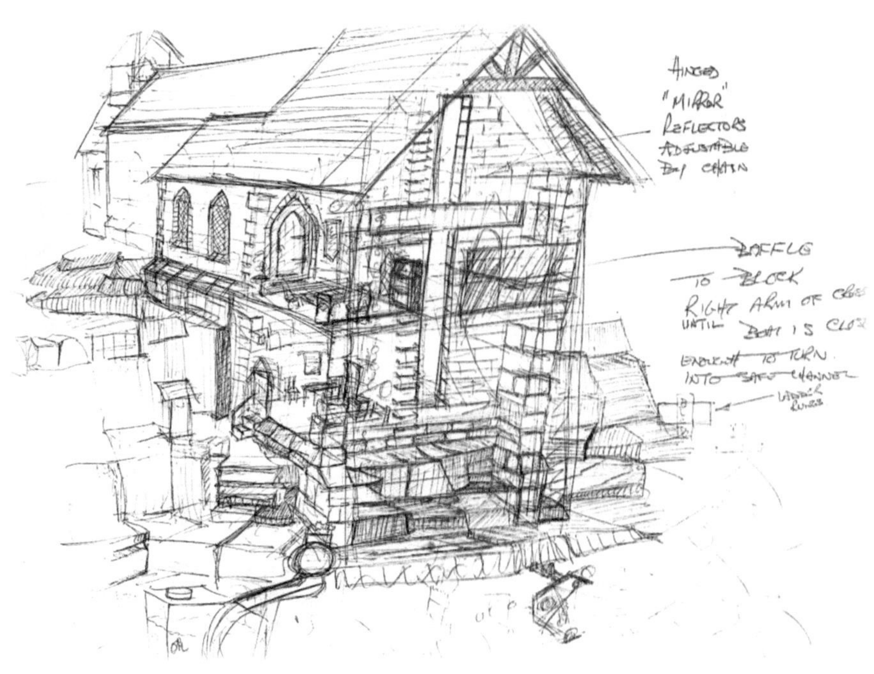

From the author's sketchbook

Roddy was quite moved. He realised that, despite all its trials and tribulations, his new friendships had made life more meaningful than he'd ever known before. Gerry and he had become very close friends and spent many an evening together, playing cards, sampling wine and enjoying Emily Rooken's tasty meals. As a housekeeper, Emily was proving a good substitute for Bessie, and although Roddy still missed Bessie's tormenting humour, he realised that he was fortunate indeed to have Emily as a replacement. There was a small side benefit resulting from Emily's new job as his housekeeper. Her husband was now in regular attendance at church and actually helped with some of the smaller chores there. When Roddy expressed his surprise at this change to Emily, she smiled and said, "'e knows what side 'is bread's buttered on, Father. I told 'im, 'I've supported you all these months, Jamie Rooken; now it's your turn to support me.' 'e soon fell in line. Times are still tough, Father, but Mr. Mason says I can look after 'is place too when 'e moves down 'ere. That'll 'elp."

Bessie's pie and preserves route had grown so well that they were able to afford a horse and wagon of their own. The vicar suspected that some of the money required for that purchase may have come from the proceeds of the secret cupboard. If so, it was money well spent. It also freed up his wagon and Slondosh for his own more liberal use. It was on one of Roddy's later visits to Pru's cottage that they decided to break their housebound routine and spend a couple of days in the small town of Mitchelhurst. This would allow Roddy to escape his clerical garb whilst they both enjoyed a couple of days on their own in a town where they would be strangers. Roddy looked very smart in Grandfather Whatson's clothes, and he had booked a room at a quiet inn on the outskirts of the town; he and Pru were looking forward to some quiet, uninterrupted time together. They were enjoying an after-dinner glass of wine in the dining room when a large and cheerful looking man breezed in. Constable Joshua Cooper spotted them and immediately crossed to their table.

"Well, well! Prudence, my dear! What a pleasant surprise." His healthy features lit up with a smile of genuine pleasure, and he bent and gave Prudence a peck on the cheek. "Please forgive my interruption, my dear. It's been such a long time since I've seen you." Then the constable turned to face Roddy, studying his face so intently that the vicar felt that the man's penetrating stare was examining his darkest secrets and drawing them from his mind. "Please forgive me, Sir," said the constable. "It was such a pleasant surprise to see Miss Prudence that I quite forgot my manners." A trace of a smile played at the corners of his mouth as his study of the vicar's face continued. "When I first spotted you, Prudence," he said giving her just a quick glance, "I thought that you were here with a younger version of your grandfather. Not only was Obidiah resurrected, but he had obviously discovered the fountain of youth. Quite a shock I can tell you. You, Sir, look very much like a younger version of my old friend, Obidiah Whatson. And you even share his taste in clothes. Permit me to introduce myself." He extended his hand to Roddy: "Constable Joshua Cooper, Sir. Your servant. Miss Prudence and I are old friends. I watched her grow up, in fact. I was a close friend of Obidiah's for many years. Surely, you must be related, Sir? To Obidiah, I mean. The likeness is quite strong."

Roddy was completely shaken. In a situation where he thought his disguise would go unnoticed, he was suddenly challenged by no less an authority than the constable. He rose and shook the constable's hand. "I am pleased to meet you, Sir," he responded. His mind whirled as he struggled for an acceptable response. "No, Sir. I am not related. I'm afraid...." Prudence quickly interceded. "Uncle Joshua, may I introduce my friend, Reverend Roddy McDowd, the vicar of Ryeport. We have been working together on projects for his village and have become very good friends. I suggested to Roddy that he should escape from Ryeport for a while. He has been working so tirelessly on the new church that he conceived for the village that I feared he would damage his health. Grandfather had left some of his clothes with me for some minor repairs. So, I suggested that Roddy borrow them and that we find a quiet little inn where we could dine incognito. Somewhere where no one would know us or recognise that he was a vicar." She laughed a sound so full of genuine amusement that it attracted the attention of other diners. "It is just our luck to have you turn up at that very inn. You are quite impossible, Uncle Joshua. I pity the poor criminals."

Cooper smiled. "I'm sorry if I spoiled your little escape plans my dear. It wasn't intentional, I assure you." Turning to Roddy, he said, "As for you, Sir, I've heard nothing but good things about you. My friend Westerhof never stops talking about your efforts on behalf of your village. You've created quite a stir amongst the congregation in Nextwest, let alone Ryeport. I don't wonder that you need a break. I am also a customer of your recent housekeeper, Bessie Drew, a most remarkable woman. She too is always singing your praises. Her business is doing very well, I understand. That was another instigation of yours, she told me. Then, of course, there is Marie: Bessie's sister and partner. She is co-habiting with Fletcher, who used to be the groom at the Nextwest Church. He too is a man I've known for many years and his father before him. You know Fletcher, of course."

"Yes," responded Roddy. "I have met Fletcher. I understand that he is a good man, although personally, I have just a passing acquaintance with him."

"Yes, indeed, a good man. He and Marie are living together, as you know. But she has agreed to marry him. They've asked me to give the bride away. You will already be aware of that though since you will be tying the knot, I mean." Roddy looked surprised. "No, Sir. I had no knowledge of that." Cooper clapped a hand over his mouth. "My God! I've put my big foot in my mouth again. I thought you had already been approached, Sir." He looked embarrassed. Prudence laughed. "No problem, Uncle Joshua. We never heard a word of this from you. Remember, we were never here! When Marie or Fletcher approach Roddy, I'm sure he will be very pleasantly surprised." She laughed again as the normally self-assured Cooper shifted from one foot to the other obviously uncomfortable.

"Thank you, Sir. I do appreciate your discretion. You do know, of course, that Fletcher and Marie now live above the carpenter's shop where the previous owner murdered Obidiah's butler, Goodman?" Roddy nodded, and Cooper continued. "Fletch' gave notice at the church recently. He now operates as a handyman in town. He's not the craftsman that his father was, but he is a hard worker and has other qualities that make up for his lack of fine carpentry skills."

"Yes. I did know about the murder," said Roddy. "Something to do with a smuggler's quarrel I understand."

"Yes, a very strange affair that. It still puzzles the doctor. He said that his training and experience suggested that Goodman had been dead for some hours when he was found on top of Godfrey. He was unable to explain his suspicions. Never will now, of course. It truly was a strange affair. Goodman was stabbed twice with a long-handled turning chisel, you know. That was another puzzle since Godfrey always carried a knife at his belt. He actually had to be restrained from using that weapon earlier that same night at The Coach and Horses. Makes you wonder what a drunk would be doing, choosing an alternative weapon when the one he habitually wore was still in its sheath. Anyway, the smuggling hereabouts was dealt quite a blow that night, with both its chief organiser and most likely replacement dead. It broke the operating chain, you see."

"So that has put an end to all the smuggling hereabouts then?" Roddy queried.

"Oh, I doubt that. Someone will come along to forge new links to reconnect that chain, I imagine. The boat's crews are still around and anxiously waiting for a wake-up-call, I'm sure. Then there's the other end of the matter the financing. There are always people willing to finance a profitable enterprise for a share of the proceeds. Like trees in the forest, I always say. One tree dies, but two or three other seedlings are waiting for a chance to take its place. Yes, I'm sure someone will come along to repair the chain. Then, we'll be off again hunting for the new smugglers.

"Smuggling is an illegal trade, of course, but, as I'm sure you know, it's a well-tolerated business hereabouts. Unfortunately, lots of people in the county depend on it to sustain their families. Illegal, it may be and impossible to condone, yet even when we catch the scoundrels, it's hard to get a conviction with our local jurors. Too many of their friends and relatives are involved, I suspect. Many of the jurors could be secret traders too. Judges too, some say." He laughed. "Run with the fox, and hunt with the hounds as the saying goes. Well, I shall leave you two young people to enjoy the rest of your 'uninterrupted' evening. It has been a real pleasure to meet you, Reverend. I would like to have a chat with you again sometime. Maybe, after your service one Sunday, might we possibly be able to have lunch together? I could use your advice on a rather delicate matter."

"Certainly, Constable. That would be my pleasure. Does this need to be a private meeting, or can Prudence and my friend Gerry Mason attend? I had already planned lunch with them for this Sunday."

"That would be fine, Father. I look forward to it. Perhaps five minutes in private after lunch if that's convenient. Well, I'll bid you both a good night, and once again, my apologies for the interruption. It was lovely to see you again, my dear." He bent and gave Prudence another kiss on the cheek before retiring to a distant table. Roddy heaved a sigh. "That was an unbelievable coincidence, Pru. Who would have thought that we would have run into the constable of all people? Every time I wear these clothes, I'm found out. I feel as though I'm wearing a billboard labelled 'imposter.'"

Prudence gave him a big smile, then giggled. "I know. I was just as shocked as you at first. The constable and Grandfather were close friends. He was always at the house on Pleasant Road. Until Grandfather remarried, that is. Uncle Joshua didn't approve of that marriage any more than I did. His visits became fewer and fewer. Eventually, he and Grandfather's new wife had some unresolved differences, and he never visited Grandfather's house after that. I was introduced to the constable at a very young age and, as is practice, I was told to call him Uncle...Uncle Joshua. He is a hard man in some ways but very fair and generous. I wonder what he needs your advice on though. That's a mystery. But Roddy, how is it that, despite all our planning, none of us remembered that Godfrey always carried a knife."

Roddy looked concerned. "I must admit I got very nervous when he spoke about Goodman and Godfrey. So, the doctor knew that there was something unnatural about that situation. We were lucky to get away with that, Pru. If the evening had been warm and dry, the result might have been danger-ously different." The rest of their evening passed pleasantly and without further incident, but Roddy discretely cancelled their room, and they left for Nextwest at the same time as the constable. The two vehicles parted company at the road leading to Pru's cottage, hopefully leaving the constable with the impression that Roddy was dropping her home before leaving for Ryeport. But the thought of the upcoming 'private' discussion with the constable weighed heavily on Roddy's mind.

• • •

In Haiti, The Seahorse was ready to sail. All hands were to be aboard before the start of the middle watch 12 midnight. Captain Currie was pacing the quarterdeck, waiting anxiously for the cook to bring him the news that Sailmaker was dead.

Latour had agreed that Sailmaker was to board first, complaining about the mugging that he'd received ashore. That and his lack of funds were to provide credibility for his return to the ship. In truth though, he was now much better off, having relieved the cook of the money that was intended to pay for his murder. He had insisted that Latour carry all of that money with him and, if necessary, use it to buy passage on The Seahorse. If Latour was unable to buy passage, he would try for a position as crew. The only position open, of course, would be that of ship's cook, although he should not be aware of that. It was also the only position he could accept because he would not allow his son to sleep in the fo'c'sle with the rest of the crew. If

Latour was unable to arrange either passage or the cook's job, it was agreed that Sailmaker would slip over the side and swim ashore. In that event, he would accept Latour's offer to stay at the mission until they could all find another ship to England.

When Sailmaker went aboard, Captain Currie stared at him in angry disbelief. "Well, Sailmaker, I'm surprised to see you here. I thought you didn't like our little ship. I was hoping to be rid of you."

"Well, you were right, Captain. This is no place for a stranger to be alone. I was mugged shortly after I got ashore. Luckily, some local people drove the thugs off, or I'm sure they would have killed me. It seems like The Seahorse is the lesser of the two evils."

"Well, you make sure you are ready for the middle watch. I don't want you complaining that you're not fit to stand duty, or I'll put you ashore for good."

"Aye, aye, Captain," said Sailmaker and headed for the fo'c'sle. The captain called after him. "Sailmaker!"

"Yes, Sir."

"Now that you are aboard, the only crewman remaining ashore is the cook. Have you seen him?"

"No, Sir. Wasn't he on the first watch ashore?"

"That he was."

"Maybe he ran into the same thugs that I did. They were an ugly bunch. I've got a couple of damaged ribs, a limp and a badly cut and bruised noggin. And I got off lucky." One of the missionaries arrived on deck just in time to hear Sailmaker's remarks. "Let's have a look at you, lad. Perhaps I can fix you up. I'm pretty good at this sort of needlework when required. I've had lots of practice."

"Thank you kindly, Sir. I have tried to clean it myself, but it's hard to see the back of my head."

"Man approaching, Sir!" called the watchman. "Too big to be the cook, and 'e's got a sprog with 'im." The captain went to the gangway and confronted Latour at the ship's side. "What do you want?" he demanded.

"I was hoping to book passage to England, Sir, for myself and my son. We have urgent personal business in England and need passage desperately. I understand there are no more ships due for quite a while now, and ours is a very urgent matter."

"We have no vacancy for passengers. Be off with you."

"Sir, this really is an urgent matter. It's truly a matter of life or death. I have money to pay for my own and my son's passage. Surely, you can find space for two people. It doesn't have to be a cabin. A corner of the hold would do."

"No. I have no room for more passengers and a minimum sized crew. In these circumstances, I'll not accept more responsibility. Besides, I don't know you. You could be a fugitive from the law for all I know. That's my last word on the matter."

"You said you had a minimum crew, Sir. I'm an able man, and I can read and write. I'd be willing to work our passage to England. I'm not a fugitive from any law. I'm the cook from the local Christian mission."

"No. Be off with you." Currie turned his back on Latour and his boy. The missionary, who had offered to help Sailmaker with his wounds, had heard this exchange and walked to the gangway wanting a closer look at Latour. "Are you Paul Latour?" he asked.

"Yes, Sir. How do you know my name?"

"I'm Reverend Palmer from the mission in Havana. My colleague and I are returning to England. As I'm sure you know, we missionaries keep each other informed of our work and lives in the islands. You were the husband of Reverend Gooding's late daughter were you not?"

"Yes, Sir. And this is our child."

Palmer turned to Currie. "Captain, this is a man of good repute and the son-in-law of a missionary to boot. Surely, you could find some accommodation for these good people aboard a missionary ship. I have personal knowledge of this man and would certainly vouch for him." Captain Currie was getting angrier by the minute. He was infuriated by having his passenger priest question his decisions, but he would take no more despite being at the mercy of the Missionary Society as far as renewing his contract was concerned. "I have given my answer, Sir. I alone am responsible for the safe operation of this vessel, and I will make all decisions." Palmer wasn't giving up that easily. "If it will help, I am prepared to give up my cabin and share with my colleague."

"I have already given my answer, Sir. good night to you." Currie turned on his heel. "Mr. Ruddock. Secure the gangway if you please and advise me if the cook makes an appearance."

"Aye, Sir." Palmer looked at Sailmaker and shook his head. "That's a good man we're leaving ashore. I know the mission has been having trouble with the local, black magic witch doctors, and I fear for this man's safety and that of his child. Come to my cabin so that I can look at this head wound in a better light, young man." They went aft, as Latour and his son retired as far as a dockside shed where they sat on some crates. "It's dangerous to walk these streets after dark," Latour said to his youngster. "We'll wait until daylight before returning to the mission." Sailmaker would now have to find his way ashore before the ship sailed so that Latour would wait for him, and they could return to the mission together. The Latours were still dozing peacefully there when the morning watch came on deck complaining that they'd had no proper meal. Hard tack and a piece of cheese was all they were given. Ruddock went to the captain's cabin. "Beggin' ye pardon, Sir. The crew's upset about their food rations, Sir. No sign of the cook at all. Did you want me to send a party ashore to look for 'im, or should I assign cook's duties, Sir?"

Currie was furious as he dressed. "Damn the bloody cook. What could have happened to him? Assign Sailmaker to cook's duties for now. He may not be fit to go aloft. We'll sort out a permanent arrangement later."

"Beggin' yer pardon, Sir, but I really need Sailmaker in the foretop. Even injured, 'e's still the best, 'and we've got to go aloft. Brannigan's my next best, an' 'e's sick as a dog, Sir. Too much drink last night. Losin' me best two 'ands up there leaves me in an awful pickle." Currie stomped out on deck and was looking amongst the crew for another man to assign to cook's duties when he spotted Latour and his child sleeping on the crates outside the shed. "You there!" he called. No response. They were sleeping too soundly. "Mr. Ruddock, tell that black man I want a word with him." Latour and his child were soon standing in front of the captain.

"I've been reconsidering your plight, my man," he said to Latour. And, in view of the good recommendation given to you by Reverend Palmer, I thought I might be able to offer you a position aboard The Seahorse as a cook. I believe I heard you say that you were employed as a cook at the mission. Is that correct?"

"Yes, Sir. I've done most of the cooking there for the past several years."

"I see. Now, what about your son? How will he work his passage?"

"Well, he could certainly help me, Sir, and serve your meals, clean your cabin too if you like. He doesn't eat much, Sir. It won't cost much to feed him. Or I can pay for his food and passage if you wish."

"Very well then!" Turning to the first mate, he said,"Mr. Ruddock, have this man sign on as ship's cook. Show him the galley, and tell him what's expected of him. Find a berth for the boy in the fo' c'sle."

"Aye, aye, Sir."

"My son and I will have to sleep together, Sir," said Latour.

"No. The cook has a berth in the galley," said Currie.

"Then the boy can share my bunk," responded Latour.

"No. He will sleep in the fo'c'sle with the rest of the crew," said Currie and turned away.

"I'm sorry, but that's not acceptable, Sir," said Latour. "I'd be afraid that my son might be abused. My first duty is to protect my child."

"You will do as I say, Sir, if you want to be crew aboard this ship," responded Currie.

Latour sighed. "Then, Sir, I must decline. Thank you for your consideration, but my child's safety has to be my first concern." He turned and walked towards the gangway. Currie looked at Ruddock, his lips set in a grim line. "Is there room for two in that galley berth, Ruddock?"

"Aye, Sir. I would say so. 'e's only a slight lad. It might be a bit tight. But I've 'ad a lot worse meself."

"Latour," called the captain.

"Yes, Sir."

"Take a look at the galley berth. Quickly now, we cast off in a few minutes. If it's sufficient for your needs, the lad can berth with you, Mr. Ruddock. No more delays. You have five minutes to sign these two up or put them ashore. If you put them ashore, assign Brannigan to the cook's job for now."

CHAPTER 2

The Guiding Light

The Guiding Light Church was closed in, and the finishing and the interior detail work was well underway. Gerry Mason had sent Albright the 'ample notice' he'd requested, and the lamp maker had replied stating that he would arrive in Ryeport the following weekend for a one week stay. He had also requested a tour of the harbour 'as described in your earlier visit.' Mason was smiling as he read the letter aloud to Roddy over lunch. "He will 'take-over,' Roddy. Albright has to be completely in charge. It's the only way he knows how to work. But we can be sure of his undivided attention to the lighting of the window. A word of advice: Don't be put off by his surly and aggressive manner. He is best known for his impatient and sarcastic manner. However, he is a devout Christian and generous in good causes. He hates to appear soft. He is a small man, physically speaking I mean, and I believe that he tries to compensate for that with his over assertive attitude. He prefers to be thought of as a tough, hard-nosed businessman. That sometimes makes him difficult to work with."

Mason had arranged for a vacant cottage to be modestly furnished and prepared for Albright's stay, and Emily Rooken had been pleased to accept the extra job of looking after the place during his visit. The accommodation would be primitive by Albright's standards, but Mason intended that. He wanted to insert Albright in the villager's living style whenever the opportunity presented itself believing that would underscore for him the value of his help to the villagers.

The lamp-house fittings had been carefully unpacked and carefully laid out in the body of the new church. Iron ladders had been permanently secured to the walls of the lamp-house, both inside and out, all as described in Albright's drawings and instructions. The ladders would facilitate maintenance and cleaning of the lighting apparatus and cruciform window. Temporary scaffolds had been strategically rigged to facilitate the installation. Now, builders and villagers alike were anxiously awaiting the arrival of the man whose design would justify or confound all the work and effort that had been put into this project. The modestly sized church had been cleaned and polished so that it almost glowed. It still lacked pews and other furnishings, however, because these were being refurbished and would be transferred from the old church in time for the dedication ceremony.

On the Saturday preceding Albright's arrival, the stagecoach that delivered Hawksworth's mailbag also had a letter for Roddy. Bishop Mason was informing him that he had received a letter from Reverend Clyde, one of the outbound missionaries aboard The Seahorse. That letter reported all the events of their voyage and the attitude and personality of the captain. It also stated that Sailmaker was aboard the vessel when it left Havana for Haiti and that Reverend Clyde had advised the homeward bound missionaries, Reverends Palmer and Swift, of the problems aboard The Seahorse and asked them to protect Sailmaker and do whatever they could to ensure his safe return to England. The letter also stated: 'The young man has suffered some abuse but was in good health and spirits when the ship left for Havana.'

Sailmaker had asked Clyde to also send his own letter for Meg. So that she could know from his own hand that he was safe and anxious to return to her. That letter was delivered, with the bishop's letter, to Roddy. Reverend Clyde had been fortunate enough to find a packet that was due to leave Havana for England only two days after The Seahorse departed for Haiti. Meg's eyes widened with surprise when Roddy handed her the letter. She hurried to the inn's kitchen, wanting privacy for the reading of it. There were tears of joy in her eyes and a broad, bright smile on her face as she returned to the bar. The whole village rejoiced at the news that Sailmaker was safe, but confirmation that Captain Currie had shanghaied him rekindled their anger for the man. The dominating feeling though was one of relief. Meg was smiling through her tears as she read and re-read the letter and told everyone her glad news.

After supper at Roddy's cottage that evening, Mason spread a drawing on the table. There was a broad smile on his face. Roddy looked at his friend and asked, "What is this then, Gerry? Another change of plan?"

"No, my friend. This is your new vicarage." Mason stood back and waited for the impact of his remark to sink in.

"New vicarage? I didn't believe that you were serious about a new vicarage."

"Well, I didn't want to say too much about it before, Roddy, until I had the plans completed and the cost established. Roddy, your new church is quite a long walk from here. It would be especially unpleasant in bad weather and not something to look forward to as a daily chore. Anyway, I took it upon myself to improve that disused cottage where we stored Albright's lamps just for you. It is less than a hundred yards from the new church, and though badly neglected, it does have a spectacular view of the sea. It will be very attractive. We have lots of material left over from the church, so I arranged to extend that small cottage." He smiled again enjoying his friend's surprise. "Actually, I have masons working on the addition already. The new section will be built at right angles to the original building so that it will become the cross section of this 'tee shaped' floor plan." He pointed to the plan on the table. "The living room will have a large window on the ground floor to take advantage of the spectacular view and also a large stone fireplace to provide some added comfort. There is even a sheltered walkway to the privy. It will be much more comfortable than this place, and the two bedrooms upstairs will enjoy the same outstanding view of the sea." Mason was revelling in his friend's astonishment. "We'll have it finished before the dedication of the new church, Roddy. Your parents will be quite comfortable in the upstairs guest room."

"But, Gerry, this was never part of our original presentation. The bishop will be most upset. He will think I'm putting on airs and graces beyond my station and do his best to destroy me. And who will pay for this extra work and expense? He certainly will not, and I never could."

Mason laughed. "Relax, my friend; if this church proves to be the success that I am sure it will be, your bishop won't have the nerve to criticise you. You are already far more popular than he. Besides, the cost is not a factor. We are well under budget for the church and have funds and materials to spare. It's all taken care of."

Sunday's weather was bright and clear. Roddy had spent considerable time polishing his sermon and arranging final details for the service. He needed this day to go particularly well because both Bishop West and Constable Cooper would be attending. The constable's impending visit had him on edge. 'Uncle Joshua' had been obliged to postpone his original meeting with him and reschedule to this weekend. Roddy was particularly apprehensive about the 'private' meeting because the constable had blamed the delay on fresh evidence found during his closing of the file on Goodman's death.

Bessie Drew, her sister Marie, and Fletcher had also put in an appearance, and Bessie, having seen the Nextwest notables arrive, had enlisted Ernie's aid to turn out any tardy members of the congregation. The old church was packed. Roddy hurried to greet Bishop West and offered to defer to him in regard to the service. The bishop declined but did agree to address the congregation before the service to make some comments about the new church. He would have been hard pressed to find any cause for complaint with the size of the congregation or the response to Roddy's service, which drew much praise from Westerhof and Cooper. Once again, the singing was very lusty; even Jamie Rooken was putting his heart and soul into the hymns. Emily was looking at her husband as though he were a stranger. After the service, the villagers set out what had now become a regular potluck luncheon. After the meal, the coaches and wagons took the guests to the new church. Bishop West was talking to Mason as they inspected the building, so it wasn't hard for Roddy and Cooper to detach themselves for that quiet discussion the constable had requested. "I said this was a delicate matter, Father, and I need your assurance that you will hold what I am about to tell you in the strictest confidence." The constable fixed eye contact with the vicar. "Indeed, Sir," responded Roddy. "Whatever you have to say will remain between us."

"Not even Prudence, Father," cautioned the constable. "As you wish, Sir," replied the vicar. His stomach was in a knot for he believed that the constable was about to reveal some knowledge of his involvement in Goodman's death. "Good man," responded Cooper. "This matter concerns a friend of yours: Reverend Tubbs."

"Oh!" The obvious relief in his simple exclamation caused the perceptive constable to pause and study his companion's face even more closely. Roddy lowered his gaze for a few seconds before resuming eye contact, then with raised eyebrows said, "Surely, Tubby is in no trouble?"

"No, Father. Nothing like that. The fact is I know that 'Tubby', as he prefers to be called, was forced into that marriage with Mrs. Whatson. I also know that he is not the father of her unborn child as she claims, although I am unable to prove it. Quite apart from the burden of injustice that her lies forced upon that gentleman, this unconsummated marriage has drained him financially. Bishop West deducted heavy support payments from his meagre income and sent them to Tubby's new wife. But I'm sure that none of this is news to you?" He raised his eyebrows in a questioning manner.

Roddy acknowledged with a nod. Cooper continued: "This whole affair has seriously damaged the man's self-esteem. I'm sorry to say he is severely depressed. He is a good man but lacking in personal confidence and assertiveness. Anyway, through sources that I am not at liberty to reveal, I know that the father of the child is actually Goodman, the deceased butler and smuggler.

"Through my ongoing investigations, I have also uncovered a considerable sum of money that Goodman had deposited in an account under an assumed name, and I believe that, in all fairness, some of this money should be used to compensate Tubby. Would you agree?"

"Why yes, Constable. I too know that Tubby was not the father. And I believe him implicitly. He has no capacity for lies or deceit."

"I agree. Now because I am legally required to seize this concealed money and surrender it to the Crown, the matter of reimbursing Tubby from Goodman's funds becomes a problem. I would have to shall we say 'adjust' the record of my discovery. I am at a loss for a safe way to do that. Now, these are not appropriate sentiments or behaviour for an officer of the law, hence my need for your absolute discretion." Again he searched Roddy's face for any hint of disapproval, but seeing none he continued: "Tubby is a nervous type; he has, as you say, no capacity for deceit. I'm afraid he would give the game away or refuse the payments if I were to try and compensate him. I cannot conceive a way to discreetly reimburse the man that would not put me in an untenable position. Do you have any ideas?"

The pair had stopped dead in their tracks and stood facing each other as they considered the problem and their new illicit relationship one that would require substantial mutual trust. "Well, Sir," Roddy eventually responded. "Reimbursing Tubby would be a great financial help, but I know the main reason for his depression lies in the injustice of being unjustly branded as a liar and lecher. It's a pity that instead of the money, you hadn't found some sort of document confirming Goodman as the father of the child or at least his intimate relationship with Mrs. Whatson." Now he examined the constable's face for a response. There was silence for a while as the two men studied each other. The constable's brow furrowed, and he looked at Roddy with a rather grim expression. "Are you suggesting, Sir, that I have fabricated this discovery? Or that I should possibly go a step further and fabricate evidence of an affair between Goodman and Mrs. Whatson?" His expression was intimidating.

"Not at all, Sir. I understand and agree completely with your sentiments in this matter. I was merely regretting the lack of evidence that would absolve Tubby from this unjust situation and possibly provide grounds for an annulment. I believe that would be Tubby's preferred outcome. I think he has accepted the financial loss, but the blot on his character is a lifelong sentence to him. I know he would like to have his name and reputation restored." Cooper stared into Roddy's unsmiling face. "I feel that I'm being offered an opportunity to falsify evidence," he said. "That would hardly be ethical behaviour for an officer of the law or for a minister of the church."

"I meant to imply no such thing, Sir. However, I do confess my belief that justice is often thwarted by the law. Sometimes it seems that the only way to achieve true justice is to step outside the law, however unpalatable that might be. But I assure you, my remarks were merely an expression of regret that no evidence has yet been found to absolve an innocent man. Certainly, I had no intention of suggesting a falsifying of evidence, even if that might prove to be the only way to correct this injustice."

The constable looked thoughtful. "Well, Reverend, I will concede that the law is not perfect. Let us leave this matter as it is for now and rejoin the rest of our party. We can mull over this problem in private and put our heads together again when we have some fresh ideas. What say you?"

"That sounds reasonable, Sir." And so, the two men joined the others on the tour. Bishop West gave a thoughtful look in their direction as they entered the lamp-house, noticing the constable's arm draped protectively across the vicar's shoulders. Mason was pointing out the various elements of the lighting equipment and explaining how they would be installed to reflect and concentrate light through the cruciform window. Despite his earlier reticence, the bishop was enthused and congratulated Roddy on his initiative, expressing his hope that everything would prove as beneficial as expected. Everyone parted on good terms, promising to return once the lighting was operational. The constable gave Roddy a wave and a broad wink as his coach turned and left the site.

. . .

Albright arrived by post-chaise the following weekend. The long uncomfortable journey from London had taken its toll on his energy, and shortly after having supper with Mason and the vicar, he excused himself pleading fatigue. The following morning, he was up bright and early. He cut himself some fresh bread, slathered it with butter and folded it around a slice of cheese. Emily had intended to prepare his breakfast, but Albright was still munching on his homemade sandwich when she arrived. "Sorry, Sir. I didn't realise you wanted such an early start. I'll be earlier tomorrow."

"No need, woman. No need. I'm quite capable of looking after myself." He hurried off to rouse Mason from his cottage. He was anxious to see the building site. Emily watched him go with a look of dismay on her face. "I think I've just lost me bloody job," she muttered. Albright did indeed prove to be a difficult and obnoxious taskmaster to the craftsmen installing the equipment. He was unreasonably impatient and sarcastic. However, it was obvious to all, that despite his constant reference to his drawings, he had the installation details completely memorised. The work went smoothly, and the equipment was completely fitted within two days. The array of lamps and adjustable mirrors was impressive.

"I just hope it all works," Mason whispered to the vicar. Despite his hushed tones, his remark was overheard by Albright. He spun around to confront them wearing a very offended expression. "Of course, it will work!" he said testily. "But, like most things of a complex nature, I would expect it to need some fine adjustment. We will need to go out to sea to get a better impression of how balanced the visible light will be. Tonight, we shall light it up. Sandwiches if you please, Mason. We will eat on the boat. You do have a boat arranged, don't you?"

"That I do, Albright. That I do," smiled Mason with a discreet wink to Roddy. The ever-obliging Benjamin Cobbe made his boat available for the trial. Ernie brought baskets of food, ale and rum. Albright seemed annoyed that there were so many people in the boat but grudgingly allowed them aboard. "Provided you all sit quiet and stay out of the way." And they did just that, anchored just off the Dragon's Tail impatiently waiting for darkness and the lighting of The Guiding Light. Then suddenly, there was a fluttering yellow glimmer beginning at the top of the crucifix and spreading quickly over the whole crucifix. The yellow glimmer quickly brightened to a stronger, more positive light. The beacons had already been lit, adding their glow to the cloudless sky. But the people in the boat hardly noticed them. They were focused on the church window. The whole crucifix was lit now, growing to a much whiter light than the beacons. It soon became an arresting sight in the night sky. Some areas of the crucifix were brighter than others, and these were duly recorded on Albright's sketch pad.

The boat moved farther out to sea, noting that the eastern arm of the cross was reducing as they went further east. Then they sailed west and saw the western arm reduce similarly as they proceeded. Cobbe's laughter suddenly shattered the quiet, and he called out, "We've got an audience, gentlemen!" Looking around, the occupants of the boat saw the riding lights of several fishing boats just astern. Cobbe waved his stern lantern and called, "Ahoy, Ryeport boats. Welcome to The Guiding Light." There arose a ragged cheer from the other boats, growing louder as more crews joined in the celebration. Then the big new bell began to toll as if it too had to join the celebration. This bell had a much deeper voice than the small one at the old church. "We'll be glad of that on a foggy night," commented Cobbe. Albright was offended by all the noise and commotion. Then, from above the crucifix window, another bright light began to grow. This was emanating from the church's tall belfry and proved visible over a far wider area than the cruciform window. Another cheer went up from the boats. "That was Mister Albright's suggestion," said Roddy. "He realised that we would need a wider light to guide the boats to The Guiding Light."

"That's a great idea," said Cobbe.

"It would be nice if we could have some peace and quiet here so that I could concentrate on my notes," complained Albright in a miserable voice. "After all, this evening was supposed to provide me an opportunity to resolve any imbalances in the light distribution."

"Oh, come on, Albright! Remember it's your work they're cheering. Who could ask for more sincere appreciation?" Mason chided. "And what's more, you even got your lighthouse. What a bonus!" Mason was grinning broadly. Albright just "humphed" and went back to his notes. "Time to celebrate when it's all finished and secure, I say." Cobbe steered for the harbour entrance, using the 'perfect crucifix' to guide him. He was keeping a wary eye on the beacons too, just until he was certain of the guiding properties of the lighted cross. "It works, lads. So it does," he said. "Just needs a little tinkering here and there to balance the brightness." Mason too was making notes concerning the appearance of the crucifix as they approached the turn into the dogleg. "We'll have to build a blind to cut off the lower part of the cross at the turning point," he said. "Or maybe we can make an arrow-head-shaped window out of the blind. Just to make people look left, at the appropriate time, and see The Harbour Light."

"That's your problem, not mine," remarked Albright. Mason bridled at the man's constant complaining. "I know that Albright – you bloody misery. You've done a great job. We're all aware the rest is up to us." "Sorry," muttered the lamp maker. It took two more nights of adjustments to the mirrors and lamps, with people signalling between the doorway of the lamp-house and the boats, before Albright was satisfied. A temporary blind had been built to mask the lower part of the cross at the turning point and proved somewhat effective but didn't satisfy Roddy or Mason. Benjamin Cobbe told them not to worry. "If we follow the cross until the western arm is completely masked by the extended sidewall, that's the time to turn left. And it's also the time that The Harbour Light comes into view. That's all we need."

Mason looked thoughtful. "Good idea, Benjamin, as far as local boats are concerned. But if we are to attract strangers in bigger ships, we shall need something more than local knowledge to keep them safe."

Cobbe volunteered to be the first boat to enter the harbour using only the 'Guiding Light.' The following night, the beacon masters remained by their fires but did not light them. Cobbe sailed into the harbour with absolute confidence. Tim Ozmund and Will Tarret were in the boat with him. They all cheered as the boat turned safely into the dogleg on seeing The Harbour Light. "Seemed only fitting," Cobbe said at the inn later, "that these two lads who lost so much to inspire this improvement should be in the first boat guided home by the new light." A procession of village boats had followed Cobbe in, all testing the various features of the light, and they were all happy with the results. The inn was soon full of villagers celebrating the success of The Guiding Light.

"Well that means I'm out of a job," grumbled Archer. "The lad on the eastern beacon too. Though 'iggins is young enough to get another job or even go back to fishin'. Don't know what I'll do now though."

"I do, Archer," said the vicar. "You can operate The Guiding Light. It doesn't work on its own, you know. The windows will need to be kept clean, the lamps too. Supplies have to be maintained, and we'll need someone here to make sure all goes well during the dark hours. You and Higgins can have a job as long as you need one. The good news is you'll be warm and dry maintaining this light. No wood to cut and carry either. You can work out duty watches to suit yourselves. Just make sure someone is always on watch in the dark hours." Archer rewarded Roddy with a rare smile. "Well, thank you, Father. Would it be alright then if I give 'iggins the news?"

"Of course, Archer. After all, as Sexton, you're in charge now."

Albright stayed in Ryeport longer than he'd intended. He was so enthused by the success of The Guiding Light that he couldn't resist extra trips to view the illuminated cross. On that first night, it was Carter who was happy to oblige him with some extra trips. Then Albright wanted a boat to take him farther west, out of sight of The Guiding Light, just to see how effectively his 'lighthouse' element contributed to bringing the boats into the narrower vector of the "Guiding Light." Sullivan's boat took him east the following night. He was most anxious to hear, firsthand, from each boat's crew exactly how much they appreciated the new light. Mason thought the man would never leave. At night, he was not much of a problem, but during the day, he was annoying: tinkering with the mirrors and fine-tuning their alignment, then fussing over details of maintenance with Archer and Higgins. Those two men were now on the church payroll as Sexton and his assistant responsible for the upkeep of The Guiding Light and all other responsibilities of the church maintenance.

Higgins had been pleased to learn that he had a job as Archer's assistant. However, he was more than a little intimidated by Albright's overzealous manner. "'e's like a bloody mother 'en," he complained to Archer. "I don't know if I want this job if 'e's goin' to be pickin' 'oles in ev'rythin' I do. 'e's so fussy. It's bloody ridiculous.' He pulled a face to mimic Albright's sour expression and then affected a delicate dusting action. "Can't 'ave a speck of dirt on the mirrors. Make sure you trim the wicks just so. Careful, mind you, don't knock the mirrors an' change the alignment. Drives me bloody mad, 'e does."

"Relax," said Archer. "He's leavin' early Monday mornin'. The vicar's goin' to take 'im to meet the eastbound coach. Then 'e'll pick up a post-chaise at the next stage. Must be nice to be that well off. I 'eard 'im talkin to Mister Mason. 'e says this is the most satisfying thing 'e's ever designed, an' 'e's done a lot of special designs for cathedrals, manor 'ouses an the like. But this one is functional 'e says. A light-'ouse is a lifesaver, not just decoration."

At that Sunday's service, Ernie nudged Doc Hudson as they stood for the hymns. "Who would have thought that the vicar would have had this effect on the village? Look at the size of the congregation. On his first day 'ere, there were a few villagers willing to kill 'im – me included." The doctor smiled. "God works in mysterious ways, my friend."

There were several trips between the two churches that day. The Nextwest people, in particular, were anxious to see the new church. Many of the congregation stayed until after dark, anxious to see the light in operation. The fishermen were quick to offer their boats as a gesture of thanks to the people of Nextwest who had become such friends of the village. Westerhof and his wife, Bessie Drew, Marie and Fletch were amongst those accepting the fishermen's offer. Bessie though was unusually quiet as she passed the spot where her son, Mick, had lost his life. She wondered if he might be alive today had the new church been built in time. But she knew the loss of the Lucky Lady had also been the inspiration for the new church. Was that the real reason that Mick had to lose his life, so that many others could be spared?

Roddy was wondering what new problems were about to confront him when he received an unexpected summons from Bishop West. But the bishop was all smiles. He had commissioned a beautifully carved oak panel on which the story of the church, from concept to completion, had been carved. A list of all who had been instrumental in the project completed the testimonial. Roddy was surprised to find that his was the first name on the list along with a glowing commendation for his dedication to the people of the village. He was a little shaken. This was a major reversal on the part of his arch adversary. He was instructed to have the panel permanently mounted, inside the entrance porch of the church, in time for the dedication service.

"Thank you, Your Grace. This is most generous. I am embarrassed and humbled by all the effort that everyone has put into this project. I feel that mine was the smallest effort in the whole business."

"Nonsense. We had all but given up on the village. Without your ideas and your concern for the villagers, there would be no new church. Off with you now. Get that mounted as soon as you can. I'll be in touch with other details for the ceremony later." The audience was over. Now there was the more pleasant business of preparing for the visitors and their entertainment At Gerry's suggestion, the old church had been cleaned and fitted with trestle tables and benches. The villagers would arrange and prepare a supper for the visitors. This would allow villagers and visitors an opportunity to mingle. The food would be paid for from the surplus in the building fund.

Roddy's parents were amongst several visitors given a tour of the church by Gerry Mason on the eve of the dedication. Roddy's mother was tearful as she read the bishop's plaque mounted inside the church entrance. His father too seemed a little choked up. "He has made us very proud," he said to Mason. "We have all come a long way since Roddy's first presentation of this project at your brother's house."

"We have indeed," responded Gerry, "and you have every reason to be proud of your son. He is much loved hereabouts and has done a great deal for this village in a relatively short period of time." Mason wished that he could be at liberty to divulge some of Roddy's more adventurous activities on behalf of the villagers, but that could never be. He had to content himself with the less dangerous exploits of their son.

Bishop West handled the dedication with splendid ceremony, and Roddy was relieved to find that the other two bishops would also address the congregation. This took quite a lot of pressure off him, and he was able to shorten his own service. "This church and its guiding light could never have been built but for the generosity and goodwill of many people," Roddy told the congregation. "Many of our benefactors were hitherto unaware of our village, yet they were unstinting in their endeavours to provide assistance for the wellbeing of strangers when they learned of the need. I would be grateful if our benefactors would allow us to express appreciation and thank them for their generosity. I now ask these good friends to stand as I call their names. Please turn and face the congregation and remain standing until the list is completed so that our villagers can recognise and thank you all."

The applause proved generous indeed. Some of the guests, Roddy's parents amongst them, were quite moved despite being a little embarrassed. Westerhof had to wipe his eyes more than once. Once the people resumed their seats, Roddy then asked that the villagers stand so that they too could be recognised, not only for their support for the new church but also for their commitment to each other in the times of great hardship and tragedy. The villagers stood and were applauded by their guests. Roddy was proud of his congregation, and it showed. They were well turned out in their 'Sunday best', and many of them now found the appropriate pages in their hymnbooks without the aid of Meg's markers. Some of them still had to pretend to be reading, of course. But they had come a long way thanks to Meg's reading and writing lessons. The packed church vibrated with the singing of the hymns, and Roddy noticed looks of approval passing between the bishops during the ceremony.

After the service, Bishop Mason managed to get Roddy alone for a few quiet moments. "Roddy, I would like to express my personal thanks for the friendship that you have built with my brother. Gerry told me that, through you, he found new meaning and purpose in his life. I'm sure you realise that he was on a serious downward spiral in terms of both his health and his associations at the time you first met. I was at a total loss to find a cure for his problems after his wife died. This has been a very welcome turn around. Frankly, I thought that you two would never get along after that first meeting. Thank you, Roddy. I honestly believe that you have saved my brother's life. You have also changed Bishop West's attitude. He is now strong in his praise for you. But he too is benefiting from the reflected glory of your achievements here. I believe you have caused him to re-examine his attitudes and disposition. You may have made a new friend."

Bearing in mind his ulterior motives, Roddy was feeling rather embarrassed. "Your Grace, I am being thanked when I should be the one giving thanks. In Gerry, I have found a true friend that I would otherwise have never known. It's true that the project brought us together, but I am hopeful that our friendship will continue even though the church is now completed."

"I'm certain it will, Roddy. Gerry is delighted to have worked with you in this, but he is even more grateful for your friendship. He intends to spend considerable time in Ryeport now. The Guiding Light Church may be a modest structure compared to Gerry's other works, but it has proved to be the building that will bring him that recognition that has eluded him all his working years." Bishop Mason was joined by Salisbury and West, and after more congratulations from these gentlemen, Roddy excused himself. All things considered, it had been a very successful day. The weather was kind, and many of the guests stayed until after dark and took trips outside the harbour and marvelled at the functionality of The Guiding Light. Albright tried to suppress his self-satisfied smile but didn't manage that very well. He did manage many trips outside the harbour though and was as excited as a schoolboy as he hustled from one returning boat into the one next departing.

On his arrival earlier and still playing the 'hard-nosed' businessman, Albright had presented Gerry Mason with his bill. However, he had been so moved by the praise heaped upon him during the 'appreciation' part of Roddy's service, and to see his name so prominently displayed on the bishop's dedication plaque, that he now asked Gerry Mason to give him back the bill. "Where is my bill, Mason?"

"I haven't even had a chance to open it yet," protested Mason as he handed him the still sealed document. "You only gave it to me this morning. I'm not prepared to pay you today, Albright."

"No need," replied the smiling lamp maker, as he tore up the bill. Mason stood dumbstruck for a few seconds. "That is most generous, Albright! Most generous indeed! On behalf of the village: many thanks. Many thanks indeed. Your generosity will be well used and appreciated. I can assure you."

Roddy was moving amongst the villagers looking for Meg. He had not seen her since the service. Finally, he learned from Kathleen Archer that she was alone in her cottage. "What's wrong, Mrs. Archer? Is she unwell?" he asked.

"As well as might be expected, Father, considering that she's been without her husband for almost a year. She was relieved and grateful to hear that Sailmaker was alive and reasonably well a month ago, but she still fears that he may not make it home. She reads and re-reads his letter constantly. She is the loneliest person in the village tonight. The celebrations have made her loss even more painful because Sailmaker isn't here to share them with her. Theirs was a true love-match. Remember too, they were very much a part of getting this new church started. They were founding members of the 'Ryeport Players' if you recall. Now they are parted when they should really be at the heart of the celebrations." She gave Roddy a rueful smile.

"Should I go to her then, Mrs. Archer? Can I help in any way?"

"No, Father. Let her be. She'll have a good cry and then pull herself together. She is a strong-minded girl. She will rejoin the party once she can keep a smile on her face. By the way, Father, when are you going to stop calling me Mrs. Archer? You've been here long enough now to know the whole village calls me Kathleen. I shall consider it a personal slight if you insist on maintaining this formality between us."

"Very well, Kathleen. I'll be sure to remember that." They both smiled.

Roddy's parents stayed for two more days. Roddy's new home, the vicarage, though very attractive after Gerry's modifications, still lacked many of the comforts of their family home. More than once Roddy had caught his mother looking wistfully around his sparsely furnished home. Her concern was obvious.

It was after one of Emily's hearty suppers that McDowd Senior turned to his son and said, "Roddy, your mother and I are most impressed by your efforts here and your well-deserved success in Ryeport. We are very proud of you. You have come a long way since those unhappy days that preceded your entry into the church. I would be most happy if those days could be put behind us forever never to be mentioned again. I want you to know that, as soon as I get back to London, I shall have my solicitor reinstate you in my Will. Welcome back into the fold, my son." Both parents raised their wine glasses to their son, and his mother had to borrow another handkerchief.

As the coach disappeared from sight, Roddy turned to Gerry Mason and said, "I suppose I shall soon be waving goodbye to you too, Gerry. I'll not look forward to that day; I have enjoyed your company these past months."

"Don't give up on me yet, Roddy," responded Gerry. "Remember I am refurbishing your old cottage for myself. And I do have a special favour that I would like to ask of you in that regard. If you and your bishop could find my idea acceptable, I'd like my residence here to be of the most permanent kind. I would like to finish my days here in Ryeport, provided that is acceptable to all concerned, of course."

"Of course, Gerry. Anything that would help keep you here a while longer shall have my undivided attention."

"Well, what I have in mind would most certainly do that, my friend. Perhaps we could retire to the vicarage for some privacy and discuss the matter over some of that excellent claret that you recently added to your wine cupboard."

• • •

It was on a cold and drizzly Tuesday morning, almost two months after the dedication ceremony, that the bishop's coach arrived in Ryeport to summon Roddy for an urgent meeting with Bishop West. The coachman asked that they leave immediately. On his arrival, Roddy was surprised and apprehensive to find that Constable Cooper was also to be party to this meeting. After Roddy had made his obeisance to the bishop, he turned to the constable, offered his hand, and wished him good morning. "Good morning to you too, Father," responded the constable rising and grasping Roddy's hand firmly. "I trust you are well and that our friends in Ryeport are enjoying the benefits of their new church."

"That they are, Constable. But I must confess that I find myself wondering what kind of trouble I'm in when I'm summoned so urgently before my bishop for a meeting in the presence of the constable?" Cooper smiled and, with a wave of his hand, deferred to the bishop for the explanation.

"Reverend McDowd," said Bishop West. "The constable informs me that you are on good terms with our Reverend Tubbs. It is in your capacity as Reverend Tubbs' friend that we seek your advice on a delicate matter this morning." The bishop paused looking a little shamefaced and somewhat at a loss for words. He broke eye contact, looking down at his desk for a few moments, before continuing. "It seems, Father, that I have committed a grave error of judgement concerning the former Mrs. Whatson's child." He looked at Roddy with a shamefaced expression. "I took that lady's word as far as the paternity of the child was concerned, and in so doing, brushed aside the protests of a good and innocent man. I confess I am ashamed of my hastiness and intolerance in that matter and will certainly make my apologies to Reverend Tubbs. I am anxious to do all that I can to make amends. An annulment of Reverend Tubb's marriage to Mrs. Whatson would appear to be a strong first option.

"Constable Cooper informs me that this lady has now been delivered of a son after a very difficult labour. In fact, the child had to be surgically removed from his mother, who died shortly after. The constable had un-covered some information concerning Goodman, the murdered smuggler, which caused him to believe that he should re-open the investigation of that man's death." Roddy felt his pulse start to race. The bishop looked to Cooper who responded with a confirming nod before he continued. "The constable believed that Mrs. Whatson should have been able to corroborate some of his newfound information and drove to Bristol to question her. It was sheer coincidence that he should arrive during this lady's struggle to deliver the child. The birth was almost two months premature I believe?" He again looked at the constable for confirmation. Cooper nodded. "At least six weeks I'm told."

"When the constable introduced himself at the house where Mrs. Whatson was staying, he was told that the lady had been in premature labour for almost two days and was very weak. The doctor was most concerned because there had been a considerable loss of blood. He concluded that the only chance to save mother and child was to surgically remove the baby from the womb. The child survived, and the doctor assured the constable that, despite his immaturity, the boy appeared to be very strong. Despite being six weeks premature, he still weighed over seven pounds. It's a small wonder then that this slightly built lady had such a terrible time. The constable tried to question the failing Mrs. Tubbs about his new information, but she refused to answer his questions, asking instead that he hear her deathbed confession that Goodman, not Tubbs, was the father of her child. She wanted to make her peace before dying." The bishop tapped a document that was resting on his desk. "The constable has sworn an affidavit as to the lady's deathbed testimony. So, you can see, Rodney – may I call you, Rodney? This being such a personal matter, a less formal atmosphere seems appropriate."

"Certainly, Your Grace, but my name is usually shortened to Roddy." He was still having difficulty accepting the bishop's changed attitude towards him. "Thank you, Roddy." The bishop gave a weak smile. "I'm very distraught over my misjudgement of Tubbs, but now my concerns are multiplied. I pressured Tubbs into that marriage taking Mrs. Whatson's word over his protests of innocence. I drove him into a relationship that I am now certain was never consummated. Now I learn that the child born since that marriage is not his after all. The lady's deathbed confession affirms that. I'm told that with due consideration of hereditary traits, given the size of the baby, Goodman would certainly be a more likely parent than Reverend Tubbs. Actually, the constable's expression was 'You shouldn't expect a Shetland pony to sire a Clydesdale.' Frankly, Roddy, I'm at a loss to know how best to break this news to Tubbs. I wondered if you, as his friend, might be able to guide me in this matter. I realise that I have done the man a grave injustice, and I am anxious to do all in my power to rectify the situation."

The constable and the bishop waited in silence for a couple of minutes whilst Roddy considered this information. Eventually, he said, "I wonder, Your Grace, if I might be the best person to break this news to Tubby. Perhaps I could have a private meeting with him to gauge his mood. He has been sinking ever deeper into depression since the marriage and certainly feels victimised. If I could prepare the ground, as it were, I could better advise you of his feelings and put you in a position to respond appropriately."

"That seems like a sound idea, Roddy. What say you, Constable?"

"I agree. It certainly seems a good way to evaluate the situation," responded the constable. "When could you do this, Father?"

"No time like the present unless there are other considerations that I'm unaware of."

"Very well then, Roddy. We will depend on your good offices." The bishop rose and extended his hand. "One other thing," said Roddy. "Who is looking after the child now?"

"The lady of the house where Whatson was staying – a distant relative I understand – has arranged a wet nurse to look after him," responded the constable. "The wet nurse cannot support an extra child on her own; however, she is a young widow. She is a lady of good repute but struggling financially since the loss of her husband. She can't afford to support this other child, and his mother's funeral is on Friday. There appear to be no family members to accept responsibility for the boy. He will almost certainly end up in an orphanage after the funeral. But there's no need for Tubbs to be concerned about that. We will look after those details."

Roddy sat in the grounds for a few minutes trying to weigh up the startling news that he'd just received. He wondered what the constable had wanted to ask Whatson so urgently that it had caused him to make the long journey to Bristol. Had he found some new clue as to the true nature of Goodman's death? He certainly seemed reluctant to close the case. Tubby managed a weak smile of welcome when Roddy entered his office. His expression changed to surprise as Roddy closed the door behind him. Tubby's door was always open. It was part of his nature to always be available and obliging. After the usual greetings, Roddy said, "Tubby, I've some news for you!" Then, as gently as he could, he relayed all of the information that he'd gathered in the bishop's office. Tubby sat dazed through the complete story. He didn't offer a single comment just a look of concern at the news of his wife's death. There was no expression of satisfaction that the bishop had admitted his mistake and was prepared to make amends. No reaction to the offer of an annulment. Nothing. No response at all for a couple of minutes. Finally, Tubby, tipping his head quizzically to one side, asked,

"So what happens to the child then? An orphanage? That is hardly a decent beginning for an innocent child." He looked troubled.

"Well, unfortunately, that's what happens to orphans, my friend. Unless a relative is prepared to step up and accept the responsibility, and no one has in this case." Roddy looked at his friend with some concern. "You are taking this very calmly, Tubby. I thought you would be pleased and relieved to be finally exonerated in this matter?"

"Well, frankly, Roddy, I've become rather numb to all these affairs over the past months, having been forcibly married to a woman that I once idolised but later came to detest. Never having the comfort or intimacy of a wife yet being encumbered with the financial responsibility. That, by the way, has left me penniless and with absolutely no hope for any sort of future. Really, I've just been going through the motions of living. Each day has been just another measure of time to pass me by. I'm not of much use to anyone really." He looked absolutely dejected, far worse than Roddy had ever seen him. "I sometimes wonder why I should even continue." He raised his head to make eye contact with Roddy. "You were the only one who believed me innocent in this matter. Bessie and Miss Prudence too, of course. Now there is this child: a new human being that bears my name – although not my son – who is about to be cast into an orphanage because no one wants him. How inhumane is that? How can I possibly allow that? These past few months have certainly taught me the misery of being unwanted."

Roddy looked anxiously at his friend. The pain of this injustice had obviously compounded over the past months. "I thought that you would be glad to have an annulment, Tubby. The child does not have to bear your name, Whatson's name most likely."

"I want to see him," said Tubby rising from his chair.

"Tubby remember this is the child of a murdering smuggler and a vicious self-centered woman who glorified in seeing you unjustly persecuted. Not good breeding, my friend. Surely you're not thinking of raising this child yourself?"

"He's a child, Roddy. Not responsible for his parents' crimes or faults. He will still need to be cared for and nurtured by someone."

"Well, how would you manage that? If, in fact, that is what you have in mind? Remember you have no wife to care for the child."

Tubby shrugged. "Don't know yet. All I know right now is that I want to see him."

And so, the two friends went to see the bishop. The constable was still there and was able to answer some other questions regarding the former Mrs. Whatson's funeral arrangements. Tubby accepted the bishop's obviously sincere apology with a quiet: "Thank you, Your Grace" and waved aside his offer to annul the marriage. "I'm single again anyway. I believe this child will need a father and a father's name. Life is hard enough even with those two simple things that we take so much for granted. It could be horrendous without them. I would appreciate leave to visit the boy, Your Grace."

"Certainly, Reverend Tubbs. When do you want to go?"

"Now would be a good time, Your Grace."

"Very well. Why don't you take Reverend McDowd with you for company? You can take my coach and driver. When should we expect you back?"

"After the funeral, Your Grace."

And so, with the bishop's blessing, the two young clerics headed for Bristol fortified with a purse supplied by the bishop. Tubby was a changed man. Roddy wasn't sure if that was good or bad. Certainly, his friend was very sober and serious, and he seemed unusually assertive and motivated.

CHAPTER 3

Reinstatement for Roddy

The bishop's coach returned two travel weary young clerics back from Bristol late on Friday afternoon. The groom asked that they go directly to the bishop's office. There was an urgent letter waiting for Reverend McDowd. Bishop West, looking anxious, waved them to chairs beside the fireplace and offered them refreshments. "Roddy, I have a letter for you. From your mother, I believe. Captain Hawksworth brought it here earlier at the request of Gerry Mason. He believed it might be urgent." Roddy read the letter and jumped to his feet. Much of the colour had left his face. "My father has had a heart attack," he said. "Mother says the doctor holds out little hope for his survival and that I should hurry home if I wish to see him." His shoulders slumped. "The letter was dated five days ago."

The bishop had been watching Roddy closely. "You can take my coach to Nexteast, Roddy. You will be able to hire a post-chaise from there. In anticipation of such a need, I instructed the groom to put up a fresh horse as soon as you arrived. Gerry Mason had a letter from his brother on the same delivery as yours. I believed it contained similar information hence Hawksworth's favour. Your housekeeper is packing a bag for you to pick up on the way. Take as long as you need. We will look after things here. Here is money for the journey." Roddy took the purse and stood for a few seconds, holding his forehead before saying, "Thank you, Your Grace" and hurrying to the waiting coach.

As soon as Roddy had left the room, Bishop West turned to Tubby. "This is most distressing news Reverend Tubbs. I do hope that he will be in time."

Tubby nodded dejectedly. "If he hadn't come with me, he could have been away a day earlier."

"Who could possibly have foreseen that?" responded the bishop as he refilled Tubby's glass. Tubby nodded agreement, and the two men fell silent for a while both feeling rather helpless in this situation. It was Tubby who broke the silence. "I should explain the outcome of our visit to Bristol, Your Grace. The funeral went quite well. It was a good service, but there were few mourners. The lady's friends were unaware of her passing until it was too late for them to attend, most of them being residents here in Nextwest. As for the child, he seems very strong and healthy, and the doctor believes that he can look forward to a healthy future. He thinks the lad's premature birth will not affect that. The young woman that was hired as his wet nurse is very pleasant. She is a widow of very limited means, taking in laundry and sewing to make ends meet. She could not afford to maintain an extra child. Indeed, she is looking for someone to care for her own daughter, so that she can seek more rewarding employment. I have paid her in advance to look after the child for one more month. It will give me time to find someone locally who can take care of him."

"So, you do intend to raise the child as your own, Reverend Tubbs?"

"Indeed, I do, Your Grace. I believe it will give purpose to my life. A reason for living, something I've lacked these past months." Bishop West dropped his gaze to the floor. "I'm well aware, Reverend, that my shortcomings are responsible for your misery over these past months. I will do all that I can to make amends for that. Should I proceed with an annulment? I am willing to follow that with a public apology if that will help."

"Oh, no, Your Grace. That won't be necessary. What's done is done. We all make mistakes. I shall raise the child as if he were my own. I would rather wait until he is old enough to understand before deciding whether or not to tell him that I am not his natural father. I might possibly find a new wife for myself before then. I may have to move to another town if local knowledge and gossip prove to be a problem for the boy. Who knows what life might bring?"

"What of Mrs. Whatson's Will? Is there money available to you from that?"

"I wouldn't imagine so. The lady was doing her best to destroy me during her last months. I hardly think she would favour me in her Will. Her lawyer will be in touch, I'm told. Most likely the only thing he will present me with is his bill."

"Please keep me informed, Reverend Tubbs. I will help. I am most anxious to make amends. What of the doctor? Did you see him? Did he present you with a bill?"

"Yes, I did see him but only briefly. He told me of Mrs. Whatson's difficult labour. It was a very distressing labour. The doctor's nurse confided in Roddy that they had blamed the stress of her difficult labour for the change in personality and manner towards them. She had called the doctor a useless quack and screamed at him that he would make a better butcher than a doctor. The nurse was offended by her foul language. She said she's never known a more vulgar and aggressive woman and was quite distressed on the doctor's behalf. He had been badly shaken by her changed personality. The genteel lady that he'd accepted as a patient had become this 'vituperative harridan' that he attended during the delivery. His exact words, I'm told.

"Incidentally, when I asked him about her deathbed confession, he seemed puzzled. He said he must have been out of the room at that time. He did recall the constable speaking with her briefly but thought that she was just as abusive and uncooperative with him. That was strange really. From what the constable said, I got the impression that she was genuinely repentant."

• • •

In Ryeport, Roddy was met by Gerry Mason. He had two bags ready packed and waiting. "Two bags?" queried Roddy. "I didn't think I had that many clothes."

"The second one is mine," replied Mason. "I'm coming with you. You might need some company."

"Oh Gerry, that's very thoughtful but not necessary."

"I'm coming. Get used to the idea. Your family and mine are good friends, remember?" The two men arrived in London two days later having hired a post-chaise in Nexteast and driven through the night, stopping only long enough to change horses and grab some quick refreshments. Unfortunately, despite their haste, they were a day too late. Roddy's father had passed away the previous afternoon without regaining consciousness. Roddy was terribly upset. Since their cooperation on The Guiding Light Church, he and his father had become good friends, and he had looked forward to enjoying his company for many years to come. His mother too was very distraught and difficult to console. Gerry offered his condolences and whatever help the family might need, before leaving Mother and son to grieve together. Bishop Mason arrived that evening, having made all the arrangements for the funeral. They had supper together, and eventually, the question of the Will was raised by Roddy's mother.

"Roddy, you must go and see our solicitor, Mr. Blackstock, at the earliest opportunity. I know your father had instructed him to reinstate you in his Will, but I haven't seen it yet. Msr. Beaucaire is also in town. Your father had arranged to meet with him to dissolve the contract that would have him purchase your father's business on his passing. That had to be done before his new Will could be effective. He told me that he had already approved Blackstock's new draft, but I don't believe they had yet cancelled the earlier purchase agreement with Beaucaire. I'm worried that that might have to precede the new Will." She looked very anxious.

The funeral was well attended, and the friendship and respect that McDowd Senior had earned over his lifetime were very evident. Everybody said the weather was lovely; the service was lovely. The funeral was lovely, and the refreshments and fellowship that followed were lovely. Roddy complained to Gerry that he had yet to find anything 'lovely' about a funeral. As they were leaving the graveside, Gerry pointed out a mausoleum in the church-yard. "That is my wife's family mausoleum. She is resting there at present. As I told you in our meeting in Ryeport, it had always been our intention to be together when we passed on. There is no room for me in there, Roddy, even if I wanted that, which I certainly do not. That is why I spoke with you about building a mausoleum in Ryeport to accommodate both my wife and me." He smiled. "You will recall my saying that I wanted my stay in Ryeport to be of a permanent nature! When I raised this matter with my brother, he said there would be no problem transferring my wife's casket there espe-cially since there are no surviving members of her family to object. Perhaps we could finalise this matter at a later time, my friend."

The solicitor, Alfred Blackstock, attended the funeral as did Msr. Beaucaire, and they arranged to meet with the family and Bishop Mason the following day for the reading of the Will. Blackstock arrived accompanied by Beaucaire. The solicitor looked very downcast as he addressed the family. Beaucaire, however, was very relaxed, his thumbs hooked into the pockets of his waistcoat as he leaned back in his chair looking very smug and complacent. Roddy unconsciously fingered the thin scar that ran down his cheek, a souvenir of their last meeting in France.

Blackstock opened the wallet-like file that he had brought with him. "Roddy your father instructed me to draw up a new Will restoring you as a beneficiary in exactly the same terms as before his purchase agreement with Msr. Beaucaire." Blackstock indicated the smug looking Frenchman sitting at his side. "Unfortunately, your father's heart attack preceded his intended dissolution of that agreement." He pushed a document across the table. This is the draft of your father's new Will. It is unsigned and therefore invalid." We have to rely on the authenticated earlier document. Your father's business will, therefore, pass to Msr. Beaucaire for the sum arranged in their purchase agreement.

"Your father's instructions regarding the proceeds of that sale are quite explicit. My office is to act as trustee, on behalf of your mother, and invest the proceeds of the sale conservatively, so as to ensure her a secure income for the rest of her life but without providing her any direct access to the capital." He looked at Mrs. McDowd sympathetically. "Your husband, Ma'am, wanted to be sure that you would be well provided for and spared the worries of money matters and investments. To that end, my office is also instructed to pay all bills that come due, including the servant's wages. Your income, therefore, will be entirely yours unencumbered of any debt or responsibilities. It was meant solely for your discretionary spending. At the time of making that Will, Ma'am, your husband was most concerned that your love for your son might persuade you to allow Roddy – from whom your husband was estranged at that time – access to the capital. He feared that Roddy's irresponsible lifestyle of those days might jeopardise your future security. That, of course, was before the reconciliation. An outcome that I know gladdened your husband's heart and resulted in his instructions to fully reinstate Roddy in his Will. Unfortunately, he was not allowed the time to dissolve his purchase agreement with Msr. Beaucaire, and that is a current and binding agreement, and its dissolution is a necessary prerequisite to the changed Will." Blackstock then addressed Bishop Mason. "Your Grace, on Mrs. McDowd's passing, whatever balance remains is to be placed at your or your successor's discretion, for use in such charities as you or they might consider worthy or deserving."

Roddy now had the draft of his father's new Will before him, and he interrupted. "Surely, with the new Will here making my father's intentions very clear, Msr. Beaucaire would be willing to void his purchase agreement with my father? Given suitable compensation, of course."

"No, Sir. I would not." Beaucaire responded with a smirk. "Your father made it quite clear, in his only legal and binding Last Will and Testament exactly what his intentions were, and they do not include you, Sir. I'm sure you understand why. Your chickens have come home to roost, young man. Mr. Blackstock here already has my money in hand to activate the purchase agreement that I made with your father. That agreement is legal and binding, and I shall rely on him to execute it. Your father's business will, henceforth, operate under my ownership and management." He rose and gave a small, courtly bow to Mrs. McDowd. I shall retain your husbands' original staff, Madam. I know it was a concern of yours that they not lose their positions. Again, Madam, I offer my most sincere condolences for your loss. I enjoyed my acquaintance with your husband, both as a friend and business associate, except of course for the tragic disruption caused by your son. In truth, I never anticipated that our purchase agreement would ever be activated. However, it was a deciding factor in repairing my damaged business relationship with your husband because it provided a remote opportunity to justly punish your son for his offensive behaviour. I offer you my condolences with regard to your son also, Madam." Turning to the lawyer, Beaucaire said, "Mr. Blackstock, I believe our business here is concluded. We should, therefore, leave these people to their private deliberations." And so, the two men left taking with them any hope that Roddy had to benefit from his father's estate. All of his efforts to be restored to his father's good graces and thereby his Will – successful as they had been – had died along with his father's unexpected demise. "It's back to stinky Ryeport again," he muttered.

Quite apart from Roddy's genuine grief over the loss of his father, Gerry was well aware of the painful disappointment at being irrevocably excluded from his Will. Gerry had, after all, had the benefit of reading Roddy's journal. He realised that he needed to help his friend now that all hope of his substantial inheritance was lost along with any dreams that may have funded. Roddy's mood was understandably apathetic and depressed.

• • •

The sudden peal of the coach-horn startled the two passengers in the bouncing coach. The guard added an unfamiliar pip-pip-pip to the end of his usual melodic phrase. That had Roddy and Gerry looking at each other with raised eyebrows. The bone shaken travellers descended from the coach into the throng of well-wishers outside The Harbour Light. Their bags were carried for them, and they were hustled into the inn, quickly followed by the coachmen carrying Hawksworth's mailbag. Soon they were seated, tankards in hand, with Ernie's generous spread laid before them.

"It feels like we never left," smiled Roddy. "That it does, my friend. That it does," responded Gerry. "Do you think they missed us?" There were expressions of concern from all around, and in response to the many questions, Roddy had to give them the sad news of his father's passing. Pleading fatigue, he asked to be excused from further questions and that the coachmen be allowed to take the floor. They entertained, as usual, and the inn was soon buzzing with the familiar conversation and laughter.

Tubby had been handling the Sunday services for the past two weeks and apparently had made many new friends in the village. Ernie commented on his changed personality.

"He seems more sure of himself somehow and more inclined to mix with us!" The coachmen left, and Roddy and Gerry quickly followed seeking an hour or two's snooze in the quiet of their cottages. Roddy collapsed on his bed and slept in his clothes until Emily Rooken woke him for supper. Tomorrow was Thursday and time for his weekly visit to Nextwest. He had really missed Prudence, but he would still have to report to Bishop West before visiting her. A few minutes after supper, he fell asleep again, in the armchair this time, and awoke to a dead fire with Moggy curled up on his lap. He stroked the cat's head. "I think, Moggy, that like it or not, Ryeport really is our permanent home now," he said.

Bishop West and Tubby were pleased to see him and anxious to hear his news. They offered their condolences and any help that he might want. Much as he appreciated their concern, Roddy found that repeating the sad news was just prolonging his agony. He would be glad when all his acquaintances were up to date with the news and he could resume a more normal life. The three men sat with glasses of wine as Tubby then related his news. "Roddy, you will remember Maud, the wet nurse that was looking after Charles? Well, I have moved her to Nextwest. We have also decided on a name for the boy: Charles Rodney Tubbs. Charles because that is what Maud has been calling him all this time, and Rodney, after a very good friend of mine whom I'm hoping will agree to be his godfather, and Tubbs, of course, being his mother's married name and coincidentally mine too." He gave a short laugh.

"Well, that really was quick work, Tubby. Getting the young lady to move to Nextwest I mean. Where will she stay?"

"With our good friend Bessie, Roddy. Dear Bessie made the offer as soon as she heard of my dilemma. As you know, Bessie has her sister's old house all to herself and is now very busy with their pie and preserves business. So, Bessie offered room and board in exchange for Maud looking after the house. I shall continue to pay Maud for looking after Charles too, so she will be much better off than she was in Bristol and have good company to boot. She was well pleased with the offer." Tubby was all smiles.

"That is excellent news, Tubby. So you are committed to raising the ch… Charles yourself?"

"Oh yes, Roddy. As I told His Grace, I now feel my life has a purpose. All I need now are godparents for my son. His Grace is pressing me for a baptism date. I am hoping that you and Miss Prudence might honour me by accepting those roles." He looked at Roddy rather anxiously.

Roddy felt his stomach twist. Tubby was asking him to be godfather to a child whose biological father he had killed, albeit in self defence. Prudence would face a similar dilemma. Obviously, Tubby read his delay as reluctance. "Of course, Roddy," he hurriedly blurted out, "if you'd rather not, I will understand. I'm sure I could find someone else." His tone of voice betrayed Tubby's disappointment. "I know you are not happy about his… breeding." Bishop West was studying the two men's faces quite intently but remained silent.

"No, Tubby." Roddy was embarrassed seeming to be caught in an act of prejudice. "I was merely trying to absorb all the implications of this responsibility and then too wondering how Prudence might react. Neither of us has had that responsibility before. I had only mentioned the 'breeding' thing earlier because I wondered if you had considered the true character of his parents before you decided to raise the boy. Of course, I'll do it. I am most honoured that you would ask me."

"Really! That is splendid!" Tubby's face lit up. "His Grace has offered to perform the ceremony for me. We only have to arrange the date. I couldn't hope for a better start for the lad. He will be baptised by our bishop, have a reverend for a father and another reverend for a godfather; he will be off to a good start indeed."

Roddy drove to Bessie's, and she rode with him to Pru's cottage. Once there, the trio had tea together and brought each other up to date with all their news. Bessie, of course, was privy to all that had transpired at Pringle's farm on that fateful day when Pru and Jed had rescued Sailmaker. So, when Roddy asked Prudence if she would be godmother to Goodman's child, a chilled silence descended on the little group. It was Bessie who eventually broke that silence. "Strange 'ow things come around, Father. The lad's father did 'is best to kill both of you, 'is mother was mean and spiteful to Miss Prudence, and now you're asked to be godparents to their son. The child ain't responsible for 'is parent's faults, o' course. But I'm sure that Tubby wouldn't 'ave asked if 'e knew all the facts. Change of subject, talking about stories, Tubby told me that when 'e spoke with Mrs. Whatson's doctor, the man 'ad no knowledge of 'erdeathbed confession. An' yet the constable said she was repentant, an' anxious to confess. 'e even swore an affidavit sayin so." Roddy and Prudence exchanged quick glances, which were not lost on Bessie. "What was that all about?" she said. "Do you two know somethin' I don't know?"

"No. Not really, Bessie," Roddy answered. "The doctor thought the constable must have heard her confession whilst he was out of the room. It's possible that the constable thought it kinder to protect the lady's indiscretion. Keep her affair private for the sake of the child. He might have seen no need to tell the doctor. The constable too knew Tubby to be a good man and believed him innocent of Mrs. Whatson's charge. I knew he wanted to help Tubby, but I certainly don't believe he would go so far as to swear a false affidavit if that is what you were thinking." Prudence shook her head. "No, I don't think so either, Roddy. He has always been a very just man. Besides, Tubby is no longer concerned about an annulment. You said yourself that the bishop made the offer, and Tubby rejected it."

"True. But that was after the baby was born." He shook his head. "Sometimes, Pru, justice and the law do not walk the same path. I wonder how I might handle that sort of a situation given those same circumstances." Bessie broke in somewhat impatiently, "Change of subject again. Maud is a really nice young woman. I really enjoy 'avin' 'er in my place. She loves the two children and keeps my place spotless, which it ain't been for a while, since I'm so busy with deliveries. 'appy soul too, never a cross word. It's a pity that Reverend Tubbs 'adn't met 'er and fallen for 'er instead of that old witch, Whatson. No offence, Miss. Didn't mean to slight your family."

"No offence taken, Bessie. You couldn't have disliked her more than I."

"Well, my dears. I must be off. I've lots of pies to deliver tomorrow. Bread too now. You certainly started somethin', Father, when you 'ad me deliver pies to warn the smugglers. Thank you." She bent over and gave him a peck on the cheek. "You too, Miss," and she kissed Prudence goodbye.

At last the two lovers were alone.

"You look tired, Roddy." Pru had noticed that once Bessie left, his shoulders had slumped, and he looked depressed. "I am, Pru. I tried not to show it while Bessie was here. She would have given me a lecture. The past two weeks have been terrible. First, there was Father's unexpected death, followed by our concerns over how Mother would manage on her own. I was still counting on my father reinstating me in his Will although that can never happen now." And Roddy told her of all that had transpired with regard to the Will and Msr. Beaucaire. "So, Pru, I'm sorry to inform you that I shall never have a fortune of my own and will never be able to offer you the comfortable life I once knew. I do miss my friends and the good times that I had in London. Those times are lost forever now. How shall I cope now that I'm condemned to Ryeport for life?"

Prudence raised her eyebrows and put on a pitying look. "Oh, boo-hoo! Poor you! What on earth is wrong with you, Roddy?" Her tone was very impatient. "You've suffered a bad loss, that's true, but it isn't like you to feel so sorry for yourself. Tell me something. These good friends of yours in London, have you heard from any of them since you came to Ryeport?"

"Well, no. But I haven't contacted them either."

"You were quite wealthy in those days, weren't you?"

Roddy smiled ruefully. "Yes, Pru. I didn't lack much; that's true."

"And I know you are not mean. So, I imagine you paid the bills most of the time when you were out with your friends?"

He thought about the question for few seconds before he answered. "Well, yes. Most times anyway."

"So maybe those were just 'rented' friends. Not true friends like the ones you've made here." A small smile was playing at the corners of her mouth as she studied his thoughtful countenance. "Do any of those friends in London compare with say Gerry Mason or our poor missing Sailmaker or Ernie, Doc Hudson, Bannerman, the Pringles or Bessie? Have any of those friends in London shared life or death experiences with you as these new friends have?"

"Well, no. There was never the occasion."

"Do you know whom I consider my best friend?"

"Well, no. You have so many friends; it would be hard to choose."

"Well, it's not! You are my best friend. There are others, like Jed of course. You and he are the only men who have risked life and limb to come to my aid as you did for your new friends. It may not have been your intention, Roddy, but you have built a good new life here. Think yourself very lucky. These friends know you don't have riches, and they still like and respect you. If you were in trouble, they would be there for you. Don't cry over lost money. Money doesn't matter that much. If it ever becomes important, we'll find ways to get more somehow. To borrow Uncle Joshua's expression: We could even forge some new links for the smugglers' chain."

Roddy looked at Prudence as the beginnings of a smile brightened his weary features. "Is this lecture over, Miss?"

"For now, perhaps. Sometime in the not-too-distant future though I shall expect you to make an honest woman of me. I'm tired of being a once a week wife. Or are you getting tired of me? Thinking of your pretty friends in London perhaps?"

Roddy reached up, grabbed her around the waist, and drew her down to his lap. "Now how could I possibly be interested in any woman other than you? You know all my dark secrets, weaknesses and desires and still keep company with me, and now you're even asking me to marry you by the sound of it. I might accept your proposal by the way, but only if you were to ask me nicely. Your proposal needs to be more romantic. I'm not won over that easily, you brazen hussy." She cuffed him around the ear. "Watch yourself, young man; I'm not one of your weak-kneed society women."

• • •

When Roddy drove his wagon to Marie's the following morning, she asked for a quiet word. Taking him by the arm, she led him to the back of the shop where Fletch was feeding more wood into the fire of her new brick oven. Then Marie went to Fletch, hooked her arm in his, and walked him back to the vicar. Fletch gave a coy smile and said: "Me an' Marie wants to get married, Father. She reckons that you're the man to do the job. If you'd marry us, we'd be real pleased. She'd like to be married in your new church. Would that be alright?"

"Well! That's wonderful, Fletch. I'd love to marry you. I hope... No... I'm sure you will have a wonderful life together. When is this happy event to take place?"

"First Sunday of next month, Father. If that's alright with you?"

"That will be fine, Fletch. You and Marie will be the first couple to be married in our new church. We shall make that a special event. I understand that you come from Ryeport originally, Marie?"

"Oh yes, Father. Our dad, Bessie's an' me, was a fisherman there most of 'is life. When 'e died – pneumonia it was took 'im – our mum brought us to Nextwest, so's she could get work. Bessie was already keepin' company with Mick's dad at the time. When they got married, Bessie moved back to Ryeport. I stayed 'ere and married that useless bloke o' mine. Nice enough fella 'e was but allergic to work'. Work brought 'im out in a rash, 'e said. 'e couldn't 'elp 'imself really. It interfered with 'is drinkin', y'see.We were married right 'ere, in Nextwest, so we were. I thought a change of church would bring me better luck next time." Roddy smiled. "I'm sure you're right, Marie."

• • •

All the way back to Ryeport, he was thinking about Prudence. I wonder if we should be the second couple married in the Church of the Guiding Light," he muttered. But he was also worried about Pru's remarks about 'forging a new link' for the smuggling chain. Knowing her as he did, he realised that she must have been giving the matter some thought; otherwise, why would the constable's phrase have come so readily to her mind?

One look at Archer's face, and Roddy knew he had a problem. "That there Mister Mason is makin' a real mess in the lamp-'ouse, Father. Stone-dust everywhere. It's all over the winda' and the mirrors. It's gettin' in the wicks of the lamps, too. 'ow are we s'posed to keep the place clean? Try as we might, we can't keep the dust off the workin's. 'iggins is fit to be tied. You gotta do somethin' about 'im makin' all that dust, Father. 'e won't take no notice of us." The scowl on Archer's face was as sour as Roddy had ever seen.

"Alright, Archer. Is Mr. Mason in the lamp-house now?"

"I don't know. Can't see for dust. 'e was there when I last looked."

Of course, the dust was nowhere near as bad as Archer was making out, but he and Higgins had been conditioned by Albright to be scrupulously clean in maintaining 'the workin's. In this area of the lamp-house, the cliff itself had been used to form the rear wall. Gerry and one other mason were now enlarging and squaring a natural cavity in that cliff just a few feet from the east wall of the lamp-house. "What's up, Gerry? You are getting my sexton all upset by making all this dust."

"Oh, we're just about finished now, Roddy," responded Gerry. "This area is nicely squared up now and ready to receive some masonry framing and then the door frame. We'll clear up the mess; don't worry. I'll even buy your sexton and his mate a pint or two at Ernie's tonight. How's that, Archer?" He nodded to the lanky scowling sexton who had just appeared at Roddy's elbow.

"That's all very well, Mr. Mason, but you must remember, the main function of this 'ere lamp-'ouse is to provide a guidin' light to the fishin' boats. Can't do that properly if the mirrors an' glass are covered in dust, and the wicks are all choked up with it too, can we now?"

"Sorry, old chap, but short of covering up all the glass and lamps, there's nothing else we could do. And that would be an impossible job. This is a one-time event." Gerry turned to his helper. "Clean up here for me, Ted. Sprinkle some water to lay the dust before you sweep. The vicar and I need to have a chat." Gerry took Roddy by the elbow and steered him to the stairs leading up to the catwalk and vestry door. Once they were behind closed doors, Gerry said, "Sorry I started this mess without consulting you, Roddy. I know we really hadn't settled this business about the mausoleum, but I needed to see if it would be practical before I could propose a plan to you. To do that I needed to make a few test cuts. And they went very well. Once I saw that, I just got carried away. There's a natural cavity in the rock that will provide ample space for an alcove sufficient to accommodate two coffins on the right and four or five on the left. I'll frame the doorway with surplus stone from our building supplies, and one oak door will provide access from the lamp-house. Nothing fancy, mind you. A couple of plaques for the door to be engraved at the appropriate time and we're all finished. No more mess. Have you spoken with Bishop West yet about us all being laid to rest in here? On the strict understanding that he waits until we're dead, of course," Gerry said with a smile.

Roddy returned his smile. "Let me get some wine, my friend. I've really had enough of this kind of dismal planning for a while. I need something more cheerful." So, the two friends sat together by the fireplace in the vicar's office and finished the conversation that Gerry had started over a month ago – also over a glass of wine – in Roddy's cottage. "Well, Gerry, I did mention the mausoleum to Bishop West before I had to rush off to Bristol with Tubby. The bishop wanted some time to think the matter over but said he couldn't think of any objection off-hand. The fact that we were both instrumental in the building of the church obviously inclined him in our favour. The only thing he was concerned about was moving your wife's coffin from her family's mausoleum to here. He was going to write to your brother about that. I haven't raised the matter with him since."

"Well, I know my brother thought that it wasn't a problem, so I will go ahead and finish the job. If it becomes a problem later, well, we'll cross that bridge when we come to it."

"Sounds fine to me," said Roddy topping up their glasses. "But what happens if Pru and I have 10 children. Even after we chuck you out, we'll still be short of space. Besides, if we don't get the approval that we need, it could end up as a broom closet." Gerry looked a little puzzled. "I thought we agreed that just the principals would be resting in there. You don't see all the king's descendants in Westminster Abbey. There wouldn't be room enough for a congregation." They both laughed, clinked glasses, and the conversation turned to the possibility of Roddy and Prudence marrying, a prospect that Gerry favoured greatly. "A fine-spirited young lady is Miss Prudence," he said. "You shouldn't let her get away."

• • •

The first Sunday of the next month, Fletch and Marie were married in The Guiding Light Church. After the service, there was a splendid reception in the old church, which was now referred to as the Village Hall. Much of the catering was done by the new company 'Fletcher and Drew' of Next-west. Topping up was provided by the local ladies on a potluck basis, and beverages were supplied by The Harbour Light Inn. It was the happiest situation that the village had shared since Meg and Sailmaker were married at the old church. As might be expected, Meg was still very withdrawn. Although she added her best wishes, and she smiled whenever she caught someone looking in her direction, the whole village was conscious of her fears and loneliness.

The following week, Roddy and Prudence attended the baptism of Charles Rodney Tubbs in Nextwest. They were surprised to find that Bishop West had accepted the role of second godfather. Just before the ceremony, Roddy caught sight of Maud holding her little daughter and dabbing her eyes with a wadded handkerchief. When he asked why she was upset, Maud told him that her daughter had not yet been baptised, and that worried and saddened her. So, he and Tubby had a word with the bishop, who was pleased to add Emily Louise Barker to the ceremony after first ensuring that Roddy and Prudence were prepared to accept godparenting responsibilities for her too. Prudence elbowed Roddy and nodding in Tubby's direction, she said, "I think Tubby is looking at Maud in a different light these days, don't you agree?"

After the baptism, the bishop asked Gerry and Roddy to join him in his office. "Gerry. I've had a letter from your brother regarding the transfer of your wife's casket to the new mausoleum. He assures me that there are no living relatives on your wife's side to object. He considers this transfer would be quite acceptable, especially in view of your service to our community. Whilst I agree in principle, convention would require that your wife's transfer await your demise. You could then be committed to the vault together without any political objection. Otherwise, critics might complain that your good lady was never a resident of the community during her lifetime or a contributing partner in the founding of the church. That distinction falls to you and Roddy alone. In that event, you would all be together eventually, but, as I said, that would be after your own demise."

Gerry started to object, but the bishop raised a restraining hand. "Hear me out, Gerry. Please. I am merely trying to avoid future unpleasantness by being ready for some disgruntled soul's objection. Were you intending to have a formal public committal for your wife, Gerry, or a private one? He raised his eyebrows inviting Gerry's response.

Gerry was silent for a while, "I understand, Your Grace. But I must confess I had never thought that there might be 'local objections.' No, I had not intended a public ceremony. A private committal with Roddy officiating would be most acceptable. At least my dear wife would be close by and where we will be together eventually. Thank you."

"We should be thanking you, Gerry. Your efforts on behalf of the village would certainly confound any objections that might arise. I do appreciate your understanding of my need to avoid problems, however. There is always the probability of someone objecting, no matter how worthy the cause. Despite my precautions, please be assured that both you and your dear wife have my personal blessing."

Gerry and Roddy both looked pleased. "Thank you, Your Grace," they chorused.

CHAPTER 4

The wreck of The Seahorse

It was Friday afternoon and time for Archer's weekly inspection of the church and all its workings. He was standing on the inside catwalk examining the reflecting mirrors when he noticed a crack in one of the upper panes of glass in the crucifix window. "If that glass breaks," he muttered, "it could cause havoc." Climbing the outside ladders was a chore Archer usually left to Higgins because of his own painfully stiff joints. But Higgins wasn't due for more than an hour, and this could be a serious problem, so Archer decided to investigate that crack for himself close up. He exited the church through the front door. A gust of wind blew his unfastened coat open, causing him to draw it closed. "That wind'll clear away the remains of last night's storm," he muttered as he scrutinised the troubled grey sky. As he made his way to the steps that would take him to the lower level of the lamp-house, he smiled, noting the sparkling windows reflecting the weak sunlight. Grasping the handrail of the steps that led down to the lower level of the lamp-house, he paused briefly and took a deep breath before beginning his descent. He lowered his left foot to the first step and carefully followed that with his right. Each step was painfully achieved in the same careful manner, left foot first, and with each footfall punctuated by a quiet grunt. "Bloody joints are seizin' up on me," he grumbled. "If this keeps up, I'll soon be a bloody invalid."

The first sexton of The Guiding Light Church took his job seriously. In fact, Archer took everything seriously. So seriously that it had earned him the title "the village sourpuss." Once on the lower level, Archer started his painful climb of the rungs of the wall mounted iron ladder. When he reached the horizontal arm of the cruciform window, he was relieved to discover that what he'd thought to be a crack was, in fact, a supple twig that lodged in the corner of the frame. He pulled it free. "Looked just like a bloody crack from inside," he grumbled. "What are the odds that would wedge there so tight?" He glanced over his shoulder for a rare view of the coastline and was surprised to see a ship – a three-masted barque – carrying just sufficient sail to maintain steerage control. It was about a mile south-west of his old western beacon. "Wonder what they're up to," he muttered. "Looks to be a lot of activity on deck."

Then suddenly, without any warning, a brilliant sheet of lightning seemed to explode from the ship's mizzen mast. The blinding light flashed outward from the ship covering a large area including the village and the church, but it lasted only an instant. Archer clung tightly to the ladder; his eyes squeezed shut against the glare. A split second later, a tremendous thunderclap shook the ground, causing him to grip the ladder extra tightly. He opened his eyes just in time to see the ship's mizzen mast collapsing, bringing down the shrouds, spars, and sail and completely covering the helmsman and a large part of the quarterdeck. The sky rapidly darkened, and the wind shifted to the west and began pushing ominous looking clouds with unusual speed towards the ship. The wind was now blowing so hard that Archer's unfastened coat cracked like a whiplash. "Where in 'eaven's name did that lot come from?" The bewildered sexton gasped as the force of the wind caused him to struggle for his breath. He checked his grip on the ladder and strained to see how the ship was faring. Now he was forced to shield his eyes against stinging rain, but he did manage to see figures frantically hacking at rigging that had been dragged over the port quarter by the falling mast. The mess of spars, furled sails and rigging were dragging in the sea, acting like a pivot and changing the ship's heading towards the coast. Archer could see that the vicious weather was making it difficult for the crew to cut the mess loose. The ship had lost all semblance of steerage control. He watched with bated breath as the waves, built ever higher by the increasing wind, pushed the ship closer towards the rocky shore. "My God. It looks like she'll be driven ashore."

Archer hurried his stiff legs down the ladder, but the wind was so fierce that he hesitated to let go of it before making the few short steps to the lamp-house door. He clung to the door frame not knowing what had happened to the ship but realising it was at the mercy of the wind. He watched anxiously as the ship – broadside to the waves now – was pushed relentlessly towards the cliffs. "My God. She's going into Sorry Cove!" he exclaimed as the ship disappeared behind the cliff where his 'western beacon' still stood. "Oh, my God! She's a gonner for sure." Inside the lamp-house, he pulled on the bell rope to alert the villagers. The new bell added its mournful voice to the noise of the wind. "I hope none of our lads have been caught up in this," he gasped as he heaved on the bell rope. "I've never seen such a vicious squall, and it sprung up so fast." Short minutes later, the sound of the ship being hammered against the rocks in Sorry Cove reached his straining ears.

Painfully he hobbled up the stairway to the catwalk through the church and out the front door. There he had to pause to recover his breath before hobbling off in the direction of the village. He had only travelled about a hundred yards when he saw Higgins running towards him. He paused gratefully, huffing and puffing, resting both hands on his knees as he waited for the younger man. Higgins was soon at his side. "You alright?" Higgins yelled. "I heard the bell. Where did this bloody squall come from? Did I hear a crash?"

Archer looked up. "You sure did!" he shouted. "There's a ship – a three-master – gone into Sorry Cove. Get some help down there. Send for Doc Hudson. I'll follow you. Hurry!" Then as quickly as the storm had begun, that terrible howling wind ceased, and the weather returned to the lighter gusts that had preceded the squall. The two men stood facing each other dumbstruck. Archer raised his arms in a gesture of shocked disbelief. There was no longer any need to shout. "It's as though someone opened a door to the mother of all storms, then quickly closed it," he said.

"I'll get some 'elp," said the bewildered Higgins. "Sure you're alright?"

"I'll be fine, 'iggins. You 'urry off to the inn right now." When Archer reached Sorry Cove, he saw several villagers wading in the shallow water, and Doc Hudson was being helped over the rocks by Ernie to examine the recovered bodies and see if anyone might benefit from his skills.

"It's The Seahorse!" screamed Meg pointing to the figurehead. "Sailmaker should be on this ship. Look for Sailmaker! Look for Sailmaker!" She splashed through the shallow water checking with all the rescuers as her eyes frantically searched the water and the ship for signs of her husband. All the fishing boats were at sea, but the village's remaining men and

From the author's sketchbook

women were not sparing themselves in their efforts to find and rescue survivors. " 'ere's the cap'n!" yelled Emily Rooken. "Remember 'im? 'e's 'alf drowned." She half lifted Currie's unconscious body from a rock pool where he'd been lying face down, dragged him to higher ground and began pumping his back, forcing water from his lungs. As soon as he started to cough and sputter, Emily left him to hurry to another man who was trying desperately to hold his head above water whilst trying to free his legs from a tangle of rigging that was holding him below the surface. Emily grabbed his collar and held his head above water as she disentangled some rope from around his feet before pulling him clear. It was Swift, one of the missionary priests. He sat up gasping his thanks as he gradually recovered his normal breathing.

"There's a black fella over 'ere," called Higgins from an area near The Chute. "Dead as a bloody doornail, 'e is. Got a bad chest wound. Looks like someone run 'im through." Gerry Mason was waist deep in water struggling to pull a submerged figure to the surface. Then he discovered that the man was impaled on a shattered length of broken spar trapped by the fallen shrouds. The spar had penetrated just below his ribcage, and almost two feet of it was now sticking out through his back. It took considerable mental effort for Gerry to keep his lunch down. "This one's a priest," he yelled. "Or was! He's impaled on a spar." Higgins responded to his call for help, and between them, they dragged the man off the shattered timber. That was when Higgins surrendered the contents of his stomach to Sorry Cove. "Look to the live ones first, people," Doc Hudson called.

Over the course of the next two hours, the villagers managed to get all of the discovered bodies off the wreck and out of the water onto higher ground, so that Doc Hudson could examine them. Only two more were found alive. The captain, thanks to Emily, was one of the survivors, but although he was now breathing regularly, he remained unconscious. Doc Hudson suspected concussion but believed he would recover. Ernie called to some nearby villagers, "Let's load the injured men onto Archer's wagon, people. There's only three, no, four, that look as though they'll make it. Doc, what say we take them to the inn? You would have better conditions there to look after them."

"Good idea, Ernie. Perhaps I could go with them. I'm soaked through and too damn tired to walk."

"Sure, old friend." As Ernie was helping Doc onto the wagon, he saw his daughter struggling to climb aboard the wreck. So he returned to the water to help Meg, yelling: "Higgins, let's take a look inside the ship! Keep your eyes open for a logbook or other ship's papers. Most likely in the captain's cabin – what's left of it." As he passed Gerry, he asked, "Gerry, when the wagon comes back, could you have someone take the dead to the old church?" Gerry nodded wearily. Ernie explained. "Sailmaker's still missing. I'm going to help Meg search the ship. God! What a mess. The vicar ain't here either. We'll need him."

"He shouldn't be long now, Ernie. He's usually back by mid-afternoon on Fridays." Gerry's voice was weak from exhaustion and he was chilled through. "By God, I'm too old for this sort of thing," he said. "Poor old Doc must have the constitution of a horse."

"Any sign of Sailmaker?!" Ernie was yelling, as he passed anxiously amongst the weary rescue team." All shook their heads. Meg was desperately dragging at fallen sail and shrouds on the quarterdeck when Ernie yelled to Archer. "Archer, ask those two survivors if Sailmaker was aboard!" Archer questioned the conscious men and called back to Ernie. "They say 'e was aboard, Ernie, but they kept lookin' at each other, waitin' for the other bloke to speak first. There's somethin' amiss, or I'm a Dutch uncle. They didn't want to look me in the eye. Neither one wants to speak up. Guilty lookin' pair, I say. Keep lookin', Ernie. Sailmaker should be 'ere. But I think there's somethin' bad they ain't tellin' us."

Higgins and Ernie entered the broken ship through a gaping hole in its side. Finding no sign of Sailmaker below, they clambered up to the sloping deck to join Meg searching amongst the mess on the quarterdeck. Both the main and foremasts had shattered and fallen when the vessel struck the rocks. The two men had to climb over a tangled mass of ropes, sail, and shattered timber to reach Meg. Higgins discovered the helmsman's feet protruding from under a mess of rigging. He and Ernie began to tear away the mess as Meg scrambled to join them. A falling tackle block had smashed the helmsman's skull and now lay on the deck by his shoulder. But it wasn't Sailmaker. Meg covered her face with both hands and began to cry. Ernie tried to comfort her. "Now, now, lass. It's not Sailmaker. Let's take another look below," he said holding her tight to his chest.

As those three struggled to keep their footing on the tilted vessel's lower decks, another group of searchers were working their way out of the cove and along the shallows of the coastline. The low tide allowed others partway into The Chute where they were sometimes bumped by floating rum casks and even a sea chest. But they found no trace of Sailmaker or any other crew. An hour later, soaked through and too cold and exhausted to continue, they were obliged to give up. But Ernie and Higgins couldn't persuade Meg that they had done all that was possible and felt compelled to stay with her as she researched all the places they had covered before.

Doc Hudson was attending to the injured, who were now in bed at the inn, while Ernie's arthritic wife had made a rare appearance to serve free soup to the grateful rescuers. A few of the recent arrivals were standing in front of the fire, drinking soup from beer mugs, as steam rose from their clothing. Most of the women had remained at home after changing into dry clothes, but a few were enjoying the hot soup, Emily Rooken being one of them. It was into this damp and depressed atmosphere that the vicar arrived. He was shocked at the scene and more so by the tragedy. But his greatest concern came when he heard it was The Seahorse that was wrecked and that there was no trace of Sailmaker. "My God!" he said to Gerry. "How is Meg handling this?"

"Well, she insisted on searching the ship again," responded Gerry. "We had a job to get her off the ship. After that, she wanted to take Sailmaker's dinghy along the shoreline. Ernie finally persuaded her to go home, change into dry clothes and take some nourishment. He told her that some of the fishing boats would be returning very soon, and they could handle the search much better than a small dinghy. He promised her that they would search immediately, adding that the fishermen would have a better idea where to look. By all accounts, Sailmaker should have been in the fo'c'sle, but a gaping hole had been smashed in the bow." "It's possible that he might have been washed out to sea," whispered Higgins as he joined their conversation.

The first of the fishing boats to return was Carter's, and his boat was heavily laden with a good catch. Two others soon followed. There was a mad scramble to unload the fish once the men heard the news, and they quickly put out to sea again leaving others to look after their catch. The men were yelling the news to each other as their boats passed in the channel. Some of the inbound boats immediately turned around to join the search, still loaded; Sullivan's being the first of those. Benjamin Cobbe's boat had two small kegs of rum on board. "Found them floating at the harbourside entrance to The Chute," he said. "They must be from the wreck."

Doc Hudson had managed to get a list of names from the conscious first mate, Ruddock. From that, they discovered that there were still seven men unaccounted for, one of them being Sailmaker. Darkness forced the boats to give up the search; the last of the boats to give up had been Sullivan's. It was a very solemn crowd that gathered at the inn to discuss how to proceed the following day. Fifteen dead crewmen were laid out in two rows on the floor of the old church. Some had been crushed between the ship and the rocks when they were thrown overboard; others had drowned trapped underwater by submerged rigging. At the end of one line of corpses was Palmer, the missionary that had been impaled by the splintered yard arm, and he was a stomach-wrenching sight. In the middle of the second row was the black man. "Never seen the likes of 'im before," said Higgins. "Don't see many black blokes 'ereabouts. Looks like a sword wound did for 'im. What d' you think that was all about?"

"Now how the hell should I know?" responded the exhausted Ernie. "I'm more anxious to know what happened to Sailmaker." Doc Hudson and Gerry were searching the bodies for identification when Doc found a letter, addressed to Bishop Mason, in the missionary's pocket. He gave it to Gerry. "This is quite a coincidence, Gerry; the man that you dragged from the water was carrying a letter addressed to your brother. I imagine that you could best arrange delivery of that. In all this confusion, I'd forgotten that The Seahorse was a missionary ship."

When they came to the black man, they found a leather pouch and a hand-carved crucifix hanging around his neck. "Well, it appears that the black man was a Christian," said the doctor. "Let's see what his purse reveals. Another letter for your brother." The doctor was amazed as he handed the wet document to Mason. "And a wedding band! Now, who would have thought that? But it's too small for his finger."

Any items salvaged from the wreck were being deposited in one corner of the old church. That salvage now included some casks of rum, two sea chests and various other items and personal effects. Brannigan's fiddle was one such item, though poor Brannigan would never scrape another tune from it. His lifeless body lay next to the black man. Higgins had discovered the logbook and some other papers in the captain's cabin and taken them to the inn.

"If the weather's good enough, we should be able to salvage quite a lot in the next few days," he told Gerry. "The hold is loaded with good timber. It's mahogany according to the manifest. However, if we get a storm, the sea will likely smash the remains of the ship and drag everything back out to sea. All that will remain then will be a few scattered pieces."

Back at the inn, the captain was still unconscious. The first mate had suffered a broken nose plus some cuts and bruises but appeared in good shape otherwise. The other crewman, a youngster named Newton, had suffered some cracked ribs plus cuts and bruises, but time would heal those. Despite his relative good fortune, Newton seemed nervous and frightened to speak, always casting anxious glances at Ruddock, the first mate, especially when questioned about Sailmaker. Doc Hudson and Ernie took another look at the captain. "He should be conscious by now," said the doctor. "In fact, I thought he was when I first came in."

"Maybe he doesn't want to wake up," responded Ernie. "This is the bastard that molested Meg and shanghaied Sailmaker. When he wakes up, he'll have me to deal with. I want to know where Sailmaker is, and depending on his answers, I may wring his bloody neck and stick him back in the wreckage."

"Can't you get any information about what happened from the other two crewmen, Ernie?"

"No. Both of them claim lost memory. I'm going to separate 'em and question them one at a time. If I have to get nasty, I can do that."

"Careful, Ernie! These are injured, men. And we don't know that they're guilty of anything."

"Not as injured as they'll be if I don't get some satisfactory answers," said the innkeeper as he stomped from the room. "Some of the villagers recognised the first mate as the cox'n of the jolly boat that was hauled aboard The Seahorse as she was leaving harbour. They believed that Sailmaker had been in the bottom of that boat." The missionary priest was recovering well. He was nervous and very depressed by his colleague's death but grateful to be safe and well cared for. Ernie decided to have Roddy – who had already been briefed by Archer – question him. Roddy was calm and reassuring and smiled as he introduced himself. "Father, we need to know what happened aboard The Seahorse. Why was she hove to just before the squall?" The missionary looked troubled. "The captain was punishing two men for mutiny," he said. "He was a stickler for strict discipline; he ran The Seahorse like a king's ship with regular musters for men under punishment." Ernie was listening outside the door as Roddy asked, "Really, and which men were to be punished?"

"A man called Sailmaker and a black man named Latour. Latour was the ship's cook." The priest looked downcast. "I understand that Sailmaker came from here. Is that true?"

"Yes, Sailmaker was a popular man here in Ryeport and a very good friend of mine. Tell me, Father, what was the punishment, and was it carried out?"

"Yes, well, partly. The captain convicted both men of mutiny and striking their officers. He had Sailmaker keelhauled. Amazingly, the man survived. It seems the men dragging him around the keel helped him somehow. The captain, however, realised what they were doing and allowed it to continue because he would use that as an excuse to repeat the punishment. He said the crew would have to keep doing it until they got it right.

"The cook was Sailmaker's friend. He kept harassing the captain and urging the crew to stop the punishment, calling them gutless cowards. Anyway, the captain changed his mind and decided to hang Sailmaker instead. Captain Currie is a vicious and vindictive man. He said he knew Sailmaker wanted to see Ryeport again so he would give him his wish. He'd hang him from the yardarm, on the port side, to give him a better view. The first mate was about to put the noose around his neck when the lightning struck, and all hell broke loose."

"So, what happened to Sailmaker?"

"After the mast came down, the ship was in turmoil. The captain threw him through the fo'c'sle door. He said he would deal with him later."

"Was there any chance that Sailmaker could have got out?"

"I doubt it. He was recovering from a keelhauling, remember."

"The black man, Latour. He seems to have been killed with a sword thrust. Do you know how that happened?"

"As I said, Latour was Sailmaker's friend. He tried to incite the crew to free Sailmaker. He even managed to break away from his guards during the squall. He shoulder charged Captain Currie and knocked him down. His hands were tied, and he was also suffering from a beating from the previous night. The captain was furious; he just lost his temper and ran him through. There was quite a build-up to this mutiny charge. Last night, the captain had molested the cook's daughter. The cook had disguised her and signed her aboard as a cabin boy. However, the captain discovered the deception on that last night aboard and was trying to molest her. She broke free and climbed into the mizzen shrouds trying to escape. This was all happening during a storm. The girl was in the shrouds with Sailmaker and the cook trying to rescue her. She had managed to kick the captain in the eye as he tried to pull her from the shrouds. When he gets angry, the captain loses all control. He smashed her tiny hands with a belaying pin, and she fell from the shrouds into the sea. Despite all our pleas, the captain refused to try and save her. Sailmaker and the cook had been overpowered by then and because they fought him – trying to save the girl – the captain had them put in irons. It was the cook's own daughter, for heaven's sake. The captain said he would punish them the next day. 'The punishment for mutiny is death,' he said. It seemed only the means was left to be decided."

Roddy's expression was grim. "So, these men were trying to save the life of a young girl whom the captain was prepared to drown?" The vicar's tone was hard and incredulous. "Where were the rest of the crew? Why didn't they stop this?"

"A lot of the crew were cronies of the captain – old shipmates from his days in king's ships. The rest were scared of them. A few of us tried but were beaten down. My colleague wrote a letter describing the incident. He addressed it to Bishop Mason. I imagine that even if you find it, the ink will have run too badly for it to be readable."

"We have the letter. Actually, the bishop's brother was part of the rescue crew from the village yesterday."

"Really, how could that be?" Swift was obviously amazed at that. "Reverend, I'm truly grateful for your help," he said. "I only wish my colleague could have been spared also. He was a good man and my good friend. We were both coming home to retire. He was quite ill, you know." Roddy nodded. "We will arrange for your return to London. You can give your report to Bishop Mason there." Roddy was desolate. His friend Sailmaker was lost. The exhausted villagers were asleep. Their efforts to rescue the crew of The Seahorse and their inability to find Sailmaker had completed their fatigue.

• • •

However, in the old church, in that dark makeshift mortuary, something unnatural was stirring. At first, it was just a sense of awareness – a disembodied sense of being, formless, and lacking purpose or intelligence – an empty vessel. Then came tiny, localised sensations of extreme cold, slowly repeated from diverse areas. Gradually those cold spots merged, blending, until the cold alone defined it as a whole body of cold, frighteningly cold. The cold intensified, and the body began to shiver, with the shivering growing increasingly violent. That sense of awareness realised that it was part of the body of cold. It is – I am – the body and in severe distress. Soon it was convulsing, and the lack of understanding became an overwhelming sense of fear. Then new sensations arrived, and they frightened the body even more. It convulsed and involuntarily sucked in great frightening gulps of air. It was desperate for more air. Gradually, the gasping grew less violent, smoother and more rhythmic. It was breathing. Then it – he – became aware that the blackness surrounding him was not absolute. There were lesser shades of darkness. Sensations now began to come, fast and furious. Before he had time to explore one, there was another and yet another. He noticed three regular paler shapes that were lighter than their surroundings. What little light there was appeared to emanate from them. The three shapes were standing in a row and had curved pointed tops.

Then he discovered he could move some cold parts, even feel one cold part touch another. *Arms!* Those parts were arms, he remembered. He tried to see them, causing another cold part to move, and the pale shapes retreated. He moved that part back again, and the shapes returned. *That's it. It's my head that's moving. That part is my head. It - I - am turning my head.* He discovered another three of those pale, pointed shapes opposite the first three. He could see. Eyes – it was his eyes that made things visible. Now he was remembering his body parts. But they had never been so cold.

The shaking had slowed again reverting to shivering. It was distressing, but it was slowly warming him. He was desperately tired. His eyes were gradually adjusting to the faint light that came from those less dark areas. Windows! They were windows – church windows – because of their shape. He laid his head down again weary from the shivering and the struggle to understand. He extended his right arm. It touched something. That too was cold, colder even than he was. He snatched his hand away fearfully and tried to see what he had touched. His eyes, now adjusted to the faint light, revealed the body of a man lying beside him. Then he made out other bodies laid in a row. He gasped in horror. His breath coming now in harsh, rapid gasps that made his throat ache. He extended his other arm, another cold contact, another body. He was part of a row of corpses. That was when he discovered he could scream. That loud unexpected noise was even more alarming and added to his terror.

He sat up and looked around. The dim moon-glow revealed another row of bodies at his feet and parallel to his row. He recognised them. There was Merry, Porter, Gomez, and the missionary Palmer. The man beside him was Brannigan, the fiddler. *They are all dead!* He held his head and screamed again. *Am I dead?* He ran his hands over his cold body, momentarily silent as he frantically tried to understand what was happening. *Is this hell?* He rolled over, scared to touch the bodies on either side and staggered, stiff-legged, to his feet looking for a door. *There!* Beyond the second row of bodies, a faint strip of light showed at floor level. *It must be a door.* He stumbled towards it, falling over bodies as he tried to get fluid movement into stiff reluctant legs and moaning fearfully.

He lifted the latch and pulled open the door to be confronted by a ghostly figure draped in white, holding a lantern aloft. He screamed again. The ghostly apparition screamed back. He turned to run and fell over a body. Seconds passed before a trembling, but very human voice said, "It's alright! Don't be frightened. You scared the hell out of me though. We thought you were dead." The ghostly figure proved to be Gerry Mason in his nightshirt. Latour's first scream had wakened him as he slept in the vicar's old cottage next to the old church. The second scream had prompted Gerry to investigate. Latour was on all fours now, straddling two dead crewmates, and still terrified. But he had recognised that voice as human. That at least was a comfort. "Where am I?" Gerry held his lantern higher. "You are in the old church at Ryeport. We thought that you were dead. We were sure you were dead!"

"I thought I was dead. Can you get me out of here?"

"Certainly." Gerry extended his hand. "Take my hand. My cottage is next door. Let's get you somewhere warm and something to eat. You are freezing cold and must be starving." Minutes later, they were sitting in front of a freshly stoked fire with Latour eagerly stretching his hands towards the flames. A blanket was around his naked body as he waited eagerly for the soup that Gerry was reheating in a kettle. His clothes were drying in front of the fire.

"You're Latour, the cook, aren't you?"

"Yes. How many others survived the wreck?"

"Only four," responded Gerry. "Five. Now we can include you. Although everyone in the village was certain that you were dead, even our doctor.

How could you possibly survive that chest wound?"

Latour looked puzzled and pulled the blanket away from his chest. The wound had healed. In its place, there was a depressed scar. The tissue surrounding the scar had a dark yellowish tinge, quite distinct against his darker brown skin. He tested his ribs expecting to feel the pain inflicted by the captain's boots and the belaying pin. Nothing! There was no pain. He had healed. Gerry was staring at Latour's chest in amazement. "That wound was wide open when we laid you in the church. No one heals that fast. Not from a wound like that."

Latour looked uncomfortable. "Where are the other survivors?" He stood up. "I want to see them. Is one of them called Sailmaker?"

"No. We never found Sailmaker. There's Captain Currie and his first mate, Ruddock. One of the missionaries and a young crewman named Newton. They are the only survivors. However, seeing them will have to wait a few hours. It's one o'clock in the morning. We can't wake up the good folks at the inn yet. They're all exhausted from their rescue efforts. There's nothing to be accomplished by waking them now anyway. Here's your soup. I'll get you some bread and cheese. Would you like a shot of brandy?"

Latour's hand suddenly flew to his neck. "My pouch! It's gone. Where is my pouch?" There was panic in his voice. "It's safe. I have it," said Gerry. "The doctor was looking for identification on the victims and found a letter addressed to Bishop Mason in your pouch. I was going to deliver it. I am Gerry Mason. Bishop Mason is my brother." Latour looked dazed. "I need that letter. It's important. Give it to me. Please. My wife's wedding ring was in the same pouch."

"Certainly, old chap. I'll get it for you." Latour followed Gerry to his bedroom where he retrieved the pouch from a small bureau and handed it to the still shaking black man. Gerry waved another letter under his nose. "This letter too was addressed to my brother. We found this one on a dead missionary named Palmer. I shall have the task of delivering that also. Would you like me to deliver yours as well, or do you need to do that in person?"

"I must deliver the letter. It's an introduction." Latour replaced the letter and the ring in his pouch, then looped the leather thong around his neck. He patted the pouch and, feeling the hard-circular shape of the ring, seemed to relax a little. Gerry rested a reassuring hand on Latour's shoulder. "Drink your soup, Latour. We can discuss what you want to do once you have warmed up. Get back to the fire for a while. I'll get you some clothes; we are of similar size."

"I want to see the captain!" Latour's face was grim.

"So, you shall in a few hours. He was half drowned when we found him. He's been unconscious ever since. Hadn't come to when we went to bed a couple of hours ago. He's not going anywhere in a hurry. Relax. Warm yourself. Sleep a little if you can."

"I'm frightened too."

Gerry felt for Latour's pulse. "You have a good, strong, regular pulse, my friend. You'll be fine. Whatever kept you below the threshold of life, as we know it, has moved on. Here, have a shot of brandy. I'll join you. Maybe we can both get a little rest before the sun rises. I've a feeling that tomorrow will be one hell of a day."

• • •

It was only minutes before this that Ruddock, the first mate, had been startled from his sleep when a hand clamped hard over his mouth. "Shh… Shh…. Quiet! Quiet now," the captain whispered. "We mustn't wake anyone." Ruddock ceased struggling, and the captain slowly removed his silencing hand allowing Ruddock to sit up. "What's up?" said Ruddock. "Are you alright? They said you were still unconscious." The captain raised a cautioning finger to his lips. "I'm alright. I just have a bad headache that's all. Come on. Get dressed. Quietly now! We've got to get away from here."

"What do you mean?" The mate's voice rose in shock, and the captain's hand quickly covered his mouth again.

"Hurry! I'll tell you more outside. Quietly now!"

The two men made their way down to the kitchen and were stuffing bread and cheese into their mouths when the captain spotted his logbook and manifest on the kitchen table. He heaved a sigh of relief as he picked them up. "These will help our case," he said. "Where are we going?" asked Ruddock. "We'll head up to the Coach Road and east from there. If a coach passes tomorrow, we'll flag it down. We'll need to be a good distance east of here by sunrise. If we see anything but the coach, we hide. Understand?"

"Alright! What brought all this about? The moonlight flit, I mean."

"When they thought I was unconscious, I heard the innkeeper say that he plans to kill us all and put us amongst the bodies from the wreck. First though, he wants to find out what happened to Sailmaker. He was married to his daughter. Sailmaker's some sort of local hero. If we're caught, we're gonners for sure. They remember you from the jolly boat."

"I knew there was somethin' afoot," said Ruddock. "They kept askin' Newton and the missionary about Sailmaker. They must know we took 'im."

"What did you tell them?"

"Said I'd lost me mem'ry. Yes, 'e was aboard, but I didn't know what 'appened to 'im. Or anyone else for that matter."

The two men slipped quietly out of the inn.

"Why don't we take their wagon?" asked Ruddock. "We could leave it in the next town where we pick up the coach. It'll stop them comin' after us."

"Can't risk the horse making a noise."

"You keep watch," said Ruddock. "I'll 'arness up the 'orse an' keep it quiet. I know 'ow t' do that. Did a bit o' smugglin' in me time. Before bein' pressed that was. We'll walk it quietly up the road 'til we're out of earshot. Then we'll get aboard. We could be in the next town, safe an' sound, waitin' for the coach by the time they find we're gone." Ruddock proved very good at keeping Slondosh and the dogs quiet. Possibly because he'd come from the inn, not from outside. The dogs didn't bark immediately. He gave each dog a piece of cheese, and they soon became friends. In the stable he wrapped Slondosh's hooves in sacking, talking softly to the animal and stroking his neck as he harnessed him to the wagon. Then he covered the pony's eyes and nostrils with a piece of wet sacking and led him quietly from the stable. He gave the dogs an extra treat from their stolen rations and walked the wagon quietly along the harbour front, past the old church and Mason's cottage, hardly making any noise at all.

Ernie and his son Tom were up at first light knowing this would be a very busy day. The first priority would be the burial arrangements for all the dead from the wreck. But when they got downstairs, they were surprised to find Doc Hudson already waiting for them. "Couldn't sleep," he said, "so I thought I'd get a quick bite to eat and an early look at the patients." "Aye! Let's do that," responded the innkeeper. "Tom, get some breakfast going; there's a good lad. We'll check on the patients and be down in a few minutes." They were back almost immediately. "The captain and his first mate are gone," Ernie told his son. "The bastard was faking it. That explains the missing food," said Tom. "Cheese, cold meat, bread and some hard-boiled eggs that I left on a plate in the pantry yesterday have all gone."

"Harness up the vicar's wagon, Tom; they'll try for the first eastbound coach, I reckon." Then he slapped his hand on the kitchen table. "Look, they took the bloody logbook and manifest too. I left them here last night." Tom came back looking very glum. "They took the wagon, Dad. I'm surprised the dogs didn't bark. I didn't hear a thing." Ernie sat at the kitchen table holding his head in his hands. When he looked up, he said,"Well, we're done for then. We don't know when they left. They could be in Nexteast by now for all we know, and we've no way to catch them. If Hawksworth comes in today, maybe he'd ride to Nexteast for us. He might get some news. I doubt they'll try to take the wagon all the way to London. That'll be where they're heading for sure. There's a chance we might get the vicar's wagon back though. At times like this, we could use more than one horse and buggy in the village."

"Dad, the eastbound stage isn't due at the crossroads for at least another two hours. We could catch it if we run. I bet they'll board the stage at Nexteast. We could be on it."

"Aye! Maybe you could run that fast, lad, but I couldn't, and you'd be no match for two ruthless bastards like those. I won't let you go alone, and I couldn't keep up with you. Let it go, lad. We'll find some other way to solve the problem. Hawksworth can let the constable know about the stolen wagon for starters."

Gerry Mason and Latour had spent the night in the wingchairs by the fire. Gerry hadn't a spare bed to offer Latour and didn't have the heart to leave the man alone after his terrible ordeal, so they had both made do with the wingchairs and blankets. Latour was still 'champing at the bit' in his anxiety to see the captain, so after a hurried breakfast, they headed for the inn. The doctor, Ernie, and his son were still eating when Gerry opened the door from the bar into the kitchen.

"Good morning, gentlemen," Gerry said. "I would like to introduce you to my new friend: Paul Latour, the cook from The Seahorse." He stood aside allowing Latour to step into the kitchen. Ernie dropped his fork. The colour drained from Doc Hudson's face, and Tom's mouth dropped open, spilling some food. No one spoke for almost a minute. It was Latour who finally broke the silence. "Good morning, gentlemen. Please, don't let me spoil your breakfast. Introductions can wait until you're finished." Doc Hudson rose from his chair, having regained most of his normal composure. "Well, Mr. Latour, you certainly look a lot healthier than when I saw you last." His eyes studied the black man's overall appearance, taking note of his self-assured stance, clear eyes and obvious air of wellbeing.

"Well, Mr. Mason here was kind enough to feed me and provide me with fresh clothing. Clothes make the man, some say."

Ernie stood and extended his hand. "Sit down, Latour. I'm the innkeeper. Call me Ernie. Can we get you something to eat or drink?"

"No, Sir, but thank you. As I said, Mr. Mason has been kind enough to feed me. Actually, I'm most anxious to see Captain Currie. We have some urgent and unfinished business." Latour's frustration when he learned of the flight of the captain and his first mate was close to anger. The fact that the village had no means to chase after them only made that worse. He explored all avenues and possibilities for following the escapees, becoming more tense and impatient at each fresh disappointment. It took quite a while to assure him that they would do all they could to assist him in his chase. They were especially anxious to help after Latour told them of the events of the previous evening and the loss of his daughter at the captain's hands.

Doc Hudson hadn't been able to take his eyes off Latour. Eventually, he said, "Please forgive my staring, Latour. Your unexpected appearance and obvious good health have stunned me so that I quite forgot my manners. I'm Doctor Hudson. I examined you yesterday and pronounced you dead. It appeared that you had died from a well-targeted sword thrust to the chest. Would you mind if I took another look at that wound? Infections can be deadly, and I confess that because I thought you dead, I didn't clean the wound."

"It's fine, doctor. There is no infection."

"Nevertheless, I would appreciate another look. Such a bad diagnosis is hard for a man of my experience to live with. Please, humour an old man."

Latour looked at Gerry who shrugged and gave him a nod. Latour opened his shirt. There was no wound. Even the yellow discolouration of last evening had disappeared leaving only a faint jagged scar. Doc Hudson took a step back shocked beyond belief. He reached out and touched the scar, gently pressing the flesh around it. "My God, I've never seen anything like it. The scar is more in keeping with a superficial cut, not a life-ending sword thrust. Who are you, Sir? How do you explain this?"

"Perhaps the wound was not as bad as it appeared, Sir. Also, my family has a history of fast healing. Possibly our lifestyle promotes that."

"Rubbish! There were several people who helped move you from the rocks to our old church, and they've all seen death before. You were dead, my friend, and I certainly can't explain your recovery. It smacks of witchcraft or sorcery although I don't believe in such things." All the men in the room were looking at Latour as though he had materialised out of thin air. Tom, in particular, looked very scared.

"Gentlemen! Please!" Latour's smile was a little strained. "There are more things in heaven and earth, etcetera. Obviously, there has been some over-sight because of my different physiology and the stresses of the rescue. I can assure you; I'm not devil spawn or some other evil reincarnation. You have nothing to fear from me." He reached for his pouch and withdrew the letter. "This letter of introduction is addressed to Bishop Mason in London. It was written by my late father-in-law, Reverend Gooding, a missionary priest in Haiti. Reverend Gooding was well known to your rescued missionary, Reverend Swift." Turning to Gerry, he said, "Mr. Mason, do you think your brother would be offended if you read this letter before he did? I wonder if you might be kind enough to read it aloud for the benefit of these good people. I'm sure it would help reassure them. I'm familiar with its contents. It was written in my presence." Gerry took the letter and looked around the group. They all nodded. Gerry read the letter aloud. It told of the events leading up to Latour's need to leave Haiti, both for his own safety and that of his daughter. It also asked for the help of the Bishop Mason in finding suitable employment for his son-in-law. "Now, gentlemen, I'm told that one of the survivors from The Seahorse was Reverend Swift, another missionary. He knew Father Gooding. I'm sure that he will be able to verify much of what is in the letter," said Latour.

"Sounds good enough to me," said Ernie. "Tom, please ask the vicar to join us. We have a lot to discuss here. Better that we hash it out together and form a plan of action." Emily Rooken arrived with the vicar. On seeing Latour, they both appeared shocked and hesitated before entering the kitchen. Emily stood partly behind the vicar as though trying to hide from the strange black man whom she knew – from firsthand experience – was 'dead as a bloody doornail' when she had helped load his lifeless body on Archer's cart last evening. Latour too was obviously uncomfortable in this atmosphere. "Gentlemen and lady," he said, giving a small courteous bow to Emily. "I'm obviously causing you all considerable discomfort. Why don't I wait in the next room so that you can discuss your concerns freely?" He addressed Ernie. "With your permission, Sir, I would like to have a word with the other two survivors. They may be able to provide me with some clues regarding the captain's destination."

"Draw up a chair, Latour," responded Ernie. "You have every right to hear whatever anyone has to say about you. Tom, please arrange for the two survivors to join us. They can add their views to our discussion. Perhaps we can even learn what really happened to Sailmaker."

By the time the westbound stagecoach arrived at The Harbour Light, the group had heard the survivor's versions of life aboard The Seahorse, the captain's pursuit of Tiny, and Sailmaker and Latour's attempts to save her. Swift, the missionary, and Newton, the youngest member of the crew, confirmed Latour's account of the events on board. In fact, Latour learned more from the missionary about his daughter's attempted escape from the captain than he had known before. He explained his reasons for disguising his daughter as a boy and the circumstances under which he had met Sailmaker. How they had contrived for him to get him passage on The Seahorse as a cook and Currie's later attempt to execute them. Hawksworth arrived midway through the session and was party to much of the story. Latour said, "One favour I would ask of you all is to call me 'Cook.' Paul Cook rather than Latour. As you now know, Captain Currie intended to kill Sailmaker and myself as mutineers. I'm sure that he will press that claim in London and blame us for the loss of the ship. Calling me 'Cook' – my job aboard The Seahorse – could prevent my immediate arrest and allow me time to confront the captain." He turned to Gerry. "Obviously, Sir, I will identify myself honestly to your brother when I present the letter."

The coachmen found that today, the patrons of The Harbour Light were not hanging on their every word. They had a more impressive tale of their own to tell. So, the coachmen took their free lunch and left, armed with the news of yesterday's shipwreck – but nothing of Latour's miraculous return from the dead. Hawksworth volunteered to ride to Nexteast and returned later that evening driving the vicar's wagon with his horse tethered behind. The innkeeper of The Star and Garter claimed he hadn't been paid for the stabling and feeding of the horse, and Hawksworth had been obliged to pay again in order to retrieve Slondosh and the wagon. "Yes, the two men had boarded the eastbound stage. Not very honest or trustworthy men, according to the innkeeper," said Hawksworth. "Said he'd only taken them in out of the goodness of his heart because they were so cold and wet." There was little else of any value that he could add. "Quite a piece of work that one," said Hawksworth. "I've met more trustworthy criminals. As I left, I heard him bragging to his son that he'd been paid twice for the stabling of Slondosh and taken a week's lodging fees for one night, from Captain Currie."

After Sunday's service, Gerry Mason and Roddy took Latour and the remaining survivors to brief Bishop West and seek his permission for Roddy to accompany them to London where they would tell their story to Bishop Mason. Roddy also needed to know how the villagers should proceed with regard to salvage rights from the wreck. Bishop West was most conciliatory and, after hearing the survivor's stories, gave Roddy his permission to proceed as requested. But first, he summoned the constable who insisted that a notary take statements from the survivors regarding the details of the loss of both The Seahorse and Latour's daughter. Copies of those statements were witnessed by Bishop West, sealed, and sent with Roddy for the attention of Bishop Mason.

The fishing fleet from Ryeport was still searching every cove and inlet and did find one more body in a cove roughly one mile east of Ryeport; he was later identified as a member of the crew. But they found no trace of Sailmaker. The wreck was re-examined to see if any clues had been over-looked but to no avail. Sailmaker was lost – presumed drowned and washed out to sea along with the other missing crewmen. Ernie tried to comfort Meg as he gave her the sad news. She broke down in tears but finally accepted that nothing more could be done and was obliged to accept the loss of her husband. Ernie and her mother eventually persuaded her to move back home to the inn.

A group of five people: Roddy, Gerry Mason, Latour, Newton, and the missionary, Swift, boarded the eastbound stagecoach on Tuesday. They made a brief stop at the 'Star and Garter' to question the innkeeper in the hope that they might glean some new information. It took them no time at all to verify Hawksworth's evaluation of the man who tried to shortchange them at every opportunity, eventually asking a fee for his worthless state-ment. Mason told the man that he would personally ensure that he got all that he deserved - after the constable had evaluated his contributions. The innkeeper suddenly became very public-spirited and waived his fees.

Gerry arranged for them all to meet with the management committee responsible for financing The Seahorse and its missionary work. Captain Currie had already spoken with them a few days earlier and as Latour suspected had blamed him and Sailmaker for the loss of the ship, citing their mutiny as the primary cause. He had used his logbook to substantiate that Sailmaker was habitual troublemaker. Fortunately, the letter written by the dead missionary Palmer was still legible and substantiated the testimonies of his surviving colleague and young Newton. Once the committee learned the truth of what had really transpired aboard their ill-fated ship, they all agreed to refer to Latour as Paul Cook pending the arrest of the captain. "Regardless of the outcome of any legal proceedings against him, Currie will never get another command from this organisation," declared the chairman. "I will also ensure that all the ship owners that I can reach will hear of this matter. We shall have the sheriff look for him and charge him with the murder of your daughter, Mister Latour. Now, regarding salvage rights. Currie has told us that salvage costs would exceed the value of any remaining cargo, Mr. Mason. Is that correct?"

"I believe that will prove true, Sir. Much will depend upon the weather. If there is another storm in the next few days, there will be nothing left to salvage. If the weather is kind, however, there might be some salvage available. I'm sure the villagers will be doing their best to retrieve as much as possible even as we speak. The food portion, of course – sugar, rice, and the like – is already spoiled or lost."

"We should write it off then?"

"I'm no expert, Sir. Why not have someone who is investigate?"

"Frankly Mr. Mason, I believe that would be throwing good money after bad. However, we'll see what the people at Lloyds say."

CHAPTER 5

A sinister new acquaintance

Bishop Mason had provided Latour with room and board plus money earned as cook's pay aboard The Seahorse. Latour was currently operating under his assumed name of Cook and was devoting every waking minute to finding Captain Currie. Bishop Mason was unable to supply him with Currie's latest address, explaining that he had been looking for new accommodation when they last met. Gerry thought that his brother might have a good idea where to find Currie but wanted to avoid Latour personally settling accounts with him. The bishop also offered Latour a position in a church in Colchester, but that was a day's coach ride from London and the captain's reputed haunts. Latour asked for time to consider the offer.

Then, unexpectedly, they received news of Currie. He had failed to keep an appointment with the insurers, and they had, therefore, sent a messenger to his last known address. From the innkeeper, they learned that Currie had been killed in a drunken brawl two nights earlier. The details were vague, but apparently, he'd been overly aggressive in his pursuit of a woman who was already 'spoken for'. Her escort had drawn a knife and quickly ended the confrontation. Ruddock had not been with him, and his where-abouts were still unknown. Lloyds had also informed the bishop which undertaker was handling the burial and realising that Latour needed to satisfy himself that it was indeed Captain Currie who was dead, the bishop had arranged for Latour to view the body. Roddy and Gerry went with him. Latour studied the face of his deceased enemy, looking more disap-pointed than relieved. Gerry took Roddy aside. "For Latour, it's not enough that Currie is dead. I believe he needed the satisfaction of killing the man himself. The guilt of being unable to protect his daughter is eating away at him."

Currie's death seemed to drain all the energy from Latour. He was listless and disinterested in any suggestions his companions made. Gerry's assessment of the situation seemed valid. He'd needed to do the deed himself or at least be responsible for bringing him to justice. As they left the undertaker's, Latour took his wife's wedding ring from the pouch around his neck and slipped it into an inside pocket of his coat. "Don't need this anymore," he said as he tossed the pouch into a pile of rubbish outside a stable. Minutes later, Latour was gazing absent-mindedly into a shop window when he felt a tug on his sleeve. Looking around, he found a scruffy little urchin offering him the discarded pouch. "Please, Sir. I saw you drop this in the next street. I fawt you might need it, Sir." Latour smiled. "No, young man. I don't need it but thank you all the same." The youngster looked downcast. "Sorry, Sir. I really did 'ope you'd need it. Fawt I might be doin' you a service, I did."

Latour felt sorry for the frail-looking youngster. "Maybe you're right. It's possible I might find a need for it sometime. Thank you, young Sir," he said and gave the boy some coppers in exchange for the pouch. "Cor! Thank you, Sir! Good luck, Sir," said the boy and took off at a run. Latour smiled as he stuffed the unwanted pouch into his pocket. The trio spent another two days in London, clarifying details of the shipwreck with the insurer's agent. Lloyds had sent an investigator to Ryeport to evaluate the salvage opportunity but with little expectation of good news. During those two days, Latour met with Bishop Mason and declined the Colchester offer. He said he knew nobody there and felt that he would rather be in the Ryeport area where he had already found some acceptance and friendship. He would also be closer to the place where he had lost his daughter. He had gained no satisfaction from Captain Currie's death and seemed like a lost soul drifting aimlessly and devoid of purpose.

Whilst in London, the vicar had, of course, visited his mother. But now it was time to return to Ryeport. Latour and Roddy said their goodbyes and left for the Coaching Inn to start the return journey. Gerry had other business in town and would follow when that was completed. At the inn, Roddy indicated a vacant table close by a large bay window that faced onto the street. "That'll suit us, Paul," he said. "Let's have an ale; then I'll buy passage on the coach." As they passed the fireplace, Latour, filching in his pocket, rediscovered the leather pouch and tossed it into the heart of the blazing fire. "I thought you threw that away a couple of days ago," said Roddy. "That I did," responded Latour and told Roddy the story of the urchin.

Latour sat with one elbow supporting his chin in a cupped hand. He looked the picture of misery. "Try to cheer up, Paul. You've had a terrible loss; it's true, but now you need to focus on rebuilding your life. I'm truly sorry that we're not able to correct the wrongs of the past, my friend, but we will help you get settled." Latour made eye contact with the vicar. His voice was flat, devoid of all emotion. "After all my efforts to save my daughter from the Bokors in Haiti, she died at the hands of someone I was depending on to save her. I was even denied the cold comfort of personal revenge." Roddy placed a consoling hand on his companion's arm. "I'm so sorry, Paul. This whole business has been devastating for you. Are you really sure that you want to return to Ryeport? I'm sure that the bishop would find you a position here in London if you would prefer."

"No, Father! My daughter is dead. Her safety was the reason for our coming to this country. I know the bishop would have helped us establish ourselves here, but I only have myself to consider now. I hope I can make myself useful in Ryeport somehow. My needs are small."

"Very well. I shall go and buy passage for two on the westbound stage, my friend. I'm sure we can find work for you. Would you like something to eat before the coach leaves?" Latour shook his head, and Roddy left the big man alone with his thoughts. Latour sat quietly for a while before he became aware that someone was standing across the table from him. Looking up, he saw a well-dressed man carrying a silver topped walking cane. His most arresting feature though was his eyes. They were brown but streaked with yellow. "Good morning, Mr. Latour." The man's smile was relaxed and disarming. "I have some news for you. May I join you for a few minutes?" Despite a certain uneasiness at the man's appearance and familiarity, Latour nodded and waved the stranger to a seat. "Certainly, Sir. Have we met? You seem to know me, but I regret that I do not recall…"

"Oh, yes, but a long time ago and far away." The stranger airily waved a hand over his shoulder, conveying the impression of a distant place and time. The man's smile became disdainful, and there was an aura about him that Latour found unnerving. "Who are you, Sir? What is your name?" he demanded.

"My name isn't important. I certainly change it more often than you do yours, Mr. Cook. My message is important, however, and believe it or not, I am here to honour a request you made." The man's eyes appeared to change colour. They were yellow, more like a cat's eyes. Latour felt a crawling sensation work its way up his spine. He looked anxiously in the direction that Roddy had gone. "Oh, don't worry about your friend the vicar; he'll be busy for a while. We'll not be disturbed. Incidentally, did you know that he is not a very sincere man of God? Not a true believer, that is. He was pushed into the priesthood by his father because he was a very naughty boy." The stranger leaned towards Latour as though to share a confidence. "He only accepted that calling because it presented him with a last opportunity to curry favours that could eventually make him wealthy. Not the best of motives as I'm sure you'd agree. Not what you would expect by the cut of his cloth." The man smiled mischievously. "However, I'm pleased to tell you that he is on a serious downhill path, has been for many years!" Then he broke eye contact as he shifted to a more comfortable position. "Please. Don't let me spoil your enjoyment of your ale, Mr. Cook, alias Paul Latour, student and past apprentice to the feared Bokor, Kulu of Haiti." His expression changed as he adopted a simpering tone. "And the husband of the late, kind, and gentle Louise Gooding and beloved father of the recently departed Tiny, or should I say Tania, Latour." He paused, staring into Latour's shocked features with a self-satisfied smirk on his face obviously savouring Latour's discomfort. However, he seemed to quickly tire of that amusement. The smile vanished, and he gave an impatient wave of his hand before continuing. "Relax! No harm will come to you today or even in a normal lifetime." He withdrew his closed fist from his pocket, turned it palm up and slowly unfolded his fingers to reveal the smouldering pouch.

Latour threw himself back in his seat as though struck by an unseen force. The stranger was smiling again, much like a magician, gratified by the amazed disbelief of his audience. "Here is your pouch, my friend. It's indestructible, you see. Indestructible, that is, until the contract that it represents is fulfilled." Latour looked anxiously around the room, hoping to find a way to escape this unnerving situation. But no one appeared to notice him or his unwanted companion. That was when he realised how silent the room was. The normal buzz of conversation had ceased, and there was no noise from the street either.

"How in God's name did you get that?" Latour nodded towards the pouch. "I threw that in the fire only minutes ago."

The stranger grinned maliciously. "God had nothing to do with it, I'm afraid. Would you like a second guess?" Latour's insides had turned to liquid fire, and his panic was starting to overwhelm his senses. "How do you know me? I'm new in this country. Practically no one here knows me. The vicar is one of the very few people who know that my name is Latour, and I trust all of those people to keep that private. They would not have told you."

"Latour, Cook, whatever you choose to call yourself, I know everything about you. And, you will never lose me." He pointed a finger directly at Latour's head as he spoke. "I can and will find you anytime, anywhere." The stranger's expression had hardened to a belligerent scowl. "A few days ago, you offered your eternal soul in exchange for a favour, and on behalf of my master, I accepted." Shock and fear were now deeply etched on Latour's face.

"Aha! I see you remember. Well, we wouldn't grant such a favour for just anyone, Latour. We get plenty of common souls, free and gratis. No need to buy them with favours. I'm sure you remember how you clutched this very pouch as you offered your eternal soul to everlasting hell – provided we arranged for Captain Currie to drown in Sailmaker's stead. That was after the keelhauling, remember." He studied Latour's face intently. "Ah, yes! I can see you do remember."

"Who are you?" Latour was terrified as he saw that, apart from himself and the stranger, everybody else appeared to be frozen. No one looked, moved or even appeared to breathe. Even the flickering flames of the fireplace were still as in a painting.

"Come now; you know who I am. You called on me, just as Kulu had taught you when he gave you this very pouch. And I responded just as Kulu said I would. Unfortunately, that stupid missionary Palmer recognised me on the ship and threw that damned heavy crucifix at me. It struck me here." The stranger fingered his right temple. "Caught me unawares just as I was about to grant your request. That was just a lucky shot on his part, of course, but the worst kind of timing really. All the energy I'd intended to distribute between Sailmaker and the crew flew out-of-control and hit the mast. Then I got mad and overdid things." He smirked. "I must confess I really lost my temper and began throwing lots of energy about. Of course, that was when I brought on the squall that wrecked the ship. I really must learn to exercise better control, learn to behave myself." He smiled as he wagged a finger in Latour's face. "I was a naughty, naughty, little devil." He laughed an ugly, cackling, noise that echoed and seemed to reverberate in Latour's head. "He recognised me, you see – Palmer, I mean. That interfering old bastard had seen me once before during a sacrificial ceremony in the islands. I got him though." He made a twisting thrust with his right arm. "I skewered him with that splintered yardarm, nearly got his mate too on the same skewer as it swung back inboard. But for Palmer's lucky shot with the crucifix, you would be in a warmer place right now, Latour. Sailmaker would be back with his bride, and Currie would be lying on the seabed in a weighted hammock." The stranger grinned, relishing Latour's escalating panic.

Latour's mouth was so dry that he had a problem forming his words. "That wasn't a wish," he said, "just an expression. Anyway, even if it had been, you didn't grant it. I owe you nothing. I want nothing to do with you." He held up a hand as though to fend off an antagonist. "I don't care about Currie anymore. He's dead anyway. Nothing can bring my daughter back now. And vengeance is pointless." Latour tried to get up and leave but found he couldn't raise himself from the seat.

The stranger smiled a grim sneering smile. "I haven't granted it yet. That doesn't mean I won't." His eyebrows raised, and a happier smile spread across his face. "It will take time now, of course, because the principals, Currie and Sailmaker, are dead. But your understanding of time is erroneous. I can wait. Several of your lifetimes if need be. We now have to wait for the reincarnation of those principal players, you see. Timing will be critical. I will guide and direct you, but you will play your part in this. Our 'contract' is a binding one. The real trick will be to locate and identify those reincarnated souls. It's not easy, but I can do it. I'm prepared to put in considerable effort on your behalf, Latour. You, your father and your 'do-gooder' missionaries caused me a lot of trouble in Haiti. Then you left my associates there – rejected them might be a more accurate phrase. That was naughty. Even worse, that denied me your daughter. Yes! You were right; it was your daughter we really wanted. You are more like second prize. It would have been quite a coup for me to 'turn' the child of a Christian missionary mother and an apprentice voodoo priest to our arts. She could have been a great asset to us.

"However, win some, lose some." He threw a hand dismissively in the air. "Although it upset me at the time, I had decided to prospect in other areas. Then," and his smile reappeared, "quite unexpectedly, you grabbed this pouch and asked for my help. You proffered a contract! All I needed to do was accept. It was like a clarion call, quite heart-warming really. It restored my faith in human nature. The game was afoot once more. Too late for your daughter, of course, but I still have you. As I said, only second prize, but a small prize is better than a boot in the arse. Especially now, after that screw up on the ship. You aren't as pure as your daughter, but you are still a Christian convert, and you were also your father's apprentice –a houngan – a do-gooding healer priest. So that's not so bad. What is it those missionaries are always preaching? 'There is more joy in heaven over one sinner that repenteth' – something like that? Well, we also know the reverse is true: 'More rejoicing in hell over one repenter that sinneth.'" He laughed again, that same eerie cackling noise as before but with a volume that threatened to shred Latour's eardrums. "This is all subject to fulfilment of our contract, of course. But make no mistake, it is binding. Once I deliver my side of the bargain, you will be bound to pay up. Your soul will be mine, and there is no time limit to our contract.

"By now, I hope you will have realised that the pouch is your communication link to me. You thought that the bits of bones and feathers and the rest of that rubbish were the essential parts of Kulu's voodoo spell bag. So you threw those bits away and kept the pouch. You believed that anything valuable, your wife's wedding band, in particular, would be safest hung around your neck especially on-board ship. Good thinking! Very smart!" He tapped his temple and smiled condescendingly.

"Do you remember the first time you threw the pouch away? It was the day you viewed Currie's dead body. With him dead, your vengeance was thwarted. The letter to the bishop was delivered, and you didn't need the pouch anymore. You decided to keep your wife's ring in your pocket and threw the pouch into a pile of rubbish. I can see you remember. You will also remember that I returned it to you, a short time later. You saw me then as a ragamuffin child hoping to earn a copper. Now you see me in a guise that would be more acceptable in these surroundings. You'll not see me very often, Latour, but you should know that I will always be close by and watching you. You will not recognise me unless I want you to. Be sure you understand that!

"Just look around you. I can do seemingly impossible things. Make time stand still, you're thinking. Actually, I have speeded up time – but just for you and me. It only seems that time stands still because we are interacting at such an accelerated rate. This way no one will ever realise I was here. I can compress hours of interaction into seconds. All it takes is a snap of my fingers. Clever, wouldn't you say?" His grin was radiant like that of a child revelling in the admiration of adults. The smile vanished as fast as it had appeared, however. Latour realised that all of his amusements were short-lived.

"Back to business," said Latour's new acquaintance. "The pouch will always be returned to you, no matter how you lose it or attempt to destroy it. In fact, the safest place for your wife's wedding band is right here in the pouch." The stranger tapped the pouch with a heavily jewelled finger as he pushed it across the table to his nervous companion. "Your wife's ring was in the pouch when our pact was joined, so my protection extends to all that it contained at that time. That's why the letter to the bishop survived so well. Not even buckled or water stained like the one in the missionary's pocket. Did you notice that? By the way, your wife's ring is no longer in your pocket. It's back in the pouch." He grinned again, obviously enjoying himself, as he watched Latour nervously examine the firm circular impression in the pouch.

"I'm so glad you got rid of the bones and feathers. The graveyard dust too." He gave a disparaging laugh. "Those Bokors come up with such theatrical additions. Anyway, the pouch and its contents will always be returned to you, be it stolen, thrown away or destroyed in a furnace. "This is enough for now." His manner rapidly changed to intolerant impatience. Latour thought he behaved like a child with any pleasure or satisfaction fleeting and constantly seeking fresh stimulation and excitement. The stranger's tone was stern now. "You, Latour, have been given immortality until our contract is fulfilled. Hence your accelerated healing ability. Did you wonder how you survived the captain's sword thrust and the shipwreck? Well, the good doctor was right. You didn't! But you were healed and repaired. And so you always will be until our contract is fulfilled.

"Unusual happenings such as that will become clear to you because I have given you this insight. You will follow the instructions you are given from time to time. For the most part, you will live a normal life, possibly several normal lives before our contract is fulfilled. You will die, but you will always be restored to the health and the age that you had preceding your first death from the captain's sword. You'll have the bruises from the beating of the night before but not for long. Any injury will heal rapidly. I shall intrude on you only to demand your cooperation as it's required to complete our contract. Then we will have to replay the keelhauling. But we have to get it right next time. We shall need to gather together that group of souls belonging to those crew members involved in the keelhauling itself. But we can do without the bloody missionaries.

"You will be required to devise ways to bring the key players together as a group and at the appropriate time. It may not occur in this lifetime though. The timing of the reincarnation for the various parties will make things difficult because lifespans can vary greatly, and so many of those we need are currently dead. It's possible that some will die and be reincarnated many times during your extended lifetime." He frowned apparently bored from his long explanation. "This meeting is over. No one here will even know it happened. I compressed our meeting into the blinking of an eye." He pointed threateningly at Latour. "But you will remember. Oh, yes! You will remember." Then he rose and left the table, walking between the furniture and frozen figures of the inn's patrons. Latour was unable to tear his eyes from his sinister visitor as he passed through the doorway into the street. All was silent and still. Latour thought that he was the only living creature in the world. Then, seconds later, his unwelcome companion poked his head around the door wearing a big grin. "Oops! Did I forget something?" he said and with a flourish snapped his fingers. Latour jumped from his seat as the silence that had surrounded their meeting was instantly shattered by the hubbub of noisy conversation and the sounds of the street. Animated diners were waving their arms and laughing, and the flames in the fireplace were dancing again. He wondered if he was going mad and covered his ears with his hands as he collapsed weakly onto the table. Surely, this had been some sort of dream. Whatever it was, he knew it was indelibly etched into his mind.

A short time later, Roddy appeared. He hurried through the rear door from the stable yard and crossed the floor to Latour. "They're harnessing a fresh team right now, Paul. We'll be leaving in half an hour. I can't say I'm looking forward to either the long journey or the fishy stink of the village when we get back." He paused as Latour's desperately shaken appearance registered with him. "My God, man, are you alright? You look absolutely distraught. Whatever happened?"

Latour smiled weakly. "I'll be alright; I just came over faint for a while. It must have been the strain of the last few days." Roddy took his companion's arm and helped the bigger man to his feet. "Some fresh air might help," he said. "That fire is awfully smoky. This place smells like a farriers. You'd think they'd been shoeing horses in here. No wonder you feel faint." Latour stumbled to the doorway still clutching the pouch returned to him so dramatically, just minutes earlier or was it seconds. No, it was much less than that. Or could it have been a hallucination? No. The pouch was real enough; it was still very warm, and he could feel his wife's wedding band through the thin leather. But, most frightening of all, the pouch was throbbing ever so gently as if with a heartbeat.

He was leaning on the wall just outside the door sucking in great gasps of air when Roddy noticed the pouch. "You retrieved the pouch? How in heaven's name did you manage that? It was deep in the flames when I left. No wonder you feel so faint; you must have inhaled too much smoke. That was crazy, Paul. I would have been pleased to give you a much nicer wallet when we got back to Ryeport." Roddy turned quickly startled by a sudden eerie chuckle behind him, but there was no one there. Frowning, he helped Latour through the archway into the stable yard and the temporary refuge of the stagecoach.

• • •

The coachman's guard added his extra 'pip-pip-pip' to the end of his post horn summons as the coach entered the approaches to Ryeport. Roddy knew what that would mean; a reception party would be waiting at the inn. Latour had been quiet and morose for most of the journey, and Roddy was concerned that he might be ill. He was certainly very depressed. The crowd of villagers that greeted them bombarded him with a seemingly unending flurry of questions. "Did you find the captain? Why isn't Gerry here? Did you know we had an appraiser here from Lloyds?" Eventually, Roddy threw his hands in the air. "Whoa! Whoa! Hold your horses. Let us get indoors and catch our breath." He was overwhelmed. Only minutes ago, he'd been dozing in the coach; now he was in the midst of an excited bunch of people clamouring for answers. "It's lunchtime," he said. "Let's take a break. Listen to the coachmen's news whilst I get my breath back. Then I'll answer your questions."

After the coachmen left, Ernie topped up their ale. Archer and the rest of the locals followed him to Roddy's table. "We had a man from Lloyds here for a couple of days," said Ernie. "He left yesterday. He asked a lot of questions. We showed him what we'd salvaged so far, then took him over to the wreck. The timber was still in the hold, but some of it was floating.

He pulled a face and wanted to know how much it would cost for labour to bring it all out by hand. Obviously, there are no derricks in Sorry Cove. Everything would have to be hand carried over the rocks. He paid Archer and Doc Hudson to sit in separate corners of the inn and estimate the man hours and other costs for salvaging the cargo. They were very close in their estimates, and the appraiser didn't look happy.

That night we had a bit of a squall. It broke the ship up even more, and some of the timber was lost through a new hole in the ship's side. The ebb tide carried that out to sea. 'Not worth the salvage costs,' the Lloyds' bloke said. It would be damaged or warped anyway. The sugar had dissolved, leaving just empty sacks. The rice had swollen and burst the sacks, and the other foodstuffs were spoiled too. There wasn't much that wasn't damaged. But just between us, I think that Bannerman and the Sullivans hid some rum casks, just in case the salvage wasn't going to give us any benefit. I saw a lot more casks on the day of the wreck. They said it must have been lost during tide changes. The appraiser was going to take the rum that we'd stored in the church until I asked him about our salvage rights – there being no crew aboard the ship. Well, to make a long story short, he wrote off the whole thing, the cargo, and the ship. If that last squall had become a full-blown storm, he would have been right, of course. The remains of the ship and its cargo would have all floated away. So what's left is ours for the taking.

"We've been talking about what to do with the ship's timbers. I'd like to extend the inn. The villagers also need a new smokehouse for their fish. Archer's old stable has seen better days too. And if we can salvage all that mahogany and stack it until it dries, it might be worth something in a year or so. I'd get the lion's share of the ship's timbers, mind you. And I'd be prepared to pay for that somehow. We'd work something out. What do you think, Father?"

"It sounds like we're in for a busy time," responded the vicar.

The rest of that month was spent on the salvage operation. The fishermen arranged to spend one day fishing, one day salvaging in shifts. Bannerman and the Cobbe brothers rigged an overhead rope from the top of the ship's broken main mast, which was still about 20 feet above water level to sheer-legs on level ground beyond the rocks. Then they hung a sling on pulleys from that overhead rope and put the lengths of mahogany in the sling. Then they hauled the sling over the rocks so that it arrived directly above Archer's flat-bed wagon. This made the salvage operation relatively easy as far as bringing the timber ashore was concerned. Most of the remaining worthwhile salvage also made its way ashore in similar fashion. "Good job the appraiser didn't see that," remarked the vicar as Archer carted the mahogany to high ground behind his barn. There it was gap-stacked to allow air circulation and covered with a canvas roof made from salvaged sails.

Then they were faced with the tough job of breaking up the rest of the ship and ferrying those heavy timbers ashore. They salvaged everything they possibly could: furniture from the cabins, lamps, spare canvas and rope, anchors and chain, plus pots and pans from the galley, even the stove, and Higgins claimed first 'dibs' on the carpenter's tools. It was a good haul. By the time the next storm came, there was precious little of value left to be washed out to sea. Most of the salvage was sold in Nextwest, and the proceeds were divided amongst the villagers. The timber was allocated to the projects that Ernie had discussed. He elected to take ship's timbers in lieu of money gained from the sale. Gerry Mason arrived back in Ryeport just as they were getting the last of the items ashore. He was driving a buggy of his own. He'd decided that a one wagon village just left too much to be desired and had bought one from a stable in Nexteast. He wanted his own transportation. So, Slondosh gained Gerry's horse Queenie as a stablemate.

Ernie was very enthusiastic about extending the inn, although he could find no real justification for the extra rooms at this time. Naturally, Gerry got the job of designing that addition and Archer's new stable. The challenge would be to use all available material to the best advantage. Latour had made himself useful during all of this but was hoping to find a job that would be ongoing once the building was finished. Since Meg had moved back to the inn, Latour had been living in her vacated cottage.

Most of the salvage activity had subsided when Archer took Roddy aside for a quiet word. "Father, I don't want you to think that I'm ungrateful, but I'd like you to consider someone else for the sexton's job. With all this buildin' that's going on, me an' 'iggins will be very busy. It turns out that 'iggins is quite a good woodworker; now 'e's got a full set of tools. They used to belong to the dead carpenter on the ship, of course. 'iggins said e'd rather be doin' wood-workin' than cleanin' winda's an' polishin' brass, so 'e'd like you to find a replacement for 'im too. As for me – well, I'm not good on ladders, as you know, and this last wreck showed me just 'ow good I was at runnin' an' jumpin' about. 'iggins an' me make a good team. I'll fetch an' carry the material in the cart, an' do the bookwork. 'iggins'l do the carperterin' an we'd get by pretty good. We'll still cut wood for fires and 'elp out at smokin' fish in the new smoke 'ut, once that's built, an' take some to market in Nextwest, I was wonderin', Father, if your new mate Latour might like the job of sexton? I feel bad askin' ye really. Your dad seemed to put such stock in me doin' that job, but I am past me best now, physically I mean."

Roddy raised his eyebrows. "Well! That's quite a surprise, Archer. Are you sure you'll have enough work? Once this building spree is finished?"

"Oh, yes, Father. 'iggins 'as made some nice bits of furniture. We plan to sell that in the market. Then, as I said, we'll pickle 'erring an' market that too, time permittin'. Then Fletcher in Nextwest has asked 'iggins to do some work for 'im too. Turns out 'e's better at the finer parts of wood-workin' than Fletch."

"Then I'll certainly ask Latour tonight. When do you want this to start?"

"Monday would be good, Father, if that's alright with you."

And so it was that Paul Latour replaced Archer as sexton for The Guiding Light Church. And he loved the idea. He would remain in Bessie Drew's old cottage until he and Higgins built a small flat for him inside the church on the side opposite the vestry. Archer and Higgins agreed to train Latour and serve as relief operators of the light for as long as required. An assistant for Latour would be arranged later. The vicar also arranged some part-time work for the Rookens at the church. The bishop accepted the modest extra expense.

• • •

Bannerman and the Sullivans crept up the rum that they'd sunk. They sold the rum through Pringle's distribution network and shared the proceeds as salvage money with the villagers. But that whetted Bannerman's appetite for more money. He longed for a return of the smuggling days. Actually, he thought he'd make a pretty good Spotsman if he could get the old organisation up and running again. So he visited the Pringles for an exploratory discussion. The Pringle's knowledge was limited to dispersal and delivery, so they had a word with Prudence. But she didn't know how the purchases were made or who funded them. Her job had been similar to the Pringles but with personal contact with a more discrete clientele. However, she did remember that Goodman used to leave messages for a Mister Birch in a derelict cottage on the Coach Road, near the White Hart. There was a broken vase in the cottage that Goodman would always place in the left corner of the front window after he deposited any message. Prudence realised that this had to be a signal to some knowledgeable passerby. On other occasions, she noticed that the vase was in the opposite corner. On those occasions, Goodman would remove the vase from the window. She assumed that, on those occasions, he had retrieved a message. What she didn't know was where the messages were concealed inside the cottage.

The four conspirators – Jed and Bob Pringle, Bannerman, and Prudence – agreed to try to make contact with that knowledgeable passerby. An unsigned note addressed to 'Whomever was interested' simply asked, "Can we meet?" Prudence placed the note under the vase in the left corner of the window. A week later, the vase still hadn't moved. She shrugged and gave up on the idea, deciding that the contact was no longer valid. At the beginning of the second week, however, she noticed that the vase was gone from the window, but she found no message. That Thursday evening, as Prudence and Roddy were having supper at The White Hart, the innkeeper brought her a letter. "Evenin', Miss Prudence. This was left for you earlier today." He knuckled his forehead. "Evening, Reverend," he said with a nod and then walked off.

Pru opened the letter. The message stated: 'There is a loose brick just above the fireplace mantel on the right side. Be very careful.'

"What is it, Pru?" Roddy had noticed her surprised expression change to shock.

"Oh, nothing."

"What nothing? I can read shock on you pretty well by now, Miss." Eventually, he managed to coax the story of her covert actions from her. "My God, Pru. You could be setting yourself up for a hanging. Who got you into this? Bannerman?"

"No one got me into this, Roddy. I do what I want. I'm a big girl now, and I know there are times when you appreciate that." She batted her eyelids and blew him a kiss. "I could do with some extra money. It looks as though the organisation might be intact but just sleeping. If we're careful – and we will be – the Pringles, Bannerman, and me too could make some extra money. Whitestone believes that I'm bound to him. I can use that to get inside information from him or give him false or stale information. Those things could help us. I believe this is a good opportunity. And we will be very careful. We're not like Goodman or Godfrey; there will be no violence. We could make this work."

"Well, obviously you're not careful enough. These people know it was you that placed the letter. But you don't know them. Someone has been watching you. It could even be Whitestone."

"Well, we'll do things a little differently from now on," Prudence responded. She went to the bar and asked the innkeeper who delivered the message. "Dunno,' Miss. We discovered it on the bar earlier on. Someone who thinks you still live here most likely."

Roddy was very concerned. "Prudence drop this. Please. You could get yourself killed." His manner was almost panic-stricken.

"Oh, alright! Since it upsets you so, I'll just pass the message on to the Pringles. They can make the choices. Do whatever they want with it."

"That's better. Although I'd rather they stayed out of trouble too. You don't know who will get caught up in this venture. Maybe even Bessie and Marie again."

• • •

Sunday's service was well attended, and Latour was applauded by the congregation when Roddy introduced him as their new sexton. Surprise! The Pringles were in attendance too. Roddy knew that the sudden religious belief that Jed had acquired because of the 'avenging angel' incident had worn off some weeks ago. Church had never been a high priority for the Pringles and given the choice of church or hard-won pleasure hours; church would always take a back seat. Bannerman, the Sullivans, and Prudence completed the little clique that discretely came together after the service. Roddy knew they wouldn't be discussing his sermon. Later, when speaking with Prudence, he said, "Pru, was it pure coincidence or a burning desire to discuss my sermon that all of your co-conspirators happened to be at today's service?"

"Roddy! You know our friends are always here to support you. But should the opportunity arise, surely you wouldn't object to their attending to other business at the same time?"

"Come on, Pru. You know what I mean. You engineered this meeting. It's the first time I've seen the Pringles here for more than a month."

"Well, I did give them the note that I got from the innkeeper at The White

Hart. What they intend to do with it, I don't know. I promise you though: I shall not set foot in that cottage again." Prudence took tea with Roddy at the vicarage that afternoon. The Pringles and Bannerman had left for home, and Latour was playing cards with Gerry. Later, he would be on duty watch at The Guiding Light.

Roddy caught a glimpse of Bridget as she ducked behind some trees when he and Prudence left his vicarage. He drove Prudence home to Nextwest and spent the night. But he worried about Bridget and worried about what she might be up to. He couldn't get her off his mind. His vicarage was remote from the village, and she never visited that area. He wondered if she was devising some scheme to pay him back for rejecting her.

True to her word, Prudence handed over all dealings with the anonymous writer to Bannerman and the Pringles. Roddy was relieved. It would be hard for her to survive a running battle with Whitestone. It would be foolish to try.

• • •

Despite the loss of his inheritance, Roddy was becoming reconciled to the fact that Ryeport was now his permanent home. He no longer considered it a mere 'stop-off' pending reinstatement in his father's Will. Pru's earlier rebuke and her insistence that he 'get over it' had caused him to re-evaluate his situation, and he had now accepted her truth that he had more real friends here than he'd ever known before. The new vicarage too was quite comfortable and had also benefited from some of the furnishings from the captain's cabin on The Seahorse. Ernie and Bannerman had insisted that he was owed some benefit for his efforts. He also had his cherished relationship with Prudence, and she seemed happy with him. Her only sore point seemed to be that he hadn't yet made an 'honest woman' of her. That plus the distance that existed between them for most of the week was very trying. He resolved to do something about that. In sharp contrast to his early days in Ryeport, the church had become the centre of many social activities now. However, he believed that credit for that belonged in large part to Bessie. Her sewing circle and Meg's reading and writing classes had brought the villagers together like never before. Meg and Pru had also set up the Sunday school. Emily and other villagers had been pleased to promote potluck lunches following Sunday service as a regular feature. There was a positive attitude amongst the congregation now. Heck, he hardly noticed the smell of fish anymore. Gerry always said he made too much of that anyway.

Roddy thought he'd test his mother's reaction to the possibility of his getting married. An elaborate wedding would be out of the question, and that might upset his mother. So he wrote and told her that he was thinking of proposing to the lovely young lady that she had met at the dedication ceremony and, depending on her acceptance, of course, the wedding would be a modest affair right here in Ryeport. They would be the second couple to be married at The Guiding Light Church. Not quite as historic an event as the first but close. He thought he would ask Reverend Tubbs to tie the knot. But he was shocked when his mother arrived in Ryeport with a travelling companion only two weeks later. Just one day after, he'd received her letter advising him that she was on her way. The two ladies were exhausted by the journey, and he now had two unexpected house guests. The worst part was that he hadn't asked Prudence yet. His mother had arrived on the day before his weekly visit to Nextwest and the day when he had intended to propose. Instead, he had been obliged to cancel the visit, sending word to Prudence via the coachman and Tubby. His guests, weary from their journey, retired early.

After settling her companion, Roddy's mother came back downstairs carrying a small jewellery box. "Roddy, I wanted a word with you in private," she said. "I wanted to explain why I dropped in on you like this uninvited. I know that you don't have much money and that will never change. I thought that you might need a ring to offer Prudence when you propose. I hope I'm not too late." She opened the jewellery box. "This is jewellery that I will never wear now that your father has passed away. I would like you to have it. If you can find a ring in there that you think your Prudence would like, it would make me very happy – provided of course that she wouldn't object to it not being new. The rest of the jewellery is yours too. Do with it what you will. Sell it if you need the money or to buy a new ring if you wish."

"Mother, I couldn't possibly take all this. Father bought this for you. I'm sure there will be plenty of opportunities for you to wear it."

"No, Roddy, there won't. Besides, your father would be pleased for you to have it under the circumstances. He was very proud of you those last few months and most anxious to have you reinstated in his Will. When Mr. Blackstock came to see me to make arrangements for paying our housekeeper, we had a chat. He told me over a cup of tea that that horrible Msr. Beaucaire had repeatedly put off your father's many attempts to meet with him to cancel that purchase agreement."

"Well, this really is a most generous gift, Mother. I'm sure that Pru would love to have a ring that originally belonged to you. Why don't I take just one?"

"Very well, Roddy. If that's what you want. Select the one you think she would like the best. Once you're married, I shall give the rest to Prudence anyway."

So, Roddy chose a gold band with three modestly sized diamonds set in a neat low mounting. "I think she would like this one, Mother. Thank you. It will mean more to me too just knowing it was yours. It will become a family heirloom." And so, Roddy proposed in the vestry after Sunday's service. Prudence pouted and refused him. "You could have found a more romantic setting than a church vestry to propose, Roddy. I would still have turned you down, but it would have been more satisfying."

"Oh! What a shame. I shall have to return the ring then."

"What ring?"

"This one!" He placed his mother's ring on the palm of his hand and offered it to her.

She gave a little gasp as she picked it off his hand and examined it with a big smile on her face. "Oh, I love it! It's so neat and classy. I don't like 'lumpy' jewellery, you know. This is lovely." Her smile quickly faded, however, and she returned the ring to his still outstretched palm. "It's too bad. I would have really loved that ring." Now it was Roddy's smile that faded. "But I thought you wanted me to 'make an honest woman of you'?"

"Well, I didn't say that should be accomplished by me marrying you, did I? I thought that you could just officiate." He looked crestfallen. She let him suffer for a few seconds before breaking into a smile. "Down on your knees, young man. I'm not won so easily." So with a smile returning to his face, Roddy made the traditional offer of marriage, down on one knee, and this time he was accepted. "But it's only because I love the ring so," she said. Then he told her the story of how his mother thought he would not be able to afford a ring and had made him a gift of one of hers. "Oh, that makes it even more special," she said. "Quick. Let's go thank her. Then we can tell everyone."

· · ·

It was late August when Reverend Tubbs tied the knot for them. Ryeport was busy with visitors, and the church was overflowing again. There were numerous guests at the potluck reception in the old church and a surprising array of gifts. The silver tea service was particularly elegant and evoked gasps of admiration when it was unwrapped. The accompanying card expressing: 'Heartfelt good wishes for a long and happy life together' was signed by Mr. Birch. Roddy and Prudence looked at each other in shock, then around the room anxiously trying to identify an unfamiliar face. There were none. Roddy held up the card. "This is a most generous and wonderful gift from Mr. Birch! Thank you so much, Sir. Please step forward so that we may properly express our appreciation." The eyes of all the guests searched the room for the donor, but no one came forward. The newly-weds looked anxiously at each other before proceeding to the next item. Uncle Joshua, the constable, had given them a handsome canteen of cutlery. Westerhof and his wife presented some very fine table linens and a pair of silver candlesticks. The two bishops were also very generous, and Roddy's mother had provided a bedroom suite. His mother's gift was already at Roddy's cottage, but the couple publicly acknowledged the gift. There were also several more modest gifts including some very attractive items of furniture handmade by Higgins but commissioned by various villagers. Pru was overwhelmed by the generosity and obvious goodwill. They did catch glimpses of Bridget at the rear of the hall. She was the only person at the reception that did not shake their hands and wish them well before she left. Her malevolent glances were not lost on Bessie Drew. "We shall have to watch that one, Marie," she told her sister.

Mrs. McDowd was very emotional. "Roddy. Your father would have been very proud of you this day. Just look at how many friends you have. How wonderful that you are so well thought of. I'm sure that you and Prudence will be very happy here. Now make me even happier. Sometime in the not-too-distant future make me a grandmother." Before she left for London, Roddy's mother presented Prudence with the jewellery box just as she had told Roddy she would. Her conditions for the gift were the same as those she had given her son: keep, sell or dispose of whatever items as they saw fit.

"Oh, no, Mother. These are family heirlooms. Because of these, we will have something of your husband and yourself with us always. I could never sell them. It means even more to me because my own parents disowned me. Now I feel I have family again." Prudence was quite choked up.

• • •

By the end of November, the addition to the inn was closed in, and weather tight. The new smokehouse had already been in use for over a month, and everyone seemed very happy with the results of their salvage efforts. One of the first to inspect Archer's new stable, albeit surreptitiously, was Bridget. She had become more withdrawn in the months following the vicar's wedding, spent little time in the company of the other ladies of the village, and was never seen again at the ladies' sewing circle or the reading and writing classes. Gerry and Higgins were helping Latour fix-up his 'digs' as he liked to call his apartment inside the church. The addition of a fireplace was particularly appreciated. Roddy and Prudence were settling in quite nicely at the vicarage, and the 'woman's touch' had made the house a home. It seemed that all the perilous excitement was now behind them. Prudence had rented her cottage on the Coach Road, and they now had income from all three cottages left to Pru by her grandfather to supplement Roddy's modest income.

Bannerman and the Pringles did not involve them in whatever they were doing as far as smuggling was concerned, and any concern over the mysterious Mr. Birch had faded. 'Uncle Joshua' visited them periodically, usually staying for lunch after the Sunday service. He was pleased to see that Pru was happy in her new life and always anxious to know if he could be of any help. Roddy always wondered about 'Uncle Joshua.' The man was obviously very fond of Prudence and had proven a good friend to Tubby. Roddy often wondered if he had fabricated Mrs. Whatson's confession in order to achieve justice. And he always had the feeling that the man knew more about Goodman's death than he declared. However, their meetings were always cordial, and the constable seemed genuinely happy for them both, so Roddy ascribed his fears to a guilty conscience and tried to dismiss them from his mind. Life was good and peaceful. Peaceful, that is, until the small hours of one morning in early March the following year.

• • •

Roddy and Prudence were awakened by a violent hammering on their door at about two a.m. Candle in hand, Roddy cautiously opened the door to discover a panic-stricken stranger, spattered with blood who addressed him in a garbled mixture of English and French. Prudence, who had followed Roddy down the stairs, was shocked by the man's appearance. Roddy pulled the man indoors before taking a quick look outside. The man did not appear to be injured himself, so it had to be someone else's blood, but he was almost hysterical.

"M'sieu. Aidez-moi, s'il vous plait. Aidez-moi!" He tried to drag Roddy through the door but Roddy, still in his nightshirt, wasn't going anywhere until he knew what this was all about. With Pru's help, he discovered that the man was a member of a French boat's crew that had met a Ryeport boat at sea to transfer 'trade' goods. This man, Henri, had been aboard the Ryeport boat helping to hang casks around the gunwale when they were spotted by a Customs cutter and called upon to surrender. The French boat had responded by opening fire with a swivel gun loaded with grapeshot. That first shot had shredded the sails and rigging of the cutter injuring two of its crewmen in the process. The disabled cutter had replied with its own swivel gun causing some injuries in both of the closely tied smuggling boats. When a second Revenue cutter was spotted approaching fast and having the advantage of the wind gauge, the French boat immediately cast loose from the Ryeport one and ran for the French coast leaving their man Henri aboard the Ryeport boat with its injured crewman.

The Ryeport boat also made a run for it dropping its weighted contraband as they went. Then the injured Ryeport man had passed out from loss of blood. "Good man," said Henri. Roddy's stomach was in turmoil. "Goodman?" he queried frowning. "Oui, ow you say eet. Bon man? Good man?" queried Henri. Prudence raised one hand to her mouth as she looked in horror at the amount of blood on Henri's clothing. "Do you mean Bannerman? " she asked. "Oui, oui, Bonman," affirmed the smuggler pointing at her. "They put me 'shore. They say, 'Henri, you go shore. Go 'ouse near church. Get priest. Tell 'im Salee say, Bon man urt. They go landin.'"

Roddy looked at Prudence. "Sully and Bannerman," she said.

"Oui! Oui! Salee an Bonman," confirmed the Frenchman. Roddy got dressed and ran to the landing. He arrived as the Sullivans were lifting Bannerman onto the jetty. He had lost a lot of blood from a wound in his left leg. Fortunately, they had applied a tourniquet; he hoped it wasn't too late. Bannerman was in shock but still breathing. "Quick. We have to get him to Doc Hudson," said Roddy. "Sully, can you take his shoulders? Henri and I will take a leg each. David, you had better stay. Wash away all the blood in the boat and leave it ready to go fishing tomorrow. Then go home. Be in bed if the Revenuers come. I'll send Sully home as soon as we get to Doc's."

"What about Henri?"

"I'll hide him."

"What if the Revenuers go to Doc's place?"

"We'll think of something. Go! Hurry now."

Doc Hudson's door was never locked, and they took Bannerman straight inside. The doctor took some waking but eventually came to the fireside chair where they had put Bannerman. "My God! What have we here? Quickly, put him on my bed and get me some light."

They sent Sully home. "Check on your brother and then go to bed. Remember, you've been there all night," said Roddy. "You know nothing about this. Check for damage on your boat in case Whitestone decides to look it over." Sully's face was a mask of anxiety, but he nodded and left without questions. Doc worked quickly. The vicar held the lantern, and in that poor light, Doc removed the shot from Bannerman's leg, cleaned and stitched the wound. It was over an hour before he was satisfied. "Now he's in God's hands," he said. "I've done all I can. But he's a tough man. I think he'll pull through. You can go home, Father. You'd better take your French friend with you."

"But what if the Revenuers come here, Doc? We can't leave Bannerman here."

"Well, you certainly can't take him anywhere else, Father. He's not that tough. He's not like your friend Latour, you know. He needs absolute rest and ongoing medical care. Infection is the biggest danger now."

"But how will you explain his wound if they come here?"

The doctor scratched his head as he searched for inspiration. That inspiration came when he saw a piece of firewood in the hearth that had a pointed piece of broken branch left on it. He smothered the jagged branch with blood from Bannerman's clothes. "There!" he said. "Bannerman staggered in here with this jammed in his leg. He said he'd tripped on some firewood as he was cutting it and fell on this piece. You make sure and tell the Sullivans that they've not seen him since they unloaded their catch earlier this evening. Hiding the Frenchman will be your problem. You don't know anything about this either." Roddy studied the doctor's weary face for a few moments. "Doc, I don't know how you do it. You know he was smuggling. Now you're risking your neck to save him."

"I brought him into the world, Father. I'm not about to let him die because the king wants more tax money. I don't have to approve of what he's doing in order to do my best for him. Besides, you've risked your neck for him before now if my memory serves me correctly. In fact, you're doing it again tonight. And I'm sure he'd do the same for us. Off you go now. I'm going to try and get some sleep in the armchair." Roddy relayed the information to the Sullivans on his way back to the vicarage. Henri slept on the floor in the spare room. He made them understand that the bed should not be warm if the Revenuers decided to search the place. They burned his bloodstained clothes, and Roddy grudgingly gave him the clothes that Sailmaker had given him on the night they lit the fireboat.

Whitestone and two of his men put in an appearance about eight o'clock the following morning. The Customs officers had stayed in Ryeport to inspect all returning fishing boats for evidence of damage, and they had found none. However, Whitestone noticed that Bannerman was missing from Sullivan's boat when it came in. "Where's Bannerman?" he demanded.

"He's at Doc Hudson's," said Sully. "He tripped cutting some firewood last night, and a stick speared 'is leg. Lost a lot of blood, so 'e did. So 'e couldn't fish with us t'day." They explained that theirs was the last boat to leave harbour that morning because they'd gone looking for Bannerman when he didn't put in an appearance. In truth though, although they went through the motions of checking his cottage, they had ended up at Doc Hudson's. They also needed to delay their departure to avoid being seen picking up Henri. The Frenchman was waiting for them on the rocks below The Guiding Light Church. They'd waited until all the other boats were out of sight before picking him up and taking him across to France. They'd put him ashore on a stretch of coastline that he knew and fished on the way home. Because of that lost fishing time, they had a small catch. Whitestone noted their lightly loaded boat. "Looks like the fish deserted you today as well as Bannerman," he said.

"Just can't find 'em some days," said Sully. "An' we were late away after lookin' for Bannerman. If we could afford it, we'd stay 'ome and pay someone else to work the boat for us. Some days just ain't worth puttin' out for. Didn't 'elp that Bannerman wern't aboard either. It's slower and 'arder with only two of us. That late start really put the mockers on us."

"Hmph," grunted Whitestone. "I'll away to see the doctor then." Bannerman was very pale but sitting up and taking a little soup when Whitestone questioned both him and the doctor. They confirmed Sully's story, and Whitestone told them they were liars. Doc gave him an angry look, searched in the hearth for the broken bloodstained stick that he claimed to have removed from his patient's leg and threw it to the officer. Whitestone studied it for a few moments, scowled, and then threw it into the fire. He had nothing solid to back his suspicions and slammed the door behind him when he left. A few days later, the vicar discovered a sealed letter on his desk in the vestry. There was no salutation. It read:

> *Many thanks for your recent assistance. It was much appreciated by many friends. Our company has many branches, each well managed but lacking efficient management. We badly need a coordinator, or mutual friends could suffer. I wondered if you might consider assuming that role.*
>
> *Respectfully, Mr. B.*

There was no return address. Roddy felt his stomach muscles tighten.

"Not bad news, I hope," said Gerry, who was visiting at the time.

"No. Just a note of appreciation," responded Roddy. Later that night he and Prudence discussed the letter in the privacy of the vicarage. "Obviously this refers to the Bannerman incident," he said. "And Mr. Birch, whoever he is, has lots of information about us. Do you think he wants us to reply by leaving a letter behind the loose brick?" Prudence was thoughtful for a few moments. "He hasn't asked you to reply. I think he will give you some time to think about it and contact you again later."

"Well, I don't want anything to do with smuggling. We are managing quite well as we are."

"We could always use a little extra money, Roddy. Besides, Mr. Birch is right about 'our mutual friends'; they are not as fortunate as we are, and they will continue to work 'the trade'. Whether they do it safely or expose themselves through poor organisation will decide how long they remain free." A week later, a second letter from Mr. Birch was lying on Roddy's desk.

> *I hope you have given some thought to joining us. Perhaps we could meet so that I can answer any questions you may have. If you are agreeable to a meeting, please leave the enclosed drawing in the window of your church porch facing outward.*
>
> *Respectfully, B.*

A black and white drawing of a birch tree was enclosed. "Might as well find out what he has in mind and who he is," said Prudence looking at him with one eyebrow raised. Roddy looked a little angry. "Yes, but he is very careful not to expose himself. And what if I refuse to join him after he identifies himself. He may decide to eliminate me. I thought I had finally got past all that. Do you realise how many people have offered to kill me since I've been in Ryeport?"

"Well. Let me see," said Prudence adopting a thoughtful expression as she placed one finger on her chin. "There's Bannerman, of course, then Ernie and Goodman. Beaucaire would have obliged too given a safe opportunity. You should be getting used to it by now." She smiled. "I've got a feeling though that Mr. Birch will turn out like Bannerman and Ernie to be a good friend. Besides, he hasn't offered to kill you yet, and we haven't had the opportunity to thank him for the wedding gift." So, Roddy was persuaded to put the drawing in the porch window.

CHAPTER 6

Mr. Birch

The church players' of Nextwest were to present a play to raise funds for local charities. Westerhof had reserved 20 seats to include a group of people that he'd invited to his home for supper before the show. Included in his invitations were Bishop West, Reverends: Watkins, Tubbs, and McDowd, and Gerry Mason, Constable Cooper, and their ladies. Tubby enquired if he might bring Maud, and Westerhof had insisted that he did. So, 20 people were seated for supper in the dining room of Westerhof's well-appointed home that evening. Prudence had been pleased to learn that 'Uncle Joshua' would be amongst the guests. They were to be there by five p.m. to allow time for sociable mingling. The meal was excellent, and Westerhof proved to be a most congenial and attentive host.

After supper, the ladies retired to the drawing room whilst the men, drinks in hand, inspected the conservatory. Roddy found himself in the company of 'Uncle Joshua' and another of Westerhof's friends, a late arrival to whom he had not yet been introduced. This tall, distinguished looking gentleman smiled, offered his hand and, with a courteous bow, said, "Good evening to you, Father. I've heard so much about you and your Guiding Light Church. I am pleased to have the opportunity to make your acquaintance at last. My name is Lloyd Willoughby. I'm in business in Bristol. Your servant, Sir." Roddy took to the man immediately. He was relaxed and courteous and very interested in Ryeport and the new church. 'Uncle Joshua' excused himself, leaving the two men in conversation. "Allow me to also congratulate you on your recent marriage, Father," continued Willoughby, nodding in the direction of the drawing room. "Your wife is a most charming and attractive lady. You are a fortunate man indeed."

However, his next remarks came as a shock. "Father, it has come to my attention that your service to your congregation often exceeds what one might expect, especially in view of your calling." Roddy's expression obviously betrayed his shock for Willoughby quickly raised a hand and apologised. "I'm sorry, Sir. I meant no offence. It is rare to find such flexibility in men of the church. I applaud your initiatives and your loyalties, believe me." He took a quick look around him before continuing. "It has become known to certain very discreet financiers that you have saved some of your villagers from the dreaded clutches of Customs men on more than one occasion." He smiled as Roddy's expression grew more alarmed. "Not a criticism, I assure you. We are well aware, Father, of how difficult it is to eke out a living from working-class employment. A subsidy is often an absolute necessity. Personally, I've always found a subsidy very welcome, no matter what enterprise or endeavour occupies one's efforts.

"Father, our private time will be very limited, so please forgive me if any of my remarks or questions appear brash and ill-mannered. I assure you, there is no disrespect intended. " He paused, looking most apologetic. Roddy nodded for him to proceed. "First, Father, allow me to extend my sincere condolences on the recent loss of your father. I understand that you and he had developed a close and particularly strong relationship as you worked together to make your dream of the new church become a reality." Roddy was frowning. Obviously, Willoughby's knowledge of his personal affairs was far more detailed than one would expect from a stranger. Willoughby continued: "Father, I am also aware of the income of a parish priest, and the fact that your father's intended new Will was rendered invalid through the malicious efforts of a Msr. Beaucaire." Again, he raised his hand as Roddy's bewildered expression changed to anger. "Please hear me out, Father. I can assure you that my information comes from sources far removed from this area of the country. No one has betrayed your confidence. I only mention these things because of my awareness that limited income will often deny the privilege of a good education for the children of caring parents. If you and your good lady have plans for any future children, I'm sure you would want them to be well-educated. However, you would need to subsidise your present income to achieve that goal. I know that both your wife and yourself come from families of means and were, therefore, ensured a good education. I imagine you would want the same advantage for your children."

Roddy's shock had progressed to anger. "Frankly, Sir, my family affairs are a private matter. My wife and I do not make a practice of discussing our personal affairs with strangers." His earlier regard for this man had disappeared. Willoughby looked sad. "Father, a man's potential in life is often limited by an inadequate education. It's not the education alone, as you well know, but the contacts that one makes whilst acquiring it that opens many doors denied to others. An adequate subsidy to your present income would guarantee such advantages to your children, in addition to ensuring, for both your good lady and yourself the benefits that you deserve. Mr. Birch is impressed by your initiatives and loyalty to your village and would be honoured if you would join us in an enterprise that would provide those subsidies." Willoughby cocked his head enquiringly but could read only anger on Roddy's face. So, after a brief pause and no response, he continued. "Mr. Birch needs an organiser you see. You have shown the skills, innovative thought, and loyalties needed for that task. The risks in a well-organised system would be minimal and the rewards substantial. If you would consider organising, on a regular basis, people whose loyalty you have already earned, it would be most appreciated. Remember, the rewards would not be for you alone but also for your friends. You could, once again, 'be saving lives as well as souls.'" Roddy recognised that last phrase as being one that he had used to describe The Guiding Light. Now he was wondering where Willoughby's information came from and who amongst his acquaintances might be part of his organisation. "I thought Mr. Birch was going to arrange a meeting with me, on a face-to-face basis, not through an intermediary. He knows me and has obviously invaded my privacy by researching my background, but I'm not trusted to know him. Even so, I am being asked to put my life and family in jeopardy. Rather a one-sided expression of trust and loyalty, wouldn't you say?"

"Father, I am Mr. Birch. Actually, Mr. Birch is a name for a collective group of financiers. It is our money that buys the goods overseas. No money changes hands in our boats. But please understand, Father, we are just as much at risk as any man running goods ashore. Many of us have prominent careers and therefore risk not only our necks but also our families' wellbeing too if discovered. We have as much at risk as anyone involved in the operation. Perhaps more, since we are also the 'target of choice' for the

Customs Service. It's true that we did research your background extensively, but that is typical of the care we exercise in all our dealings. That level of caution will help keep you safe as well as ourselves.

"Please, Father, take time to consider our request. Again, I ask you to forgive my bad manners in being so direct in my approach, but, as I said earlier, our private time together has to be limited and above suspicion. Our meeting under these circumstances would appear quite innocent, wouldn't you agree? If you decide to join us, we will arrange another meeting. Just chalk across on your church's gate post if you agree. A circle if you don't. Thank you for your time, Sir. Whatever your decision, I wish you and your good lady every happiness." At this point, Westerhof's call to "Please assemble for a short walk to the church" ended their conversation. Prudence noticed Roddy's sour expression as they joined the other guests. "What's wrong?" she asked. "Later!" he responded curtly.

At home that night, they discussed the whole matter at length. "We should join the organisation," said Prudence. "You will always risk your neck to save your people and for no reward at all. You've proven that time and again. If you do the organising, the risks will be fewer, minimal in fact. And it is only fair that we share in the benefits." It was hard for Roddy to refuse Prudence anything so, despite some resentment at her pressuring him into this dangerous commitment, he chalked across on the gatepost the following morning. It was still there when Tubby visited the church on the following Saturday. His first comment was: "Roddy. I have a really fine brass crucifix I could give you for that gatepost." Roddy laughed. "That's not what it seems, Tubby. Not a religious symbol at all. It was just a signal to let some people know that I'm in the church. I should erase it. Now to what or whom do I owe the pleasure of this visit, Reverend Tubbs?"

Tubby blushed a little, but Roddy pretended not to notice. "Actually, Roddy, wanted your opinion on a personal matter."

"Really, and you drove all the way out here for that? I seem to recall that my advice has served you poorly in the not-too-distant past."

"Roddy. Would you think it proper for me to ask Maud to marry me?" Roddy drew back in surprise. "Why, Tubby, this is quite sudden, isn't it?" His friend looked crestfallen. "Oh, I'd hoped you wouldn't say that."

"Come now, Tubby. That doesn't mean 'no.' I merely meant that this was unexpected news. Actually, Prudence and I agreed that you and Maud made a fine couple at Westerhof's supper party. She is a really nice lady."

"Oh, I'm so glad you think so, Roddy. I'm afraid I've fallen head over heels for her. But I was anxious about it being so soon after Mrs. Whatson's death."

"Not in the least bit relevant, old chap. That marriage was never consummated. The bishop is willing to annul that marriage whenever you ask. Do you think Maud would accept your offer of marriage?"

"Oh, I do hope so. We do seem to get on well together. But I must confess, I am nervous to ask her."

"Well, you must ask her, old chap. I can't think of a single soul who would think ill of you for that. In fact, they would all cheer for you. You have a good heart. You've proven that by taking on young Charles as your own. How is he, by the way?"

"Oh, he is doing very well, Roddy. Maud and I both love him. Her daughter too, of course; she is a sweet child."

"Well, my friend, it looks like you will have a ready-made family. You will be streets ahead of Prudence and me."

"This is great news, Roddy. I'm so glad you approve. You are a good friend. I shall ask her just as soon as I can afford a ring. Mrs. Whatson left me a little short. All her demands, you know."

"Tubby, come and tell your news to Pru. Join us for something to eat and a glass of wine to celebrate." Prudence prepared the food whilst Roddy explained. "Tubby is going to ask Maud to marry him, Pru," he said raising his eyebrows. "Just as soon as he can afford a ring." Prudence paused in her preparations. "Why that is wonderful news, Tubby. I'm sure you will both be very happy." She looked at Roddy. "As soon as he can get her a ring, you say?"

"Yes, the whole Whatson affair has cost him dearly. He is still in recovery." Roddy and Prudence locked eyes for a few moments. Roddy smiled. Pru nodded and went upstairs. When she returned, she was carrying Mrs. McDowd's jewellery box. "Tubby," she said, "Roddy and I would be happy and proud if you could find a ring in this box that you think Maud might like. It would be our secret engagement present to you. If you don't see one that you like, feel free to choose one that you could sell or exchange for another that would suit you better." Tubby's jaw dropped as Prudence opened the box. He looked from one to the other of his friends without speaking for quite a while before saying, "That is too generous. I couldn't possibly accept such a gift. It's too much." Prudence explained how Roddy's mother had given her the jewellery and her instructions regarding the use or disposal of the items. "So, you see, Tubby, we would be happy if you and Maud could share our good fortune. Remember 'It's more blessed to give than receive.'" Tubby finally chose a gold band with a small diamond. Not the most expensive in the box but quite elegant. He was so grateful; they were embarrassed.

"Remember, Tubby. This gift is strictly between us. We will admire the ring with as much pleasure and surprise as anyone else when Maud shows it to us," said Prudence with a smile. They sat down for their meal with their very happy friend. He declined the third glass of wine and said, "If you wouldn't be offended, I would like to get back to Nextwest and ask Maud as soon as possible." They both smiled. "Of course, Tubby; away you go with all our best wishes." Tubby turned at the doorway. "Roddy, would you officiate at the wedding. Please?"

"I would be very happy to Tubby; where will it be?"

"It should be Nextwest. His Grace would expect that."

"Then with Bishop West's permission, Tubby, I would be pleased to." And so, a month later Tubby and Maud were married. The bishop provided a generous cash engagement present and two gold wedding bands. Tubby's smile lit up the church. Maud too, looking radiant in one of Bessie Drew's modified creations, was smiling her shy smile, and the couple looked very happy. The reception was in the church hall catered by Bessie Drew and Marie and financed by Bishop West.

When Roddy returned to Ryeport, he found an unsigned note on his desk in the church. It asked that he meet with Bannerman and the Pringle brothers on Thursday at their farm. The four men discussed the areas of the smuggling operation that each was responsible for and what rules and disciplines were to be applied. After that, Roddy gradually shaped the operation to become his own, safety being his first priority. A note behind the loose brick initiated a final meeting with Mr. Birch. They were ready.

• • •

Things went extremely well for more than a year. Roddy received no money for his efforts, but his account with a Bristol Investment Broker was growing nicely.

Bannerman smiled as he noted the brass vase in the left window of the old church in Ryeport. The vicar had adopted the 'vase-in-the-window' system of signalling between himself and Bannerman in order to maintain the impression that they still didn't talk to each other. The vase placed in the left window meant that Roddy wanted to meet him in Archer's stable. Had the vase been in the middle window the meeting would have been at Sailmaker's old rigging shop. However, Archer and Higgins were away selling smoked fish and pickled herring in Nextwest so they should have the stable to themselves. Bannerman entered the new stable and called Archer's and Higgin's names aloud several times. There was no response. The small office was empty, and Bannerman was at the top of the hayloft ladder intending to check that space when Roddy came through the door. Bannerman took a cursory look around before climbing down and extending his hand. Roddy smiled as they shook hands. "Good to see you, Bannerman. Are we all set for Thursday?"

"Aye, everythin's set and secure. I'll be looking after the beach. The run will come ashore at Wyno's Bay about 10 o'clock on Thursday. Tackle is greased, oiled and muffled. With one exception, we're using Goodman's old crew to lift the goods up the cliff. I've moved Trevelyan to the dispersal team. 'e gets a bit loose mouthed when 'e's 'ad a few, so I didn't want 'im knowing anythin' more, or sooner than 'e 'ad to. I've put 'im on the last delivery; that's to Wicksted, the longest run. And the only notice 'e'll be getting before 'e takes over a loaded cart is when we bang on 'is door and 'and 'im the reins. It's safer that way. I've also warned 'im that if 'e ever breathes a word of our operation, 'e won't live long enough to see 'is children grow up. But 'e'll be no problem now. Better this way than if I'd cut 'im off completely. 'e's not a bad bloke really and 'is family needs their share of the proceeds. 'e might've got bitter if I'd cut 'im right out of the team. If 'e stays loyal and close mouthed, we'll look after 'im. If he doesn't..." He drew a finger across his throat. "We'll still look after 'im. Archer would call that the carrot and the whip method."

Roddy gave a wry smile. "If I thought it would come to that, I'd quit. But you've good measure of the men, Bannerman; I doubt there will be any trouble. The operation runs well since you took over the beach. I understand you had the crews practising the assembly of the lifting gear for hours before you were satisfied with their speed." It was Bannerman's turn to chuckle. "Not just speed...quiet is just as important. We've got it down to an art. The men are goadin' each other to faster times, but if it ain't quiet, it don't count. It's a source of pride to go faster and quieter. And none of 'em drink before a run anymore. I told 'em that the Spotsman gave orders that anyone turnin' up drunk for a run was to 'ave a bad accident. Said you wouldn't allow a drunk to put us in the 'ands of the Revenuers." Roddy's forehead creased into a frown. "Any chance of that? Drunken slips of the tongue, I mean?"

"Always! We can only watch for signs of trouble and take steps to scare the hell out of any loose-lippers. If scarin' doesn't work," Bannerman gave Roddy a grim look, "we 'ave to resort to stronger measures. If someone's careless 'yappin' could leave' good people danglin' from a gibbet, well...we'll just 'ave to protect ourselves." He drew his finger across his throat again.

"Remember, Bannerman, we said we would never use violence. That's how Goodman came unstuck." The vicar had had enough of this subject. "Look, I really wanted to talk to you about a small change of plans. An urgent order needs to be delivered the day after the run. The client insists that it be delivered in time for an affair he's hosting at the weekend. He doesn't want to be known to any of the crew because he holds an important public office. Pru has arranged to leave it in his gatehouse. To make this work, we'll have to load his box onto my wagon directly from the run. I'll take it back to Ryeport and have the coach take it to Nextwest the next day. Pru and I will pick it up later at The Coach and Horses so that she can make the delivery on Saturday. I'll spend an hour or so with Reverend Tubbs, to give me a legitimate reason to be in Nextwest. So, I'd like you to arrange for that box to be the first one off the boat without any of the crew seeing us, of course. It's not a big box. It weighs about 12 pounds. Just leave it behind the big oak at the cliff top. Bannerman looked at the vicar as though he were a stranger. "Vicar, that's madness. You can't change plans this late in the game, let alone drive your wagon in the dead of night with trade goods aboard. Any man would think twice about that. Any roughnecks would see a man alone as an easy mark, and Revenuers would stop any cart at that hour."

"There will be two of us, Bannerman; Pru is coming too. We'll be disguised, not dressed as a cleric and his lady, and we'll travel by back roads. It's an important deal and promises to be the first of many. The client wants to impress his dinner guests. If anyone asks about the goods, he will say that he bought them at an estate sale. Bannerman looked at the vicar in stony silence for quite a while. "We shouldn't do it!" he said. "It goes against all our planning. Your planning. Your rules. This is the last thing I would expect from you. Rehearse and follow the plan, you always said. And it's worked well for us. I see Pru's 'and in this, she's impulsive but not you. You know 'ow important it is to stick to a well re'earsed plan. It's been the reason for our success. Everybody drills and follows the drill. Make no decisions during the run you said. Just follow the drill. Now, too late to re-drill, you want to break your own rules. This is Pru's 'andiwork for sure. We're doing well and safely. Why risk it all for a little more profit than we need? A little greed could get us all 'ung."

Roddy was silent for a while, but when he spoke again, he ignored Bannerman's remarks as though he'd never made them. "Look, the crate is numbered 17. I would really appreciate it if you would bring that one up first. Arrange for it to be the last item loaded on the boat. You could carry it yourself up to the knoll on the east side of the cliff top. My wagon will be hidden behind the knoll out of sight of any crew. They'll be working on the western side at the tackle. You'll be able to return to your business straight away. It won't take you more than a couple of minutes. I'll put the crate on my wagon. We'll be gone within a minute of you setting the box down. It's important. Please make this one, small exception to the plan." Bannerman had come to know that Roddy, the Spotsman, was a very different person than Roddy, the vicar. Once the Spotsman had made a decision, he'd always been immoveable. Despite Roddy's well-mannered tone, Bannerman knew he would brook no refusal on this change. You could argue with the vicar, but once his 'Spotsman' mind was made up, you couldn't change it unless you were Prudence, of course. Bannerman shook his head. "I'll do it this one time. But I don't like it. It could bring us bad luck. But you're the Spotsman, so since you insist." He threw up his hands. "I'll put the crate be'ind the big oak, on your side of the tree, to keep you from being seen. I'll not look for you or speak if I see you. If anyone else sees you, it could finish our whole operation. Don't ever ask me to break my routines again at such short notice. I won't do it. You'd better be be'ind that knoll 'alf-an-'our before the dispersal crew's due at the field. I'll 'ave a 'watcher' 'idden along the west side of the Coach Road, so you'll 'ave to come in through the copse on the east side of Pringle's farm. I'll arrive, by boat a little after that. If all is clear, I'll be givin' the signal that'll be relayed down the line, and the lads'll start comin' in, trustin' us because of our past record. I just 'ope we don't let 'em down. You make sure your wagon is well greased and quiet too, Vicar. Keep that old nag of yours a bit 'ungry through the day an' put the feedbag on 'im when you arrive to keep 'im quiet. You be quiet too. And make sure Prudence sits still and keeps 'er mouth shut. No noise at all." He leaned towards the vicar as he wagged a menacing finger in his face. "None." He rose from the feed sack that had served as his seat and made for the door. "Oh! Be careful. Remember, the loose shale close by the cliff edge, and it's rocks and water 30 feet below. That's where I met them two smugglers, remember?" He left without another look or parting word. The vicar had the distinct impression that he had used up any credits that he'd earned with Bannerman. He watched his beachmaster leave and sat holding his head for a few more minutes. Bannerman had been correct in seeing Pru's hand in this. It had been her idea that they exploit this unexpected opportunity to do more business with one of the upscale clients that Goodman had introduced her to. Roddy knew Prudence was impulsive by nature; opportunistic might be a better word. She was also impatient of his planning and drilling. Bannerman had spotted that without having spent much time around her. He was quick to see strengths and weaknesses in people. Roddy suspected that Bannerman would also be aware that Pru was his personal weakness and reasoned that was most likely why he had given in this time. But that also gave him the right to say 'never again'. Roddy allowed Bannerman a few more minutes to clear the area before he too left for The Harbour Light.

A few minutes after he'd gone, there was a rustling in the loft. Bridget waited until she was sure the vicar was out of earshot before surveying the area and descending the ladder. The vicar's arrival had interrupted Bannerman's usually thorough security check. The fact that they both knew that Archer and Higgins were away had lulled them into an erroneous sense of security. Bridget's eyes were wide and gleaming, and she was muttering to herself as she hurried from the barn and headed for the sanctuary of her cottage. "I know who the smugglers are! An' I know where the vicar and 'is tart are going to be durin' a run on Thursday night. Too good for me, is 'e? But 'e'll take up with the likes of 'er. I'll teach 'im! Pay 'im back, I will. I'll teach 'im for snubbin' me." There was a malicious grin on her face. "I'll see 'im 'ung. 'is tart too. Then 'e'll be sorry. I'll tell the whole bloody village. See what they think of their precious vicar then." Suddenly she stopped and clapped a hand over her mouth. "But Bannerman's from our village. Who else? Who else? Who can I trust? If I tell someone an' they tell Bannerman, 'e'll kill me, 'e will! 'e'll kill me for sure!" Panic began to grip her now, and she ran the rest of the way to her cottage trembling and sweating with fear. Once indoors, she drew her forefinger across her throat in imitation of Bannerman's gesture to Roddy. "If they'll kill one of their own, what chance do I stand? I'll 'ave to tell a Customs man. That's what I'll do. Then I'll be safe. They'll keep me safe, may even give me a reward. I'll move away, to a big town where they can't find me. That's what I'll do. T'day's We'n'sday. I've got a bit more than a day. Where can I find a Customs man in just a few hours?" She sank into the chair by the cold fireplace and held her head in her hands. "I've got to think, and I'm not good at that."

• • •

Roddy was feeling chastised by Bannerman's reluctant concession. He was the Spotsman after all. It was his job to run the show. He planned all other parts of the operation and arranged for misinformation to be fed to the Customs officers, so they were often miles away when the goods were run ashore. Dispersal arrangements too were made with his usual painstaking care. Nevertheless, it was Bannerman's crew management, local knowledge, and experiences with the men that made the transfer at sea, the run ashore and dispersal work so smoothly. Bannerman still intimidated him a little despite their friendship and mutual respect. He knew that he could never make the hard decisions that his beach master might. He could never 'take care' of someone in the manner Bannerman indicated. Fortunately, that had never been necessary since he'd become Spotsman. He promised himself that he'd quit if that was ever needed.

Pru had been helpful in setting up a system of misinformation for the Customs people, and the results had been very satisfying. She would tell Whitestone about some 'rumours' that she'd overheard, and Roddy would make sure that a different source would give corroborating information to another Customs officer. Because of this, the Revenuers were often lying in wait, scores of miles away from the actual run and sometimes on nights when there was no run. The smugglers themselves were unaware of this side of his planning of course. His role in the smuggling was known only to Bannerman, Pru, Bessie Drew, and the Pringles. Bannerman and the Pringles were known to the smuggling crews, however. In fact, most of the smugglers believed Bannerman was the Spotsman as well as beach master.

Bridget's discovery that the vicar was the 'Spotsman' had her excited but fearful. At last, she had knowledge that would enable her to punish the vicar for rejecting her. On the other hand, Bannerman's reputation for violent physical reaction was well known. And his gestures when referring to 'looking after people' were too graphic to misunderstand. She was sure Bannerman would kill her if he found out what she knew. Eventually, she fell asleep in the chair by the fireplace and awoke hours later cold, terrified and in complete darkness. She grabbed her throat, expecting to find a horrendous gash delivered by the angry fisherman. When she realised it was only a dream, she calmed down, and since her throat wasn't cut, she ate some bread and cold meat from her pantry. She needed to get the information to Whitestone and without the village knowing. She decided to send him a letter. "That's it," she muttered. "I'll send him a letter on tomorrow's stagecoach." Feeling better now that she had a plan, she kicked off her shoes and lay on her rough bed fully dressed and hoping for a more restful sleep than she'd had in the chair. She awoke at first light, glad to be up and about. After a cautious look outside, she made her way to The Harbour Light. It was already Thursday. The run was tonight. She had only this one chance to trap the vicar and his 'tart.' "I must find out if the coach is expected today," she muttered. "But I've never 'ad business with the coach. Those nosy villagers would want to know what I'm up to. Bannerman would like to know for sure. Find me out, so 'e would."

Meg was backing through the kitchen door of the inn carrying slops for the pigs when she bumped into Bridget. Meg's mind was elsewhere, and the unexpected contact startled her. She cried out as she spilt slop from the bucket all over the steps. "Bridget! What in God's name are you doing here? You scared the hell out of me."

"Sorry, Meg. Sorry. Sorry. Sorry. Didn't mean to scare you. Oh, Meg… I've had a terrible night. I'm so scared. I don't know what to do." Bridget adopted her 'poor-me' face.

"What's wrong, Bridget? Are you sick?" Meg was genuinely concerned as Bridget knew she would be. Meg was always nice to everybody. Bridget found her a bit sickening really even though she was glad for her compassion right now. "Meg, I keep having this awful nightmare. Someone was trying to kill me. It was scary; there was blood everywhere… my blood. I didn't know what to do. When I woke up, it was pitch black. I thought I was dead." She buried her face in her hands and started to cry. Crying was something she was good at. She practised it often. It helped her get her own way. Meg put her arm around Bridget's shoulders. "Oh, come on into the kitchen. I'll make you some warm milk." She half carried the bigger woman into the inn.

"What's the problem here?" Ernie, never pleased to see Bridget, was standing in the kitchen eating breakfast. Meg explained Bridget's plight, but her father was unsympathetic. "Take your problem to the vicar, girl.

The inn is no place for these matters. Be off with you. Go see the vicar." Bridget collapsed in a fresh fit of crying. Finally, she blubbered, " 'e was one of them trying to kill me. 'im and that 'awksworth man – the one that meets the coach sometimes. I'm scared of them. I'm sure it's a warning. It's a warning!" Meg gave her some warm milk. "Here drink this. It was just a bad dream, Bridget. Take your mind off it, and you'll soon be alright."

"Will the coach and that cap'n 'awksworth be here today?" Bridget asked wiping her eyes.

"Thursday. Hmm, yes, I think it's quite likely," said Ernie. "Why? You going on a trip?" He made no effort to conceal his impatience.

"No. It's just that in my dream, cap'n 'awksworth was one of them that was 'urtin' me. I don't want to see 'im."

"Enough of this nonsense, Bridget. We've got work to do. Take your dreams to the vicar." Ernie didn't understand why Meg smiled so broadly at that. A disconsolate looking Bridget left the inn shortly after. "So the coach is expected today." Bridget smiled as she said it, and once she was out of sight of the inn, she straightened her back, and her stride became more purposeful. She would write the letter and have the coachmen deliver it to Nextwest for Cap'n Whitestone. But her writing skills were limited. She had been a student in Meg's classes at the old church, and Meg had been extra patient with her, but she didn't cope as well as the others. Then after the wreck of The Seahorse, Meg had given up her role as teacher, and the vicar's tart had taken over. She scowled at the memory. There was no way that she was going to have that tart, Prudence, telling her what to do. So Bridget had quit. Now sitting at her kitchen table, she discovered that she couldn't spell Whitestone or Revenue or officer, and she started to cry again. But she remembered the words Customs and reward from posters in the village, so she scrapped her first attempts throwing the paper towards the fire, but they fell short and landed on the hearth. She sat down for another try and wrote:

> *Customs ofser Ther b a run ashawfursdee. Nyt*
>
> *Y noze Beech. Sined Bridget, Ryeport.*

She paused, admiring her work. The first thing that Meg had taught her class was how to write their own names and the name of the village. Now Bridget thought she deserved a reward. She knew how to spell reward from the posters. Then a chill ran up her spine as she realised that if the letter fell into the wrong hands, Bannerman might hear of it, and she had signed it. She screwed up that note and threw it to the hearth with her earlier attempts. But she really would like the reward, so she decided to draw a fish. She knew how to draw a simple fish. She'd use that as her signature. If all went well, she would be the only one who knew the signature was a fish. That would prove she wrote the letter and earn her the reward. So, she rewrote the letter trying to be neater and added: *REWARD PLEEZ*, then drew a fish and sealed it. On the outside, she wrote 'Customs ofser.' That looked much better. She felt quite pleased with herself. Tucking the letter into the pocket of her apron, she took a bucket to the well and did a little laundry whilst she waited for the coach.

When Hawksworth rode in, she was confident that the coach would soon follow, and it did. An elderly couple alighted from the coach and entered the inn for some refreshment. They were followed by the coachmen and the familiar mailbag. After some reflection, Bridget decided that the lady passenger, rather than the coachmen, would be a better choice to deliver her letter. She would have to pay the coachman. Besides, they were too friendly with Ernie and the vicar. Her letter should be none of their business. The lady passenger was happy to oblige the attractive but seemingly slow-witted young woman who asked a favour, and about an hour and a half later, she gave the letter for 'Customs Ofser' to the innkeeper of The Coach and Horses and with a wink said, "Some girls just can't resist a uniform."

Whitestone was farther west, however, following another piece of misinformation. The letter might have sat there for days had the innkeeper not spotted young Albert Starr, one of Whitestone's new recruits. He called him over. "Here's a letter for the Customs officer from someone who can't spell and can 'ardly bloody write. You'd better take it." Starr smiled as he looked at the clumsy writing and bad spelling. "I guess I can open this," he said. "I'm a Customs Ofser, but I didn't realise I'd been spelling it wrong all this time." But as he read the message his smile disappeared. He left half his ale in his hurry to get to Whitestone's office where Lieutenant Bennett had been left in charge. Bennett read the letter and scratched his head. "No signature," he said, "unless a fish wrote it. This could be another piece of bad information. Lord knows we've had too much of that these past few months." The two men looked at each other trying to decide on an action that their critical superior wouldn't ridicule. "Tell you what," said Bennett. "You ride to Wyno's beach, see if there's any evidence of preparations for a run, possibly a prepared signal fire or even just the makings. That is a beach where they'd have to use tackle to lift the goods to the cliff top. If you see anything like that, hurry back here. Meanwhile, I'll get some men together and see if I can arrange for a cutter to cover that beach from seaward. Don't take the smugglers on single-handed now. Just ride over there and try to look casual. Hurry back if you see anything suspicious but do nothing to attract attention. Keep your eyes open as you approach the cliff top. They might have watchers hidden close by. Can you handle that? If it's a true lead, it'll be your first encounter with smugglers; all the other times having been false alarms." Starr was excited. "Yes! Alright, I'll be fine. I'll be away then," said the enthusiastic young man as he checked his pistol.

• • •

Back in Ryeport, Doc Hudson saw Meg leave the inn and head out along the broad harbour front and hurried to catch up with her. "Hello there, young Meg," he called. "Where are you off to in such a hurry? I was coming to see how you were getting along." Meg paused, allowing the doctor to catch up. "Good mornin', Doctor. I'm fine. I was just off to see Bridget. She was in tears this mornin'. She'd had some dreams about people cutting her throat. I thought I'd see if she was better now."

"Really? Then I'll walk with you. Provided that you slow down a little that is. My old legs couldn't keep up with your young ones." There was no answer to their first knock on Bridget's door and no answer on the second attempt either. Doc peeked through the window. "Looks like she's not home."

"Maybe she's sleeping," said Meg. "She had a bad night, remember? Let's check." She opened the door, and they walked in calling Bridget's name. But still, there was no answer. As Meg made her way to the bedroom, Doc picked up a crumpled piece of paper from the hearth. "Looks like she's been practising her writing, Meg. It was good of you to teach the villagers. Quite a few of them can read passably well now. A little slow, but that will improve with practice." He smoothed out the crumpled paper, and his face paled as he read the message. Just then they heard the latch lift on the back door. It was Bridget. Meg gave a little wave. "Hello, Bridget. We were worried about you. When we couldn't get an answer, we thought we'd better check to make sure you were alright." Meg looked relieved. Bridget's eyes though flashed to the crumpled papers on the hearth. Doc had concealed his piece behind his back. "I'm fine," said Bridget. "Just had to go, that's all. When you gotta go, you gotta go." Meg's gaze went to the crumpled papers.

"Been practising your writing then, Bridget? That's good! Maybe you'll go back to class again?" Meg moved to pick up one of the pieces of paper, but Bridget hurriedly beat her to it and quickly threw all the pieces into the flames. "Oh, Bridget! I did so want to see how well you were doing."

"Not good, Meg. I don't want anyone to see them. I might come back to class but only if you start teachin' again."

"Oh! Well, maybe in a little while," she said with a smile, but she looked a little hurt. "Well then, provided you're alright, Bridget, I'll get back to the inn. I've got lots of chores to do. Bye for now." Meg waved, and both she and the doctor left. "I wonder what all that was about?" Meg said to Doc. No reason why she wouldn't let me see how she was doing. I spent a lot of time with her."

"I know you did, Meg. Strange woman, that one," responded Doc. Meg returned to her chores at the inn, and Doc hurriedly pulled Ernie outside. "What's the matter, Doc?" Ernie was puzzled by his friend's furtive haste. Doc showed Ernie the letter. The innkeeper's hand went to his mouth in shock. "This is tonight," he said. "Yes," responded Doc. "Where do you think she got her information?"

"I've no idea unless she's been rolling in the hay with a smuggler. Do you think any of our lads are involved?"

"Who knows? Where's Bannerman?"

"Selling smoked fish, I think. East of here."

"Due back when?"

"Tomorrow sometime."

"Well, that fits," said the doctor. "It could be just the cover they need to be out overnight. How in God's name can we find out for sure?"

"Jed Pringle might know."

"I'll take the vicar's wagon and get over there," said the doctor. "Maybe Pringle can stop it. I'm pretty sure he knows people in the trade."

"The vicar and Prudence took the wagon to Nextwest early this morning," said Ernie.

Doc waved Bridget's note in front of Ernie's nose. "This was only one of several papers on the hearth in Bridget's cottage. She hurriedly threw the rest on the fire when Meg went to pick one up. I think this was a practice piece. I happened to snag it before she came into the room. Do you think she actually sent a letter? One she was satisfied with perhaps?" Ernie thought for a while. "She would have had to pay the coachman to take it, so I wouldn't think so. Wait! Come to think of it, I did see her pass something to a woman passenger before the coach left. At the time, I thought she'd just picked up something the passenger had dropped."

"Would the vicar know anything about the run?" Doc was very worried.

"Who knows, Doc? He's saved a few necks here in the past even though he wasn't involved. Maybe he won't be as willing to risk his neck now he's married." The two men were suddenly shocked by Latour's deep and unexpected voice. "Can I be of any help?" They had been so engrossed in their speculations, they hadn't seen him approaching and were shaken by the interruption. "Where in God's name did you come from?" the doctor snapped. He was shaken and angry at Latour's intrusion into their furtive discussion. "Sorry, gentlemen. I've just come from Archer's stable. I've arranged for Higgins to look after The Guiding Light for a couple of nights. I didn't mean to startle you."

"You were eavesdropping," accused the doctor.

"Hardly, Doctor," responded Latour. "You two were in such agitated conversation, it seems you were oblivious to all about you."

"No! There's nothing you can do," responded Doc tersely. "We have urgent and private business to discuss." Latour's chin dropped to his chest as he considered his response. When he looked up again, there was an unfamiliar assertiveness about him. "Gentlemen, I know what a 'run' is. I've also heard all the stories about Customs officers coming to this village suspecting the vicar and Sailmaker, even you Ernie, of being involved in smuggling. Sailmaker told me all about his involvement during our last hours aboard The Seahorse. Neither of us expected to live past noon the following day, so he didn't believe he was breaking any confidences. I know about the fireboat and the Spotsman's attempt to kill Sailmaker and how the vicar, Miss Pru, and Jed Pringle saved him. There are some things you need to understand about me. First, Sailmaker was my best friend. He helped us escape from Haiti when our very lives were at stake. He also tried to save my daughter's life and lost his own as a result. This village also took me in at a time when I felt I had nothing to live for. You gave me a living, friendship and a reason to go on with my life. So, if there are problems for the people of this village, I consider them my problems too. I need to help – to repay, if you like – and I will owe a debt to Sailmaker for as long as I live." He fixed his eyes on Doc Hudson. "As for you, Doctor, you have nothing to fear from me. It's my skin that's black not my heart." The two men looked embarrassed. Latour continued: "If it would help, I could drive Gerry's buggy to Pringle's farm, provided you tell me how to get there. Gerry is in London for a few days and won't need his buggy. I'll also need to know what to do or say when I get there." He gave them a wry smile. "I'm afraid I missed that part of the conversation."

Ernie locked eyes with Doc, who answered his unspoken question with a grudging nod. So, Ernie showed Latour the note and told him of their suspicions and fears. It was finally decided that Doc and Latour would both go to Pringle's farm to see if they could find out if a run was planned and, if so, what they could do about it. It was late afternoon when Latour and Doc trotted the buggy into Pringle's driveway. The two brothers looked anxiously at Latour. They had heard stories about his 'rising from the dead' and were rather nervous about this strange man. They had never actually spoken with him before. A nod of acknowledgement when Roddy introduced his new sexton was as close as they'd come. Doc explained the reason for their visit, and Jed Pringle became fidgety as he read Bridget's practice note. "Quick," he said. "We've got to go to Nextwest. Latour, if you agree, I'd like you to go to the field above the landing beach. We can drop you off just west of the field and point the way. But be careful and keep under cover. There may be soldiers or spies hidden there. Come straight back here if you see anyone and tell my brother Bob. Remember, watch for spies, and be careful.

"Doc, you drop me off at The Coach and Horses. I'll see if I can find out if a letter was delivered and if so, what has come of it. You should go to Marie's bakery at the bottom of Church Street hill and tell Bessie what's happened. I'll meet you there as soon as I can. If I'm not there by eight o'clock, you must say to Bessie: 'A leopard can't change its stripes.' Will you do that? Latour, you can say that too if you happen to run into Bannerman but don't say it to a Customs officer."

"You mean spots. 'A leopard can't change its spots," Doc corrected: "Leopards have spots, not stripes."

"No! You must say stripes! A leopard can't change its stripes," Jed insisted. "And you make damn sure you say it that way. 'A leopard can't change its stripes.' Whatever you do, don't say spots. Then do whatever Bessie tells you."

Doc was shocked. "So, Bessie is in on this?"

"No. But she has contacts and is very close to the vicar. Remember, just the way I said it: stripes, not spots." They let Latour off the buggy with instructions to follow the same route that Bannerman had used to take the injured Sailmaker down to meet Sully's boat. Pringle carefully described the lay of the land to Latour and warned him of the loose shale on the cliff top. Then they headed for Nextwest.

About three miles farther west, Jed Pringle spotted a man leading a lame horse who quickly ducked behind some brush. "Did you see that bloke, Doc? A 'uniform, leadin' a lame 'orse, is 'idin' be'ind the bushes on your left. I 'ope Latour keeps 'is eyes peeled." Doc dropped Jed at The Coach and Horses and continued the short distance to Marie's bakery. Marie and Fletch were there, but Bessie had already gone home. Doc said nothing to them about Bridget's letter. But Marie, seeing how anxious Doc was, climbed into the buggy and directed him to Bessie's place. She realised something had to be wrong because Doc rarely left Ryeport. Now he was here, obviously worried and anxious to talk to Bessie. Doc showed Bridget's letter to Bessie and told her of their fears that it may have got through to the Customs office. He asked if she knew if there was a run tonight. Now it was Bessie's turn to look worried. "Doc, I honestly don't know. Let's talk to Fletch; 'e might know if somethin's on tonight. Besides, Jed'll be going there with any news he gets at The 'Coach.'" Doc was growing more anxious by the minute. Precious time was leaking away, and daylight was already fading. "The vicar came to Nextwest today. Do you know where he might be?" he asked. Bessie shook her head.

Jed arrived at Marie's just as they did. "Shields, the innkeeper at The Coach 'n' 'orses, said 'e'd given a letter to Lieutenant Starr addressed to 'Customs Ofser.' He'd enjoyed a laugh when he described the spelling." That spelling, of course, was confirmation that Bridget's letter had got through. Starr had been seen shortly after that riding fast towards Ryeport. There was nothing more the innkeeper could add. Fletch said, "I'd best be goin' then. Thanks for the information, Doctor. You'd best see if you can find the vicar. When you find 'im, tell 'im, 'A leopard can't change its stripes.'"

"There you go again," said Doc. "It's spots, not stripes. Tigers have stripes; leopards have spots."

"No! You be sure to say stripes – not spots – it's important. It means the run's bein' warned-off. After tonight it won't mean anything. Find the vicar.

If you can't find him, go home. You'd best be in bed or in a very public place before dark." Fletch hurried from the shop. The doctor and Jed drove to the manse, then The White Hart and back through the town, but they found no trace of the vicar. Reluctantly, he and Jed headed back to Pringle's farm. Jed was still concerned about the 'uniformed man' with the lame horse that he'd seen on their way into town. He was sure it had to be Starr. It was after 10:30 when the pale moonlight revealed Jed's barn. The two men were startled as, somewhere off to the west, a red rocket screamed into the air. Minutes after that, there was a small explosion from the direction of the cliffs, and a sheet of flame shot skyward. That flame soon settled down to become a strong, steady glow. "That's the warning-off fire," said Jed. "I wonder who got the job of lighting that. You'd best stay with us tonight, Doc. We'll make up some excuse for you visitin' us."

On the cliff-top, Latour had watched Starr lead his lame horse into the field and conceal it behind some scrub. Then the officer had furtively made his way to the edge of the cliff, pistol in hand. That cut off any possibility of Latour getting back to the Coach Road, so he stayed in hiding, watching Starr's shadowy figure as he searched the site and examined the tackle. With a lame horse, Starr would be unable to ride for help, and it was too far to walk back to town, so he too decided to hide. He had orders not to tackle the smugglers single-handed, so he would stay concealed and, hopefully, be able to identify them later. He had waited quietly for about an hour before deciding to look for boats approaching the shore. It was just as he reached the edge of the cliff that the rocket that startled Doc and Jed had screamed into the air. Then, after a short delay, a small explosion from the cliff below him shot a sheet of flame into the air and ignited the warning-off fire. It had shaken Starr so badly that he would have fallen over the sloping cliff top had he not managed to grab a piece of the lifting tackle.

Someone had lit the fire remotely using a length of fuse and a small charge of gunpowder. Starr hadn't seen anyone, and he was prevented from putting the fire out because it had been set on a ledge under the overhanging cliff top. He was not even able to drop anything down to smother it. But now he heard hushed voices coming from behind the oak tree on the east side of the field. Cautiously, Starr made his way towards the voices, keeping behind scrub wherever possible. Roddy and Prudence had arrived well ahead of the lead time that Bannerman had requested. They had been sitting quietly, strictly observing Bannerman's strict instructions when they too were startled by the rocket and warning-off fire. Roddy quietly dismounted from the wagon, and Prudence called to him to be careful. It was her caution that Starr had overheard. Roddy tiptoed around the oak tree to see what was happening at the cliff top.

"Stand – in the king's name – or I'll fire!" called the 17-year-old Starr, in as gruff a voice as he could muster. Roddy's figure, still in the shadow of the great oak's canopy, was indistinct to Starr – merely a pale human shadow overlaying the darker shape of the old oak tree. The young officer moved closer; his pistol raised. He was far more visible in the pale moonlight than the silhouette of the man he planned to arrest. Roddy ducked and yelled to Pru, "Go! Go! Go!" as he ran towards her. Prudence slapped the reins, and Slondosh pulled away. That was when Pru heard the bang of a pistol.

Starr hadn't meant to fire. He'd been charged by a big man who had leapt at him from behind a bush. Latour had decided to take the officer down before he could fire his pistol at Roddy. Starr had turned to face his attacker, and his pistol had fired as their bodies collided. Roddy looked back and saw the two figures on the ground. His first thought was for Bannerman. He came running from the oak, screaming like a banshee. Starr, with his weapon discharged and thinking he was about to be attacked by a horde of smugglers, scrambled to his feet and took flight. He took with him a distinct impression of a large, featureless, black man attacking him, but he felt sure he had killed his attacker. When Roddy reached Latour, he was bleeding badly. The pistol had been jammed against his chest when it discharged. Roddy looked up and saw Starr drop his pistol as he ran for the road. Roddy yelled after him assuming different voices just to keep him motivated – before returning to his injured friend. "My God, Paul, wherever did you come from? No. Don't answer that. Let me get you to the doctor."

"No time, Roddy," Latour mumbled weakly. "It's bad. Roddy, please hide me. Promise! Don't bury me for…th…three…daaay…daaaays." His voice faded to the barest whisper as blood drizzled over his lips. "Prom…ise." Roddy cradled Latour's head in the crook of his arm. "I promise, Paul. I'll hide you. I'll look after you." Latour gave a gasp, and his head rolled to one side. Roddy ran to the oak, "Quick, Pru. Help me." Pru had stopped the wagon as soon as she heard the pistol shot and was quickly at his side. "Oh, Roddy! It's Paul. What can we do? Who did this? Was it a smuggler, or a Customs man?"

"He wore a uniform, but I think he was alone. Let's get Paul into the wagon. Quickly now, help me." Together they dragged the big man to the wagon and eventually managed to get him into the back. Only then did they remove the feedbag from Slondosh before leading the horse quietly from the cover of the small copse and onto the Coach Road. They were soon making good time towards Ryeport. Prudence was in the back with Latour. His clothes were soaked with blood, and there were no signs of life. No breath or pulse. He was dead. "Roddy, what can we do?" she said. "Where can we go?" There was panic in her voice. "We're going home, Pru. Gerry is in London for a few days. We'll hide Paul in his cottage. But we have to do it without anyone seeing us. Then we must get home and change. The run has been warned-off. The Revenuers must have sent a scout to the cliff top. Listen," he said softly. "Whoa! Slondosh! Whoa!" He put a warning finger to his lips to silence Pru. They both heard the distinct sound of many hooves, coming from farther west on the Coach Road. "That man must have been a scout or a look-out," said Roddy. "Now the main party is riding in. We must hurry. Giddup, Slondosh, Giddup." He slapped the reins on the horse's back, and Slondosh moved off at a fast trot.

• • •

In Ryeport Bridget had been standing at her back door, looking west, for more than an hour. If her letter had got through to the Customs officers, there would be a lot of action there by now. Her fate could well depend on the outcome. When the rocket soared into the air, her hands flew to her face, and she had to lean against the door. She was in no position to see the warning fire because that area was hidden by the nearer cliffs. Obviously, something unusual was happening. But would she be safe? Ernie was pacing back and forth in the kitchen of The Harbour Light, worried about what was happening with Doc and Latour and wondering where the vicar and Prudence were. "If there is a run, where is Bannerman? Who else in the village might be caught in the trap?" he muttered.

At Pringle's farm, Jed and Doc were scrambling out of the buggy. The sound of drumming hooves was being carried to their ears also by the westerly breeze. It had to be Customs men, but were they heading for the farm or the cliff-top? Bob came hurrying from the porch, where he'd been waiting for Latour all evening. He had seen both the rocket and the glow of the warning fire. "What gives, Jed?" he called as he ran towards them. "Have the Revenuers been tipped off?" He cocked his head to one side listening attentively. "Those 'orses, are they after you?"

Jed's mind was racing. "I'll explain later, Bob. They can't be far be'ind us. We'll say Doc came to see me 'cause I've 'ad a bad dose of the shits these past couple o' weeks. We've been 'ere all afternoon, and when it got late, Doc agreed to stay the night 'cause it could be dangerous drivin' back on 'is own with all the villains about these days."

Doc interrupted: "That won't do, Jed. Too many people have seen us in Nextwest today. Whitestone will blow that story out of the water. Say I came to see you about the diarrhoea by all means, but we'll have to admit we were in Nextwest if we're asked. Let's say that I gave you the last of my tonic for the diarrhoea and wanted to find the vicar because I wanted him to open an account for me at the apothecaries. I can fake something from there. The vicar will back me up if I ask him."

When Lieutenant Bennett knocked on the farmhouse door, the three men were seated at the kitchen table, and Jed was dealing cards. Glasses of rum sat close to hand, and there were a few coppers on the table. "Good evening, gentlemen," said Bennett. "Or should I say good morning? I must admit I was surprised to see your lights burning this late. Were you waiting up for a delivery perhaps? We're having a little excitement hereabouts tonight, and since you happen to be up late too, I thought I'd make sure you were well. Rather unusual for farmers to be up so late, wouldn't you say? I thought: 'Early to bed, early to rise' would be your routine." He raised his eyebrows and smiled, certain that they were involved and that he'd caught them off guard.

Jed responded casually: "Doc 'udson came to see me 'cause I've 'ad a dose of the screamers for over a week now. Gave me 'is last dose of tonic, so 'e did. Good stuff that. Then we tried to find the vicar in Nextwest, so Doc could get some more. But we didn't find 'im, an' that made it too late for Doc to go back to Ryeport tonight. With all the villains lurkin' about these days, it would be too dangerous." But Bennett wasn't interested in Jed's health. "There was to be a run ashore, just across the road tonight, and one of my men shot one of the smugglers, a black man, on the cliff-top. Did anyone come here for help? We believe he was badly wounded."

"No one came 'ere," Bob responded. "I did see a rocket a little while ago. Was that one of your signals? Then there was a small explosion and a sheet of flame. I imagined that was a warning-off fire. Was I right?"

"Yes, but the smugglers' boats would have been too close inshore to escape our cutter. It shouldn't take long to run them down. I'd really like to find this black man though. There aren't many black men hereabouts, but I do believe there is one in Ryeport, Doctor. What is his name?"

"That'll be Paul Latour," said Doc. "He's a good man though, Sexton at our church. He wouldn't be involved in smuggling. He hasn't been here long enough to know anything about it." Jed laughed, " 'old on a minute," he said. "Not many black men 'ereabouts, you say." He reached inside the chimney breast, and then withdrew his hand, covered with soot. Jed rubbed the soot over his face. "ow about me then? Am I the black man your officer shot? This smuggler's trick of blackin' their faces is well known in these parts. Makes people 'arder to spot on a dark night, but maybe you Customs blokes never 'eard of that. I'll give you another tip: Lots of Dutch smugglers are usin' dark sails now. They don't show up in the moonlight like the white ones. That's already catchin' on east of 'ere, I'm told. Feel free to ask me more questions next time you're at a loss. Obviously, they don't teach you much in Customs school."

Bennett looked at Starr. "Well, Starr. Any chance that the man you shot had blackened his face?"

"I don't think so, Sir, but it was very dark."

The Customs officers searched the farm, including the barns, stable and chicken-coop but found nothing suspicious. Bennett doffed his hat, to the trio playing cards. "Thank you, gentlemen! I apologise for any inconvenience, but we must be diligent in keeping the king's peace." As Jed moved to close the door behind them, he heard Bennett say to Starr: "First, you ran your horse so fast on that rutted road that he came up lame. Then against my instructions, you decide to take on the smugglers by yourself and had to run from them, leaving your horse and pistol behind. Then to top that off, you claim that, before you ran, you fatally wounded one. Yet there was no trace of him when we arrived, only minutes later. Not a good performance, Starr. Captain Whitestone will be furious." He turned to face another rider as he approached the house. "What did you discover at the cliff-top? Any sign of the person that lit the fire?"

"No, Sir, but it could have been the man that Starr fought with. The fire was set below the cliff-top, Sir, on a ledge below the overhang. It's too treacherous to reach in darkness. It was most likely fuse lit. The lifting tackle is set up though. This was a valid tip alright."

"Very well! We ride on to Ryeport. Let's see if we can find this Paul Latour.

Starr, you ride with me."

Back in Ryeport, in order to minimise any noise, Roddy was leading Slondosh past the darkened cottages to Gerry's empty one. He and Pru dragged Latour's lifeless body from the wagon and into the bedroom. "Let's slide him under the bed, Pru. Anyone looking through the window won't see him then."

"Oh, Roddy, that is so heartless!" Pru was very upset; Paul Latour had become a close friend. Roddy hung his head. "I know Pru, but he is dead. I wish that wasn't true, but it is. He won't feel the hard-stone floor. Hurry now. We have to stable Slondosh, and then we've a long walk to the vicarage, and the Revenuers could be right behind us." But Latour was a big man and not in any condition to help. He was difficult to move. Roddy propped Latour against a chest of drawers whilst he laid a blanket on the floor, and then he rolled Latour onto it. "Pru, help me pull the blanket from the other side of the bed with Paul on it." That worked quite well, and they folded the surplus blanket over the body, cleared away any dirt they'd tracked in and walked the wagon to the stable behind the inn. But Ernie was waiting there for them. "Oh, my God! So much for trying to sneak in," whispered Roddy. Ernie was on his feet in an instant. "Father! Where the hell have you been! I've been worried sick about you. Doc Hudson and Latour went looking for you hours ago. Have you seen them?"

"No, Ernie. Our errands took longer than expected, or we would have been home earlier." Roddy noticed that Ernie was studying his clothes. How could he explain why he was not dressed as a vicar? "Father, I've got some news for you. Can I have a private word?"

"Certainly, Ernie, but can we put Slondosh away first? I think there might be some trouble brewing back around Pringle's farm. We saw a rocket fire into the air a short while ago. Then we heard the sound of several horses. I expect the Revenue men might be here shortly. They might misconstrue the fact that I'm not wearing my clerical clothing and that my horse is sweaty."

"Oh, really! Might they?" Ernie's feigned surprise made it clear he wasn't 'buying' the vicar's story. "Let's put the horse away then, or should I take you home first?"

"Well. Yes, that's a better idea. Let's take Prudence home first." They dropped Pru at the vicarage and hurried back to the inn to stable Slondosh. On the way back, Ernie told Roddy about Bridget's letter and their suspicions and how Doc and Latour had gone looking for him. Now Roddy was at a loss for what to say. Should he tell Ernie that Latour was lying dead under Gerry's bed? Or about his trouble on the cliff-top? Or the real reason why he was not dressed as a vicar? Ernie was a good friend but strictly opposed to any involvement with smuggling. Was it fair to burden him with information that Whitestone's incisive questioning might draw from him? That knowledge might serve to convict him, despite his lack of involvement.

"Ernie, I haven't seen Doc. Sometimes Prudence and I like to go out incognito. We just like to be two ordinary people, out for a quiet evening meal. We just wanted some time to ourselves without being recognised. When we do that, I shed my clerical clothes and wear ordinary clothes. Mind you, I'm sure the Customs people would try to attribute different reasons to that. Remember their last visit?"

"Yes, I do remember. I also remember that their suspicions were right on the mark that time. Let's put Slondosh away. Then you get home and into bed before the Revenuers arrive with their terrible suspicious minds. I've got the feeling that they'll be here sooner rather than later. You hurry home now. I'll rub the horse down." He gave Roddy an accusing look. "Just in case they try and attribute some improper reason for Slondosh being so sweaty."

Roddy was still getting undressed when Lieutenants Bennett and Starr came knocking at his door. He quickly changed into his nightshirt and rubbed his eyes, to make them look bleary, before answering the door. "What's this all about, Officer?" Roddy stifled a manufactured yawn as he let the two men in. "Sorry to disturb you, Father," said Bennett. "We are looking for a black man. I believe his name is Latour. We don't know where he lives in the village."

"Oh! Paul lives in the church. He looks after The Guiding Light, you know. Very good at it too; he's a good man."

"Well, one of my officers shot a black man tonight, Father, during a smugglers' run. Not too many black men in these parts so when he escaped, we thought we'd check up on the ones we knew of first."

"Oh, that wouldn't be Paul. He's almost certainly asleep. He'd arranged for Higgins to tend the light for him tonight. Tomorrow too, I believe."

"Well Sir, please, take us to him right now."

"Let me get dressed first, Officer. You surely don't expect me to go traipsing all over the cliffs in my nightshirt." Needless to say, Latour wasn't in his 'digs'. His neatly made bed hadn't been slept in, and Higgins had no idea where he was. Questions about a possible lady friend drew a blank. "He's our man right enough," said Bennett. "Maybe he crawled away and died somewhere. Or maybe his friends carried him off. What is it, Father?" Bennett thought the vicar's puzzled expression meant he might be concealing something.

"Well, it's only a thought, Lieutenant. Do you know how Latour came to our village?" Bennett confessed that he didn't. So Roddy told him of the wreck of The Seahorse and how Latour had lost his daughter the night before the wreck. "And so, Officer, I've noticed that periodically he gets extremely depressed. On such occasions, he's taken a bottle of rum and disappeared for a few hours. I believe he may have found a place, somewhere close by, where he can drown his sorrows in private. Paul is a very good man, and though he's new here, he's become a popular and valued member of our village. I can't imagine him doing anything unlawful."

"Well, if we find him – alive, that is – he may be glad of you as a character reference, Father. Incidentally: There seem to be very few fishing boats at the landing. Why would that be, Father? Do those good fishermen think they might catch more fish by sneaking up on them in the dark? Perhaps whilst the fish are asleep?" Starr smiled at Bennett's sarcasm.

"Actually, Lieutenant, some of the fishermen earn a little extra money selling smoked and dried fish, pickled herring and so on, in coastal towns east of Ryeport. Once they have accumulated sufficient stock to make the trip worthwhile, they sail east, and depending on how quickly they sell out, they could be gone for two or three days. If time and conditions permit, they fish on their way home. I understand they left on such a trip today. But surely you knew that was a long-standing practice here." Bennett looked a little downcast. "Good night to you, Father. We have seized a considerable amount of tackle tonight and apparently killed one smuggler. However, someone did manage to light a warning-off fire. We shall be back tomorrow to check on your enterprising fishermen. The smugglers can't hide forever." In fact, Bennett left Starr and some men to watch the overnight comings and goings in the village.

CHAPTER 7

Hide the body

Knowing that Whitestone and his men would be in Ryeport early the Pringle's had roused the doctor at first light. Jed stuffed a sandwich in his hand as he climbed aboard the buggy. They knew he needed to bring Ernie up to date before the Customs officers arrived. Lieutenant Starr had drawn the luckless job of keeping surveillance on the village during the night and recorded Doc Hudson's arrival, as Queenie trotted Gerry Mason's buggy to the inn.

Doc found Ernie outside the inn waiting for him, just as he had for the vicar. "Where the hell have you been?" said Ernie. Tom put Queenie away, while a very worried innkeeper took Doc aside and questioned him about Latour. Doc was worried too. "Ernie, I think he's dead," he said. "The Lieutenant said his officer had shot a black man on the cliff-top last night. He claimed it was a full shot to the chest, at close range. We had sent Latour there to see if there were any Revenuers waiting to ambush the smugglers. If Latour saw anyone, he was to go back to the farm and tell Bob Pringle. But no one has seen him since. So, Latour would have been in the right place, and at the right time, to be the man the officer shot."

Ernie looked crestfallen. He asked: "Where were you all night? I was worried sick that Lieutenant Bennett didn't mention you." So, Doc told his friend all that had transpired since he left yesterday. "So, she did send the letter." Ernie was furious. "That's what we get for helping to support that useless bitch and teaching her to read and write."

"Yes. But Ernie, we mustn't say anything about that letter to anybody." Doc put his finger to his lips. "Bannerman would likely kill her on the spot, should he find out. Quite apart from the fact that we can't condone murder, there would be more intense investigations. We don't need that right now."

"But what if she's questioned by the Revenuers?"

"I'll take care of Bridget," said the doctor. "For now, no one knows anything about the letter but us. Best leave it that way. What they don't know, they can't reveal. I'm sure Whitestone will be here shortly. He left men here overnight, you know. I spotted the officer who supposedly shot Latour as I came into the village. They'll want to search the boats and the village again. They told us they were coming here last night to look for Latour. Did they search?"

"Well, yes. I spoke to the vicar this morning. He took them to the church and some cottages, but they didn't find Latour. They said that proved they were looking for the right man. But Whitestone wasn't here. It'll be more thorough today. No one knows where Latour is. It looks bad." Just then, they heard the sound of approaching horses. "Quick. Into the kitchen. Doc grab some breakfast. I've got a feeling this is going to be a very long day."

Whitestone strutted into the inn, impatiently slapping his riding crop against his high leather boot. He was furious. He had given Bennett a tongue lashing as soon as he heard of the affair of the night before. As far as he was concerned, they should have been combing the area all night, not merely hiding and watching. That could have given the villagers time to coordinate their stories and hide any contraband. He sorted his men into teams. Bennett was to supervise a search of the village. Two men would search the buildings along the harbour front whilst a second pair searched the backyards and outbuildings. They would start at the west end of the village and move east. "We have to find the black man. Be sure to investigate every possible hiding spot, woodpile, haystack or pile of junk. Look in the attics, under boats and beds, any space at all!" Bennett shouted. "That doesn't mean that you can ignore any kegs of rum you fall over or any freshly disturbed earth. Be sharp. Tell me if you see anything even remotely suspicious – anything at all. I've left some men at both ends of the village. You start in the west. That way we'll nab anyone who tries to run ahead of you."

The vicar could feel his panic level rising. They were bound to find Latour. They had only to look under Gerry Mason's bed. Whitestone and two officers were at the landing. Those fishing boats not involved in selling dried or smoked fish along the coast had left at first light, unaware of the drama of the night before. They were gone long before Whitestone got there. He gritted his teeth. His officers hadn't even made a list of the boats that hadn't returned last night. They had merely accepted the story that they were selling smoked fish in the eastern coastal towns. That was very sloppy investigating. This valid tip had come in on the very day that Whitestone had followed another false lead west of the town. He couldn't believe his bad luck. The tackle and warning-off fire proved that this tip was sound. When Bennett had tried to find a cutter in Nextwest Harbour yesterday, he discovered that they were all operating westward, in support of Whitestone's false tip. His remarks at Pringle's farm had been made to scare people he believed were involved into a slip of the tongue or some ill-considered remark. So, now the only evidence that they had to work with was the tackle on the cliff-top and Starr's claim that he had shot a black man. However, a black man, Latour, was missing from this village. That seemed like solid evidence of the villager's involvement.

The officers assigned to search the houses had reached the inn, and Tom had stayed with the officers searching the inn itself whilst Ernie followed the 'backyard team' into the stable. Whilst they were prodding hay and checking the loft, Ernie noticed a glint of silver from the pocket in the dashboard apron of Gerry's buggy. Gerry usually put his pocket flask there when he was driving. That could be a tempting trinket for a light-fingered soldier, so he removed it, waving it at the suspicious soldiers as he did so. "Mr. Mason's flask," he said. "I'll keep it safe for him. If a thief happened by, he might walk off with it."

He left the stable, walking along the path behind the cottages, intending to return the flask to Gerry's liquor cabinet. As he entered the back door of Mason's cottage, Moggy rushed between his legs. Ernie had to clutch the door jamb to save himself from falling. Moggy hadn't yet accepted the fact that he'd moved to another home and would frequently pester Gerry for food and a fuss. So, Moggy now enjoyed two homes. "I'll kill that bloody cat," fumed Ernie. "I can't leave him locked up in here. If he gets shut in, the place will stink by the time Gerry gets back." He put the flask in Gerry's cabinet and went looking for the cat. Obviously, Moggy didn't want to be found. But Ernie spotted an inch or so of a black tail poking out from under the bed. He was on his knees, trying to grab the cat when he found Latour. The shock caused him to jerk his head up, striking it on the bed frame. "Oh, my God!" His head hurt, but his heart was racing as he rolled back the blanket for a closer look. The bloodied shirt certainly verified the Customs officer's claim. Starr had indeed shot a black man, full in the chest. Ernie jumped up, his mind in a whirl. "The vicar must have put Latour here. Why the hell didn't he tell me? The soldiers are almost here. Only one more house to go." He peeked through the back window. The team searching the backyards was well ahead of those checking the cottages. They had just finished poking around the woodpile and were now checking the privy. He could hear the vicar talking to the soldiers searching the cottage only two doors away. They would soon be here. The backyard team had already moved east and were now in the old churchyard cemetery next door.

"No time to waste," he muttered as he dropped to his knees and pulled on the blanket that Roddy had used to slide Latour under the bed. It moved fairly easily. Ernie quickly dragged Latour, on the blanket, to the back door. A hurried look outside verified there was no one watching. He propped Latour against the door post, dropped down on one knee, pulled Latour's right arm over his shoulder, put his right arm between the dead man's legs, grabbed Latour's right wrist and struggled to stand up. "By God; you're a heavy bugger, Latour," he gasped. Finally, he was upright, with Latour across his shoulders. He struggled through the door to the privy. Fortunately, the soldiers hadn't bothered to latch the door. He dumped Latour unceremoniously onto the seat and latched the door. No one had seen him. But he had no time to catch his breath. He still had to hide the blanket, catch the cat and close the door to the cottage. He was dragging the blanket out the back door when the latch clicked on the front door. He could hear the vicar trying to persuade the soldiers that, since Gerry was in London, and no one had used the cottage whilst he was away, it would be pointless to look in there. They just ignored him. Whitestone had made it very clear to his men that they would pay dearly if they missed anything. "Sod the cat," muttered Ernie and snatched the blanket through the door, softly closing it behind him. He leaned against the wall and tried to catch his breath.

The vicar followed the soldiers into the cottage. Ernie, peeking through the rear window, could see the anxiety on his face. One soldier stood on a chair, raised the trap door into the attic whilst the other checked the rooms. After a quick look around, the two men were about to leave the cottage when the last man at the door hesitated. 'ang on a bit, Fred." He went back into the bedroom and looked under the bed. Ernie watched the vicar's shoulders slump. He looked guilty and exhausted. Then the soldier got off his knees and returned to the front door. "It was just a bloody cat," he said. "I knew I 'eard somethin.'" They left, closing the door behind them.

Ernie nearly collapsed with relief. "I could sure use a drink," he said. Then he realised that, with the soldiers being here all day, they would be more likely to revisit the privy than the cottage. "Got to put 'im back," he groaned. And, after another cautious look around, he spread the blanket on the floor beside Mason's bed, retrieved Latour and pulled him back under the bed. Then he caught Moggy and threw him out the back door before returning to the inn. Going behind the bar, he poured himself half a tumbler of brandy. He was enjoying that when the very puzzled looking vicar entered the inn. Ernie was angry at having been 'kept in the dark', but his dominating feeling was one of relief. Having survived his recent dance with a cat, a corpse and the soldiers, he thought he would tease the vicar a little just to see how forthcoming he might be. "What's up, Father? You look even more frazzled and haggard than you usually do."

"Oh, it's nothing, Ernie. I could use a drink though. All this bother with the soldiers. They just searched Gerry's place and the old church. Whitestone came back and asked me a lot of questions that I couldn't answer, mostly about the fishermen. Looks like the soldiers will be here all day. I understand he has sent two cutters out to meet the boats and escort them back in. This promises to be a very trying day."

Ernie gave a little smile and tried to look casual. "Did they find Latour?" The vicar, still looking puzzled, took the half tumbler of brandy from the innkeeper. "No. Not yet anyway."

"Any idea where he might be?"

"No."

"Elusive bloke, ain't 'e?" That was when Doc Hudson entered the bar. "By God, I really need a drink, Ernie." The innkeeper obliged with another half tumbler of brandy. Doc gave Roddy a thorough scrutiny. "Well, Father… What do you think of all this commotion and excitement? I imagine that life down here in the country is rather dull compared to what you were used to in the big city." Roddy really didn't know what to say. His full attention wasn't even available to his companions. He was still wondering where Latour's body had gone and how his cat had got into Gerry's cottage. Moggy had been curled up on the mat in front of the fire at the vicarage when he had left that morning, so he knew they hadn't locked him in there last night. The doctor was still studying his face as he waited for an answer. "Oh! No, doctor. Sorry, my mind was elsewhere. This is far too exciting for me." Ernie leaned towards him. "Don't worry, Father. Everything is just as you left it, and Whitestone is still stumped – for now, at least. And all thanks to your bloody cat." Roddy frowned, as he looked at the innkeeper, wondering how many drinks he'd already had. Ernie turned to the doctor. "Doc, what's the news about Bridget?"

"Oh, I've been to see her, Ernie. Of course, she knew that the run had been warned-off. That's common knowledge in the village now. I took her aside and told her that one of the officers had shown me the letter and asked her if she knew anyone who could have written it. I said: "They don't know yet who wrote the letter. But I know Bridget, and I showed her my copy of her letter. I told her: Our village has been good to you, Bridget, but you choose to reward that friendship by causing trouble for the village. I warn you, if you ever try to claim any reward or say that you wrote the letter or claim knowledge of any 'run' ever again, I shall pass this letter around the inn. That way, you can be sure that any smugglers in the village will know who set the Customs men on them.""

Doc's companions were hanging on his every word. "What did she say to that?" asked Ernie.

"She grabbed her throat and started crying! Then I told her, 'Provided you keep your mouth shut, no one will know it was you, Bridget. Unless the Revenue people are successful of course. In that case, I will pass this letter around the inn, I promise you.' She fell on her knees blubbering and asked me to protect her. I said I would, provided that she pleaded ignorance of this business. I think she will keep her mouth shut. She's convinced Bannerman will cut her throat if this ever leaks out.

"You know, I've delivered most of our villagers, less than 40 years of age that is, including Bridget. I wouldn't want anything bad to happen to any of them, but she is certainly numbered amongst those that sorely try my patience. Incidentally, Father," he said as he turned to Roddy, "she was in the hayloft at Archer's stable when you and Bannerman were discussing the run. That's where her information came from." The vicar stepped back in shock. Then he hung his head, and his shoulders slumped. "So now the whole village knows I'm involved in the smuggling?"

"No! Just us three – and Bridget, of course."

"Well, there is Latour, of course, but he won't say anything," said Ernie, dryly. "Is there anything you want to tell us, Father? Roddy looked sheepishly at the two older men. "It seems there's not much you don't already know."

"Come now, Father. We've been protecting your sorry arse for a couple of days now. We took you on trust. Surely, you can do the same for us." Ernie was looking definitely hostile.

"Well, alright. I honestly didn't want you chaps to have to lie or cover for me. I thought that if you knew nothing, Whitestone couldn't incriminate you. I thought you would never need to know." He pushed his glass across the bar. "Another please, Ernie."

"Me too," said the doctor.

"Well, I'm not going to be the odd man out," responded the innkeeper and dutifully refilled all three glasses. Then he took a disappointed look at the severely depleted bottle that he'd opened for his first drink, as Roddy explained his recruitment into the new smuggling ring. They also learned that their vicar had retrieved Latour's body after he had jumped in front of a pistol aimed at Roddy and how he and Prudence had concealed their friend's body under Gerry's bed. Ernie laughed when Roddy said he was amazed that the soldiers hadn't seen the body when they looked under the bed. "You may laugh, Ernie, said the disgruntled vicar. "But believe me, you wouldn't have found it so amusing had you been there." The brandy was relaxing Ernie, and he managed a grim little smile.

"Believe me, Father! I know it wasn't funny because I was there. Latour was a heavy bugger to handle on my own. I barely had time to carry him out to your privy, right after the soldiers had inspected it, and then I carried him back again after you and the soldiers left the cottage. Then I caught your bloody cat and tossed him out the back door. To be honest, though, I would never have known Latour was there, but for the cat. By the way, in view of mine and Doc's efforts on your behalf, I think you should be paying for these drinks, not me." He passed the sadly depleted bottle across the counter. Roddy stood there in shocked disbelief. "You did all that? You moved the body? On your own?"

"I did. Not once but twice. Into the privy and then back out again." Then the innkeeper explained, in detail, his activities concerning Gerry's cottage. "What do we do with the body now?" Ernie said. "I think we should bury him at sea."

"I think that would be the safest thing," said Doc. "Not for two more days," stated Roddy, emphatically. "I promised Paul." Doc frowned. "Why?" he asked. Roddy shrugged. "Paul asked me to hide him for three days. He didn't say why, and he died before he could explain." All three men were showing some effect of the quickly downed drinks at this point, and Ernie commented: "You two had better have something to eat. You've knocked those drinks back too fast. I can tell 'cause you're both gettin' blurry 'round the edges."

Back at the vicarage, Whitestone was quizzing Prudence; he wanted to know if she had any idea who wrote the letter. "Frankly, my dear," he was saying, "you are a major disappointment to me. This one letter, signed with a fish, is worth months of any effort on your part. And it was written by an illiterate at that."

"Well, I've told you everything I've heard," said Prudence. "Goodman was my main source of information, and he's dead. If you aren't satisfied, I'd be quite happy to be off your 'informer's list.'" There was a knock at the door. "A soldier saluted as he presented himself. "Captain Whitestone, Sir; a cutter has been seen in the channel; it's escorting two fishing boats."

"Thank you, Sergeant." Turning to Prudence Whitestone said: "We will continue this later, Madam. Excuse me."

• • •

It was almost noon when the sound of the posthorn announced the arrival of the coach. The three drinkers at the bar walked to the door to meet the coach. Hawksworth wasn't here, and he'd already received one mail delivery this week. Two deliveries in one week were not unknown but unusual. To their surprise, Gerry alighted from the coach, a day ahead of his scheduled return. The three conspirators exchanged anxious glances. "We'll keep Latour's present location strictly between us, right?" The vicar was relieved when both his companions nodded their agreement. Gerry was puzzled by all the activity and the soldiers. "What in heaven's name is going on here?" he asked. They took him into the inn, poured him half a tumbler of brandy and explained everything. Everything, that is, except for the fact that a very dead Latour was lying under his bed and the vicar's involvement in smuggling. The coachmen took a quick jug of ale and excused themselves. Obviously, the villagers needed no entertaining today. Besides, they didn't want the Revenuers thinking they might be too friendly with possible smugglers. After a second drink, Gerry picked up his bag. "I could use a nap," he said. "That journey always wears me out. I'll see you lads in a couple of hours." No matter how they tried to detain, distract or tempt him with brandy, he insisted on his nap. Ten minutes later, he was asleep on his bed. The cat had curled up behind his knees. Neither one of them disturbed Latour.

Whitestone met the boats at the landing. The captain of the cutter, an assertive, fresh-faced young man, was giving orders to the fishermen as though they were his own crew. That did not sit very well with Joshua Cobbe who, at the time of their arrest, had been busy hauling in full nets hand over hand. The other fishing boat was John Morris, who had been fishing just a few boat lengths away and having an equally good day. Joshua Cobbe leapt out of his boat and went storming up to Whitestone, demanding an explanation, an apology and compensation. He was quickly joined by Morris and his crew, but they didn't ruffle Whitestone's composure in the slightest. He had sufficient men to handle a few unarmed fishermen if needed. "Sergeant! Oversee the unloading of these boats. I want to know if you discover any smuggling implements: Creepers, weighting stones, anything suspicious." Turning back to the fishermen and addressing Cobbe, he said: "As for you, Sir, I shall apologise if I find nothing suspicious, not before. There are smugglers operating out of this village. If you want to stop these inconvenient searches, I suggest you help us find the culprits. They are the cause of your problems, not I." He turned to the captain of the Cutter. "Well! What are you waiting for? There are other boats out there. Go and bring them in. I particularly want to see Bannerman's boat. I suspect that he and the Sullivans are partners in more than fishing."

Whitestone had sent Starr back to the cliff-top where Latour had been shot. He was to supervise the men stripping the lifting tackle from the area and loading it on to a wagon. After that, they were to comb the area for further clues. Whitestone had instructed Starr in front of his men: "You have this assignment, Starr, because you know the area better than any other officer here. Remember? That is the place where you left your pistol and your horse. All in your hurry to tell us that you had certainly killed a black smuggler, who after his death apparently lit the warning-off fire and promptly escaped."

Starr, who'd had very little sleep last night, was now trying to redeem himself by being extra thorough in his search for clues. Looking behind the big oak, he found cart tracks. "From a light wagon by the look of it," he said. A little farther on there was a spillage of chaff and oats. "From a nosebag, to keep the horse quiet," he muttered. He followed the tracks back to the road, where they disappeared amongst dozens of others. Going back into the field, he found a stain that he took to be dried blood. Then some parallel drag marks, leading from the stain to the cart tracks. "Could be heel marks from a dragged body," he said. But that was the extent of all the clues he could muster.

In Ryeport, the second cutter had escorted three more boats of irate fishermen into the harbour; Bannerman's was the first to tie up. He and the Sullivans had been dragging in a good catch when they were ordered back to Ryeport. Carter and Benjamin Cobbe, Joshua's brother, skippered the other two boats. "Good to see you again, Bannerman." Whitestone feigned goodwill as he approached the boat. "I understand you have been selling smoked fish along the coast. I hope you are well, although you look as though you've had no sleep for a month. You really should take better care of your health. It can't be very restful: catching a few 'winks' in an open boat. That will hardly refresh a weary body." He waved his sergeant to the boats. "Same instructions as before, Sergeant." But Sullivan's boat had as much fish as Joshua Cobbe's. Carter's too was well loaded. Standing on the dockside, Ernie, Roddy and Doc wondered how that could be. If they'd had to unload and conceal contraband carefully enough to ensure recovery, that would have taken time. They would have also been closer to the coast than the richer fishing areas that Cobbe had been working.

There was nothing suspicious in any of the boats. Unless Bannerman's and Carter's large catches could be considered suspicious, but that only served to alibi those boats. Whitestone was plainly frustrated. He particularly hated listening to the griping of the angry fishermen, who persistently reminded him that this was not the first time he'd been proven wrong when he had harassed them. Now they were demanding compensation – not that they'd get any. Eventually, Whitestone instructed Bennett to remain at the landing with a party of four men, to check the remaining boats as they came in. Then he had two men accompany him into the village. He carried a slate and some chalk, and, knocking on every door, he asked the tenants to write the words Customs officer. Many couldn't write at all but those that could all spelled the words correctly. Bridget claimed she could only write her name. Doc ensured that he remained very visible to her as he accompanied

Whitestone on his rounds. As dusk fell, the frustrated Customs officer mounted up and, leaving Bennett in charge, rode back to Nextwest. Gerry Mason, having been roused for Whitestone's test, returned to the inn, seeking the reason for the Customs officer's search. Eventually, he declared that he was famished and ready for a good supper.

Ernie, thinking ahead as usual, had Tom help him take a kettle of hot stew and dumplings to Bennett and his soldiers at the landing. He had included a gallon of ale with the much-appreciated meal. "We've got no quarrel with you lads," he said. "We know you have to follow orders." He returned to the inn and, after ensuring that Gerry and Doc were well looked after, he excused himself, quietly slipped out the back door and headed for Gerry's cottage and the waiting vicar. "Are you sure you're alright with this, Ernie?" asked the vicar.

"Aye, I'm ready," responded the innkeeper. The vicar who had improvised a stretcher from poles and fishing nets said: "Prudence is going to walk a few paces ahead of us. It's dark enough that we should go unnoticed. But she'll warn us if anyone approaches. But it's a long walk to the vicarage, on an uphill grade at that. I'm not looking forward to it."

"Best get on with it then," responded the innkeeper. The two men rolled Latour onto the stretcher whilst Prudence checked around the outside of the cottage. "All clear," she called softly and led the way behind the old church, through the cemetery and on towards the most open and danger-ous part of their route, the landing. The burly innkeeper was at the front of the stretcher, and the much smaller vicar was at the rear. The ground was rough and uneven, and just as they were about to step out from cover, Roddy twisted his ankle in a pothole. "Sorry," he groaned as he dropped his stretcher handles. "Don't worry," responded the innkeeper. "Latour didn't notice." "Shhh!" Prudence hurried back to halt them. "Quiet! There is a soldier just ahead," she whispered, and they all hunkered down behind some scrub. The man chose a nearby bush just yards away, grunted and began to relieve himself. "That was good ale," grumbled Ernie in a hushed voice. "You'd think he'd hang onto it a bit longer than that." The soldier soon headed back towards his camp, allowing the stretcher-bearers to resume their stealthy journey to the vicarage. They arrived without further incident, struggled up the stairs and laid Latour on the bed in the spare room. "Let's clean him up and change his shirt," said Ernie. "He tried to help us and paid for that with his life. The least we can do for him now is clean him up. Tomorrow night, we'll get Bannerman to bury him at sea. Let's wash the blood and dirt off his chest. Did you notice, Father? He's not stiffening up at all." Ernie was frowning. "You'd think he'd only just kicked off." Roddy got a bowl of water and started cleaning the area of the wound, removing the dried blood and the grime it had attracted. "You're right," he said. "He hasn't stiffened at all yet." Then Roddy took a shocked step back. "Look at the wound, Ernie. It's almost filled in, just a sort of hollow. Not very deep either." His voice was hushed and awestruck. "It seems that he's healing! They rolled Latour on his side. The ball went right through," said Ernie. "But even the wound in his back is closing." He examined the wound more closely. "Never seen anything like it," he said. "Doesn't look like a gunshot wound anymore. It was a lot worse than this earlier." He turned his worried face to the vicar: "You don't think he's coming back to life again, do you? It wouldn't be the first time."

"Now, Ernie… You don't really believe that," answered the vicar. But his words lacked conviction, and he sounded nervous. Prudence came into the bedroom. "It's all clear outside," she announced. "I believe the soldiers are still busy with Ernie's ale. That really was a good idea, Ernie. You kept their attention focused on their bellies instead of their duties. There's a sail in the channel. The last of our boats I imagine."

"Pru, take a look at this." Roddy moved the candle so that she could get a better look at Latour's wound. Some hot wax dripped onto Latour's chest; he flinched, and they all jumped back nervously. After a long pause and many anxious glances, they plucked up enough courage to touch Latour again. "No pulse," said Ernie. Prudence held a small mirror to his mouth and nostrils. "No breath," she said. Ernie rolled back Latour's eyelid. "He's dead!" he said in a confident, dismissive voice. "That must have been a reflex or something. Let's get a shirt on him. I want my supper! And then… I think I'll get drunk. I deserve it after a day like this."

Roddy had no shirt large enough for Latour but said he would fetch one from Latour's 'digs'. Then he and Pru would change their friend's shirt. So, Ernie bade them good night, leaving them alone with Latour. Roddy turned to his wife. "Pru, will you be alright if I go to Paul's 'digs' now and get him a shirt? I also need to look in on Higgins. Just to be sure everything is alright. I'll not be long. Then we can have something to eat and a glass of wine." She nodded. "I'll be fine, Roddy, but hurry back; I'm getting hungry." As Roddy left, Prudence threw the dirty water out the window and started to clean up.

She was replacing the bowl on the washstand, with her back to the bed, when a frighteningly deep chill permeated her whole body. The cold felt animated, as though thousands of icy insects were crawling all over her, invading every pore, and sucking every last scrap of body heat from her. She was frightened to turn around yet terrified to remain blind to whatever it was behind her. She screamed – a panic-stricken cry that she didn't recognise as her own.

At that moment, Roddy was entering the lamp-house to find Higgins singing happily as he polished a cupboard that he'd made. It was a well-crafted piece, and he was rubbing the wax into the wood with almost loving care. He was so intent on his task that he didn't hear the vicar enter. "Good evening, Higgins. You're in fine voice tonight. You must be enjoying yourself." Higgins was startled. "Oh! Oh, yes, Father. Sorry! Didn't 'ear you come in. 'ope you don't mind me doing this in 'ere, Father. It gets borin' just 'tendin' the light. Everything's workin' real good, by the way. I do keep my eye on things while I'm polishin'."

"That's fine, Higgins. You're doing a good job. I just wondered what it was that was putting you in such a good mood. Nice cabinet, by the way."

"Thank you, Father. I really enjoy workin' with wood. This is made from off-cuts from the broken bits of mahogany from The Sea'orse. That wreck improved a lot of things 'round 'ere. Even gave me the tools to do this work." The vicar pulled a wry face. "Well, that may be true, Higgins, and I'm happy for the good that has come from the wreck. But we must remember that it also cost a lot of lives. A pretty steep price to pay for the benefits it bestowed, I'm thinking." Higgins looked a little shamefaced. "Yes, Father. Sorry! Didn't mean to sound 'eartless. Of course, we're all very sorry about Meg's loss too, Father."

"That's alright, Higgins. I understand. Life goes on after all. Well, good night, Higgins. I'll see you tomorrow."

"Yes, Father. Good night to you too. Oh, Father, any news of Latour?"

"I'm afraid not, Higgins. Let's see what tomorrow brings. He was another casualty of that ship, remember? His daughter drowned the night before the wreck. I'm sure he gets very depressed at times."

"Of course, Father. Must be 'ard, 'specially with no other fam'ly 'ereabouts."

"Well, good night again, Higgins. Keep up the good work. I'm just going up to Latour's 'digs' to see if I might have missed some clue as to where he may have gone."

• • •

There was a sense of awareness building. At first, it was merely a vague, disembodied sensation of existence, like a drifting receptor lacking purpose or intelligence – formless and devoid of stimulation. Then gradually the sensations came. First a small, localised sense of intense cold, soon repeated from different parts, until they eventually became a defined area. It was when the shaking began that he remembered. This had happened before. It was familiar. He was desperately cold but sensed an area of warmth across the room. Then he became aware of something far more frightening than the unbelievable cold that had alarmed him so. There was something beside him – another intense, pulsating, cold body. Fearfully, he opened his eyes to find the demon, 'Nick', staring down at him. That same frightening being that had so terrified him at the Coaching Inn in London. The full realisation of what was happening flooded his mind. He remembered the cliff-top, the bang of the pistol, the crushing pain in his chest and asking Roddy to hide him. Obviously, he'd kept that promise.

Nick's quiet but menacing voice was penetrating his consciousness. "I'm disappointed in you, Latour; fancy putting yourself at risk for that half-baked user of a priest. This is the second time in a few months that you have publicly recovered from a fatal wound." Nick was so focused on Latour that he'd ignored Prudence, but when she screamed, he had turned angrily towards her and flicked the back of his hand in her direction. She flew through the doorway and onto the landing at the top of the stairs. Immediately, he returned his attention to Latour. "You had better realise that the villagers will start to regard you as an evil threat, Latour – an immortal. They will fear your ability for self-healing, and when that happens, they will turn on you. All sorts of religious freaks will be invited here, each one claiming that they alone can permanently destroy you – the evil one – in various unpleasant ways. They will want you to remain dead. Pieces of you may end up in different parts of the country. It's happened before – entertainment for an otherwise boring afternoon. Your destruction will become an amusing distraction from the villager's petty, humdrum lives. So! I'm here to caution you against enlightening these fools with details of our contract. That would really seal your fate. And – more importantly – could delay the completion of our business."

"Since you have chosen to compound our problems by aligning yourself with the vicar and his woman, the innkeeper, the doctor and who knows who else, you will need a plausible story for your recovery. This excuse of yours that your people are quick healers is too ridiculous. Better to confess that you don't understand this gift yourself. Tell them you suspect that the lightning that brought down the ship's mast must have changed you somehow and given you the gift of speedy recovery. They may not believe you, but they won't be able to disprove it either. Who amongst them would know what effect the absorption of a diffused lightning strike might have on a human body?" Nick lifted his head. "Aha! The vicar has arrived. He'll be up here at any moment. You should pretend to be asleep. Wake slowly. Let them revive you and become a part of your recovery. When they question you, remember the lightning. If you don't – I may be obliged to send more of it. It could make your new friends… 'crispy'. Remember, if you need me, I'm as close as that pouch." He snapped his fingers and was gone.

  Roddy was re-entering the vicarage, with Latour's clean shirt, when Prudence screamed for the second time.

Latour heard hurried footsteps on the stairs. He closed his eyes, realising that Nick had speeded up their time again. Just for the period of their conversation. He wondered why Prudence had screamed and what she might have seen.

• • •

Lieutenant Bennett and his officers had completed their search of the returning boats with the same disappointing results they'd experienced with the earlier ones. The fishermen had unloaded their catch and headed for the inn. Bennett could hear them cursing and complaining on the way. That innkeeper was smart, he thought. That heavy meal and the ale he had given his men ensured that they would make no attempt to go to the inn. Otherwise, there might have been a confrontation, possibly a brawl, especially with alcohol involved. Bennett took his men to the church for one last search of the building. His main focus was Latour's 'digs' and the lamp-house. Higgins was very co-operative, but they found nothing suspicious or useful and wearily retired to their tents.

At the vicarage, Roddy was bounding up the stairs, two at a time, in his haste to help Prudence. He found her crouched and sobbing on the landing outside the spare bedroom. He was soon on his knees beside her, one arm around her shoulders. "Pru'! Pru'! What's wrong? Are you hurt?" She clung to him. "Oh, Roddy, I'm sure there was someone in there beside Paul. First, though, I sensed hundreds of tiny, ice cold fingers, crawling all over me, sucking all the warmth from my body. I couldn't do anything about it. Then there was this awful smell. A foul stench, like something dead and rotted putrid. It was suffocating me. When I turned around, I swear I saw a horrid little man beside Paul. It was just for a moment. He seemed unaware of me until I screamed. Then he turned and waved me away with the back of his hand. The next thing I knew, I was out here. It lasted only seconds, but it was the most terrifying experience of my life. Roddy, I'm too frightened to go back in there. It was awful; it seemed absolutely evil." Roddy waited patiently for his wife to calm down. After a few minutes, the tears stopped. Just the fact of his being there seemed to reassure her. He stroked her hair, hugged her tight and whispered his words of comfort. Several minutes passed before she recovered her composure well enough to let him check on his dead friend.

Latour was lying just as they had left him, still and undisturbed. There was no sign that anyone else had been in the room. Certainly, he smelled no foul odour or found it excessively cold. He decided that the strain of the past days had caused Pru's mind to magnify the sensations and fears of attending to Latour's dead body. He called her in. "Pru, come on in. It's alright. There's nothing unnatural here. It's safe for you to come in." Hesitatingly, she entered the room, pausing at the threshold to fearfully survey the room. Roddy motioned her closer. When they were both standing at Latour's bedside, Roddy pulled the blanket aside. There was no wound. In its place, there was a shallow depression. The flesh was lighter there, but even that seemed to be gradually darkening as they watched.

Prudence moved behind Roddy, one hand covering her mouth. "He's healed!" she gasped. Roddy nodded as he touched his friend's chest. "He's very cold," he said. "But you're right. The wound has healed." The disbelief and awe in his voice revealed the fear that he was feeling. He placed his fingers on his friend's neck, feeling for a pulse. "I think there is a faint but steady throb," he said. "Where is that mirror, Pru? Quick!" He took the mirror and held it to Latour's nostrils. Small traces of vapour condensed on the cold mirror. "He's alive!" exclaimed the bewildered vicar and took a guarded step backward. Prudence retreated towards the door, one hand over her heart. Roddy got another blanket and laid it over Latour, tucking the edges under him to improve the entrapment of what little warmth there was in that cold body. He began rubbing the outside of the blanket to create some frictional warmth. The body moved slightly. Again, Roddy jumped back. Latour gave a low moan. Then he whispered: "Cold! So cold!" Roddy rubbed the outside of the blanket even harder, creating more heat. "Quick, Pru, see if you can light the fire." She complied, pleased to be away from the bedside. About five minutes later, with the fire starting to blaze, Prudence returned to Latour's bedside. "The wound?" she queried. Roddy cautiously peeled back the layers of coverings to expose Latour's chest. The yellow appearance had all but disappeared, and the flesh appeared whole again. Prudence bent closer for a better look. Latour began to shake. Then he let out a great gasp. Startled, her head jerked back in shock, and she found herself staring straight into the eyes of this man who, only minutes ago, had been very dead. She screamed. Latour screamed, and so did Roddy. They jumped away from the bed. All three of them froze, remaining stock-still and staring at each other for what seemed an eternity. Prudence edged her way around the bed to stand slightly behind Roddy again and grabbed his hand.

Latour was gradually recovering his breathing. It progressed from erratic shallow breaths to a deeper, more regular rhythm. His eyes though were wide open and scared. Roddy went closer. "Paul, are you alright?" He reached out and touched the man's hand. It was warmer now, almost as warm as his own. Latour's eyes focused as he looked from Prudence to Roddy and back again. "I'm so sorry…I…I was in a really deep sleep. You startled me." He took some deeper breaths. Roddy said, "Paul. You were more than sleeping. We… We thought you were dead."

"Was it like before?"

"What before? I mean before what?" said Roddy.

"Like when I woke up in the old church. When Gerry came and got me?"

"I don't know, Paul. I wasn't there."

"I was dreaming," said Latour. "I was back on the ship. The lightning seemed to surround me. I felt a tingling run all through my body. Then the captain drove his sword into me when I tried to open the fo'c'sle door. It felt really bad. I was sure I would die. Then the tingling got stronger. The tingling seemed much stronger around the wound. Was it like that?"

"Paul, I don't know. There was no lightning this time. Here or on the cliff-top. We all believed you dead. But we hid you, just as you asked." Roddy turned to his wife. "Pru, do you think you could warm a mug of milk for Paul? He's still very cold." Prudence almost ran down the stairs to the kitchen. "You brought me a clean shirt," said Latour. Roddy nodded.

"Cleaned me up too!" Latour smiled weakly. "Do you think you could help me to the fire? I'm still terribly cold."

"Of course."

Prudence returned with a tray, bearing three mugs of hot milk, a bottle of brandy and some cakes. "I thought you might be hungry," she said, offering the cakes but at arm's length. He smiled. "Thank you, Miss Prudence. You are very kind. I'm so sorry if I scared you." Roddy was looking at his friend as though he'd never seen him before. "Paul, I don't know how to thank you. You saved my life back there on the cliff top. I thought I was done for. Then you came out of the darkness and took the shot meant for me. I can never repay you."

"I didn't mean to take the shot," confessed Latour. "All I intended to do was knock the man down. It was just bad judgement on my part."

But Roddy was confused and scared, and he looked it. "Paul, we thought you were dead. Ernie and the doctor will swear you were dead – by all the tests and measures that we could apply. In fact, we were making arrangements to bury you – after the third day. How can you heal like this? It just isn't natural."

"Roddy… I honestly don't know. This has only happened since that lightning strike. As I said: I felt a strange tingling all through my body. Somehow, I knew that the wound would heal. The tingling was stronger there, and it felt that the wound was mending, but I knew I was dying. I also knew that was a fatal shot I took on the cliff-top, but I felt that tingling again. Not more lightning but the same sensation that the wound was knitting together. I wonder if that lightning had the effect of speeding up my healing process." The three friends hashed and re-hashed that idea for over an hour. But they were no wiser at the end of that time. But Latour had sown the seed of a possible explanation.

Eventually, the conversation got around to the Custom's raid and how the officers were still searching for him. "We will still have to satisfy White-stone that you were not the man on the cliff-top and explain your absence from the village," said Roddy. "I did try to plant the idea that you were given to periods of depression, which I blamed on the tragic loss of your daughter. God knows that's reason enough for the hardiest soul to be depressed. I said that there were times when I sensed you needed to be alone, but I didn't pry into your whereabouts. I added that on those occasions, you usually took a bottle of rum with you. Paul, I know that isn't true, but I had to give them something to chew on. Mind you, I don't know who could corroborate that story." Latour studied his friend's worried face quite intently. "Well, the wound has healed, so it seems that I could not have been the man that was shot. The need for time alone is plausible too. But where was I? It would have to be a place that the soldiers hadn't searched surely."

"What about the beacon huts?" Prudence interrupted. "The soldiers only took a quick look inside. Could he have been asleep behind the woodpile?"

"The soldiers were pretty thorough," responded Roddy. "Whitestone threatened them with dire consequences if they weren't."

"Better they suffer his anger than Paul end up in prison," Pru said. "All we need is a speedy and plausible answer for his absence. No one goes to the huts these days."

"I'll take a look at the eastern beacon hut," said Roddy. "Maybe we can make it look reasonable to miss seeing someone hiding behind the woodpile." In the hut, Roddy restacked the wood, creating a cavity large enough to accommodate Latour. He also arranged a door of sorts – four lengths of timber that Latour could set from inside the cavity to make the pile of wood look full and complete. And so Latour, with a half rum jug, plus the remnants of some bread and cold cuts and a heavy blanket were hidden in the woodpile of the eastern beacon hut. The following morning, one of the soldiers noticed smoke spiralling from the chimney of the hut. He roused his mate, and together with Bennett, they discovered a black man wrapped in a blanket, eating some stale bread and cheese, sitting by the brazier.

When questioned, Latour confirmed Roddy's suspicions of his need for occasional privacy and stated that he had been in the hut all along. He smelled of rum and wood smoke and admitted to leaving the hut on a couple of occasions, just to answer nature's call. Bennett pulled Latour's shirt open, but there was no wound. The soldier's protests that they had searched the hut fell on deaf ears until Latour demonstrated how he 'closed his door' from the inside. The sadly depleted rum jug and food remnants added substance to Latour's claim. Bennett also recalled the vicar previously mentioning Latour's periods of depression and his tendency to disappear for hours on such occasions. However, they tied Latour's hands and stated they would take him to Whitestone. The vicar saw them passing his vicarage and rushed out to enquire after Latour's health. He insisted on going with them to Whitestone, and Bennett waited whilst the vicar collected his wagon. Then the prisoner and troopers climbed into the back whilst Bennett rode behind.

News of Latour's capture had reached the village, and a large crowd had gathered to watch the soldiers and their prisoner depart. Doc and Ernie – looking as though they had awoken from a nightmare – were front and centre. Latour nodded to them as the wagon passed, but they hurriedly crossed themselves and backed up a pace or two. Under different circumstances, their awed expressions would have been laughable. But Roddy knew that they would face real problems on their return, regardless of the outcome in Whitestone's office.

Starr immediately identified Latour as the man he'd shot. However, once Latour's shirt was removed, Starr was forced to recant. Nevertheless, he steadfastly maintained that he had definitely shot his attacker and that the shot had been squarely in the chest. Whitestone's lips were set in a grim line. "You may go, Latour," he said. "Bennett, bring me the men responsible for searching the hut where Latour was found." Latour tried to excuse the men, saying that they could have searched whilst he was outside relieving himself, and the hut would have been empty. But Whitestone needed a scapegoat. Roddy and Latour left Nextwest. On the way home, they gave their news to the Pringles.

It was late afternoon when Slondosh turned onto the Ryeport Road. The sun was back – lighting a scattering of grey clouds, colouring the space between them with pink, orange and various shades of blue. The evening was a little cool, but the vicar and Latour felt far more chilled than the weather could justify. Both were concerned about the villager's response to Latour's reappearance. Nick's warning about the violent response of fearful villagers had made a strong impression on Latour. He wondered how far his newfound healing abilities would help him if he were burned at the stake. Would his blackened bones grow new flesh but remain chained to the stake to await repeat performances, or might Nick send more lightning to 'crisp-up' the villagers?

Because both men were concerned about what sort of reception they might get at the inn, Roddy decided to drive directly to the church. They both agreed that allowing some time before the inevitable round of questions might give them both a chance to prepare their answers. However, that plan was dashed when they found Ernie sitting on a fallen tree just off the church driveway.

Ernie stood and raised a hand to the horse's bridle. "Hello, Father, Latour. How did things go in Nextwest?" Ernie was a hard man to un-nerve, but he had never known a dead man come back to life, and this was not the first time that Latour had accomplished that. The anxiety on the innkeeper's face was plain to see. Ernie always seemed fearless when facing danger, but those dangers were natural ones. He had no idea what he was facing with Latour. He wanted to know what had happened after he'd left the vicarage last night. After all, no one knew better than he just how dead Latour had been. Ernie had committed to burying him at sea today. Now here was the 'dead man' as large as life itself and looking every bit as healthy as before the shooting. And these two were the only ones able to shed light on the mystery.

The vicar spoke first. "All went well, Ernie. Once Latour took his shirt off, Whitestone's man conceded that Paul could not be the man he'd shot. There was no evidence of a wound. Whitestone concluded that it must have been a smuggler with a blackened face that had attacked Starr. Apparently, Pringle had already ridiculed Bennett for not knowing that blacking one's face was practised by some smugglers. Whitestone was furious. That young officer, Starr, won't live down his part in this affair for many a year. Other soldiers will be punished too for failing to find Latour in the beacon hut."

"We need to talk," said the innkeeper in a dismissive manner. "Mind if we go to your place, Father? Or would Latour's be more convenient?"

"Let's go to my 'digs'," said Latour. "We'll be less likely to be disturbed. I'll make us some tea. I'm told that I owe you many thanks, Ernie. I really appreciate all that you've done for me. Hop up here," he extended a helping hand. Ernie hesitated for a few seconds. Then, with an anxious look at the vicar, he grasped Latour's strong hand and was hauled aboard the wagon. Once at his 'digs', Latour prepared tea and brought out some food before sitting with his guests. "Well, my friends," he said, looking very anxious. "I hope you will still allow me to call you 'friends'? No one has ever helped me more than you have, and that was certainly the action of friends. I hope too that you might consider me a friend." Ernie ignored Latour's remarks and fixed eye contact with the vicar. "Father, just what happened at the vicarage after I left you last night?" And so, Roddy told Ernie exactly what had transpired after he had left, excluding only Pru's horrific experience. Latour poured the tea. "Ernie," he said. "I know that my healing this way worries you. Frankly, it worries me too. I can't explain it. As I told the vicar, when the lightning struck the ship, I felt a tingling, almost a burning sensation, run through my whole body. It was particularly strong in the area of the wound. Almost like a cauterising iron. I knew somehow that the sword wound would heal. I didn't think I would survive, mind you. I just believed that the wound was healing. I felt that same tingling sensation when I was shot. I certainly never had that power of healing before the lightning. I can't explain it. I wonder if the lightning strike did something to change my body. Our bodies all heal, given sufficient time. But to survive the injury, we must heal faster than the wound deteriorates. The only happening that I can think of that might have caused the change in me was that lightning strike. It must have speeded up my healing process. I've got no other explanation. This never happened before the shipwreck, certainly not in Haiti. I was mauled by a mad dog there and nearly died from my injuries. I still have the scars." He rolled up his sleeve to reveal groups of large dark scars. "That healing took many weeks."

Ernie's expression was very grim. "I can understand someone healing a wound, Latour. But you were dead. You don't heal dead. As far as the lightning is concerned, why didn't the rest of the crew come back to life as you did? They were on the ship with you."

"Maybe I wasn't dead. I've heard of that happening before. In Haiti, we have known men to be buried alive because they were dead by all normal measurements. In one case, a coffin was exhumed days after the burial. The inside of the coffin lid was gouged from the corpse having tried to claw his way out. There were slivers of wood under his fingernails." Ernie didn't look convinced. "He couldn't have been dead when they buried him."

"Maybe, I wasn't dead either, Ernie. Just in a deep coma."

"Never heard the likes of that before."

Roddy interjected. "However Paul came around Ernie, the fact remains he is alive and here now. He saved my life on that cliff-top, and I'm convinced that he is a man of goodwill who has the best interests of this village at heart. So how do we deal with this situation? Who amongst the villagers believes he was dead? And who believes he was involved in the smuggling? How do we satisfy everyone's curiosity, without alarming them or the Revenuers?" Ernie's expression was very grim. "I must say, Father, I'm surprised and disappointed to find that you are in league with the smugglers again. I backed you on the first occasion because you were only trying to save some of our villagers. But now you are doing this for your own personal gain."

"Ernie, the smuggling was already going on, and you know full well that Bannerman and the Sullivans would have been in Whitestone's net long since but for a stroke of good luck. And there have been other instances since then where I had to step in and save the situation, even though I wasn't involved. Because of that, I was approached to organise the group, simply because I was more careful and methodical than the smugglers themselves. They intended to proceed with or without me. It seemed the best way to keep them out of trouble was for me to organise part of the operation. It's true that I do share in the proceeds now. My income from the church is small. Certainly not sufficient for me to keep my wife in the standard of living she was used to. We're hoping to have children and will want them to be educated, and that is where my share of the proceeds will be spent. Frankly, Ernie, I can justify that reason a lot easier than money spent on a king's extravagances." Ernie wasn't backing down. "Well, I want nothing to do with it. And I don't want my family to be touched by it. So, from hereon, you're on your own. As far as smuggling is concerned, I'll not lift a finger to help any of you in the future." Roddy hung his head. "Ernie, I will be eternally grateful for the help you have already given me. You have been a great friend, in all matters since I came to Ryeport. And, believe me, it was never my intention to involve or hurt you in any way. For that, I'm truly sorry. I hope we can still be friends."

Ernie stood up. "We can be friends – provided you observe my conditions. I never want to hear another word about smuggling in this village, not from you or Bannerman, Carter, Sully or whomever else might get involved."

"I understand, Ernie. Thank you." Roddy stood and extended his hand. Ernie shook it and turned to leave. "By the way, Ernie," said Roddy. "Paul was never involved in the smuggling."

"I know that. He learned about your problem from Doc and me."

"Of course!" Roddy smiled. "One thing I still can't understand though is how Bannerman and Carter came in full to the gunn'l's with fish, after having to spend time hiding trade goods." Ernie paused with his hand on the latch. "Doc asked the same question. It seems that after sinking the trade goods, Bannerman ran into some boats from Nexteast that were returning home full of fish. He paid them a good price for their catch, using money they'd got from selling the smoked fish. They pretty well filled his and Carter's boats right there. Then they made sure to wet their own nets as he got closer to Ryeport. Luckily, they were pulling in some fish as the cutter approached. That was quick thinking on Bannerman's part. But mostly luck. The Revenuers had seen our other boats with good catches. They would have given him a hard time if his boat had been too light."

And so the three men parted, their friendship strained and uncomfortable but still intact. Ernie sought out Doc Hudson and apprised him of their conversation, also seeking Doc's opinion of the 'lightning strike phenomenon', and the 'deep coma' part of Latour's theory. Doc was shaken by Latour's recovery. "Yes, it's true that people have recovered from deep comas," he said. "Some had even shown some healing during the coma, but they had all retained evidence of vital signs whilst unconscious." On the subject of the lightning strike having infused Latour with special healing capabilities, he was derisive. "Never heard of lightning having any beneficial effect on a human body," he said. "In my wildest dreams, I couldn't even conceive of any way that it could stimulate healing. If there had ever been any instances of such a thing happening, you would see forests of tragically sick people standing out in thunderstorms, with their arms raised to the heavens."

The rest of the village, not knowing of Latour's involvement or actual wound, accepted the story that Latour had escaped from his duties during a fit of depression to seek the comfort of some rum in the solitude of the beacon hut. Most of the villagers had suffered bitter personal losses in their lives, but they'd all had friends and family to help them through their despair. Sympathy for this quiet and helpful newcomer and his painful loss came easy. At least he'd arranged for Higgins to look after the light. He hadn't neglected his duty to their safety.

Roddy's main concern was Bannerman. The smuggler was furious to learn there was a spy in their midst and convinced that the spy must be the same one that had betrayed Goodman. His obsessive and not too subtle questioning was beginning to arouse unwelcome attention from some of the villagers. Eventually, to prevent further damage, Doc had to take him aside and tell him the story of Bridget's letter. As expected, Bannerman was determined to kill her. Doc arranged a different solution. He met with Bridget in her cottage and convinced her that she was now to be included in the smuggling ring. If the Revenuers ever caught the smugglers, they would name her as part of their distribution group. She would then suffer the same fate as a smuggler. Doc told her that evidence had been planted that would prove her role in the smuggling, and she would never know where or what that evidence was. He pointed out her back window, and she saw Bannerman burying a cask in her backyard. "There will be other evidence," said the doctor. "You can dig that cask up by all means, but you won't know who might be watching." She was even more terrified now and tearfully promised to keep silent. Doc Hudson waved Bannerman inside, assuring Bridget that he wouldn't allow any harm to come to her. She huddled near the front door as Bannerman entered from the rear, and she told the two men that she'd meant no harm to the smugglers but only wanted to get even with the vicar because he'd humiliated her when she asked for his help. Doc persuaded Bannerman to pay her a small fee occasionally and to record those payments, just to further implicate her as a smuggler. As they were about to leave her cottage, Bannerman grabbed Bridget by the hair, pulled her head back and drew his thumb hard across her throat. "If you ever mention one word of what has passed between us today, Miss, then one of our group will find you and silence you for good." She ran from him, clutching her throat and sobbing.

The two men left the cottage. "Was that brutal display really necessary, Bannerman?" Doc was upset by the incident. "I believe it was, Doc. She just loves to talk at the well. That's what killed our last preacher, remember? That's what did 'im in really. She'll always try to look important to the other women of the village. Not 'avin' a man of 'er own is 'er biggest problem."

• • •

Life in the village soon returned to normal as the drama of Latour's disappearance and the Customs officers search became mere memories. Ernie's main concern now was Meg. Since Sailmaker had been shanghaied, she had been less than her usual, prankish, happy-go-lucky self. A little of her previous personality had returned, when she'd received Sailmaker's letter from the missionary. And she always kept that with her, tucked in her apron pocket. Ernie would pretend not to notice when he'd spot her reading it with tears in her eyes. Her hopes and dreams had all died with the wreck of The Seahorse. Latour had confirmed that Sailmaker was on board that fateful day and that he had been locked in the fo'c'sle when the ship was wrecked. His body was one of five that was never recovered. Although she had now accepted her loss, she had grown ever more morose and less sociable. Ernie was troubled. "She needs to get on with her life," he told Roddy one day. "I pray for some insight on how to help her."

A couple of weeks after Latour's recovery, Hawksworth arrived at The Harbour Light, in a buggy. The fact that the athletic Hawksworth was driving a buggy caused a few raised eyebrows because he always rode in on one of his fine hunters. 'Buggy rider' was not his style at all. The patrons chided him, asking if he was reduced to 'buggy rider' because he had 'a bone in his leg'? Or some other disability. He was saved further harassment when the sound of the posthorn drew his tormentors outside to meet the coach. Four passengers alighted, the last being a stocky, well-dressed man in his mid-forties. Hawksworth offered his hand as the man carefully placed his right foot on the small iron step and swung his wooden leg down to the ground.

"Hello, Will! Did you have a good journey?" Hawksworth said as he steadied the man when his stump skidded on a stone. His friend replied, rather testily, "It's bad enough being shook up over these rough roads but getting in and out of the damn coach is inviting disaster." But once he was standing on firm ground, he smiled and extended his hand. "Good to see you again, Hawksworth. But I'm not sure you're worth the pain and suffering involved." He paused to survey the broad harbour front, the inn and the small gathering of people. "So, this is Ryeport. You must show me around. But first – I need a drink. Maybe more than one, and you're buying."

The coachmen proved quite entertaining this day, but Ernie knew that the more enduring attraction would be the newcomer, Hawksworth's friend. "Well, aren't you going to introduce your friend?" he asked, once the coachmen left. "Certainly," responded Hawksworth, "but first everyone should please charge their jugs. My expense, Ernie." The innkeeper beamed. This promised to be a good day.

Hawksworth raised his jug. "Gentlemen: May I introduce my good friend, Doctor William Horatio Simms, physician and surgeon, late of his Majesty's ship 'Whisperer' and soon to be the acclaimed author of the adventure novel *Wishful Sinking*. I invite you to drink to his success and continuing good health." The barroom reverberated to the repeated toast, and Will Simms rose to acknowledge the welcome. "Thank you one and all. Especially the one who's buying the ale." He raised his jug to Hawksworth, who responded similarly. Then, with a big smile on his face, Hawksworth took the floor again.

"Dear patrons of The Harbour Light: I just had to introduce my good friend Will Simms to you because he is the mysterious correspondent who sent me those suspicious mailbags that caused you all so much consternation and gave me so much amusement. I've written about you so often to Will that he feels he knows you all. Especially, after Gerry Mason forced me to reveal the secret of the official-looking mailbag. So, gentlemen: Please, be so kind as to stand as I call your names so that my friend can put a face to the characters he has come to know so well." And the assembled patrons stood in turn and quietly raised their tankards to Will Simms. He repeated their names as each one stood, and they all felt a sense of camaraderie and inclusion because of that.

Will told them that he had finished his book and that he and Hawksworth would be editing it together to prepare the final draft. He would be staying at Hawksworth's farm until the book was finished, but he intended to spend some time in Ryeport, enjoying a jug or two as he became more familiar with the village and the people whose names he knew so well. He also wanted to take a trip or two outside the harbour and see The Guiding Light in action. Ernie did manage a quiet word with Hawksworth before they left. "I take it that this is the doctor you spoke to me about some months back – a possible relief for Doc Hudson?" Hawksworth nodded. "I love the idea of having my old friend living close by. I also believe he would be a good replacement for Doc Hudson, but only time will tell. Don't mention anything to either of them about that though. I'd rather it be their idea." It was a good meeting, and Ernie sold a lot of ale before Hawksworth and Will Simms drove off in the buggy.

CHAPTER 8

Re-awake in modern times

The cycle of chimes, performed by Father Eggleton's grandfather clock, roused Earl Whitt from a dreamlike state. He stirred, stretched and stifled a yawn as he lazily opened his eyes. Suddenly, he realised that Sexton and Father Eggleton were staring at him. He excused himself and feeling self-conscious and embarrassed said, "Sorry, I don't usually feel tired during the day, but it is very warm in here, and I guess I'm still having problems with jetlag." As he straightened up, he caught a brief glimpse of that other figure – the one standing behind Sexton – snap his fingers and disappear. Whitt looked around the room, but the fellow was nowhere to be seen. But he was relieved to see the flames in the fireplace were dancing again. I must have dozed off, he thought. But his dreaming had been so vivid and realistic it had meshed with Father Eggleton's reading from the old journal. Even now, he remembered the sounds and smells of the old village. "Are you alright, Mr. Whitt?" Sexton enquired.

"Er, yes! I just thought I saw someone standing behind you there for a moment. Must have been a shadow."

Sexton smiled. "Well, I think you dozed off for a while. Maybe a dream figure came back from the 'land-of-nod' with you. It's lunchtime, Mr. Whitt. Our good lady of the kitchen, Sarah Bass, should be here shortly with something tasty to tempt your palate. Are you ready for something to eat?" Whitt rose from the chair and stretched. "Yes, sorry for dozing off. Too much sitting around, I guess. That, plus the coffee, the warmth, and jetlag, I imagine. I'm not usually tired during the day."

"No problem. Even our young vicar here is a bit dozy-eyed. It must have been all that reading from the journal. It couldn't possibly be the coffee? That's supposed to keep you awake." The vicar smiled, as he too stretched. "Amazing how sitting can be so tiring, isn't it, Earl? I hope we didn't bore you too much with our story of the village. Those early days of The Guiding Light really are key to our village history. But we really shouldn't expect outsiders to share our interest. If we bored you, I apologise."

"Oh, no, it's an interesting story," said Whitt, "and realistically told. But I do think I need some fresh air now. I need to get my circulation going. How about a stroll outside before Sarah gets here?" Whitt's companions nodded. "Certainly," said Sexton. "That sounds like a good idea," and opened the kitchen door. Whitt stepped out into the fresh air, inhaled deeply, stretched and touched his toes a couple of times. "There, that's better." The three men then began a casual stroll to the cliff top. "So, what happened with Will Simms?" asked Whitt. "Did he ever sell his book?"

Sexton laughed. "So, you weren't asleep after all. Yes, to cut a long story short: Will sold that book and three more after that. He and Doc Hudson also became good friends, and after a few trips back and forth to London, Will closed his house there and moved in with Hawksworth. Then one stormy night, about a year later, Doc Hudson stumbled through the door of The Harbour Light and collapsed. Ernie put him to bed at the inn and sent his son to fetch Will Simms from Hawksworth's farm. Simms tended his friend for three days and nights. Doc Hudson had developed a severe case of pneumonia. They did all they could for him, but he passed away on the third night. He was 86. The villagers were devastated. There was never a more popular or better-loved man in the community. There had never been any mention of Simms taking over Doc's practice, although he had helped him out from time to time. But it seems that the villagers all accepted that Simms would eventually do that. It appeared to be an unspoken understanding between the two men. They really had become fast friends.

"Before signing on as a ship's surgeon, Simms had travelled and read extensively. He was able to bring his friend up to date with the latest medical news and stories of exotic herbal cures from around the world. He was always a popular figure at the inn and entertained the patrons there with stories of his travels or books that he'd read. He also helped alleviate Doc's suspicions and fears about Latour. One of the stories he told the patrons of the inn was of men in India, who could slow their heart rate to an imperceptible level so that people believed them dead. And then, two or three days later, the vital signs of those men would be restored, and it would appear that they had risen from the dead. Tales of strange practices from far-off places had the villagers sitting on the edge of their seats. Simms also claimed that he'd heard tell of some people being healed of various ailments when lightning struck close by them. He always stressed the 'close by' part of the story, emphasising that it would be stupid to try to attract a lightning strike. No one knew for sure if he'd heard about Latour's 'rising from the dead,' and the second event was never common knowledge anyway. However, Simms had become very close with both Latour and the vicar. It's possible they may have shared some secrets.

"As far as the other characters in the story are concerned: It was about two years after the wreck of The Seahorse that Hawksworth and Meg were married. He'd courted her for about a year. Roddy married them in The Guiding Light Church. The entry is in the register. They went to live at Hawksworth's farm and had a good and happy life together. But, although it was obvious that Meg cared deeply for her new husband, she was sometimes seen at Sailmaker's deserted rigging hut, wistfully handling some of his things. Those two young people had been true soulmates. The death of Sailmaker destroyed a rare and special relationship, leaving the villagers with a strange sense of unfinished business. Meg and Hawksworth had two children, and their descendants still live hereabouts.

"When Hawksworth and Meg married, Will Simms decided to get a place of his own. So, he moved into Doc Hudson's cottage. He had Gerry Mason design and build an extension, a large piece of which became an infirmary." Sexton laughed: "Bridget became his live-in housekeeper and nursing assistant. Will taught her to clean, dress and stitch wounds, and she was apparently very good at it. It gained her some prestige in the village. As you might expect, there were also suggestions that she warmed Simm's bed. But that was pure gossip. Neither of them ever married, but Bridget told no more stories at the well.

"Latour gave up the job as sexton when he was fifty. He wanted to go to school and become a lawyer. He too had become very involved in the 'trade,' and his share of the smuggling proceeds were invested in the same manner as the vicar's. He told Roddy that he needed to build a life for himself away from the village before he died of natural causes. He wasn't sure if he would recover from a natural death. His previous recoveries had followed fatal wounds, and they had occurred long before old age had robbed his body of its youthful restorative powers. In the event he did recover after dying from old age, he certainly wouldn't want that to happen amongst people who had grown old with him. Just imagine the shock of watching an old man die and then see him suddenly restored to life as a healthy 36-year-old! So, he bought a house outside London and would visit his friend in Ryeport occasionally. He and the vicar did very well financially. The money that they earned from the 'trade' had been well invested in property in London." Sexton smiled happily and continued: "Latour accepted a position with the same law firm that handled the trust fund for The Guiding Light Church. After gaining his legal accreditation, he bought into that firm and then bought Blackstock's share when he retired. That firm has been in our family ever since, eventually passing down to me. The name was first changed to Blackstock and Latour. Then Latour and Cook. More recently, it became: Latour, Cook and Sexton.

"Roddy and Prudence had five children – three boys and two girls. They were all well-educated and did very well for themselves. None of them chose the church as a career, however. That had to await the arrival of Father Eggleton here. When Ernie, the innkeeper, died, his son Tom took over the inn. Sam Bass is actually a descendant of his through Tom's daughter's line. Hence the name change. Sam Bass is no Ernie, I'm afraid. No leadership qualities there. Many of the other villager's children married and settled here. Some of the physical characteristics have been handed down through the generations. The most startling ones, of course, are Archer and Rooken.

"The smuggling continued quite successfully until one day, there was a running battle with Revenue cutters who caught villagers sinking contraband just a few miles east of here. Five of the villagers died in that battle. Their leader was a descendant of Bannerman's and one of those killed. He was a hard-headed man, who lacked the planning abilities of the previous smugglers. He also had his crews armed. That was a big mistake. The cutter's captain gave no quarter when the smugglers killed one of his men. He used his swivel gun, loaded with grapeshot. That put an end to smuggling hereabouts."

Sexton's story was interrupted by the sound of a car, scrunching over gravel. "Ah! Here is our good Sarah Bass," he said. "Oh! She has Sam with her. What a treat." Sexton's sarcasm was obviously heartfelt.

Sarah soon had the table set with steaming, homemade soup plus attractive choices for their ploughman's lunch. Sam had thoughtfully brought along some bottled beer. "Thought you might need a change from coffee," he said, as he took a seat at the table. But Sarah immediately grabbed him by the ear and lifted him out of the chair. "No one invited you, Sam. You've got plenty to do back at the inn. Beggin' yer pardon, gentlemen. I hope you enjoy your meal." And Sarah propelled her protesting husband through the door. Whitt laughed. "I wonder who wears the pants in that house." He was surprised but relieved to find himself laughing in Sexton's company. "Whatever happened to 'Tubby' and Goodman's boy, Charles?" Whitt wanted to impress them that he had been listening after all.

Sexton smiled as he poured them each a bottle of Smithwick's beer. "Well, Tubby and Maud had a good life together. They also had three children from their own union. Tubby adopted Maud's daughter and, of course, they also had Charles. The children all considered themselves one family. Tubby and Maud treated them all as their own natural children. When Charles was older, he was told his birth mother had died in childbirth, and Maud had raised him from his first day. No mention was ever made of the unpleasant facts of Tubby's first marriage. Charles eventually grew to well over six feet tall and weighed over 18 stone – almost 300 pounds on your scales. He towered over Tubby but never seemed troubled by any lack of family resemblance. He did enter the church and ended his career as a bishop. Tubby's letters revealed his pride in Charles and in their other children. There was never any evidence of the 'bad breeding' that Roddy had feared. They all enjoyed a good life. Roddy McDowd, the original vicar of The Guiding Light, died at eighty-two. Prudence lived a further five years. They are both resting in the vault that Gerry built in the lamp-house. Well, that just about closes the chapter on that generation."

"No, it doesn't," said Whitt. "What about Latour?"

"Ah! Latour." Sexton looked thoughtful for a few moments. "Well, his diary states that he was 89 when he realised that he was growing unnaturally weary. He suspected that old age was about to close the book on him. He was living near London – in the Hampstead Heath area actually. He'd decided to end his days there, and this was only a few years before Roddy died. As I said before, Latour didn't know if he would recover from death of old age. But, according to his 'contract' with Nick, whenever he recovered, he would be restored to the age and physical condition that prevailed before his death aboard The Seahorse. Since that wouldn't allow him to return to an area where people had watched him grow old, he enlisted the aid of his old friend Roddy McDowd. They would allow the usual 'three-day-wait' and follow that with the burial of a weighted but otherwise empty casket in London.

"The timing of that death could have proven disastrous. Latour was alone, riding his favourite horse across the heath quite near his house. It had started to rain about half an hour before he collapsed and fell from the saddle. This happened close by an historic inn called 'The Spaniards Inn.' His diary states: 'I remember the fall. Then nothing more until I felt that same sense of disconnected awareness that always preceded my earlier recoveries. It was less violent than before but still accompanied by the intense cold and violent shaking. Each successive recovery had been faster and less traumatic than the previous one, and this one proved by far the easiest to date. I became aware of voices:

"'ere 'e is ! Just like I told yer! Black as yer 'at, dressed like a toff an' dead as a bloody doornail.' The voice belonged to a skinny little man who was prancing around him as he signalled two other men to draw closer. One of them bent over Latour. 'Are you sure he's dead?' he queried. The skinny fellow sounded offended. 'O' course 'e's dead. I'm an undertaker's assistant. I knows dead, I do. Seen plenty of stiffs in me time. Should be a reward, I shouldn't wonder. For findin' 'im, I mean. Tyin' up 'is 'orse an' all.' Sexton smiled. "I remember that part pretty much verbatim, but I will paraphrase the rest of the diary. To continue: Latour chose to fully open his eyes at the very moment that the third man decided to investigate, causing the man to jump back in alarm. 'This fellow isn't dead,' he said to the skinny intendant. 'No! He certainly isn't,' agreed his companion. Latour wrote that he began to shiver and shake again. 'Of course, I'm not dead,' he said as he roused himself and sat up. I just had a bad fall.' But actually, he was wondering how long he had been 'dead' this time. He patted his coat, seeking the reassurance of his wallet. It was missing. Taking a chance, he said: 'He knows I'm not dead,' nodding towards the skinny man. 'I asked him to look after my wallet for me. Just in case someone took advantage of my condition, while he went for help. I take it that you two gentlemen are those he summoned. I'll have my wallet back now if you please,' he said, extending his hand to the skinny fellow. Skinny stepped back, one hand clasped over his mouth. 'Come now,' Latour said impatiently. 'Give me back my wallet. I'm freezing cold from lying in this rain. I can't reward you until I have my wallet, and you certainly deserve something for your help and above all your honesty.'

"'Do you have this man's wallet?' demanded the second man. 'er, yes. I was keepin' it for 'im. Like 'e said.'

"'Then hand it over." So Skinny cautiously handed Latour his wallet.

"'ere! You look younger,' he said. 'You were an old man when I left you. There's somethin' funny goin' on 'ere,' said Skinny. Latour reached into his wallet and found what change he had. 'Here is a generous reward for your assistance, Sir. Thank you. Now I shall mount up and go home for some dry clothes before I catch my death of cold. Thank you, gentlemen! Please forgive my haste. If I weren't soaked through, and so damnably cold, I would love to share a glass or two with you at The Spaniards, but I really do need to warm up and get into some dry clothes. Please accept my sincere gratitude for your concern. Perhaps I shall see you at the inn another time.'

"Skinny jumped forward and held the horse's bridle. "ere 'old on. There's somethin' wrong. I'm tellin ye. This ain't the same man that I saw lying 'ere dead an hour or so ago.' Latour looked at Skinny rather derisively. 'Gentlemen,' he said, addressing the other two men. 'Would an old man be riding such a fine-spirited animal? Am I really as black as your hat'? I always considered myself a fine, deep-toned brown myself. This fellow obviously has cognitive deficiencies. Goodbye, gentlemen, and thank you again for your concern, but I must change out of these wet clothes soon lest I come down with pneumonia. Then I really might end up: 'dead as a bloody doornail.' He smiled as he mimicked 'skinny's 'comment, touched the brim of his hat in salute and rode off."

Whitt looked at Sexton with a big grin on his face. "Come now, Sexton, do you really think we're that gullible? How could you possibly expect us to believe all that? You quote the complete dialogue and the interaction too. You need to beg artistic licence for that story!"

"Why?" responded Sexton, raising his eyebrows in surprise. "All this information is contained in the letter Latour wrote to his friend the vicar. It's all on file with his other documents in our archives. I'd be happy to show them to you."

"So, he didn't die?" said Whitt with a smirk. "How long did he take to recover this time? Usually, he wanted three days."

"Well, it appears that this recovery took only an hour or so. He believed that was because there were no wounds to heal, no trauma to repair. The 'three-day' request was always an exaggerated precaution anyway. His longest recovery period was from the gunshot wound from the Customs officer, and even that took less than 24 hours. But once again, he experienced full recovery, having reverted back to the age and health he'd enjoyed aboard The Seahorse. I'm sure the skinny undertaker's assistant had a few sleepless nights pondering the changes in the man that fell from the horse that day. Anyway, Latour rode home and changed into dry clothes before riding on to Colchester where he had purchased another house in preparation for this event. He'd assumed a new identity for that purchase: Paul Cook.

"Roddy arrived in Hampstead and presided over the burial of the weighted coffin. At the time of that death, Latour's law firm was ably managed by a trusted employee, who had been with the firm for roughly 10 years. Latour's last act before retiring was to complete a purchase agreement with Paul Cook, so his ownership of the firm continued."

"But did he return to Ryeport again? After all who knew him had died, perhaps?"

"So his diaries say. That was in his capacity as legal representative for The Guiding Light."

"Now who on earth would you expect to believe that story? You will be spinning yarns about werewolves next. Or aliens from outer space, coming down here for the smoked fish." Whitt was growing derisive again. Sexton laughed. "Actually, they don't like smoked fish. The aliens, I mean. However, they were quite partial to Ernie's bitter ale." Eggleton laughed and poured refills of Smithwicks. Whitt had never felt so insecure and lacking in control of his life. He decided to enjoy the meal and not take issue with these stupid stories any longer.

• • •

The luncheon group at the vicarage was relaxing with their second beer as Al Chernak's station wagon turned off the highway onto the Ryeport Road. Al and Heather were weary to the point of total exhaustion. The past week's harried events had consumed all their reserve energy. Had it not been for the fact that they had been able to utilise the costumes that Sexton had already arranged for the theme park, this colourful wedding would have been impossible. Sexton also arranged early delivery of horse drawn carriages and the participation of some students that he had originally engaged to be costumed attendants at the park.

Neither Al nor Heather had uttered a single word for the last 20 miles. Al was having a struggle just keeping his eyelids open. He was steering with one hand and massaging and slapping his face with the other, all in an effort to stop himself from falling asleep. Heather's last remark before finally fading off to sleep in the seat beside him was: "I'm all used up and grubby." Al glanced at her enviously as she dozed in the reclined passenger seat. He would have loved to allow his eyes to close right now.

Following Chernak's station wagon was a bus carrying the college students. They had been only too happy to accept the additional job as attendants for the wedding. They would don their costumes from the theme park inventory, add swords and other seaman's apparel and act as honour guard and ushers for the costumed wedding. Extra income was always acceptable, and a few days away from the city, all expenses paid, would be a great gig.

He was relieved when the church steeple appeared over the hill to his left. His sigh of relief was loud enough to rouse Heather. Her bleary eyes studied him for a few seconds before she sat up, yawned, stretched theatrically and said: "Thank God."

"Why, thank God? He wasn't doing the driving," responded the weary Chernak.

"No, he was too busy holding up your heavy eyelids. That would be a tougher job than driving."

"Tell me about it."

A large marquee had been unloaded at The Seahorse Inn, and the lorry that brought it, along with tables, chairs and other rented items, had backed up to the elevated, rock-walled 'side-garden' of the inn. The so-called 'garden' was really just an unkempt field that had been graded level and strewn with straw for the occasion. Ground level of that area was about the same height as a loading dock, so the lorry was backed up to that at right angles to the road partially obstructing Chernak's route to the parking spaces on the far side of the inn. The hustle and bustle of the delivery crew had attracted a crowd of spectators.

As he waited, Chernak spotted a woman with copper coloured hair, squeezing out of a slightly rusty Ford that she'd reversed into the last remaining space on his side of the lorry. Her driver's side door could only open about 15 inches before striking the vehicle next to it. However, by sucking in her stomach and stretching her arms above the roof, 'Copper-top' managed to squeeze out of her car and between the next vehicle, transferring quite a lot of road dust from both of them onto her otherwise smart, dark green coat. He'd been in similar situations himself and by now would have been unpleasant to deal with. 'Copper-top', however, was smiling, albeit a little ruefully, as she brushed herself down and made her way to the boot of her car. Backing in had not been a good choice. Despite the fact that she was older, maybe mid-40s, and about 25 pounds heavier than most of the ladies that Chernak was normally attracted to, she had an air about her that drew his attention. Nor was he alone in that. The other men in the crowd had also stopped watching the marquee crew to focus on her. Those that caught her eye quickly returned her smile and were rewarded by a warmer one in return. It was infectious. Tired as he was, Chernak would have liked to join the crowd. He had the feeling that he was somehow missing something. Heather, however, had noticed his distraction, followed his gaze and spiked his ribs with her elbow. "Don't stare. What's wrong with you?" Holly Maxwell, the source of Al's attention, was oblivious of this little by-play, of course. She had started her new live-in job at The Seahorse Inn only a couple of weeks before and still carried the advertisement that Sexton had given her during her last evening as barmaid at a nightclub in Plymouth.

It was Sexton who had warned Sam Bass that the extra business expected from the upcoming wedding, plus the launching of the Ryeport tourist park, would require more help in the bar. "Better to try out that help early, rather than late," he'd warned. "The wedding could be a great opportunity. People don't complain so loudly about poor service when it's delivering free booze. The tourist trade can be rewarding, Sam, but you need to make them feel welcome. A good barmaid would add charm and personality to this place. God knows, you could use some of that." Holly opened the boot of her car, heaved out a large shopping bag and squeezed through the cars towards the inn. Strong too, thought Chernak. "I bet…" Heather's elbow broke his chain of thought again, and they wearily followed Holly into the cool, dim confines of The Harbour Light Lounge. Sam Bass was in conversation with Holly when they entered, but as soon as he saw them, he turned from her and gave them the benefit of his grungy smile. "Hello, Miss Heather, Mr. Chernak. It's good to see you back again. Don't let the confusion out there scare you. Everything's well-organised here. We'll be ready in plenty of time for the big day. Don't you worry!" He partly turned his head towards Holly. "Take those goods into the kitchen, lass. Be ready to work tonight; the marquee crew will want feeding."

Sam returned his attention to Al and Heather. "How was the trip to London, folks? You do look tired. Did you get all the costumes arranged? This place has been like a zoo. I don't know how I've kept everything organised. I suppose it's just my nature to rise to a challenge." Chernak's lips twisted in a wry smile. He knew full well who had the organisational skill in this village, and none of it belonged to Sam. "Before I answer any questions, Sam, I need three things: a drink, then another drink and then a visit with my best man. I trust he arrived safely?"

"Yes, Sir. Mr. Whitt arrived last night. Rather tired from his journey, I assume, and a bit disorientated like, judgin' by 'is manner that is. Right now Mr. Whitt is at the vicarage with Father Eggleton and Sexton. Sexton's taken 'im under 'is wing', you might say. 'e's been showin' 'im 'round the village. 'ow about a nice draught, Sir?"

"No, Sam. I fancy something sweeter. We need to relax with a sweeter, long drink: one that will flush that long, boring drive out of our bodies. We'll have two Bacardi and cokes, please. Regular coke – not diet – with a twist and lots of ice. But before you do that, please have your son go outside and direct the students and the coachmen to their lodgings." Before Sam could respond, however, the door opened, and the bus driver stumbled into the room, closely followed by the students. "Boy, I could really use a wet," said the driver as he bellied-up to the bar. "That was one boring drive. I'll have a lager and lime please, barkeep." Then a student piped up. "Make mine a rum and orange, lots of ice." Suddenly, they were all crowding the bar, calling their orders as though this might be the last drink of their lives. Sam groaned; he hated fiddling around with mixed drinks! However, he was smart enough to realise that he would make more money in one week from the tourist's 'fancy' drinks than he would slopping draught for the locals for a month. They'd learned to nurse a pint all night long as they talked or played dominos or cards. Then inspiration struck. He threw open the kitchen door. "Holly! Come and look after these customers. You can put that stuff away later." Turning to Chernak, he said: "I'll look after the bodies outside. My boy is helping to get the community centre set up, and Sarah's busy makin' supper."

Chernak was sure that Holly's smile preceded her through the kitchen door into the bar. "This gal is going to be a real asset to this place," he thought, "provided Sam doesn't drive her away". It took Holly a few moments to get some lemons and limes from Sarah's kitchen, but all the while her smile and air of confident goodwill warmed the space between her and the customers. Once the clients were served, Holly directed her attention to Heather, the bride to be. Holly was genuinely interested in the costume arrangements and details of the wedding, and Heather was only too pleased to describe, in a very animated manner, the alterations to her dress and the unique arrangements concerning the event. Al wondered where her newfound energy came from. He raised his empty glass to Holly, and fresh rum and coke with ice and a twist were quickly before him. There wasn't even a pause in the conversation, just that quick warm smile.

Al saw one of the students counting coins onto the bar and – feeling magnanimous – said to Holly: "Miss: Please buy the house a round – on my tab. These guys deserve a drink after that drive." The ragged cheers and raised glasses from the crowd were reward enough, but Holly's smile and raised eyebrows were a welcome bonus.

"Where's my best man, Sam?" Chernak, having finished his second drink, had gone outside to find Sam Bass and Whitt. "At the vicarage, Sir. I'll run you over there if you like."

"No, Sam. Just point me in the right direction. I'll take the station wagon. I need him to try on his uniform." Ten minutes later, Chernak was getting an earful from Whitt as to how bad mannered it was to keep a friend so in the dark, especially, when that friend had travelled thousands of miles to be your best man. However, a couple of drinks later, all had calmed down, and Chernak was able to go to the car and retrieve the costumes. He backed through the doorway on his return, suit bags folded over one arm and balancing hat boxes with the other. The first bag held Whitt's uniform. "Would you mind, Father?" asked Chernak – holding up a bright blue and white jacket, trimmed with gold braid – "if Earl used your bedroom to try on his uniform? It would set my mind at ease." "By all means," replied Eggleton. "I'm sure we are all anxious to have a preview of the wedding costumes." Chernak took the bags into the bedroom. He had to show Whitt how to dress appropriately but, in about 20 minutes, they both emerged as officers of the King's Navy, dressed as Post Captains of the late eighteenth century.

"Wow! You two look magnificent!" said the vicar. "Quite dashing!" Whitt, despite all his complaining, thought so too. He paraded in front of the large mirror by the front door, posing with his sword and his hat, adjusting his breeches and so on. He was obviously impressed with his appearance, and Chernak was relieved. Sexton though was looking very thoughtful, and his lips were set in a grim line as he studied Whitt. He would allow a small smile and a nod of approval whenever the others looked in his direction, but he did appear fixated on Whitt especially since he'd donned that uniform.

"Okay, Father. You're next," said Chernak rushing him to the bedroom. Eggleton returned wearing clerical garb appropriate to the period. "Not as glamorous as ours, I'm afraid," said Chernak. "But appropriate to your calling, nonetheless. Now, the 'piece de resistance', for the man who made it all come together. Sexton, your costume is on the vicar's bed. I hope you'll approve." Sexton dutifully retired to the bedroom and shortly re-emerged, dressed as a gentleman of the times, complete with sword, plumed hat, lace cuffs and cravat. He looked very dashing, in a long scarlet coat, trimmed with gold braid and pale gold breeches. His silver buckled riding boots added a fine finishing touch to the picture. His appearance was impressive. More so, because of the way his colouring complimented the clothing. Whitt was quietly shocked. "I think I would have preferred that outfit," he commented to Chernak.

"It wouldn't look as good on you," said Sexton. "You'd need a much deeper tan to do it justice." They all laughed. "This calls for a toast," said Chernak. A couple of hours passed, and they were nursing a third refill when Chernak spotted Heather, peering through the door's sidelight. "Oops! I forgot about Heather," groaned Chernak. "I'm in trouble. You lads had better back me up in this. You all insisted on trying on the clothes. Remember now!" Heather was not alone. Her stern-faced mother was with her.

"You can't come in," said the vicar, as he answered the door. "It's bad luck to see the bridegroom in his wedding dress before the wedding."

"Father, you've been drinking," accused the bride to be.

"Not at all! I've only had coffee all afternoon," protested the slightly inebriated vicar.

"Oh, I've heard about Sexton's coffee," Heather responded. However, the ladies were very impressed by the gallant attention paid them by the gentlemen they found in the vicarage. They even forgot the scolding they'd intended to deliver and gracefully accepted coffee, courteously served by the handsome gentleman in the scarlet coat. There was just a hint of 'sunshine' in the coffee this time. And it was spoiled by cream and a little sugar. "Dress rehearsal is tomorrow," announced Heather. "Provided that's alright with you, Father, of course."

"Certainly, my dear. I look forward to it. What time?"

"Three p.m. Provided you boys have sobered up by then!"

"We'll be there with bells on," slurred the vicar.

"We must be leaving," said Heather. "We have to get the rest of the clothes to the other members of the wedding party. They will need to try them on before tomorrow. I guess you had forgotten that, my dear," she said as she delivered a rather hefty pat to Chernak's cheek. He rolled off his chair and collapsed on the floor. "If you intend to abuse me this way once we're married, I think I'd best call the whole thing off," he said. "Get up," responded Heather, "before you make your pretty panties dirty. I'm taking the car. You guys can walk back to the inn. The fresh air will do you good. We'll see you at the inn for supper at seven. Wear your civvies," and then she left. "That went well," said Chernak as he refilled their glasses.

• • •

The following morning, Father Eggleton joined Heather, Al Chernak and Whitt for breakfast. After his second coffee, Eggleton said: "Okay, folks. If you are ready, let's get started. I'm anxious for Sexton to show you what our church is all about. He is a fantastic storyteller and a walking history book when it comes to this village and the surrounding area. He often entertains the locals with stories of the smuggling days and valiant exploits at sea, and you feel a familiarity with the characters that he describes, almost as though you sweated with the smugglers as you helped them 'run the goods ashore'. I'm sure he could have made a fortune as a professional storyteller. I just love to listen to his tales. It's more like hearing the story from someone who had experienced it all firsthand. He seems to immerse you in the story somehow." Whitt made no comment but, reflecting on yesterday's experience, he could hardly disagree. The vicar seemed unable to get off the topic of Sexton's skills. Looking somewhat puzzled, he continued. "Sexton manages to breathe life into his stories of this village. His skill is quite uncanny. I count myself very fortunate to be involved here at this time." Heather interrupted: "I've had the church tour, Father, so please excuse me. These two boys can see The Guiding Light without me. Keep an eye on them though. They aren't very responsible." Eggleton acknowledged with a wave and a smile, and the three men rose and headed for the church.

Eggleton was still talking as they entered the church. "Earl, this church doubled as a unique sort of lighthouse two hundred years ago, and the stories that have evolved concerning it and its founders are almost legend." Eggleton led the way to a door in the back of the vestry and, stepping aside, allowed Whitt to precede him. Whitt smiled at Eggleton as he stepped through the door but suddenly caught his breath, feeling as though he had stepped into an open elevator shaft.

Whitt had stepped onto a catwalk halfway up a stone-built, rectangular tower about 40 feet tall. "Quite an experience, isn't it?" chuckled Eggleton. "Sorry for not warning you, but that's the way Sexton introduced me to the lamp-house. I just wanted to be on the other side of the joke for once. There's no danger of course. The guard rails are very safe and secure." They were on a narrow wooden catwalk and stepping onto the catwalk without being warned felt like stepping into space. There was a waist-high, steel handrail and railings, which proved to be very sturdy, but they weren't obvious when you took that first, unsuspecting step.

Eggleton was explaining: "This chamber is more than twice the height of the church. Its foundation was built 20 feet or so farther down the cliff than the church foundation. There was no way the founders could afford to build the whole church as tall as the lamp-house. So, to accommodate the large crucifix window, the mason started the lamp-house lower down the face of the cliff. Then he joined that to the main body of the church, at the top of the cliff. Crafty, eh?"

In the wall opposite the catwalk, the seaward wall was a massive cruciform window, about 30 feet tall. The glass sparkled, reflecting the careful attention of the sexton's crew. The room was elaborately fitted with adjustable mirrors, plus rows and columns of brass cased oil lamps, all with multiple wicks. Everything was spotlessly clean and polished to perfection. A blend of odours, brass-polish and pine-scented floor cleaner were strong, but both had to compete with the pervasive smell of lamp oil.

"Well, Sir. What do you think of our Church of the Guiding Light now? I bet you've never seen the likes of this before." Sexton had joined them, having stepped onto the catwalk from another door farther along. His broad smile reflected his obvious pride in the lamp-house. His enthusiasm, as he explained the workings of the oil lamps and the adjustable mirrors, was contagious. "The mirrors focus and concentrate the maximum available light through the cruciform window," he said. Despite his attempts to remain 'cool,' Whitt found himself caught up in Sexton's explanations. It wasn't hard to imagine the relief and gratitude of the fishermen for this bright and distinctive guiding light in these perilous waters. Sexton finalised his explanations with: "There is just no way to estimate how many wrecks this light prevented or how many lives it saved."

The three men descended the stairs to the lower level of the lamp-house. There Sexton showed them the crypt that Gerry Mason had built as a mausoleum for himself and the founding vicar's family. "I've had a new lock and hinges fitted now, of course, but this is the door that fell from rusted hinges to reveal the coffins and time-capsule that the founding vicar left behind. But I'm forgetting my manners. The rest of the story can be better told over a good cup of coffee. Please, come on up to my 'digs,' I can even provide some hot apple pie and cheese to compliment the coffee."

"Sexton calls his quarters the 'digs,' explained the vicar as they climbed the stairs, back up to the catwalk that gave access to both Sexton's 'digs' and the vestry. "As lodgings go, my 'digs' are rather small," said Sexton. "More like a bachelor flat."

"When Sexton retired from his law firm to become our sexton, he upgraded the 'digs' at his own expense," said Eggleton. "Actually, he built an insulated apartment within the cave-like, single room of the original apartment, adding all the mod-cons, of course." Whitt frowned. "I can't imagine why he would go to such expense. It's not as though he had any ownership in the place."

"Actually, he wasn't concerned about ownership. As I said before: he is a very wealthy man. He said he can afford to indulge himself in some extravagancies. About two years ago, he even bought an established law firm in Toronto. To service his personal investments in Canada," he said. "He still makes occasional trips over there."

Sexton had followed them through the catwalk door. "What do you think of my 'digs', Mr. Whitt? It's really luxurious compared to what my ancestor enjoyed. It's small, but I don't entertain as a rule. Today is a pleasant exception." He took a cheese dish from the fridge, put a fresh apple pie in the microwave and set up the percolator. Hot apple pie and a slab of old white cheddar cheese complimented the coffee very well. A touch of 'sunshine' added its special glow to the snack.

• • •

It was Wednesday evening, and the wedding party had all gathered in The Seahorse Lounge for supper. Apart from a small group of technicians in Ryeport to set up the TV crew's equipment, Chernak's group had the place to themselves. The wedding party included Heather's parents, her bridesmaids and the college students. Sarah finished her bobbing and weaving, allowing the diners to finally relax with their meals – without needing to dodge the enthusiastic Sarah. However, she was growing with the job. The diners all had cutlery, even napkins.

It was Heather who broached the subject of the bachelor party. Placing her right hand over her heart, she said in quivering tones: "Poor Al's last night of freedom is rapidly approaching. He has only two more days before he becomes a bonded slave to his beautiful but demanding wife." She wiped an imaginary tear from her eye. "So, I was wondering what exciting and fun things have you guys arranged for poor Al that will indelibly etch his last night of freedom into his memory? There aren't too many places in the Ryeport area where you can arrange for a stripper to jump out of a cake unless Sarah might oblige. She could even make the cake. You might even get a package price." She gave a quick snort of laughter. "Maybe even group rates." There were a few snickers around the table as mental images were entertained. The vicar looked uncomfortable. "That was unkind."

"Sorry, Father. Just joking. I didn't mean to offend or conjure up any mental images of Sarah leaping out of the cake in the 'altogether'." The technicians at the next table had obviously tuned in to the conversation, and their laughter blended with that of the wedding party. "Hmm! Even if I hadn't intended to conjure them up… it seems mental images are alive and well tonight." In the adjacent Harbour Light lounge, Sam Bass heard the laughter and turned to Sarah: "I bet that was a dirty one," and gave her a knowing wink and the charm of his grungy smile. "Not used to 'earin' wimmin laugh much 'round 'ere."

"I wonder why." Sarah's reply was accompanied by a disapproving survey of her husband.

Chernak turned to Whitt. "I believe that 'bachelor party' falls under your jurisdiction, Mr. Best Man. Pray tell: what special event have you arranged for my last night of freedom?" Borrowing from Heather's theme, he placed the back of his hand on his forehead and dejectedly hung his head. Whitt looked embarrassed. "Frankly, Al, I thought that with all the driving and shopping that you've been doing for the past week, that you would have just wanted to relax." Whitt had completely overlooked that aspect of his 'duties'. Sexton's unnerving presence had driven all such considerations from his mind. "Someone has to consider your health and wellbeing," he said as he tried to recover some composure. "You need to save your energy for the honeymoon. Someone with as many miles on the clock as you have needs nourishment, not punishment."

The technician's laughter proved they were still listening in. Struggling to divert attention from his shortcomings as 'best man,' Whitt said: "Why don't we invite those guys to join us? They're sharing the fun; perhaps they'd share the tab. Seriously though, it's been hectic for you guys, and it's going to get worse before it gets better. I thought that we could just settle for a good meal, right here, a few poker hands and some drinks. Even if we went to a place that passes for a large town somewhere within driving distance of here, you couldn't come up with much excitement. I'm sure Sarah would be glad to fix us up right here." That started the group laughing again. "There go those mental images again," said Heather. "Boy, if Sarah thought she was busy before, wait 'til Friday night."

Chernak was staring at Whitt as if he were an unwelcome stranger. "You forgot about it, didn't you? You dropped the ball. I can't believe you." He shook his head in obvious disappointment. In trying to bypass Al's remark, Whitt caught the vicar's eye. "Don't you think that would be a good evening, Father? Even without the cake? Although, if there happened to be one, we might all prefer that Sarah stayed inside it. In fact, I think we should pay her to stay inside it." Sam Bass heard the laughter again and made for the hallway. Sarah moved to block his way. "No, you don't, Sam. It's their party. No eavesdropping." Reluctantly, Sam went back to his bar.

Heather took the floor again. "Whatever you want to set up, Mr. Organiser, you're too late for this location. You missed the boat. The girls and I have this place all sewn up for Friday night. The TV boys are all going to Nextwest that evening, and Sarah has agreed that we can have this lounge exclooooosively." She hung the word out, just to ensure the guys knew they weren't invited.

Al knew the signal and that objections would be a waste of time. "Okay, where else can we go? Our rooms are too small, even for our small group." He threw his arms up. "Why don't we just settle for a few drinks in The Harbour Light and an early night? That'll be something to boast about to our grandkids." Whitt felt ashamed and embarrassed at having let his friend down. By contrast, his own bachelor party had been a wildly varied affair, only parts of which he could remember. Al had done a great job for him, but that was back in Toronto. Ryeport had none of those facilities. And Al had not had to contend with this black sexton, haunting him and keeping him on edge.

Eggleton raised his hand, and Whitt seized on the opportunity to deflect any further examination of his failings. "Yes, Father, you may leave the room. Please hurry; we don't want any accidents." Eggleton was becoming more comfortable with their banter and just smiled. Treating the vicar like one of the boys was not disrespect; it was the price of membership in this circle of friends. "I just wanted to offer you fellows the use of the vicarage," he said. "Provided you guarantee 'no strippers', mind you. Sarah would deliver our supper, nothing more. Besides, I don't think there is sufficient time between now and Friday to build a sufficiently large cake."

The laughter brought Sam Bass's head around again. He was halted in his move towards The Seahorse Lounge by an order from the bar. "I'll have a pint of your best, Sam," said Archer. "You're not a bad bloke, Archer, but you've got a bloody rotten sense of timing," said Sam. He resented being left out of the party. Archer scowled. "Okay, Archer! Okay!" But Sam hadn't quite given up on the idea of eavesdropping on the party, and the pint he poured Archer was far too foamy. Archer gave Bass a wry look but didn't pick up the glass. "We'll let that sit a while, Sam. See how close that comes to a pint when all that fizz collapses."

In the lounge, the vicar still had the floor. "So, some drinks, good food, good friends and an evening of cards. That sounds good to me and, on the plus side, we'll all be sober and right here in Ryeport when we wake up. No excuses for being late for the ceremony." Heather was smiling, and her eyes flitted from one guy to the next, as she toyed with her meal. She was enjoying the predicament of this self-opinionated male group. It was so unlike Whitt not to have this event all planned and sewn up tight. He certainly seemed nervous and unsure of himself since he'd been in Ryeport. She'd noticed he appeared particularly edgy when Sexton was around, but he wasn't here tonight. It seemed to her that Chernak and Whitt were trying to resolve their dilemma by staring at each other. Finally, Al broke the mini silence: "Sounds good to me, Father, provided that you don't surprise us with any wild women. I guess it's too late to ask you to be my best man. Or would that be a conflict of interest?" Al extended his hand to the vicar. "Thank you, Father. You're our saviour. Oops! Sorry. No disrespect intended."

"None taken, and you're welcome. Just make sure and let Sarah know what you want to eat tomorrow before we leave. I'm sure she's never been so busy." In The Harbour Light Lounge, Sam had topped up Archer's pint and was looking, disappointedly in the direction of the party. The laughter had subsided now, and he'd been left out. He wondered how he might insert himself in all the fun that seemed about to erupt in Ryeport.

It was seven p.m. on Friday night, and Al Chernak's friends were gathered at the vicarage for his bachelor party. Sarah was busy in the kitchen with last minute preparations for their supper. Father Eggleton had improvised a small bar in the corner of the room, and a borrowed fridge was keeping the beer cold. It was all very cosy and organised. Sarah had remembered the napkins, cutlery and a large assortment of condiments. She was enjoying the challenges of the new clientele. Heather's father, Fred McDowd, had been the first to arrive. The groom and his best man followed shortly after. Whitt's face fell when Sexton came through the door carrying a case of wine. His absence from Wednesday's meal had raised his hopes that Sexton would not attend tonight's gathering.

"My contribution to the celebration," Sexton said, "some amusing reds, and subtle white wines and, just for the toast: some champagne. Good stuff too. I'm sure you'll enjoy. Oh! I've also brought some of my wonderful coffee and some 'sunshine', of course – 'Cafe-a-la-Sexton'. I'm sure we can trust Father Eggleton to be our designated driver, provided he only drinks coffee." Sarah poked her head around the kitchen door. "All present?" she queried. "Aye, Ma'am, the gang's all here," replied the vicar. The group was soon sitting before large steak dinners with all the trimmings. After many phone calls, Whitt had arranged special delivery of the steaks. He had even instructed Sarah on how to marinate them in wine, sauté the mushrooms and prepare garlic toast. Sarah had provided the fresh vegetables. Sexton filled their wine glasses, and everyone was set.

Sarah excused herself. "I'm leavin' you boys to yourself now," she said. 'Afters' is all set up on the kitchen table. 'elp yourselves. Leave the dishes in the sink. I'll come by to 'elp Elsie clean up in the mornin'." She closed the door behind her. By eight o'clock, the dishes were all in the sink, and the table was cleared for their poker game. "That was a most excellent meal," said the vicar, holding his stomach. "I can't remember ever having such a good steak." The group echoed their approval but looked a little lethargic after the big meal and the wine. So Eggleton suggested some fresh air. "Why don't we stretch our legs a little? Take a walk before we sit down to play cards. A little fresh air would brighten us up a bit. Help blow the cobwebs away."

Their walk took them to the eastern side of the churchyard; an area where Whitt and Chernak had not been before. The ground was level, and there were no trees, only scrubby pieces of brush. The only object rising more than a few inches above ground was an antiquated looking door, still mounted in its frame and staked so as to stand upright. It was about eight feet from the edge of the 40 feet tall cliff, and set against a backdrop of sea and swooping, screeching seagulls. "What's that: the doorway to the great outdoors? Or a suicide's way out?" asked Chernak. Fred McDowd was quick to respond: "Neither, that's the original fo'c'sle door from the port side of The Seahorse, a ship that was wrecked here more than two hundred years ago. It's an unwanted piece of Ryeport's history and nearly three hundred years old."

"Looks like it too. It's green with mould and has little clumps of fungus growing on it," commented Chernak. "Why is it staked upright out here?" McDowd explained: "When The Seahorse was wrecked, the owner of the inn fitted this door as a replacement for a damaged one in the 'Harbour Light'. The new door served very well until the first anniversary of the wreck! From village records, we learn that on that clear afternoon, an unexpected flash of lightning covered the whole area, and this door was blown open by a fierce wind. Then a ghostly figure stepped through. From what we've read, there was a storm raging on the other side of this door, but nowhere else – only outside this door." He put heavy emphasis on those words and looked around the group as if hoping they appreciated the significance of his words. "There were no signs of a storm anywhere else, only through this door. The ghostly figure was bloodied and exhausted. His wrists were tied, but his arms were raised, pointing in an accusing manner, and he appeared to be shouting something. Apparently, the whole bar panicked. They recognised the 'ghost' as a local man called Sailmaker, a villager who'd been shanghaied aboard The Seahorse nearly two years before. After a few seconds, the figure stepped back through the door, and it swung shut. All evidence of the disturbance vanished, and every-thing returned to normal until the next anniversary of the wreck when the whole eerie scene was repeated. That was one too many ghosts as far as the innkeeper was concerned. His daughter was present this time, and she too recognised the ghostly figure as Sailmaker, her lost husband, and she passed out on the barroom floor.

"The innkeeper had the door removed and tried to burn it. But it just wouldn't burn. So, they towed it far out to sea and cut it loose, but the sea wouldn't accept it. The tides always brought it back here. No matter what they tried, they couldn't get rid of it, and that terrified the villagers. So, the vicar had it brought here, staked upright on consecrated ground, as you see it now. The group that set it here said a prayer over it, and it's been here ever since. For a few years, people used to come here on the anniversary of the wreck, just to see if the incident would be repeated. It never was, and all interest eventually died out. However, the incumbent vicar has always attended here on that anniversary to say a prayer just to satisfy the villagers. I understand that Father Eggleton intends to keep up that practice. Isn't that right, Father?"

"Yes, Fred," responded Eggleton. "It's just a superstitious story, of course. But I'll honour the tradition while the door is still here. I believe there was some talk of selling it to an antiques buff at one time. Current opinion though is that the old tale has no credibility." The vicar nodded to Whitt. "Maybe you would be interested, Earl. Al was telling me you were looking for some unique artefacts to 'tiddly-up' the entertainment lounge of your new house in Canada. There's a good story to go along with the item, wouldn't you say? We could even have the story written up in 'olde' English script. You could frame it and hang it on the wall beside the door." Sexton was standing off to one side, but he hadn't taken his eyes off Whitt whilst McDowd told the story. "Why the door is nailed shut!" Whitt said. "That's crazy. The ghost would only have to walk around the door to get out."

"The innkeeper nailed it shut as soon as they tore it from the inn all those years ago," responded McDowd. He swore that there was a curse of some sort attached to the door. Some unpaid debt that the ghost wanted settled he reckoned." McDowd's expression was deadly serious. "But Father Eggleton is right about the door being for sale. If anyone's interested, one hundred Canadian dollars would buy it, cash and carry, of course. As an antique, it's really worth a lot more."

Whitt was looking thoughtful. He touched the door but jerked his hand away as a tingling sensation ran up his arm. "Just like the journal," he muttered. Sexton's eyes narrowed. Then the vicar broke the spell: "Well! If there are no takers, I guess we'd better be getting back to our card game and, perhaps, a little liquid refreshment, gentlemen. His smile seemed a little nervous, as he cast a backward glance at the mould encrusted door and noticing that Sexton still hadn't taken his eyes off Whitt. That visit to the door had set the atmosphere for a few ghost stories whilst the guests enjoyed some of Sexton's coffee, all safe and secure in the vicarage. Despite Al's initial disappointment at the lack of a spectacular bachelor party, Chernak and his guests thoroughly enjoyed the evening. He was in such a good mood that he made a bet with Whitt. "One cut of the cards, Earl. High card wins. If I win, you owe me a hundred dollars. If you win, I'll buy you the fo'c'sle door for your recreation room." Chernak smiled when he turned up the King of Diamonds, but Whitt turned up the Ace of Spades. The room erupted with laughter as the vicar said: "You get to take the door home, Earl – but the ghost goes with it!" Whitt's smile was somewhat contrived. He had mixed feelings about the door and no intention of claiming it. "Doo-doo-doo-doo," chanted Eggleton, mimicking the creepy music of a horror film. He'd been enjoying Sexton's coffee since supper.

CHAPTER 9

A picturesque wedding

It was Saturday, 29th of March, 2003 and when they awoke, the villagers of Ryeport were relieved to discover a beautiful morning with a gentle breeze was drifting picture perfect, white clouds across a pleasant blue sky and a temperature in the mid-sixties. The earnest prayers of all involved, from wedding party to TV crews, had been answered. Had the weather not cooperated, today could have been a disaster. Contingency plans had been made, of course, but a cold, rainy day could never have done justice to the colourful wedding they were all eagerly awaiting. This televised wedding should provide a great jump-start to the village's entry into the tourist industry.

However, Father Eggleton was not feeling at all well. He was sitting on the edge of his bed, holding his head in both hands and wishing that the walls of his bedroom would keep still. "Too much coffee," he grumbled. "I've got to straighten up." The naive young priest hadn't understood Chernak's warning last evening when the well-meaning groom-to-be had tapped him on the shoulder and whispered: "Be careful, my friend. Too much 'sunshine' will have you falling on your knees and sacrificing your all to the porcelain god." But Eggleton had never experienced the effects of too much alcohol before, and 'the porcelain god' was an expression he hadn't identified. He was relieved, however, that he was already in the bathroom when he had to perform his first act of sacrifice to that newfound deity. The horrible churning sensation in his stomach and the foul taste in his mouth was a frightening experience for the naive vicar. Fortunately, he managed to get to his knees before his stomach propelled some foul looking stuff from his mouth at great velocity. He hadn't realised how powerful his stomach muscles were until that moment. The other members of the bachelor party – all more experienced than he – were coping quite well, even though headaches predominated, and although they would manfully deny hangovers, most were looking forward to the time when they could face 'a hair of the dog'. But that was not yet. No one could face such medicine this early in the day. No one was hungry either. Coffee, just plain coffee – no 'sunshine' – and a slice of toast was a popular breakfast.

 Sexton decided to visit the vicar. He too had suspicions that the young man had been exposed to too much 'sunshine' than was wise last night. Now he was concerned that the man whose job it would be to 'tie the knot' might come unravelled before the young couple were properly 'spliced'. The vicar's door was not locked and after no response to his repeated knockings, Sexton let himself in. "Hello, Father! Where are you?" There was a mess of dishes in the kitchen. Obviously, the vicar's housekeeper and Sarah hadn't been here. He was about to go upstairs when he heard some uncomfortable sounding noises from the bathroom. "Uh-oh," he muttered. When Eggleton made his appearance, he didn't look at all well. It might have been funny had this not been such an important day. "Father, you need a tonic," said Sexton. "Let's go to my place, and I'll get one for you. I'll come back later for your costume. Elsie and Sarah will soon be here to clean up. I wouldn't want them to see you like this. Might think you were ill or, God forbid, hungover." Sexton got Eggleton into his dressing gown, draped one of the young man's arms over his own shoulders and walked him off to the 'digs'. Once there he made him swallow a concoction of his own invention, largely tomato juice and herbs, and put him to bed. Then he returned to the vicarage and collected the vicar's costume and a change of underwear. Sarah met him at the door. "Good mornin', Sexton. Where's the vicar? You boys 'ave a good time last night?"

"Yes, thank you, Sarah," said the smiling Sexton. "We had a great time. The food was excellent, as always. The vicar is getting changed at my place. We're checking each other out as far as costume is concerned. Bye." Sarah followed him to the door, looking very disappointed. "You could do that 'ere," she called after him.

The wedding ceremony was scheduled for 11 a.m. It was already 9:30 and, Sexton suspected that the bishop's horse drawn coach from Nextwest might be approaching the village already. The camera crews were already positioned to record every detail of this well publicised event. Eggleton, however, was feeling very sorry for himself. Sexton's 'tonic' had already been sacrificed to the 'porcelain god' and there had since been a few re-checks just to make sure his stomach wasn't withholding anything of value.

The groom and his best man, dressed in all their finery, were playing 'sword fighting' in the forecourt of The Harbour Light when suddenly, Chernak held up his hand for a cessation in play. "I've just remembered the size of the deposit I had to leave on the return – in good condition – of all this gear," he said. "We'd better take it easy with the swords, or I may have to cancel the honeymoon." So, he and Whitt began a leisurely stroll along the harbour front, where they met up with students. These young men were now dressed as eighteenth-century sailors and carrying the swords required for the nautical 'honour guard'. They all boarded the square-rigged ship where they had their photographs taken before resuming their walk to the church. "Okay, men," said Chernak, snapping to attention. "Fall in, in a column of threes or fours – or whatever's good for you. Then, follow me." He drew his sword, and, pointing it towards the church, commanded: "*CHARGE DEATH BEFORE DISHONOUR*." However, he'd only gone a few steps before he stopped abruptly, clutched his stomach and, in a much quieter voice, said, "*But ever so gently*." Whitt was amused. He'd never seen Chernak this playful. As this was happening, Sexton was wiping the vicar's face with a wet cloth and hoping to get the young man into a condition where he could don his costume.

A stagecoach arrived at the vicarage, and the bride's party alighted and went inside to get dressed. Following the tradition that had been handed down over the years, Heather and her attendants would walk the short distance to the church. The stagecoach turned around and headed for a 'staging' area at the junction of the Ryeport and Coach roads. This staging/ parking area had been set up to allow guests to park their cars and arrive in style aboard the stagecoach. On the way, they passed the bishop's coach, also fully loaded and on its way to the church. Sexton was keeping a wary eye on all comings and goings and was very concerned when he saw the bishop's coach arrive. "Oh, God." he said. "I hope we won't have to ask the bishop to perform the ceremony." A crowd was already forming in front of the church, many of them in homemade costumes appropriate to the eighteenth century. There were even two horses tied to the old hitching rail at the boundary wall, adding a touch of restless colour to the gathering.

Sexton stepped outdoors for a quick overview of the situation. "This looks very much as it did when you were preaching here, Roddy," he said quietly. "I've missed you so much, old friend." But then, a broad smile slowly crossed his face as he said: "But I do believe you have been returned to us at last."

His expression became serious again on re-entering the church. "I wonder how our vicar's faring now. I think it's time for drastic measures." His pace quickened, and his manner became more attentive. Back in his 'digs', he poured a tot of rum and, concealing it behind his back, took it to the bedroom and helped the vicar into a sitting position. "Here, Father, this is the second stage of the cure," he said. "Bottoms up!" And he poured the neat rum into the unsuspecting man's mouth and held his jaw tightly closed. "You're a mean old bastard, Sexton. You nearly killed me." Sexton smiled. "Now, that's better! I was beginning to think you might not make it. Now I'm sure you will. Can you remember the service?"

"Yeah. Urgh!" Eggleton shuddered. "I'll never drink rum again."

"I'm sure you mean that – today anyway. Now, wash your face, and get dressed."

"Shower! I must shower."

"Okay. But time's getting very short. The bishop is already waiting for you. Go!"

The bishop thought that Father Eggleton appeared a little stunned when he congratulated him on the village turnout, but before he could engage Eggleton in conversation, Sexton appeared. "Please excuse the interruption, Your Grace, but Father Eggleton is required most urgently by the groom." He gave the bishop a quick smile, took Eggleton by the elbow and led him through the church, grabbing Chernak on the way just to give credibility to his actions. Once out of the bishop's sight, he excused himself to the bewildered Chernak and led the vicar back to his 'digs' via the cliff-face steps and the lamp-house catwalk. Eggleton was being led around like a zombie by his anxious mentor, who was constantly wiping his friend's face with a damp towel. The bishop was not given another opportunity to speak with Eggleton until after the ceremony.

The groom's party entered the church, and the ushers began seating the people. When Reverend Eggleton eventually emerged from the vestry, he seemed a little unsteady on his feet, but he smiled as he faced the groom and best man and asked: "Are you two ready?"

"Yes, Father. But maybe we should wait for the bride," said Chernak.

"As you wish," responded Eggleton. "It's your day after all."

There was a signal from the front door, and the organ began to play the wedding march. The congregation turned to face the door as the bridesmaids slowly led the procession down the aisle. Heather's tastefully modified gown suited the period perfectly, and she looked beautiful as she moved gracefully into the nave on the arm of her colourfully dressed father, Fred McDowd. Concealed movie cameras discretely recorded the event.

Heather thought that Father Eggleton's face looked greenish and rather 'waxy'. His eyes too appeared off-focus, almost glassy. She stole an anxious look at Chernak, who smiled and discretely held a forefinger to his lips as he gave a slight shake of his head. "You look absolutely beautiful, Heather," he said.

"So do you," she whispered. "But do you think the vicar knows where he is? And why is his face so green?"

"There's nothing wrong with my ears, my dear," the vicar whispered, as he inclined his head towards them. "It's just the walls won't stay still!"

"Oh, God!" said Heather.

"I'm sure He's watching," responded Eggleton. The music stopped, and the vicar braced his shoulders and began: "Dearly beloved. We are gathered here today, in the sight of God and this congregation, to witness the joining together of these two people in holy matrimony." The ceremony went without a hitch. After the signing of the register, Father Eggleton introduced the happy couple to the congregation as Mr. and Mrs. Chernak, and amidst polite clapping, the glamorous newlyweds took their first steps as man and wife. All eyes were on them and their entourage as they exited the church, where they were greeted by a well-practised salute from two post horns and an honour guard that raised their swords to form an arch as confetti and rice showered over them. "It's just like watching Hornblower," called one of the crowd. "How wonderfully romantic," commented a tearful woman. Chernak smiled as he turned to face his bride: "Did you remember to sign the prenuptial agreement, my dear?"

"Not funny," responded Heather, as her elbow found his ribs once again. All attention was on the bride and groom. Only Sexton noticed Father Eggleton disappear into the vestry where he made a beeline for the toilet. He refused any further ministrations from Sexton until he was shown the label on the sealed bottle of pink stuff that proved it wasn't one of his own concoctions.

Eventually, the newlyweds noticed the vicar's absence and, insisting that he be in the group photograph, sent people looking for him. "Would they mind if I bring a bucket?" asked the vicar, as Sexton led him from the 'digs'. Fortunately, Sexton had the young man quite presentable by that time. He looked well composed and a much paler shade of green when he took his place beside the bishop. Sexton gave him a 'thumbs-up' from the sidelines, before being drafted into the group himself. Chernak nearly ruined all their efforts at composure when he introduced the vicar as The Reverend Kermit Eggleton, but at least the smiles captured by the photographer that day were genuine.

Fred McDowd had a surprise for the newlyweds. A sparkling white, open carriage pulled into line ahead of the coach, and the bride and groom were driven on an extended tour around the village to wave to all the well-wishers before returning to the inn for the reception. There were lots of family 'heirloom' pictures taken that day. The coach and open carriage – together with wagons and buggies that had unexpectedly appeared – were filled and refilled many times over as people posed and cameras clicked. The TV people worked frantically to capture as much of the event as possible.

It was another two hours before the wedding party was seated in the marquee for the reception. A string quintet played quietly in the background, pausing only for the speeches. Chernak was prolific in his praise for Sexton's help and guidance but smiled as he said: "Father Eggleton has also asked me to extend his gratitude to Sexton for helping to make his appearance more colourful."

Eggleton and Sexton walked home together. Outside the vicarage, the vicar paused and fixed eye contact with Sexton as he said: "Sexton, I can't explain why, but I've had this awful feeling that something tragic would happen today." The young vicar gave a violent shudder before continuing. "There were times when I would experience a terrible chill – a feeling that something was sucking all the heat from my body. And that sensation was accompanied by a strange odour. Faint but repulsive. It may sound overly dramatic, but I had the feeling that something evil was lurking about, looking for an opportunity to inflict some vile act. But I first noticed those unsettled feelings when I saw how intense you were around Whitt on the cliff top. You two appeared 'connected' somehow – no one else – just you two and that damned door. When Whitt touched it, he quickly jerked his hand away. I'm sure you noticed. What do you think that's all about? I can't get that image out of my mind. I feel unsettled around that damned door. It sits on the cliff-top like some brooding, malignant, gateway, just waiting for the opportunity to open and expose us all to hell's demons. I had the feeling that today might be that day. I will really be glad when that door goes to Canada."

Sexton smiled. "You worry unnecessarily, my friend. Obviously, your mind was troubled by the stories surrounding the door. That, plus the aftermath of all that 'sunshine' – which was most likely responsible for those chills as well. I'm sure that Whitt was affected by the stories too. More than his macho personality would allow him to concede." Sexton gave the vicar a reassuring pat on the shoulder. "Everything was quite safe. We were on consecrated ground after all. And, if it was the stories that troubled you, remember that the door only opens for Sailmaker's ghost and then only on the anniversary of the wreck." He gave a quiet laugh. "Despite your fears, today went off very well. And you did an excellent job, by the way." Eggleton, however, looked very troubled.

But Sexton was disappointed. In having to take care of Father Eggleton, he had been unable to watch Whitt enter the inn in his captain's uniform.

• • •

By Wednesday of the following week, Sexton was busy at Archer's stable, overseeing the packing of three crates, one to hold The Seahorse figurehead, another for two old ship's lanterns and the last one for the fo'c'sle door. Some old fishing nets that Sexton had brought along – splashed with different coloured paints – were also being packed with the door. Archer was grumbling. "Why anyone would want this decrepit old junk beats me. Then to go to the expense and trouble of carefully packing and shipping it by airfreight is madness. Discarded fishing nets too! It's just a wicked waste of money!"

Sexton was quietly thoughtful. It had been almost two years since he had met a man who, working on behalf of a local orphanage, was trying to recruit mentors for children who had passed the preferred adoption ages and were consequently facing the prospect of remaining in the orphanage until they reached adulthood. Actually, the man wanted individuals who were prepared to become 'big brothers' to such children. He explained that those children badly needed an opportunity for a special, personal relationship – one on one – with an adult figure. He'd praised Sexton for his other charitable work and wondered if he might consider involvement in such a project. Sexton was well aware of the problems faced by such orphans and how much harder it was to place a child who had any form of disability. Such was the case with one 13-year-old boy, Jamie Farr. Jamie had a below average IQ and a poor attention span and, because of this, had spent nine years at the orphanage. Sexton met and felt sorry for the quiet, well-mannered boy who, despite the best efforts of the administration, had so often been bypassed. So, Sexton had taken him 'under his wing', hoping to compensate for some of those disappointments.

Some months after he had undertaken this responsibility, 'Nick' had appeared. "So now you have the last one," he'd said with a big, self-satisfied grin. Don't you think it was neat, how I led you by-the-nose to the orphanage? He's the last one, you know. The boy completes your required group of souls. He must go with you to Canada, of course. Bye for now. I'll see you at the restaging of the wreck." Then, before Sexton could respond, he'd given that cackling laugh that grated so on Sexton's nerves and disappeared.

Jamie had enjoyed many outings with Sexton but had been particularly thrilled when he was called to the orphanage office and asked if he would like to go to Canada for a few days. Jamie always enjoyed his time with Sexton, who took him to shows, sporting events, the movies, mini golf or boating. Now, in preparation for that visit to Canada, he was helping Sexton with the packing of the artefacts from The Seahorse. He looked up from wrapping corrugated cardboard around the figurehead and asked: "Why are we sending all this stuff to Father Charlesworth in Toronto, Mr. Sexton? I thought you said it was for Mr. Whitt."

Sexton tapped the side of his nose with his forefinger as he replied: "Because, young Sir, this 'stuff' happens to be an important piece of Ryeport's history and I intend to explain that to Mr. Whitt to ensure he fully appreciates this 'stuff' as you so eloquently describe it. You may recall from the wedding that Mr. Whitt is an impatient man, not a willing listener. He won this door in a card game. But to be truthful, I don't think he was very excited about it. Certainly, he'll not be expecting anything more than the door. Anyway, I made arrangements for my good friend, Father Charlesworth, to hire a van and collect these crates from the airport. He will help us deliver the 'stuff' personally. With a priest present, I'm sure Mr.

Whitt will mind his manners long enough for me to explain things to him. Father Charlesworth is an old friend of mine and has agreed to do me this favour. We met many years ago at a seminar."

Jamie's forehead creased in a frown. "What's a seminar?"

"Oh, it's just a gathering of students, listening to a teacher speak about a particular subject. Rather like going to school but for a short period."

"And that's where you met Father Charlesworth?"

"Yes, he was the teacher."

"What was he teaching?" Sexton heaved a theatrical sigh. "Boy, you're full of questions today. My friend is an expert on different religions and was talking about the way that the natives of the West Indies had accepted the Roman Catholic religion by blending it in with their own African religion. But that was hundreds of years ago."

"Why would you be interested in that? Religion's boring. Two would be twice as boring, especially having to go all that way to hear about it." Sexton smiled and rubbed Jamie's head. "Yeah, I guess you're right. But my ancestors are from the West Indies, and I was interested. Besides, that wasn't the only reason I went to Canada that time. I happened to be there on other business, and the seminar just happened to fit in with my other plans. Now, if you've finished with all your questions, perhaps we can get 'this stuff' into the boxes and be done with it. I could use a cup of my special coffee. How about you, Archer? Care to join Jamie and me in my 'digs' for coffee and a good, toasted ham and cheese sandwich?" Archer nodded. "Best offer I've had all day. Let's get this lot on my lorry. Then we can stop off at your place on my way to the shippers."

• • •

Sexton and Jamie Farr arrived in Toronto a week later. Jamie was overawed by the luxurious hotel on Toronto's airport strip. As long as he could remember, he had lived in the orphanage just outside of Nextwest in Cornwall. Now, in the past 24 hours, he'd been driven in a limousine to London's Heathrow airport, experienced his first plane flight – first class, no less – and was presently a guest in a world class hotel. He was living his most exciting adventure. In the hotel, he was allowed to push the buttons in the elevator and use the key card to enter their spacious suite with his own bathroom, lounge area, and TV. His excitement as he assimilated all of the new experiences was refreshing and contagious. Sexton was smiling as he experienced these familiar things anew because of the lad's obvious pleasure. Later, comfortably seated in the dining room, Jamie still appeared to be in a wonderland. The menu was so varied that making a choice had been difficult for him. He had followed his full meal with strawberry cheesecake and had struggled to finish the last of his dessert. "Stuffed to the gills," he said as he downed the last mouthful. Sexton teased the lad. "I bet it's not as good as the food at The Harbour Light, Jamie. You always told me how much you enjoyed that. Here, Jamie, take the keycard and enjoy the 'telly', while Father Charlesworth and I talk. You won't get lost now, will you?"

"No, Sir," replied Jamie. "I won't get lost; I know my way now."

As the lad disappeared, Father Charlesworth said: "Now that we're alone, Paul, we need to have a serious talk. You, my friend, have got me worried over this reenactment business. Although we've spoken of it before, I must confess I never believed you intended to go through with it. Until you asked me to see those crates through Customs, I thought that idea would fizzle out, and die a natural death." Sexton smiled. "Did you have any trouble with Customs, Doug?"

"No. Not at all! They opened the crates, of course, and were puzzled by the condition of the door with its film of mould and little clumps of vegetation. I told them that if they'd stood in a churchyard on England's Cornish coast for as long as that door had, they'd have grown roots as well, never mind gather mould. No, the goods are not the problem. What I'm concerned about is your motivation for all this. When you last spoke about restaging the wreck of The Seahorse, I thought you were just extrapolating some reincarnation theory. If I remember correctly, you originally intended to have that take place in Ryeport. Wasn't that why you bought the tall-ship and then connived to have the wedding changed to a costumed affair?"

"You're right, Doug. Actually, I leased that ship with the intention of fitting her out with The Seahorse figurehead and door and rewriting the name on bow and stern. She was to suffer the same fate as the original Seahorse and on the anniversary of the original wreck. But I needed certain 'souls' to be aboard at that time, and most of them were in Canada. I was contriving ways to get them to Ryeport in time for the event when Heather totally wrecked my plans by bringing her wedding date forward. Her grandmother is terminally ill with cancer and becoming more frail every day. When she told Heather how badly she had wanted to see her married in Ryeport's

Guiding Light church, and thereby maintain the family tradition, Heather determined to grant her that wish. Well, that destroyed my plans for this anniversary. It was impossible to overcome all the obstacles in time. But then Nick showed up. He said that although the wreck did have to be on the anniversary, it didn't have to be in Ryeport. All I needed to do was identify some representation of the ship as The Seahorse and he would stage the wreck anywhere I chose I didn't even need a complete ship. The door and figurehead would be ample identification for his needs."

Charlesworth was looking very concerned. "Paul, you have let this reincarnation theory become an obsession. You are sounding like the script for a cheap horror movie. I never thought you would go this far." Sexton hung his head – trying to conceal his impatience. "Doug, I know we'd had our share of wine when we last discussed this, but you've heard the full story of The Seahorse many times. My biggest disappointment has always been that in all the years we've been friends, you have never managed to visit Ryeport. Your background in paranormal studies would have helped you recognise that there was unfinished business there; I'm sure of that. If only we had both been there when Whitt entered The Harbour Light, I'm sure his reaction would have convinced you." He gave a shrug of resignation. "Doug, I really was desperate for your guidance in this matter. Why is it that your planned visits are always cancelled?" He raised his hands in an expression of frustrated disbelief. "Take this last time, for instance. You were actually leaving for Heathrow when your bishop called you back, cancelled your vacation and ordered you to Boston so that you could run a seminar there. What lousy timing! What happened to cause that? You seemed rather vague when we spoke on the phone."

"Paul, my first instructions were also vague. And please understand, I wasn't asked to handle the seminar in Boston – I was 'instructed' to. Father Jattori was scheduled to give the intended lecture there, but he and his assistant were involved in a freak accident. A window fell from a large office building as they were passing underneath. The assistant died when he saved Father Jattori by pushing him to safety. Well, almost safety. Father Jattori was also injured. At that time, I was the only person available with seminar material prepared, so I was instructed to take his place as a speaker. When I arrived in Boston, I made a point of visiting Father Jattori in the hospital. I learned that, aside from the seminar, he had also been asked to investigate a bizarre series of events in a house in the city – a demonic possession. He had been on his way there when the accident happened. If he thought it necessary, he had permission to perform an exorcism. Now, that is a rare event, and before I met Father Jattori, I had never met anyone who had been involved in an exorcism. Another priest, Father Lucas, had since been assigned to replace Jattori as the exorcist. He has done this work before. However, I was very nervous when I heard that I was to be his assistant. But, as it transpired, events at the house had escalated, and the exorcism had already begun – with the priest who had initially reported the possession assigned to assist him. It was all over by the time I arrived. The first thing I noticed when I entered the house was the awful putrid smell and the freezing cold. It was unlike anything I had ever experienced before. Both priests were exhausted, absolutely drained, but I had a chance to talk with them later."

'Remember the smell!' Father Lucas said to me. "It's always the same. If you ever wonder if there is an active demon present, the smell will confirm it. It might be faint at first, but it grows stronger during the confrontation. However faint though, you will recognise it now because you've experienced it. Everyone in the room will experience a dreadful chill – a deadly cold that seems to invade every pore of your body, draining all warmth in the process. The demons also have a faint halation around them, but unless you'd seen it before, you might not notice it. But it's always there, no matter how they try to conceal it. The demon can appear in many forms, but to people that have confronted demonism, those two things will give them away. People with heightened psychic abilities are especially sensitive to it. They have been known to detect that awful smell, even if they've never encountered a demon before." Charlesworth's expression was very serious. "Believe me, Paul – it was frightening. And I was only there at the very last. The confrontation was already over."

Sexton was leaning forward in his chair, his attention fixed intently on his friend's face. "Did you actually see the demon?" he asked in an anxious voice.

"No! As I said, I arrived after it was all over." Sexton sighed and sank back in his chair, disappointment clearly written on his face. Charlesworth shrugged. "I understand the halation is barely perceptible, to the inexperienced eye at any rate. Father Lucas said you might think it was a light reflection."

"That must have been quite an experience."

"Once in a lifetime is enough, believe me, brief though it was."

"So, does this experience give my story of 'Nick' – as my demon labels himself – more credibility? You were always sceptical about him." Charlesworth looked puzzled. He raised his eyebrows, and there was a suggestion of a smile on his lips. "You never told me you were possessed, Paul. Just that Nick turns up now and then with instruction."

"No, no! I'm not possessed. Nick visits when it suits him or if it will advance his agenda."

Charlesworth looked uncomfortable. "Paul, I must confess, I am worried about you and this project of yours. I honestly thought you were obsessed about this shipwreck business and that that maybe caused you to attribute supernatural causes to some coincidences. But what you're proposing for tomorrow is like calling on the devil to raise the dead. I dread to imagine my bishop's reaction if he ever learned of it." Sexton's expression was very grave. "I realise that this could put you in a serious predicament with the church, Doug." He shrugged. "You shouldn't participate in this. I can manage from here on my own. There's no need for you to be involved any further."

Charlesworth raised both hands despairingly. "You are guaranteed my help, Paul. Our friendship is too deeply rooted for me to turn my back on your problems. Besides, my interest in the subject of reincarnation makes this a 'can't miss' event. I am intrigued by your plans. Especially all the money and effort you have expended to make this come to pass. Not that I believe it will, mind you. However, I am sure that I would be cast out of the church if news of my participation ever came to light. I can just imagine trying to explain myself. 'My friend and I were only trying to resurrect some dead guys, from two hundred odd years ago. One of them was killed in a brawl when he should have drowned, and we needed to correct that. Unfortunately, we needed the help of a demon to arrange that. But this was a one-time event; we'll not do it again, I promise!'"

Sexton was quiet for a few seconds before making fresh eye contact with his friend. "Look, Doug, I don't want to put you on the spot. I'll drive the van tomorrow. I can take things from here. There is no need for you to be involved any longer. And believe me, Doug, I couldn't be more grateful for the help you have already given me." Charlesworth sat back and raised his eyebrows. "You'll drive the van! I've seen you drive. More like a teenager trying to prove he's worthy of a Formula One car. Just imagine how great you'd be driving on the other side of the road in a strange van where the controls are on the other side of the vehicle from what you're used to. Quite apart from anything else, I've decided I like Jamie too much to let you do that to him."

"I still intend to drive, and maybe you should wear civvies. Take off the collar."

"Why?"

"You shouldn't be seen to be involved in an act such as this. It would end your career and destroy your reputation and credibility. And it doesn't have to succeed for you to get into hot water, does it?"

"No! But tell me again to be sure I understand it. You are going to set up a skeletal representation of The Seahorse using those genuine artefacts, hoping that they will sufficiently identify the 'ship' to the dark powers that will be assisting you. That door, etcetera, is to provide a positively identified target for them to aim at, so to speak. A variation of the voodoo doll routine." Charlesworth did a theatrical Bella Lugosi imitation, accompanied by some creepy, musical, doo-doo, doo-doo noises. "Then you plan to tell the story of the wreck and get the people at the building site to stand in for the original sailors. Because, you say, these people are reincarnations of the original crew?"

"Correct."

"Does that mean that they are reincarnated souls?"

"Yes."

"How can you know that?"

"As I said before, Doug: The 'demon', Nick, says that all souls aboard The Seahorse were 'marked' at the time he wrecked The Seahorse. He can read that mark on a person. He has a job to know where to look for them in the first place, and even when he finds them, he can't identify the individuals. All aboard, crew and passengers carry the same mark."

"And one of these reincarnations is the original captain. The one you say killed your daughter in that past life?"

"True."

"Which one is the captain?"

"I believe it's Whitt. But I won't be positive until he steps up and takes the captain's place. In fact, I don't know who is who of any of them. I tried hard to prove or disprove that it was Whitt when he was in Ryeport. I thought his reactions at the inn would be my best chance for positive identification. That's why I wanted you there. But that didn't happen. Whitt certainly responded fearfully in The Harbour Light Inn though. He almost threw a fit. He also reacted strangely in the old church. That was where the dead from the ship were taken."

"Have you got the whole crew accounted for?"

"No. The reincarnation timing is affected by who dies prematurely and who lives beyond normal life expectancy. There are too many variables, especially when compounded over several generations."

"Then you may not have the captain at all. What about Sailmaker? Is he amongst the assembled group?" Sexton hung his head. "I can't be sure. Whitt certainly behaves like the captain. His character is in keeping with Captain Currie's, and he responds in a fearful way in The Harbour Light."

"Can't your friendly little demon help? After all, if we are to believe any of this, he's the one who screwed up all those years ago. A little extra effort on his part would go a long way towards his making amends." Sexton sighed, looking weary. "We don't live in the eighteenth century any longer. Families move, emigrate, marry, break-up, remarry and have affairs. It's not as simple as following a family tree. We have been searching for over two hundred years, several generations, and this is as close as we've come to forming a quorum."

"A quorum? What is this, some sort of management meeting?"

"Oh, cut me some slack, Doug." Sexton was getting exasperated. "'Nick' said we won't be able to get all the crew as living beings. Some souls will be in limbo somewhere." He waved a hand in a despairing gesture. "Others may be newborn, whilst some might be on their deathbed. Who knows? But I must get a core group together; Nick can 'borrow' the other souls – his words – for just a brief period. They will black out, or something, whilst their souls are with us. Then they'll be returned none the worse for wear. We will have a full crew, but some will have less substance than others, he says."

Father Charlesworth was looking at Sexton in shocked disbelief. "Just listen to yourself. You really do sound like some cheap horror novel. None the worse for wear, you say! What if one of those souls happens to be landing a 747, when Nick 'borrows' him' or driving a high-speed train? My God, man; if one of these guys gets 'borrowed' just as he is about to abort a nuclear strike, you could even start World War III. If he's such an expert, why doesn't Nick know where to find these souls? This event has to take place tomorrow afternoon on the anniversary of the wreck." Sexton nodded. "Yes."

"How will you arrange that?"

"I won't. Nick will."

"Oh, your friendly little demon. Really, Paul, I think you're headed for the funny farm."

"Oh, I think my final destination will be a lot worse than that and warmer than I'd like but unavoidable. I could never have got my core group together in Ryeport; they are too scattered. It was a lot of work and very expensive just getting them together here, where most of them live. Nick found one member of the marked crew in a hospice in Sydney, Australia. He was eighty-seven years old and dying of lung cancer. There would have been no chance of my bringing him to England to be a member of our core group. But, if he is still alive, Nick will "borrow' his soul for a few seconds of real time for the re-enactment. Another is a schoolteacher in Hong Kong and a third is in prison in Arizona. How could I have arranged for these people to get together in Ryeport – and in time for tomorrow's little show? And should I tell them: 'By the way, one of you – we don't know who – won't make it home because we'll have to drown him. But do have a nice day!' No, Doug. Nick's idea of the 'quorum' and 'borrowing' the rest for a few 'accelerated' seconds seems like the best way."

Charlesworth looked grim. "And, of course, you know you can trust good 'Old Nick'. He's one of the good guys...right? Just look at his impeccable references. But what if one of your essential bodies doesn't show... Whitt, for instance? Or, what if tomorrow, the captain's latest reincarnation is a newborn?"

"Well, Whitt will show. I'm sure of that."

"How can you be so sure?"

"Because I sent him the bills for the air freight, the van rental and my own and Jamie's airfares and hotel suite. He will be raving mad and want to get at me. Money is his God. He becomes a raving lunatic if he thinks he's being screwed. He'll be there. About two hours after me."

"How can you be sure of that?"

"I sent him a couriered message, special delivery, bills attached, saying I'd be at the building site at 1 p.m. I've arranged for him to get that message at noon on the dot. I know he has a lot of paperwork to catch up on after his trip to the UK, and he'll be stuck in his office all week. But I shall be at the site by 11 a.m. I need to get things set up and rolling before he gets there. Then, when Whitt arrives to confront me with the bills, I'll tell him it was a clerical error and that I've already paid the bills – which I have, by the way. That should allow him to enjoy the show until he gets 'on stage' anyway."

"What if the other guys at the site leave?"

"They won't. They have two or three days' work left, and Whitt is 'phoning' them every day, threatening penalty clauses, withheld payments and goodness knows what else. They'll be there. They badly need their payment. They're stretched to the limit financially."

"How do you know all this?"

"I arranged for a lunch truck operator to chat with them daily. He's become the contractor's buddy. I pay him to call me every day with every fresh piece of news, no matter how trivial: work-in-progress, who has a cold, dental appointment, whatever."

"Who did you get to do that?"

"Todd, the coffee truck guy. He too was 'fingered' by Nick as from The Seahorse. You wouldn't believe how difficult it's been to get and keep these people together for this anniversary. I needed Whitt and his contractor, Smitty, also an ex-con named Denton, and Todd. None of these guys even knew each other before I set this up. The fact that these four were all in Ontario helped enormously. There is one more 'crew member', quite local Nick says, but he wouldn't let me contact him. It's too sensitive he said, and I could prejudice the whole deal. But he will make sure that he'll be there.

It's a good job that I have plenty of money; otherwise this could never have come together. Through a law firm that I purchased; I stole Whitt's original contractor away by paying him a big bonus if he agreed to work exclusively on a house that I'd purchased just for that purpose. Then I offered another contractor, Smitty, a fat contract to finish Whitt's house, but he had to employ another of my 'crew' for the life of the contract. Whitt, of course, is number one in my group. Smitty was number two, and the employee that was bound to the contract was number three. But I had to get rid of Smitty's original helper first. To do that, I gave Smitty's helper a farm outside Calgary, with strings attached that would keep him there. That tied three of my crew together. Then I overpaid Todd to go miles out of his way to provide coffee and food at Whitt's place. That was number four. This has been expensive, but now four of my 'essential group of six will be 'on deck' at Whitt's house in time for the restaging of the wreck. Nick will provide the fifth." Sexton paused, looking a little shamefaced, as he added quietly: "The sixth is Jamie. He completes the minimum sized 'live' quorum."

"My God! You've set up Jamie for this fiasco too?"

"Doug. I know it sounds mean, but Nick says that all the souls of The Seahorse crew were locked into a sort of endless holding pattern in the reincarnation cycle that prevents them from moving on. They have been sidetracked. All of those aboard The Seahorse at the time of the wreck, me included, are living less than normal lives, because of all this unfinished business."

"This has really become an obsession with you, hasn't it?"

"Well, you could say it's a matter of life and death. My several lives and deaths, in fact. I'm tired, Doug. Not naturally tired but empty somehow. I need to move on. This version of immortality is like living with a deadly debilitating disease."

"You scare me, Paul! You know I give some credibility to reincarnation theory, but you've really gone overboard with it. And the revenge aspect isn't good. 'Vengeance is mine, said the Lord.'"

"I know! I know!" The impatience in Sexton's voice was clear. "Believe me, Doug, if I could get out of this, I would. Honestly! I have no interest in revenge. When I saw Captain Currie's dead body, my need for revenge just drained away. But my daughter drowned before the wreck of The Seahorse and my unintended pact with the devil, so she was untainted by Nick's marking. She will have been reborn several times over by now. In fact, I believe I know her in her present reincarnation. If I'm correct, then you know her too. But those souls that were marked during the wreck of The Seahorse will have led troubled lives. That 'marking' even extended into the village of Ryeport because of Nick going berserk on the ship. He paid no attention to how wide an area he was affecting. However, this event should lift whatever curse that his 'marking' has imposed on people in the village too. I can't know that for sure, of course, but I am pretty sure that I will not be on that plane back to England later this week. I'm sure that

I'll be dead. I hope so anyway. I've had enough of this style of immortality. So! Can I prevail upon you for one last favour, Doug?" Sexton inclined his head, questioningly, towards his friend. Charlesworth sighed. "Of course, but only because I think that you are deluded, Sexton. I hope so anyway. I was looking forward to many more years of discussion and arguments with you. They're always entertaining."

"Well, I would have liked that too, Doug. However, my present concern is for Jamie. Will you see that he gets home safely? I had no choice but to bring him. He too was 'fingered' by Nick and has had a poor quality of life to date. I've left money for expenses and a return ticket for you from Toronto. It's in an envelope that I have given to Jamie. I had hoped to see the lad set up with a family that would adopt and love him, but the timing will not allow me that pleasure. I would really appreciate it if you would be kind enough to keep in touch with Jamie and make sure he's okay. I've set up a trust fund for him. My lawyer also has your address and my instructions."

"Of course, I'll look after Jamie, Sexton – should that prove necessary. Enough of this morbid talk though. I hate misery. One more glass of wine to end this evening on a happier note. Then I must be off. Good job I didn't drive today. I'll get a cab at the door. Let's all breakfast here tomorrow, about eight-thirty. I'm looking forward to seeing what Jamie might have to say about a hearty Canadian breakfast, hash browns, beans and all. Then we can set off on this crazy mission of yours. By the way, did you bring any of your famous rum? Supplies must be getting pretty short by now."

"Oh, yes. I've brought enough to 'whet the whistles' and stimulate the listening appetites of the building crew. As a rum and orange beverage though. Not straight up." The two men finished their extra glasses of wine, laughing and talking of old times. Eventually, Sexton signed the bill, put his friend into a cab and watched it disappear into a maze of weaving taillights. He shook his head sorrowfully as he headed for the elevator. "By God, Doug, I'm so sorry that our time together is almost over," he said quietly. "It's a long time since I had a good friend like you. I do hope we meet again."

. . .

Shortly after eight o'clock the following morning, Father Charlesworth called Sexton's room from the lobby of the hotel. "Is young Jamie ready to entertain us with his enthusiastic appetite, Paul? I'm looking forward to enjoying breakfast in his company – especially since you're still buying. By the way, how's your head? Mine's a little muggy." Father Charlesworth's voice was upbeat, despite a mild hangover. "Serves you right," responded Sexton. "You chose the wrong vice, my friend. You don't get hangovers from sex." Sexton enjoyed getting in his digs on the celibacy issue. "How would you know?" responded Charlesworth. "Certainly not from experience? Get down here before they run out of coffee."

After breakfast, Jamie was given the key card again, and the two friends settled down to organising their arrangements for when they got to Whitt's building site. Two coffees later, they collected Jamie, and the trio and their 'antique' cargo were en route. At 11 a.m., right on schedule, the van pulled into Whitt's driveway. Smitty's truck was already there, also an electrician's van, but the workers were busy inside. Half an hour later, the crates containing The Seahorse's artefacts were open, and Sexton began pulling fishing net from one of them. "What in heaven's name are you planning to catch with these?" asked Charlesworth.

"Oh, these are my floor plan, Doug. Or, more accurately, my deck plan. Full scale too," replied Sexton. "These old nets are cut to the exact size and shape of The Seahorse's upper deck. We'll spread these on the ground, green painted edges to the right – green for starboard side of the ship. Red painted edges to the left; that's the port side. You'll see that the net is pointed at one end and sort of square at the other. Pointy-end, yellow paint, is the bow or front, and square end is the stern, or back end if you prefer. Now, we must lay this on the ground and point it to the same compass heading that The Seahorse was using all those years ago. The net is folded down the centre of the ship, the white line. That parallels the keel. We straighten the net out and align that first."

He pulled a small compass from his pocket and, moving to the 'pointy-end', dragged the net to a new orientation and secured it with a tent peg. Then he moved to the rear, stretching the net to its full length as he went. Once he was satisfied with the alignment, he secured that too. Then he invoked the aid of his helpers to unfold the net to its full width. "Looks like you've done this a few times before," said Charlesworth. "Yes, my friend. I certainly have, but this time I've got help. Makes things move a lot faster." Returning to the packing crate, he removed two, hinged, wooden frames, which opened to form four-foot high gate legs. He set these up on the back of the net – one at each corner. Going back to the crates, he returned this time with two old ship's lanterns. One was badly battered, but the other was in fairly good condition. These he hung on the corners of the gate legs. "Guess what, lads? That's the back of the ship, and these are the original stern lanterns. Get the idea now?" Charlesworth and Jamie looked at each other as though Sexton was a little mad. Charlesworth even used his finger to draw a few circles alongside his head, as he winked at Jamie. The youngster laughed. "Mr. Bass will be mad when he finds you've pinched the lamp from the front of his inn, Sir."

"Don't worry, Jamie. I've already bought him new ones. They are actually being installed today, by a firm called Albright Lighting from London." Sexton was growing more excited now. "It's beginning to take shape," he said.

"But it will never float," responded Charlesworth with a smile. Jamie laughed, but Sexton was too focused to join in the fun. "Would you get me the remaining lumber from the crate please, Doug?" The next assembly was set at the bow of the ship –the pointy-end. "Here's our bowsprit, lads," said Sexton as he bolted another eight-feet long piece to the assembly. "Now that's set up, we can mount the figurehead." Sexton and Jamie supported the rather distressed looking Golden Seahorse, whilst Charlesworth hooked it to two pieces of chain dangling from the two-by-four 'bowsprit.'

"There, my friend, now we have the front and the back of our ship all set up and pointed in the right direction." Sexton was smiling. "We have to exercise a little imagination from hereon though because we don't have the ability to build more than one level of deck. Now we're ready to set up the fo'c'sle door on the port side, lively now. Rum ration and victuals are due after this." Re-enforcing bars were driven into the ground, at two painted spots, leaving about three feet sticking out of the ground. The door frame was soon secured to these supports. "But now the door can't open," protested Jamie.

"It's nailed shut anyway, lad, compliments of the innkeeper from a couple of hundred years ago. He didn't like what came through it one night. But it will open when it has to regardless of the ropes and nails." The Sexton was upbeat now. His skeletal ship only needed three more timbers, all 'spiked' eight footers. Those spikes were also pushed through the net at marked locations. "These represent the three masts: fore, main and mizzen," said Sexton.

At this time, the coffee truck announced its arrival by playing its little signature tune on the horns mounted over the cab. The basement door soon opened, and Smitty, Robbie Denton and the electrician exited. They all froze in their tracks as they saw the strange 'confloption' that Sexton had set up. Then there was an outburst of laughter as they all pointed at the 'ship' and tried to outdo each other with witty observations. Sexton just smiled and, ignoring their remarks, retrieved a large cooler from the van, together with an insulated bag. It was five minutes after noon when he announced: "It's lunch break, lads!" as he set the cooler and insulated bag on an upturned crate.

• • •

In Ryeport, England, however, it was already five minutes after five p.m., and the working crew were beginning to filter into The Harbour Light for some liquid refreshment. Some dark clouds were gathering off to the west, hinting at the possibility of rain. Opening day for Ryeport's theme park was only three days away, and there was some anxiety about being ready on time. Some workers and costumed attendants were hurrying to complete their tasks in time for this evening's dress rehearsals. The jobs all had to be completed by tomorrow, no matter how late the crews would have to work. Trelaw and his buddy were amongst the costumed attendants still working. They were rowing a dinghy through The Chute into Sorry Cove where they needed to put the finishing touches to some wiring in the skeletal 'wreckage' of a ship that had been set there to dramatise the dangers of the cove. In The Harbour Light, Holly was attending the bar when Mike Rooken stepped through the door. "Afternoon, Holly. Seen anythin' of Archer yet?"

"No, Mike, I haven't seen him yet. Can I get you something, or will you wait for your friend?"

"I'll 'ave a pint-o-best please, dear. I'll wait at the bar 'til 'e turns up. You're a much nicer picture than that ol' bean pole. Brighten the place up, so you do. Just 'avin' you 'ere gives new meanin' to the term 'appy 'our." Holly smiled as she set a pint in front of her stocky admirer, then coyly placed a forefinger under her chin and gave him her trademark curtsy. "Well, thank you, kind Sir," she said, then laughed and ruffled his grey hair.

CHAPTER 10

Re-stage the wreck

By this time, the building crew at Whitt's building site in Canada had exhausted their witticisms about Sexton's ship and were now plying him with questions. Robbie Denton, having recognised Sexton as the man who had offered the contract for Whitt's house, excitedly grabbed Smitty's arm to introduce him. "Smitty, this is the gent that arranged this contract for us. Say hello to Mr. …er." He struggled to recall the name.

"Sexton… My name is Sexton, Robbie. So, you must be Alexander Wilton-Smythe," said Sexton, extending his hand. Smitty looked puzzled as they shook hands. "Call me Smitty," he said. "Everybody else does."

"Very well, Smitty; pleased to meet you at last."

"Likewise," Smitty said as he scanned Sexton's features thoughtfully. "So, you're the mysterious guy that got us this contract? It was also your firm that brought my last helper, Andy, the good news that he'd inherited a farm. That news came out of the blue. Andy said, 'It was like finding a winning lottery ticket.' Now, by coincidence, you're here again? You seem familiar somehow and appear to be influencing my life in many subtle ways. Not always for the better!" He raised his right hand in a questioning gesture. "Have we ever met before?"

"I don't believe we've met before, Smitty. Not in this life anyway," Sexton responded with a smile. "In a past life possibly?" Smitty frowned and pointed at the mock-up ship as he asked: "Mr. Sexton, what's this setup all about? Whitt never mentioned anything about you being here today or this." The electrician and lunch truck operator, Todd, had joined the group awaiting the answer.

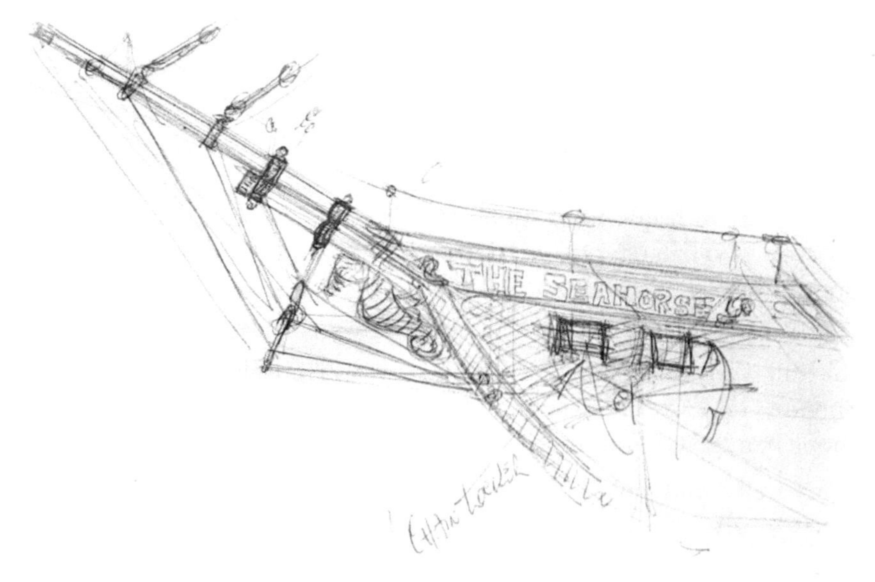THE SEAHORSE Co

"Oh, just a little light entertainment, Smitty. Mr. Whitt won that door with a cut of a card deck whilst he was in England. It's a genuine antique, the figurehead and lantern also. They were salvaged from a ship called The Seahorse that was wrecked there in the eighteenth century. Ever heard of it?" Sexton studied Smitty's face now as though expecting a reaction. Smitty shook his head, but Robbie Denton was looking very puzzled, staring first at the figurehead, then at Sexton, and then back again to the ship as though trying to focus on a distant memory. Sexton continued: "Mr. Whitt thought these items might add some colour to his new recreation room. He'd decided on a nautical theme, I understand. These genuine parts rescued from the wreck of The Seahorse are over 200 years old. Intriguing, wouldn't you agree?"

"Looks like pretty crappy stuff to me, Mr. Sexton. We could have made new ones for him in pretty short order, and they would have looked a lot better than these."

"Ah! But they wouldn't be original. The genuine articles are always more valuable, you know, and help bring the past to life. By the way, you can forget the 'Mister'. Just call me Sexton. Everyone else does." He smiled at the bemused Smitty as he borrowed his words to dispense with formality. "You see, Smitty, the history of our little fishing village in England – where this ship was wrecked – is a particular passion of mine. When Mr. Whitt won these artefacts and expressed an interest in using them in his entertainment lounge, I thought I might add some dimension and interest by telling the story of the ill-fated Seahorse. Setting up the items in this way helps people realise how small such ships were. It helps to provide a sense of proportion and atmosphere. Wouldn't you agree?"

"It'll never float," interrupted Robbie, laughing loudly as he looked around him for appreciation of his wit. "You're not original, I'm afraid," responded Sexton drily. "Come, gentlemen, it's a warm day, and I have brought some really good, cold orange juice in my cooler. It's nicely flavoured, I might add, with a little 'Caribbean Sunshine.'" He smiled. "That's what I call my special rum, Caribbean Sunshine. It's very old – matured in the cask – of course. I also brought some excellent pork pies, fresh buttered rolls, cold cuts, cheese and pickles. Why don't you lads pull up a crate and join us in a nice free lunch while I tell you a little about this dead ship? I'm sure you'll find it interesting. I even have a journal salvaged from the wreck. It was written by a survivor, the ship's cook. There are also some letters penned by two missionaries who were passengers at the time of the wreck. So, I can promise you, the story will be authentic." Smitty looked troubled. "Mr. Whitt is on my ass to finish this job on time, Sexton," he said. "He'll not take kindly to us sitting around listening to stories while there's work to be done. He'll withhold the payment due to us for completion of this stage. That could make life very difficult. I have bills to pay."

"Well, you're entitled to a lunch break, my friend. And you need have no fear as far as withheld payment is concerned. My office has already taken care of that for you, Smitty. Mr.Whitt will reimburse my office later. I should have thought to set up that arrangement sooner. Sorry."

The coffee truck driver was looking 'put out' as he watched Jamie and Father Charlesworth serving pies and orange juice to the crew. "Hey! What's goin' on then?" he said to Sexton. "I go out of my way to be here every day, come rain or shine. I make my livin' by sellin' food and drink to these guys. You're depriving me of my livelihood!" Sexton took the man by the elbow and turned him away from the others. "Relax, Todd. Have I ever treated you unfairly? Here, take this to compensate you for today's lost sales." He took a one hundred-dollar bill from his wallet and handed it to the lunch truck operator. "Don't I always send your cheques on time?"

"Oh!" Todd looked a little shamefaced as he took the money. "That's okay then, Sir. Just so's I know where we stand. Thank you. Er... could I try one of those pies perhaps?"

"Certainly, Todd, be my guest." Sexton waved towards the improvised table where Jamie was already building himself a ham and cheese sandwich as he popped the last of his pie into his mouth. Charlesworth was amused. "You are becoming a bottomless pit, young man," he said. Some of the crew were already coming back for refills of orange juice whilst others were joining Jamie in building fresh sandwiches. "Whew! I didn't realise how much I liked orange juice," said Smitty.

The crew were all seated, enjoying their free lunch when Whitt's Lincoln sped into the driveway, spraying dirt and gravel from under the tires. The vehicle was still settling on its springs when a very angry Earl Whitt stepped out. His gaze took in Sexton's improvised ship and the relaxed work crew enjoying their lunch,' and his body language left no doubt about his anger. "What the hell is this all about, Sexton?" he said, waving a fistful of bills at the mocked-up ship. "And where do you get off sending me airfreight bills and hotel expense, for delivering this pile of junk? And your personal travel expenses to boot?" Silence immediately settled over the work crew as they waited to see how this confrontation would play out.

Sexton smiled. "Ah! That was a clerical error, Mr. Whitt. Actually, I've already paid those bills. Consider it my treat. Good day to you, by the way. Sorry if I caused you any aggravation. I wanted to bring young Jamie to Canada for a visit, and this seemed like an excellent opportunity to kill two birds with one stone, as the saying goes. So here we are. Again, I apologise for the error. As I said: It's already corrected. The good news is, you have your goods early and at no expense to you. Feel better now?" He smiled and waved his hand dismissively at Whitt, paying his anger as much attention as one might expend on a bothersome fly. But then he fixed eye contact with the belligerent looking Whitt and, in a slower, more measured tone said: "Don't worry about the bills. They're all taken care of. Have a pie; they're very good…you'll like them. Some orange juice too…it's laced with Caribbean Sunshine."

Whitt's anger dissipated immediately. He nodded, collected a pie and a glass of juice, gave Smitty a nod and sat beside him. "Just like throwing a switch," said the dumbfounded Charlesworth. Everyone was looking at Whitt in amazement, shocked by his abrupt change of demeanour. "What switch, Father?" asked the puzzled Jamie. "Don't worry, lad. It's only an expression," replied the priest.

Jamie opened the journal. "Hey! Today's the anniversary of the wreck of The Seahorse!" he yelled. Sexton was quickly at his side. "Never give away the punchline, lad," he said as he took the journal from the lad. "It spoils the story." He stepped onto the fishing-net 'deck' of The Seahorse and turned to face his audience, pleased to see that Charlesworth had moved the cooler to a position easily accessed by the 'crew,' and then, without further ado, he began his story.

"Our story of The Seahorse really begins in 1792 in Ryeport, a small fishing village located on a hazardous stretch of coastline in Cornwall, South-West England. The arrival of the ship was eagerly awaited as it was carrying building supplies for the village's new church. After The Seahorse had discharged her cargo, the captain and his crew spent their free time between the ship and Ryeport's only inn, 'The Harbour Light'. Later that evening, after most of the crew had already returned aboard, the captain became inebriated and indecently manhandled the barmaid, Meg. Now, Meg was the innkeeper's daughter and the recent bride of a local hero, Stephen Riggs – known locally by his nickname: 'Sailmaker'. Well, Sailmaker happened to enter the inn just in time to see the inebriated captain taking liberties with his wife and knocked him down. A fight ensued, and the captain got the worst of it. Some crew members would have gone to their captain's aid, but the villagers rose to ensure fair play, and the crew backed down. Embarrassed, the captain and his men left the inn.

"It was intended that The Seahorse would sail at first light, but the captain wanted revenge for his humiliation of the night before. So, just prior to departure, he staged a fight on the ship's upper deck – to keep the attention of any village onlookers focused there. This gave his first mate and a couple of cronies the opportunity to slip ashore unnoticed, in the jolly boat to 'shanghai' Sailmaker. They surprised him, alone in his rigging shop, and soon returned to the ship with their unconscious victim lying in the bottom of their boat. None of the villagers realised what had happened. In fact, Sailmaker wasn't missed until noon, and by then The Seahorse was many miles away. In case any of you are unfamiliar with the term 'shanghaied', it's a nautical term for kidnapping.

"Now, as you can see from this very realistic reconstruction, The Seahorse was a handsome, three-masted barque. She was under the command of an ex-Royal Navy officer, Captain Currie. The captain was an excellent seaman and navigator but deserved his reputation as a sadistic bully. Much like the infamous Captain Bligh of His Majesty's Ship: The Bounty." Sexton held the journal aloft. "This is the cook's journal. It begins when the cook, a black man named Latour, was signed aboard the ship in Haiti. The ship's original cook, from the outbound voyage, had failed to return from shore leave, and the captain, who was not prepared to delay his departure by sending a party to search for him, gave passage to England to Latour and his young son, in exchange for their services as cook and cabin boy. As I said: Captain Currie was a sadistic bully, and he exercised every opportunity to terrify his crew with unjustified and harsh punishment. But the man he singled out for the worst treatment was the man who had bested him in Ryeport's inn: the shanghaied Sailmaker."

At this point, Whitt raised his empty glass to Sexton, in a questioning manner. "By all means, Earl, help yourself. Please, everybody, help your-selves. I don't intend to take any orange juice or food back." Sexton continued with his story. "During the outbound voyage, it had become clear that the captain had no intention of allowing Sailmaker to return to Ryeport. He took every opportunity to place him in the most perilous situations, hoping for a fatal accident. But he was often frustrated in the matter of punishment because The Seahorse was owned by the Missionary Society and carrying two missionary priests as passengers on this voyage, and they had made it clear that they would be reporting all the events of their journey to the owners of the vessel. The captain well knew that an unfavourable report would cost him his command.

"The Seahorse was homeward bound and only three days sail from London when it became clear that a storm was imminent. That caused the first mate to rig safety lines and prepare the ship for rough weather. The captain was alone in his cabin, enjoying a generous measure of rum, whilst he waited for this evening snack; a meal regularly served in his cabin by the cabin boy, Tiny. By the time darkness fell, The Seahorse was being buffeted by gusty winds, and rain was stinging the faces of the watch on deck. The crew had been fed and a foretop man, Brannigan, was entertaining the men below by singing ribald songs as he played his fiddle. Brannigan used to couch his fiddle in the crook of his left arm, rather than tucked under his chin. This allowed him to sing and play along at the same time. After months at sea, however, the crew, soon tired of Brannigan's overworked repertoire, and faced with an uncomfortable night ahead, they abandoned his entertainment in favour of sleep.

"In the galley, the captain's snack – hot soup, plus bread and cheese – was now ready. Tiny placed the linen-wrapped bread and cheese in his apron pocket and donned the oilskin coat that Sailmaker had cut down for him. Taking the handle of the soup kettle in his left hand, he reserved his right for the safety line. 'Careful now, Tiny,' said his smiling father, 'Remember we are only three days away from freedom and a new life, little one. Play it smart; our dark days will soon be over.' Tiny smiled back. 'Don't worry, Father. I'll be careful.' Opening the galley door, he grabbed the safety line with his free hand and Latour watched the youngster make his way safely across the heaving deck and through the door below the quarterdeck. Tiny passed the missionary's cabin and knocked on the captain's door. "Enter!" slurred the captain. Tiny, familiar with the captain's volatile temper, whispered his father's warning: 'Be careful!'

"In the galley, Latour smiled as he anticipated their arrival in London and patted his chest for the reassuring feel of the thin leather 'pouch' that he wore around his neck. That pouch contained a letter of introduction to Bishop Mason in London and was their ticket to a new life. One other item in the purse left the impression of a circle in both the letter and the soft leather of the pouch; that was his wife's gold wedding band. On her deathbed, she had made him promise to pass it on to their child at the appropriate time. The letter was grubby now, from the constant chafing in its often-sweaty hiding place. But there was another secret to Latour's pouch. It had once been his spell bag, for Latour had once been an 'apprentice' to his father, a voodoo priest skilled in healing, who had been gradually teaching his skills to his son.

"But the young Latour's ego had surpassed his social skills, and when his father had tried to teach him patience and humility, they had quarrelled, and in a fit of temper, young Latour had left home. A black magic priest (a Bokor) had seized this opportunity to flatter him and make him his apprentice, believing that the young man would be helpful in expanding his own area of control. However, when Latour discovered the black magic priest's real ambitions included a plan to kill his father, he had left him. But that had made a dangerous enemy of the Bokor."

• • •

Whilst Sexton was telling his story, life in Ryeport was going on much as usual. The arthritic Archer had just stumbled into The Harbour Light, saving himself by grabbing the supporting post that 'doubled' as a coat rack. "That door's a bloody death-trap. Someone will 'ave a bad accident over that step one o' these days," he grumbled as he perched on a stool beside his stocky friend, Rooken. But his friend gave him a derisive look and said: "I see you're still trippin' over yer own feet, Archer?"

"It's like a bloody obstacle course," moaned the arthritic beacon master. "First, you 'ave to smack the top o' the door so it scrapes free of the lintel. Then you 'ave to duck under that an' step down about a foot just to get in the bloody place. And it's bloody dark in 'ere, 'til your eyes get used to it." Turning to Sam Bass, he said: "You mark my words, Sam. Someone will sue you over that doorstep one day. Anyone would think you're tryin' to kill off your customers."

Sam Bass drew Archer his customary draught and set it before him. "No, they won't, you miserable old sod. People 'ave been steppin' through that door safely for over three 'undred years, an' you're the only one that's ever complained. Just look where you're goin'." Holly gave Sam Bass a scornful look and smiled at Archer as she mopped up the foamy overflow from his glass. "It would be easier, Archer," she said, "if the door didn't stick. I've asked Sarah to have a carpenter trim a bit off the top. It'll be fixed in a day or so. "Thanks, dear," responded Archer. "You're a pleasure to deal with, that's for sure. This is a much nicer place since you've been around. You look pretty in your costume too. Really look the part, you do. Where did you get the idea for the dress?"

"Oh, thanks, Archer! I copied it from a picture of Meg, the innkeeper's daughter, drawn by the wife of the vicar that designed the church. She drew a picture of your ancestor too, remember? Actually, I thought it was you when I first saw it. Then I saw the date."

"You were right the first time, dear," interrupted Rooken. "That was 'im alright. 'e's a bloody antique, 'e is."

"Well, you're in the same drawin'," snapped Archer. "Same date. But you never did look as good as me, short-arse!"

"Now, now, boys! Be nice," said Holly with a chuckle. "No one would believe you were such good friends, from the way you talk to each other."

"They'd be right too," said Archer. "Come on, short-arse. Let's get to a table and chairs. These bar stools make me walk funny."

"That's got nothin' to do with the stools," responded Rooken. "You've always walked funny." But he got down anyway, and the two costumed men made for their usual table and a game of cards.

• • •

Back at the building site in Canada, Sexton was continuing with his story. "Tiny's delivery of the captain's snack would prove to be the catalyst for the disastrous consequences that overtook The Seahorse the following day. Tiny entered his cabin at the captain's command. The missionaries, in the next cabin, reported that the captain's speech was slurred when he shouted at the lad: 'Where the hell have you been, boy? A man could die of starvation waiting for his next meal around here. Get over here before I take a belt to you for your tardiness.'

'Yes, Sir. Sorry, Sir.'

'Don't stand there dripping all over my table, boy. Where are your manners? Bloody black heathens, you're all alike. Get that bloody oilskin off. Leave it on the deck outside the door.' The priests heard Tiny open the door and drop the oilskin. They were familiar with the lad's regular routine, having been present on occasion to see Tiny set a placemat, then put a bowl and spoon upon it, while always avoiding eye contact with the captain and scared of being accused of dumb insolence.

'Come on, boy, come on. The bloody soup'll be cold,' they'd heard the captain yell. The missionaries had exchanged sympathetic looks, imagining the youngster's dread. Then they heard Currie shout: 'That bowl's dirty!' But that was quickly followed by his loud scream, causing the priests to rush into the captain's cabin. They found him standing beside the table, holding his steaming, soup-stained britches away from his thighs. Then he turned on the cowering cabin boy, and the anger on his face was frightening. 'You filthy black heathen! You did that on purpose. I'll flay you alive.'

'I'm sorry, Sir. But you pulled the bowl away, Sir, just as I poured the soup, Sir.'

The captain stumbled around the table, grabbed Tiny's shirt with his left hand and delivered a heavy, backhand blow to the child's face with his right. The force of the blow sent the youngster reeling and as he fell, his shirt tore open to the waist. All three men stood aghast when the ripped shirt revealed the developing breasts of a young girl. Tiny, the cabin boy, was actually a cabin girl. The shock caused the captain to release his grip on Tiny's shirt, allowing the child to scramble between the priests and run for the outer door. 'Well, well, our cook's been hiding secrets from us all this time!' slurred the captain. My nights could have been more entertaining had I only known.' He crashed past the priests, knocking one to the deck, before tripping on Tiny's discarded oilskin. 'Stop her!' he bellowed. 'Stop her!' Tiny had made it through the outer door to the upper deck, intending to run for the safety of the galley, but unfortunately, Ruddock was coming towards her on the same safety line, blocking her path to the galley. Tiny turned about and scrambled up the ladder to the quarterdeck with the first mate hurrying towards her. The captain arrived at the foot of the ladder at the same time as the mate, knocking him to the deck. Sailmaker heard the commotion and, seeing the youngster's plight, rushed to help.

With no place else to go, Tiny had climbed into the mizzen mast shrouds. She screamed when the captain reached through the shrouds and seized her ankle. Sailmaker struggled with Ruddock as they both tried to climb the quarterdeck ladder. The helmsman, distracted by the commotion, relaxed his grip on the wheel, allowing the ship to lurch violently. 'Mind your business, you bloody fool,' the captain screamed at him. Sailmaker had reached the quarterdeck, where a quick glance over his shoulder revealed Latour rushing from the galley. Other crew members were coming on deck, roused by the watchmen. Ruddock had regained his feet and tried to stop Latour and received a broken nose for his efforts. And so began a running battle with Sailmaker and Latour trying to rescue the girl and Currie and his cronies trying to beat them off. Tiny was tiring and having trouble holding onto the ratlines as her hands grew cramped and cold in the stinging rain. For a while, it appeared that Latour and Sailmaker would bring her safely to the deck, but they were eventually beaten down by greater numbers wielding belaying pins.

The captain was forcing Tiny to sidestep across the ratlines to the aftermost shroud. But as he released her ankle, to reach around the next shroud, she swung a kick outside them and connected with the captain's left eye. The blow tore flesh, and the blood flowed freely. Currie reeled away from the pain of the blow. Then, in a fit of extreme rage, he grabbed a belaying pin from one of his men and smashed Tiny's small hands with vicious, overhead blows. She screamed in agony as her broken fingers lost their grip. She fell into the sea and was quickly lost from sight. Latour was on his knees, both arms twisted behind his back, each held by a different man. He screamed through his pain. 'No! No! Put about. Pick her up. Please! Please! Pick her up.' The captain covered his bloodied face with his left hand and, ignoring the pleas of those asking him to save the popular 'cabin boy', said to Ruddock: 'Put these two men in irons,' as he kicked both Latour and Sailmaker on his way to the ladder. 'Are we to come about, Sir?' asked Ruddock. 'There's a chance we could find the boy.'

'No! We certainly will not come about. I'll not waste more time on deceitful, lying trash like these. Replace that helmsman with someone capable of holding the vessel steady. Trim the ship, men, and clean up this mess.' The two missionaries were kneeling in prayer at the foot of the quarterdeck ladder, and Currie grabbed the older missionary, Palmer, by the collar, dragging him to his feet. 'Come to my cabin and dress this eye.'

Many of the crew had witnessed the maddened captain smash Tiny's fingers with the belaying pin, and the missionaries had been party to virtually the entire incident, having heard the start of the captain's tirade through the thin partition that separated their cabin from his. But their efforts to help Tiny had been roughly brushed aside. The first mate and others jumped to obey the captain's orders and dragged Latour and Sailmaker below decks, hung a single candle lantern in the chain-locker and shackled them to a bulkhead there. Then they left, securing the door behind them. The eyes of the two men gradually adjusted to the poor light, and Sailmaker took stock of their surroundings. He was sure this would be their last stop before execution. 'How badly you hurt, mate?' he asked anxiously, as the swinging lantern splashed light and shadows across Latour's face.

Latour's grief was far more painful than his injuries. He was moaning softly. 'Oh, God! My poor Tiny. Oh, Tiny! Tiny! I'm so sorry! Louise, I failed to protect our daughter. Oh, God. Please help her. Please, please, help her. Why did you allow this to happen? Just a few more moments and we could have saved her. Why?' He collapsed and broke down sobbing. Sailmaker knew that Louise was Latour's late wife, but his friend had referred to Tiny as his daughter. He repeated his earlier question. 'How badly you hurt, mate?'

'I'm alright. Maybe a couple of broken ribs. Cap'n's boot did most of the damage. Are you alright?'

'I've been worse. Latour, I'm so sorry about Tiny. I couldn't get to him. Don't know how to tell you how sorry I am.'

'No need, my friend. I saw you trying to save her. Your actions spoke louder than any words. There's no hope now. She will be miles astern; a dozen ships couldn't find her now.' Even in that poor light, Sailmaker saw his friend's face twist into a mask of pure hatred as he said: 'Did you see that cowardly bastard smashing her small hands with that pin? He intended her to fall overboard. That was a vicious, deliberate murder of a child and in full view of the ship's company. What a gutless bunch they are. There was time to come about and save her. But why weren't they trying to help her before that? They just stood and watched. Why didn't that cowardly bunch toss Currie over the side and come about?'

'Because that would be mutiny, and they know that's a hanging offence.'

Latour was hugging his left ribs with his manacled arms, trying to cushion them against the jarring of the ship as she bounced and pitched in the rough sea. 'There were enough men witnessing Tiny's murder to convince any jury that there was just cause,' he said. 'That gutless bunch didn't even protest until she fell from the shrouds. Then it was too late.'

'Latour, why didn't you tell me Tiny was a girl? I suppose you didn't trust me any more than the rest of the crew.' Latour was silent whilst he struggled to find a position that would lessen the searing pains that pierced his chest every time he tried to breathe or speak.

Latour turned to face his companion. 'I'm sorry for not trusting you with the fact that Tiny was a girl. I signed her aboard as a cabin boy because I thought that the captain wouldn't accept a cabin girl as crew. I was also worried about the crew finding out Tiny was a girl. I honestly believed this ship would be our only chance to escape from Haiti, so I couldn't risk losing your help, Sailmaker. We really were desperate to escape the black magic priests. On this ship, I was able to keep Tiny with me. We almost made it though, didn't we? Only two or three days short.' Latour gasped in agony as his emotions demanded more air for his damaged lungs, and his wracking sobs brought frothy blood to his lips. 'I'm really grateful to you for helping me get this berth, Sailmaker. It wasn't your fault that things turned out so badly, and we wouldn't have survived in Haiti. In months of trying, we had never managed to get passage away from there. But you found a way to get me aboard The Seahorse – as crew. I was so relieved to get Tiny away from the Bokors. They had killed her mother and her grandfather and almost killed me. It would only be a matter of time before they would have captured her. So! Now you know the whole story, my friend. I will always be in your debt for getting us away from Haiti and for all the times that you helped us on this unhappy ship with her despicable captain. After all, you could have stayed at the mission and waited for another ship to take you home. I know you only re-joined The Seahorse to help us. Now, my friend, let's get some rest. Talking is too painful.'

The storm abated during the night, and Latour and Sailmaker finally found some relief in fitful sleep. The wind gradually subsided, and the waves eased to a rolling swell. That reduced the pain they'd experienced the night before as the ship crashed from crest to trough. The Seahorse was making roughly seven knots as she ploughed steadily towards her home port, and the watchmen saw the coast of Cornwall take shape off the port side at first light.

The two prisoners were wakened by the first mate – with his badly swollen nose – and two other crewmen. 'Time for you two sleepin' beauties to rise an' shine,' said Ruddock. 'An' shine you certainly will. You be stars in the mornin's 'men under punishment' parade. But don't worry, like you, all your troubles will be short-lived.' He laughed, as he nudged his companion. 'Mutiny – not many people get to do that twice – eh, matey?'

Sail was being shortened as the prisoners were brought on deck, and the vessel's speed fell away until it was just sufficient to maintain steerage way. The crew was mustered around the mainmast, facing aft. Captain Currie was standing on the quarterdeck, facing them and wearing his naval dress uniform complete with a sword and pistol. The other officers were also armed. Then, much to Currie's obvious annoyance, the missionaries put in an appearance. Reverend Palmer was carrying his Bible and a heavy brass crucifix, and just as Currie was about to address the assembly, Palmer spoke up: 'Captain, I would like to offer my services as a priest for these proceedings. These men deserve the comfort of knowing that God will....'

'Be silent, priest. You have no place in these proceedings.' The captain dismissed Palmer's words with a curt wave of his hand and addressed the crew. 'We are assembled this morning to witness punishment for the crime of mutiny. The accused men are: Stephen Riggs, known to you as Sailmaker, and Latour, the cook. These men conspired together to kill their captain and his first mate, intending to wrest control of this vessel from its lawfully appointed officers. Such conduct places the ship and all aboard in grave peril. This crime is well deserving of the capital punishment demanded by the laws of seafaring men, and there can be no doubt as to their guilt. Their conduct was witnessed by practically everyone on board. I have considered punishment appropriate for their crimes and decided that for Sailmaker – a well-documented troublemaker – that punishment shall be keelhauling. He will be dealt with first. Latour shall suffer death by hanging. Sailmaker's punishment will be carried out immediately. Latour will hang once the keelhauling has been dealt with. There are different versions of keelhauling procedure. This will be the simplest one. Sailmaker will be passed under the ship, starting on the starboard side, and drawn back up on the port side. Are the lines ready, Mr. Ruddock?'

'Aye, Sir. Ready.'

'Then proceed.' Sailmaker was brought to the starboard side of the ship, just below the fo'c'sle. His hands and feet were bound together. A rope had already been passed under the ship, and one end was now made fast to his wrists; the other end was brought from the port side, below the quarter-deck, and secured to his ankles. He was to be drawn under the ship with the ropes held tightly against the vessel, so as to scrape his body against the barnacle encrusted hull as he made the journey. Two men, Brannigan and young Newton, were to control the line at the starboard side whilst Josh Merry and Bellew, on the port side, would drag Sailmaker slowly around the keel. Brannigan and Newton would be responsible for keeping their line taut to prevent Sailmaker from effecting any swimming action – such as kicking his legs. 'Are you ready, Mister Ruddock?' asked the captain. 'Aye, Sir, ready,' was the response.

'Proceed!' Brannigan and Newton lifted Sailmaker to a horizontal position, above the ship's rail, preparing to cast him over the side. Once Sailmaker's body hid Brannigan's face from the captain, he whispered to Sailmaker: 'We'll hold the line slack, lad. Swim with yer legs. Jerk twice on the hand line when you're past the keel. Merry will pull you in faster then. Big breath now. Good luck.'

'What are we waiting for, Brannigan?' bellowed the captain. Sailmaker entered the water with a splash, and the men on the lines took up the slack. 'Heave away,' called the captain. 'Handsomely now.' Josh Merry and Bellew made a good pretence of pulling the line in slowly, but, in fact, they slid their hands along the line, allowing it to sag a little. On the starboard side, Brannigan was trying to give the appearance that he was keeping the line tight, but he'd positioned Newton so as to block the captain's view of his hands. He left enough slack for Sailmaker to 'kick-swim' his way down, going deeper under the keel than he was meant to. Once Merry felt the tug on the line, he brought Sailmaker up quite quickly. A faint smile played around the captain's lips as he watched the proceedings, but he said nothing. Sailmaker was brought aboard and laid on the deck, gasping, coughing and bleeding from several cuts. He remained still, giving the impression that he was worse off than he actually was.

'Well, well! It appears there's been some sort of conspiracy here,' said the captain as he descended the ladder. He inspected Sailmaker's condition for himself, ensuring that his boots struck the prone Sailmaker's ribs as he stepped alongside him. 'Surely, Mister Ruddock, you instructed those men on how to handle the lines before we carried out punishment.'

'Aye, Sir, that I did.'

'Well, it seems that they are slow learners. They didn't keep the lines tight. That allowed the prisoner to swim instead of being held against the hull. We'll just have to do it again.' A loud groan went up from the assembled company. The captain whirled around and, glaring at the assembled men, he raised one hand and slowly traversed the whole crew pointing a warning finger and pausing whenever he recognised any friend of Sailmaker's. 'And we shall keep doing it until they get it right. Wait!' He lowered his head and raised a restraining hand. 'Let's try a variation – feet first this time, Mister Ruddock. Toss him back in, right here. Well pull him feet first back to his starting point.' The crew had been silent during the keelhauling, but now there was a howl of protest. But the officers, all cronies of the captain, were armed so truthfully, there was little the crew could have done to prevent the punishment.

Once around was usually considered full measure in keelhauling. Few survived that and were rarely sent around a second time. Latour was particularly loud as he incited the crew to rebel and free Sailmaker. Captain Currie crossed the deck and slapped him across the face. 'Quiet, you. Your turn will come soon enough.' He turned to the first mate. 'This time, Mr. Ruddock, you will man the starboard line with Newton. Brannigan shall watch to learn how it's done. This shall be a training exercise for the crew. We'll teach them the proper way to haul a man around the keel. Then, if need be, we can start over, from the starboard side again. They should be getting the hang of things by then.'

The missionary Palmer stepped forward from the assembled men. 'I must protest, Captain. This punishment is inhuman. There has not even been a trial to convict these men. Practically the whole crew saw that these men were trying to save the life of a child, not seize control of the ship.' The captain's face was livid at this unwanted intervention. 'You, Sir, are a passenger aboard this ship,' he screamed. 'You have no voice here. Hold your tongue, or I shall have you locked below decks.'

'I may have no voice here, Captain. But I will certainly have a voice once we dock. You would be wise to remember that.'

'Your opinion, Sir, is just that, an opinion. And your opinion does not carry any weight in these matters. I alone am responsible for the safety of this vessel, and I will take whatever action I deem necessary to discharge that responsibility.' All through this confrontation, Latour was inciting the crew to rebel. Some of the men – emboldened by the missionary's words – were becoming increasingly vocal in defence of the prisoners. 'Enough of this,' shouted the captain, drawing his pistol. 'I shall shoot the first man that breaks ranks before I dismiss the crew.' His anger was boiling over, barely controlled.

When Currie returned to the quarterdeck, he paused thoughtfully before turning to face the assembled men again. 'Very well, since you obviously have no stomach for justice, I shall make a concession to your petticoat values. We all know how much Sailmaker wanted to see Ryeport again. We heard about it continuously. So, I shall grant him that privilege just to prove I am a compassionate man. Ryeport is just off the port bow. Sailmaker shall see his home again. On reflection, I think it only fitting, that his punishment should be carried out in view of his home. Raise him up, Mr. Ruddock.' Ruddock and another hand lifted Sailmaker to the ship's rail. 'Look, Sailmaker,' said Currie, 'you can even see the church they were building when we were here last. But I shall give you an even better view.' He turned to address the crew. 'I hereby change the punishment for Sailmaker to death by hanging. That should be an easier task for this inefficient crew.' Another howl of protest went up from the assembled men, but this time the captain ignored it. 'Send him up, Mister Ruddock. His last memory shall be of Ryeport."

Ruddock dragged Sailmaker to a position level with the mainmast. The noose that had been prepared for Latour was looped over a belaying pin there. The running end of that rope ran through a block secured to the outboard end of the topsail yardarm, about 20 feet above the deck. 'You should get a good view from up there,' Ruddock said to Sailmaker, grinning as he nodded towards the yardarm.

The injustice of these proceedings was robbing Latour of all reason. He was almost hysterical as he screamed at the assembled crew: 'What's wrong with you? This is murder, plain and simple. This is only happening because Sailmaker defended his wife from your drunken captain. Some of you even witnessed that. Any one of you would have done the same – or should have.'

'Gag that man,' bellowed the captain and again descended the ladder from the quarterdeck to strike Latour. The cook's wrists were bound in front of him, and he was being restrained by two men, each holding an upper arm of his. The only thing that Latour's desperately groping fingers could reach was the purse that hung around his neck, and he gripped that tightly as he screamed at the captain.

"Reverend Swift's letter to his bishop closely follows that in Latour's journal and this despite the fact that they never had time or opportunity for collusion in this matter. I'll ignore the opening salutation. Listen up now!"

Reverend Palmer and I were horrified almost daily by the ugly and unjust punishment of the ship's crew but never more so than by that selected for Sailmaker and Latour on the day these two men were unjustly condemned for mutiny. On the day that sentences were to be carried out, sail was reduced, and the ship was making only steerage way on a calm sea. The sky was clear with no hint of impending bad weather. Latour, the cook, had been sentenced to hang immediately following the keelhauling of Sailmaker, and he was inciting the crew to rebel and prevent these unjust punishments. He screamed at the captain: 'You are a vicious, cowardly bastard, Currie. You corrupt the very meaning of the word justice. True justice would have Sailmaker safely reunited with his wife and you keelhauled in his place. I'd willingly give my immortal soul to everlasting hell to see that!'

On hearing that last sentence from Latour, Reverend Palmer and myself crossed ourselves and prayed for his soul. Then suddenly, Palmer gasped, grabbed my arm and pointed to a stranger who had appeared beside one of the men restraining Latour. My Lord, I have never seen fear on my friend's face before, but his obvious recognition of that man terrified me.

Latour, the cook, was still raging at the crew, when the stranger pointed one hand at the captain and held his other – in a restraining gesture – towards the grouped crew. That was when Reverend Palmer stepped forward and hurled his heavy crucifix at the stranger. His aim was true, and the cross struck the stranger in the temple, knocking him off balance just as a blinding streak of light flew from his hand, narrowly missing the captain and striking the mizzen mast. The mast exploded, as though struck by a cannonball. Flames erupted amongst the debris, and panic and confusion reigned as tackle and broken spars fell like rain. One shattered spar narrowly missed Reverend Palmer and myself and hung close by, dangling from a rope that had snagged on a backstay. The helmsman had been completely buried under the debris, and the ship was no longer under control from the helm.

Men began to respond to the mate's calls to cut free the fallen mast and shrouds that now hung over the port quarter. That mass of material was dragging in the water, causing the ship to pivot around it and changing our heading towards the coastline. The eerie stranger was crouched against the ship's side, fingering his wounded temple and glaring hatefully at my friend. I rubbed my eyes and tried to convince myself that what I was seeing was merely a trick of light, but I swear to this day that the stranger was outlined by a glowing reddish haze that matched his every movement. He looked demented as, half-crouched and baring his teeth, he scowled and pointed to the splintered yardarm that had so narrowly missed us and motioned it outboard over the port side. My Lord, that broken spar followed his hand movement as if they were connected. When the spar reached the outermost limit of its arc, the stranger aggressively waved it back inboard and still obeying the stranger's hand, the spar hurtled back inboard to spear Reverend Palmer just below his ribcage. The force of the blow carried him, screaming, over the starboard rail before it swung back again, dragging his lifeless body head down, and arms trailing, across the deck. Eventually, it stopped amidst ship where it began slowly to rotate, as though intent on displaying my friend's agony to all quarters of the vessel. His eyes were wide and staring and his poor body soaked with blood, with the jagged end of the spar protruding from his back. I stepped forward fearfully, wanting to help him. But I was so overwhelmed with the horror of it all, I fell to the deck vomiting.

When I raised my eyes again, the angry stranger was prancing about crazily, making frantic, stabbing gestures towards the sky, as sparks flew from his fingers. Then, as if responding to his gestures, angry looking clouds gathered about the ship, and the sky darkened. Lightning began to flash all around us, and rain stung my face like a whiplash. My Lord, this all appeared to be a response to the stranger's bidding. A howling wind circled the ship with a noise that was made more frightening when the panic-stricken cries of the crew blended with it. It seemed that the gates of hell had opened, and hordes of tormented souls were clawing their way onto the ship. I covered my ears with my hands, fell to my knees and froze, petrified by the demented howling and my dead friend's eyes that begged me so desperately for help that I was unable to give. I could only watch as he slowly rotated on that hideous skewer. All aboard knew that the ship was beyond the help of human hands. My senses deserted me.

Sexton looked up from the letter. "Well, what do you think, lads? That hardly sounds like a natural shipwreck to me. Something evil had to be at work there." He scanned the group once more whilst tucking the letter back into the journal. They all looked uneasy, but Todd looked as though he'd just woken from a nightmare.

Sexton continued: "Sailmaker was lying against the ship's side when Josh Merry staggered to his aid and dragged him towards the fo'c'sle. He was about to cut the cords binding Sailmaker's wrists when Currie stumbled across the deck and knocked Merry down with the butt of his pistol. Then he opened the fo'c'sle door and pushed Sailmaker down the ladder, screaming: 'I'll deal with you later.' Sailmaker's hate-filled voice screamed back: 'I'll come for you, Currie, through this very door. This I swear by all that I hold dear. You shall pay for your evil sadistic ways.'

Sexton pointed to the old, mould covered door now staked upright on the deck of his mock-up of The Seahorse. "There stands the very door that we are talking about, lads. It has been staked upright, just like that, but on consecrated ground, for two hundred years because Sailmaker's ghost had come through it on the anniversary of the wreck for two years in succession following the wreck. The villagers believe he was looking for Currie then and that he is still looking for him today." The building crew was silent, looking anxiously at each other.

"There was no chance to cut the fallen shrouds free. The two men holding Latour abandoned him and stumbled to the quarterdeck, intending to free the ship's wheel. Latour, now unrestrained, managed to trip Currie and pinned him face down on the deck. Then he pulled his bound wrists under Currie's chin and heaved back hard, choking him. Currie was losing consciousness when Ruddock hurried to his aid, kicked Latour in the head and dragged him off the captain. Ruddock then helped Currie to the ship's rail where he began to regain his breathing and his senses. Latour had just regained his feet when Currie plunged his sword deep into Latour's chest. Latour screamed, and the ship heeled heavily onto her port side, shipping water over the rails just as he lost consciousness."

Sexton paused. "Well, Smitty, no matter how much nicer you might make a new door or figurehead, it could never bring that much atmosphere to Mr. Whitt's recreation room." Todd, the lunch truck driver, called out: "Hey, Mr. Sexton. Did the Sailmaker ever make it back through that door and give the captain his just desserts?" Sexton smiled. "No, Todd. Not yet anyway."

"That's a 'bummer'. I guess the captain died when the ship got wrecked?"

"No, Todd. He was one of the few survivors."

"That's a lousy story, Mr. Sexton. The good guys are supposed to win out over the bad guys."

"Well, Todd! There's a famous American saying: The game ain't over 'til it's over."

"Well, it's over. You can't fix something two hundred odd years later."

"Who told you that?"

"Stands to reason."

Jamie piped up. "Mr. Sexton, Sir. I didn't really understand the thing about keelhauling. Could you explain that again?"

"Certainly, Jamie. Perhaps it would be better if we acted out that scene. Why don't you fellows come aboard? Make out you are part of the crew. Take your places on the ship, and we'll keelhaul Captain Currie – in place of Sailmaker. That's the outcome that Latour was prepared to sell his soul for, and that would satisfy Todd's values too. 'The good guys would win out over the bad guys.' His audience looked embarrassed as they scanned each other's faces, each waiting for someone else to be the first volunteer, but no one was prepared to make that first move. Sexton looked disappointed. "Oh, come on, lads. It's just a little amateur theatre. There's no water, not even an audience to boo a bad performance." That was when he saw Father Charlesworth – standing behind the rest of his audience – crossing himself and looking very scared. His eyes were focused somewhere behind Sexton. Todd looked terrified too. Sexton then became aware of a sudden chill, then a foul, putrid odour. Looking behind him, he was surprised to see 'Nick', and only then did he recognise him as the 'stranger' that had appeared aboard The Seahorse all those years ago. "Don't mind me," said the grinning demon as he snapped his fingers. "I do enjoy a good story, and you're quite entertaining really. Needs a touch more atmosphere though, a little more background scenery perhaps." Nick lowered his head, raised his arms and tapped an invisible baton on the invisible podium, in the manner of an orchestra conductor. Then he extended his left hand and, with a slow, 'pulling' motion, appeared to summon a breeze that rustled the trees and spun little dust clouds on the dry, sandy lot.

Then, feigning an intellectual expression, he raised his eyebrows and grinned, as he said to Sexton: "That's my wind section." Then he began rhythmic, lateral motions with his other hand. Back and forth, and back and forth again, and Sexton heard the sound of water slapping with a slow, regular beat against the ship's hull. "Percussion," said 'Nick', his grin growing broader. Next came the smell of the sea, tar and hemp, as Nick 'gathered' handfuls of the surrounding air and swept it towards his nostrils. He was really enjoying himself now, gloating over Sexton's obvious bewilderment. "Aroma therapy," he said and almost doubled up with laughter. Then Sexton heard a sound like the crack of a bull whip from high above and, looking up, he saw a topsail straining at a ghostly, yardarm, high on the foremast. Salt spray splashed over the deck of The Seahorse. Sexton's flimsy representation of the ship evaporated. Now he was aboard the real Seahorse. The waves, growing ever higher, caused the ship to plunge and lift, plunge and lift, and he clung to the rail, struggling with his balance. A fearful sense of panic gripped him, and he looked anxiously at Nick. The demon was grinning broadly, obviously enjoying Sexton's disbelief. "Don't you just love this?" said the demon. "Worth the wait, wouldn't you say?"

Sexton's 'audience' had disappeared. The ship was complete now, heaving and twisting on a rough sea. He was no longer the storyteller. Now he was the ship's cook, reliving those last hours of The Seahorse. Sexton looked for Charlesworth and Jamie, but they were gone. So too was Whitt's house; the cars, the trees and building crew were all gone. There was nothing now but sea and the heaving deck of The Seahorse, and, off to the port side, a hazy coastline about a mile or so distant.

"Too rough," said Nick. "That was the night before." He raised his arms, grinning like a mischievous schoolboy as he glanced over his shoulder, anxious to savour Sexton's disbelief and discomfort. He made the quietening gesture of a conductor, and the sea responded, calming to a rolling swell. "That's more like it," he said. "Now, places, everyone," and he began pointing his baton to various locations on the vessel. Sexton found himself on the port side, just forward of the main mast, hard against the ship's rail. His hands were bound, and a hangman's noose hung over a belaying pin nearby. Todd stood just feet away, wearing a blank expression. Jamie appeared at the starboard rail, just below the fo"c'sle. Whitt took a position on the port side, below the quarterdeck and was immediately joined there by Smitty. Robbie Denton, arms folded, stood just abaft the main mast; all their faces were expressionless. Nick focused his attention on Sexton as Father Charlesworth appeared and took a quick look around before making his way aft, to climb the ladder to the quarterdeck. The expression on the demon's face was one of pure delight and anticipation. He snapped his fingers, and Charlesworth turned to face forward. He wore a captain's uniform, sword and pistol, and a most malevolent expression. Sexton was dumbstruck for a few seconds but then screamed at Nick. "No! No! Not Charlesworth. He's not the captain. He can't be."

"But, of course, he is," said the gleeful demon. His clasped hands were in front of him, and he was shaking with delight.

"No. He's a good man. I would never have gone along with this if I knew you were going to make him the captain."

"I know that. That's why I didn't tell you. Besides, I didn't make him captain. He WAS the captain. Surprise! Surprise! I just love surprises!" Nick was clapping his hands now and chuckling wildly, like an excited kid at a birthday party. Sexton tried to move towards him, but he couldn't budge. "You said all the people on the ship were marked the same way. You said you couldn't pick out individuals. I tell you, Whitt's the captain."

"No, actually, Whitt was Josh Merry in that previous life. I was concerned that his massive shudder when you took him to the 'makeshift morgue' in Ryeport might have given the game away. If you recall that shudder hit him just as he passed over the spot where the villagers had laid his dead body. You failed to pick up on that. But there – I do deserve to get lucky sometimes. You just didn't connect the dots – for want of a better expression." He smiled as he made an apologetic gesture, slightly raising his hands and giving a small shrug. "Smitty was Bellew," he said. "Those were the guys who did their best to save Sailmaker during his keelhauling. Young Jamie was Newton in that past life, another one of your friends. And that stupid lunch truck driver was the stinking do-gooder Swift, the missionary, another friend of yours. I could have done without him, but you needed your daily reports on the situation at Whitt's house, so I went along with that. Charlesworth was Captain Currie, and Robby Denton was his psychotic first mate, Ruddock." He laughed. "Your error was assuming that people do not improve with each incarnation. That might have been the object of the exercise, but it doesn't always work that way. The captain certainly followed that game plan. He was sickening. With each successive reincarnation, he became more of a goody-goody. He disappointed me, big time. That's why this is so much fun now. Josh Merry, on the other hand, learned to appreciate the good life, and if it was at other people's expense, so be it. He became the Earl Whitt that you dislike so much today. He's more my kind of guy. The others just muddled along, sometimes bad, sometimes better. Not making any significant changes overall."

"You lied to me," fumed Sexton. "You said you didn't know who the captain was. You let me struggle all these years trying to identify him, and you knew all along."

"I know...it just goes to show: You can't trust anybody these days. Not even your friendly, in-house demon." Nick spread his arms and laughed aloud. The noise of his laughter reverberated all through the ship. It was almost concussive. Smitty and the rest of the building crew were still motionless, seemingly frozen in time. "But now we need the rest of the crew," said Nick. "I've got them all tagged and waiting."

"You can't do this," said Sexton. "I won't be a part of this."

"But, of course, you will. Actually, you no longer have any say in the matter. You set this up, remember? So just sit back and enjoy the show. It is a command performance after all, and by your command. Remember, it was you that assembled the quorum. This couldn't have happened without your cooperation, you see. Your active participation was necessary to establish that you were a willing contributor to all this. It confirmed our contract, in fact. You can't go back on that now. Besides, I've waited too long for this moment. It's a pity you didn't read the small print. But then, there wasn't any, was there?"

Nick was smiling again. "You did quite a good job with the 'quorum', Latour. Grouping them all together and keeping them that way. We needed the keelhauling party, you see. You couldn't have done it without my help, of course, and lots of your money. But never mind about the money! You can't take it with you, as the saying goes."

He turned his back on Sexton, lowered his head and began chanting. It sounded as though he was making a roll call, and as he pointed his baton around the ship, ghostly figures took their places at the helm and around the mainmast. On the deck lay the bound and torn figure of Sailmaker. All were lifeless.

"The tough part was keeping Charlesworth close, without you realising who he was. It was particularly hard keeping him away from Ryeport. If he'd walked through the door of The Harbour Light" – Nick threw his arms in the air – "I know his response would have betrayed him. That's why I had to drop that window on Father Jattori. Just to give Charlesworth a job away from Ryeport. Actually, I've wanted to get rid of Jattori for quite a while. He's been a real thorn in my side at times. Then that stupid assistant of his shoved him out from under the full weight of the window." He grinned. "Well, he won't do that again.

I've 'borrowed' all the rest of the crew, except for two that is. I imagine they're in limbo somewhere. I can't find them. I'm rather proud of how this all worked out, and to top it all off, you'll be coming home with me, Latour. It was a good thing that Sailmaker survived that first keelhauling. Otherwise, you might not have called on me. But he was too much of a goody-goody to let him off without some punishment anyway."

There was panic in Sexton's voice as he yelled at Nick. "You're the one who screwed up all those years ago. Not me. You're the one that messed up back then." Despite his fear, he was furious. "You're incompetent. You should pay the price for that, no one else, just you."

"I know! I know! Life isn't fair, is it?" said Nick, laughing and clapping his hands. "It's more fun this way though. Besides, it wasn't really my fault. That do-good missionary, Palmer, recognised me and threw his crucifix at me." He rubbed his head. "It struck me in the temple. He barely missed my eye," he added crossly. "I had only intended to loose enough power to disable Currie, revive Sailmaker and put some fire in the bellies of the weak-kneed crew. Palmer's crucifix knocked me off balance, spoiled my aim and made me lose control over the energy. So, I hit the damned mast instead. Not what I wanted at all. That brought the mast down. It was that missionary, Palmer, that screwed up everything. He made me mad! I lose control when I get mad – as you know."

Nick pointed at the ghostly, immobile figure of the missionary, Palmer, and then raised both his arms. Palmer's arms followed suit, allowing the Bible and crucifix tucked under one arm to fall to the deck. Nick pointed to the fallen items and, with a 'brushing' motion, swept them into the scuppers and over the side. "There, he can't repeat that now. I fixed him though, didn't I?" He grinned again as he made a thrusting, twisting motion with his arm. "I skewered him real good – nearly got his mate Swift, too – on the same skewer. I barely missed him when the spar swung back inboard. I might have had two missionaries on the same skewer." Suddenly, his expression changed, his features darkened, and he became impatient. "Time's getting short," he said. "I have to return the 'borrowed' souls quickly." Then a smile crossed his face again. "I did enjoy Charlesworth's extrapolation about the borrowed souls though. Unfortunately, none of them was an airline pilot or aborting a nuclear strike. That could have been fun." He imitated the sound of an aircraft engine – brrm - brrm - cough - brrm - cough - brrm – as he used his hand to mimic an aeroplane falling from the sky and ending with a loud 'ker-smash'. Then he convulsed with laughter. Sexton's insides were in a knot. He said: "You're like some bratty kid that was spoiled rotten and never grew up!" Nick rolled his head onto his shoulder and gave him another big grin. "I know," he said. "But we kids do have more fun."

Nick turned to face the assembled crew, described a wide arc with both arms and then clapped his hands. There was a brilliant flash, like a horizontal sheet of lightning. Their features and clothing were changed to those of the original crew, and they all came to life. Nick satisfied himself with a quick look around, and then, pointing at the captain, snapped his fingers. Some of the crew rushed the 'captain' and his officers, and the men holding Latour released him to help Sailmaker.

'Captain Currie' was dragged down to the port quarter and secured to the line taken from Sailmaker's ankles. His wrists were fastened to the other end of that line – going to the starboard side. "Heave him over the side, lads," bellowed Nick, and Currie was unceremoniously dumped feet first into the sea. "Heave away, lads. Handsomely now," yelled Nick, smiling, as he strutted on the quarterdeck in a pompous imitation of Currie. The crew heaved on the keelhauling line, drawing it slowly from port to starboard, keeping it taut all the while.

The captain's lifeless body was dragged aboard on the starboard side. His clothes and flesh had been torn by the barnacles on the ship's hull, and he had no vital signs. The ship's crew fell silent. "There you go, Latour. Just as you requested! Justice has been done," said the demon, triumphantly.

"Time to go, lads," he said and called names, as he pointed to the individual crew members, chanting as he waved them away. Brannigan had been the first 'ghost' to appear and was the last to go. That seemed to concern Nick. "He was the first one I 'tagged'," he said to Sexton in an accusatory manner. "You kept me talking too long. Sailmaker! Go home," he called as he waved him towards the fo'c'sle. Sailmaker walked, as in a trance, to the fo'c'sle door and then turning to face them, paused, as if unsure of what to do. Nick motioned him away, and he stepped through the door, closing it behind him.

• • •

Back in Ryeport, there was panic. Unexpected sheet lightning and a violent squall had taken everyone by surprise. Dave Trelaw and a buddy had just rowed through The Chute into Sorry Cove to finish wiring fake wreckage, installed there as part of the background for the theme park. His buddy said later that Trelaw had 'gone blank', stood up in the stern and ignored him when asked to sit down. He'd given no indication of hearing or understanding. Then, when the lightning flashed, he fell into the water close by The Chute and disappeared. Buddy searched frantically for a few minutes and then rowed like mad through The Chute, screaming for help.

Mike Rooken was at the bar in The Harbour Light, holding two empty jugs, awaiting refills from his favourite barmaid when the sudden flash of lightning and crash of thunder startled everyone. In the arched entrance to The Seahorse Lounge, the image of a door appeared. Then that door flew open revealing the figure of a man in old-fashioned seaman's clothing. The ghostly image lasted only seconds, but that was long enough to petrify the patrons. Other ghostly apparitions appeared briefly in the bar at the same time. There was nothing solid about any of the images, but despite the short duration, they shook the patrons badly.

Holly was between Rooken and the ghostly door, so he was given a double shock. Not only did he have to contend with the ghost in the doorway, but he also saw Holly lose nearly two stone in weight, and 20 years off her age, in those fleeting seconds. The 'laughter lines' at the corners of her eyes and mouth, together with any other delicate marks of her maturity, instantly vanished.

Then – as if someone had flicked a switch, all the apparitions, the man and the door and the ghostly figures in the bar, all vanished. But the new and younger Holly remained. But this was not the Holly that Rooken knew. This young lady could well have been her daughter. She looked about 19 years old and was slimmer and lighter than Holly. Unlike anyone else present, she seemed completely unfazed by what had transpired. "Two more pints, Mr. Rooken?" she queried.

Jamie was stunned. "Er…ye…yes, please, Holly," he stammered.

The barmaid gave him a teasing sort of smile. "And just who might Holly be, Mister Rooken? Have you got another girlfriend that I don't know about? I'll thank you to remember that my name is Meg." She leaned forward to pick up his jugs from the countertop, only then noticing how loose her blouse was. "Oops! Modesty forbids that I should bend in this blouse, Mister Rooken. I must change!" Rooken, white as a sheet, stumbled back to the table where Archer was waiting. His friend's eyes were wide and staring, as he sat shocked and motionless. "Did you see that?" Rooken asked. Archer nodded, seeming incapable of speech. Some other patrons in the bar had scrambled to their feet and out the door, sucking in great gasps of air as soon as they were outside.

Meg had gathered the front of her blouse in one hand and gripped the waistband of her skirt with the other. "I'll get someone to serve you, Mr. Rooken," she called and, passing Sarah in the kitchen, she asked: "Can you watch the bar for a few minutes please, Sarah? Wasn't that lightning weird? It came out of nowhere." She hurried to her room for a solution to her modesty problem.

• • •

Back on board The Seahorse, Nick was in a clean-up mode. He had returned all the 'borrowed' souls. Now he turned to Sexton and said: "We have to leave these people here. They will be confused. Some may not handle it too well, Robbie Denton in particular." He made the familiar quote sign as he said: "But his sanity was always borderline anyway. The mock-up of The Seahorse has to stay too. You and Charlesworth must also remain. And, more importantly, I'm not able to take any more liberties with the timeline. So, all the 'original crew' will retain the same age and health as they had aboard the ship. No immortality, just a one-time age and health adjustment. Some good," he smiled, as he raised his hand, palm up; "others, not so good!" This time he waggled his hand, palm down. "One old man on his deathbed in Australia will be happy with my work today."

He walked across the deck and picked up Captain Currie's sword from where it had been dropped prior to his keelhauling. "You and the captain end here," he said and without another word drove the sword hard into Sexton's chest, in the same spot that Currie had, all those years ago. "See you in hell, Latour. Contract completed." Sexton collapsed and died instantly. Nick withdrew the sword, took one last look around and then 'snapped' his fingers. The Seahorse was replaced by the mock-up that Sexton had set up on his arrival.

Sexton's 'audience' were left standing on the netting 'deck' of The Seahorse, bewildered and looking as though they had awoken from a nightmare.

They remembered Sexton's story and being asked to play-act in the keel-hauling. But that had happened so quickly that they all believed they had imagined it. Some wondered if the orange juice had been drugged. Then they saw Charlesworth and Sexton, and panic set in. Todd examined them both and tried artificial respiration on Charlesworth but to no avail. Sexton too was beyond their help. Robbie Denton did not look like the same man. His hair was iron-grey, and he seemed to have aged about 20 years, as he frantically swung an imaginary axe at an invisible target on the port quarter of the mock-up ship. He was completely unresponsive and appeared to have left part of his mind aboard The Seahorse. Jamie Farr, sporting a short ponytail and looking about three years older, was kneeling by Sexton's side, crying. "Who did this? Get an ambulance. Quick! Someone get the police and an ambulance."

Smitty was disorientated. He kept bending his legs, kneeling, doing squats, first bending his 'good' leg and then the 'stiff' one. "My leg's healed," he kept saying, incredulously. He dropped his pants and examined his previously stiff knee. The scars were gone. He rubbed, pushed and probed the knee, seeking the familiar bumps from the heads of the screws that held the steel plates in place. They were gone as was the pain and stiffness. He pulled his pants back up and, still in a daze, went to see what he could do for Robbie Denton.

The electrician, the only non-reincarnation from the original crew, sped his pickup out of the driveway, the wheels spraying gravel in all directions. On this hot June day, he was freezing cold and shivering. He had an urgent need to do two things – call the cops and change his underwear and not necessarily in that order. He remembered the storytelling, the free lunch and orange juice and the crazy mocked-up ship that seemed to become real for just a few seconds. But how could he explain all the things he thought he'd seen? He stopped his truck and checked his watch. The storytelling lunch and this other experience had all happened in about half an hour – like a fast-forwarded movie – but surely, they'd spent that long eating lunch. All that business with the ship could have lasted only seconds. It wasn't possible. There were also two dead men to account for. He hadn't imagined them. He searched his clothes and the truck to make sure the cops wouldn't find any 'pot'. They were sure to look for that, once he told his story.

CHAPTER 11

Crowley and Sarah discuss the unexplained

Sexton's funeral was scheduled for 11 a.m. that morning, and the village seemed eerily quiet. A miserable, overcast sky, ominous dark clouds and sporadic drizzling rain provided a fitting backdrop for the prevailing mood in Ryeport. People seemed to be holding their breath as they waited nervously for the event. No boats had put to sea today; nor was there any other work-like activity in the village. Small groups of people were gathered here and there, talking softly, almost furtively, amongst themselves as though fearful of being overheard. Some villagers had gathered in The Harbour Light, but they too were unusually quiet. Sam Bass, conspicuously clean and well turned out in a dark suit and black tie, was serving tea and coffee. It appeared that the total population of Ryeport was waiting for the funeral. From the whisperings and guarded conversations, it seemed they were anticipating something even more dramatic than a funeral. The mysterious circumstances and rumours surrounding Sexton's death had them speculating on something...supernatural.

Chief Inspector Crowley and young Jamie Farr were the only guests in The Seahorse Lounge, finishing their late breakfasts. Crowley's appetite had been satisfied by toast and coffee, but now, as he watched Jamie enjoy a large meal of sausages, bacon and eggs, home fried potatoes, baked beans and toast, the savoury aroma and the lad's obvious enjoyment was tempting him to reorder. Jamie had described his favourite Canadian breakfast to Sarah, and she had enjoyed obliging him. Crowley was smiling at his young companion's enthusiasm for the meal and secretly wishing he still had his own youthful appetite.

Several weeks had elapsed since the mysterious deaths of Father Charlesworth and Sexton. The post-mortems and forensic investigations had delayed the release of Sexton's body for interment but done nothing to explain the bizarre events of that day. In fact, they had compounded the mystery. Crowley had asked the forensic laboratory to establish Sexton's age because, in death, he had the appearance of a man in him mid-thirties. That conflicted with both his travel documents and the evidence of people who knew him. These all stated his age to be 76. But the laboratory had declared Sexton's remains to be approximately 260 years old, and a second laboratory had confirmed those results. Crowley, therefore, had those tests discreetly repeated by two other laboratories – without disclosing the reason or original findings – but they too had confirmed the earlier evaluations.

A letter found in Sexton's wallet stated that Father Eggleton had agreed to act as next-of-kin. Accordingly, Crowley's office had notified the vicar of Ryeport of his friend's death, and Eggleton had arrived in Toronto the following afternoon. He told Crowley that Sexton had asked him to assume the next-of-kin responsibilities during a light-hearted conversation after the bachelor party. Sexton had inserted his request out of context to their conversation. Eggleton had laughingly declared that Sexton would outlive him but had been pressured to agree. However, he had been surprised when Sexton smilingly handed him a large, sealed envelope a few days later saying: "This contains a copy of my Will, Father, and a letter of explanation. I'd rather you didn't open it until at least three days after I have been officially pronounced dead. It might prove embarrassing." The vicar had also agreed to assume temporary responsibility for Jamie should Sexton die whilst the lad was in his care. Jamie, who had no family to name as next-of-kin, would then have to return to the orphanage and would be without the friend and mentor he so admired upon Sexton's death.

It was obvious that Sexton had expected that he – but not Charlesworth – would die at the building site. The plane tickets confirmed that Sexton was relying on his friend to see Jamie safely back to Ryeport.

During Crowley's first telephone conversation with Father Eggleton, the vicar had explained that he was particularly concerned about Jamie because of the youngster's below average IQ and short attention span. However, despite some obvious educational shortcomings, Crowley had found Jamie to be an intelligent and self-assured young man, well-mannered and helpful. But he was puzzled that the youngster's trousers were almost three inches too short and his other clothing too tight. He had remedied that with a visit to a local sporting goods store, and as a result, Eggleton did not immediately recognise Jamie – until the lad bade him: "Good morning, Father."

In the absence of a legal guardian in Canada, the Crowleys had obtained permission from the orphanage to look after Jamie until Father Eggleton arrived. They also accommodated and assisted the vicar with the legalities involved concerning the repatriation of Sexton's body. However, once it became clear that Sexton's body would not be released for weeks, Crowley had suggested that Eggleton and Jamie return to Ryeport without Sexton's body, volunteering to personally accompany the body back to Ryeport once it was released. Jamie, however, had insisted that he should remain in Canada until he could return to England with his friend and mentor. So, again, with the consent of the orphanage, the lad had been living with the Crowleys ever since.

Eggleton had been shocked by the difference in Jamie. He was a very different young man from the one he had bidden 'Bon voyage' when he left Ryeport a few days earlier. He was about three inches taller, looked about three or four years older and seemed very confident and mature. He also had a healthy tan, was more muscular and his hair was much longer. "This is long enough for a ponytail!" Eggleton had chided as he gave it a playful tug. Jamie's IQ had apparently 'grown', along with his body, and he was quite cool and self-assured concerning his own wellbeing – unlike the more childlike youngster that Eggleton had known in Ryeport.

Crowley and his wife had developed a strong affection for the bright and personable youngster during his stay with them. In fact, Mrs. Crowley, who admired his good manners and considerate attitude, was treating him like a long-lost son. "Pat," she'd said to her husband, "I'd like you to explore the possibility of our adopting Jamie, provided both you and he agree, of course. I enjoy having the chatty youngster around, and he's certainly no trouble. With both our sons living overseas now, it would give you some-one to share some leisure time with. You would have a fishing and golfing buddy again." Crowley admitted that he liked the idea, and the lad certainly seemed comfortable with them. Right now, it would be inappropriate to mention it to Jamie, of course. Crowley would have to bide his time and be sure that the boy got over the loss of Sexton. However, he had discreetly checked with the orphanage whether adoption might be possible, and they had been happy to give him the 'green light', subject to Jamie's approval, of course.

The bizarre details of The Seahorse affair intrigued Crowley to the point of obsession. Having had no luck in solving the complexities of the case using conventional methods, he had obtained permission to extend this visit to Ryeport to explore any local knowledge for insights that might aid his investigation. His superiors were very uncomfortable with the 'supernatural' theories that were being bandied-about and dead set against using a psychic, but although Crowley was also a sceptic at heart, he was beginning to think it might be their last resort.

One of the eminent experts in the paranormal field that they would have chosen to consult would have been Father Charlesworth. The fact that he was one of the victims complicated the issue even further.

Obviously, Jamie, despite his involvement, knew nothing of any hidden agenda regarding Sexton's visit. As far as he was concerned, they were only at Whitt's house to deliver The Seahorse artefacts. The startling, dreamlike flashes he'd experienced, he attributed to Sexton's legendary storytelling, enhanced perhaps by the two glasses of Sexton's fortified 'orange juice' that he'd enjoyed. Alcohol was a new experience for Jamie, and any reference to 'Caribbean Sunshine' had been attributed to the oranges. His growth spurt and long hair he had taken in stride, as though he had no knowledge of his earlier physique. The fact that so much detail had been compressed into seconds of real time had not registered with any of those involved, except perhaps for the very disturbed electrician.

Crowley intended to put all enquiries on hold until after the funeral. He wanted to enjoy the visit and Jamie's company, as far as the circumstances would allow. He teased the lad as he finished his meal. "Make sure you leave nothing on the plate, Jamie. Sarah might think you don't like her cooking." The youngster just grinned, as he said: "Mrs. Bass knows better, Sir. Don't you, Ma'am?" Sarah had arrived behind Crowley and began removing the dishes. "That I do, Jamie Farr. My plates all had patterns on them before I served them to you. I'm sure you've licked them all off. Don't even leave a stain on the plate now, do you?" She gave Crowley a broad wink and a nudge. "Cost a fortune to satisfy 'is appetite, Sir. Since 'e came back from Canada, that is. Don't know what you did to 'im over there, but 'e came back bright as a new penny. Never seen such a change in a body. Growed a bit too." She returned her puzzled expression to the lad. "Been standin' in a manure pile, 'ave ye, Jamie?"

Jamie rose from his seat. "Thank you for breakfast, Sir. I really enjoyed it.

You too, Mrs. Bass. You really do make great meals, whatever the occasion. Here, let me take those dishes to the kitchen for you." Then, not allowing time for an objection, Jamie took the dishes from Sarah's hands and was gone. Sarah looked after him thoughtfully, then sat in Jamie's vacated chair, took a nervous look about them and fixed Crowley with a challenging stare. "Whatever did you people do to that lad in Canada?" she demanded. "When Jamie left 'ere, 'e was slow as molasses in January. Couldn't keep 'is mind on anything for more than a minute or two. Then he'd be off, playin' some silly game. 'e was never picky with 'is food, mind ye, but 'e was easily distracted from that too and rarely finished a meal. Now 'is appetite is about double what it used t' be. An' just look at 'im. Bright as a button, eats enough for two men, grown about three inches taller and always eager to be busy. You'd never believe it was the same lad. Do you know what 'e said to me the other day when I asked 'i 'ow 'e liked the food in Canada?" Crowley shook his head.

"'e smiled an' said: 'It sure beats figgy-duff, Mrs. Bass."

"So, I asked 'im: 'What's figgy-duff? 'Figgy-duff is ship's biscuit, crushed up with figs or dates,' 'e said. You get that when rations are short on board.'

"It turns out 'e's right too. But only if you were ships' crew about two 'undred years ago. Now, wherever would 'e pick up an expression like that? Not 'round 'ere, that's for sure. What, in 'eaven's name, 'appened over there, Sir? The village is all shook up by Sexton's weird death an' the changes in people. Not just them that went to Canada neither. It don't seem natural. Take our barmaid, Holly, for instance." Sarah nodded in the direction of the bar. "She lost nearly two stone in a matter of seconds. Right 'ere, in the 'arbour light bar, right in front of everybody. Mike Rooken watched 'er shrink a few dress sizes an' drop about twenty years off 'er age in seconds. Suddenly, 'er dress was much too big, an' – 'onest now – she looked twenty years younger. 'ow do you explain that? The people in the bar 'avn't 'ad a good night's sleep since that day. It turned some of 'em right off their drink, so it did. Mike Rooken for one. 'e was stood right in front of Holly as 'e watched the weight – an' the years – fall off 'er. Really shook 'im up, I can tell ye.

"At the same time, whilst Rooken was stood there with 'is mouth 'angin' open, ghostly figures started appearin' in the bar. One came through a door that suddenly appeared in that archway, right there." She pointed towards the entrance to The Harbour Light bar. Her voice rose in pitch and volume as she leaned towards Crowley, staring intently into his face. "The people in the bar said there was a storm bangin' an' crashin' be'ind the ghost in the ghostly door. That would be right 'ere – right where we're sittin'. But there weren't no storm in 'ere. The people in 'ere didn't see or 'ear any storm. Everyone in the other room saw the bloke in the doorway, but no one in 'ere did. They didn't even see the door. Other ghostly figures appeared in the bar too, right beside some of our regulars who were already sittin' there. The ghostly comin's an' goin's only lasted a second, mind ye, then." (Sarah snapped her finger in front of Crowley's face.) "Suddenly, everythin' was back to normal. Just like that." (She snapped her fingers again.) "Except that everyone was lookin' at each other wonderin' what the 'ell was goin' on. Some of 'em got up an' run outside, lookin' real scared. They were all sayin': 'Did you see that?' Or, 'What the 'ell was that?' real worried like. When Rooken turned to look at 'is mate, Archer, 'e said, 'a ghostly image of 'imself was already sittin' there, right next to 'is mate. But 'e was still standin' at the bar.

"An out-of-body experience, 'e said. Then there's the scar on 'is cheek. It wasn't there before all this 'appened', but now 'e's got a three-cornered scar on 'is face. One of 'is ancestors got that same scar over two 'undred years ago' when he fell against the beacon brazier durin' an 'eart attack. You watch Rooken t'day. Can't leave that scar alone, 'e can't. Keeps touchin' it, 'e does. Rooken always 'ad a 'dickie' 'eart too. But 'is doctor says it's different now. No better, no worse, just different. Specialist can't understand it. It's a different part of 'is 'eart that's damaged now, they say.

"They tested our beer, y'know. Once the word got out, people from the government came down 'ere, sealed up everythin', took samples away an' tested 'em. We were shut down for over a week. They must 'ave thought we'd put drugs or somethin' in the beer. All the tests came back negative, they said. Nothin' wrong anywhere. The people in the bar that claimed to 'ave seen these things were given medicals an' x-rays, an' magnetic ray things, but they were all okay. They all got a clean bill of 'ealth.

"Ye know, there did use t' be a door in that archway," she nodded towards the entrance to The Harbour Light lounge. "But that was 'undred's of years ago, before this part of the inn was even built. That door led straight outside in those days. An' the people in the bar who saw the ghost said it came in through that very same door. Turned Rooken right off 'is beer – an' that's no easy job. Swore right off drink, 'e did. That only lasted a couple of weeks, mind ye." She paused, searching Crowley's face as if expecting him to be able to explain it. Crowley raised his hands in a despairing gesture and shrugged, as he said: "Sarah, I honestly don't know what happened. There were reports of strange happenings at Whitt's new house in Ontario. In fact, I'm hoping that you folks over here can shed some light on these happenings. We're at a complete loss for explanations. Lots of theories, lots of scientific investigations but no answers."

Sarah's concerns weren't satisfied. She said: "I'm told that Sexton died from a sword wound, while 'e was in a group of seven people, but no one saw it 'appen or found a sword. Then, Sexton's friend, Father Charlesworth, drowned at the same time." She threw her hands in the air. "In a place where there was no water." She leaned towards Crowley, her hands now imitating Crowley's despairing gesture. "It all seems creepy. Unholy some'ow. Witchcraft, some people 'round 'ere are saying. The village ain't been the same since." Crowley, caught a little off guard by Sarah's unaccustomed persistence, took a few seconds to respond, but Sarah's eyes never wavered.

"I can understand people's confusion, Sarah," he said finally, "because we share it. But let me assure you that Canada had nothing to do with these changes. We have tried our best to determine what happened, but every investigation only deepens the mystery. For instance: you are right about Father Charlesworth. He drowned in an area where that should have been impossible. However, when the laboratories examined the water from his lungs and clothing, it was found to be sea water. But he died over a thousand miles from the nearest sea water. It was not just any sea water though. It contained materials that were native to the waters from this very coast about four thousand miles from where he drowned. As for Jamie and Sexton, I didn't know either of them before these events took place. Or any of the other people that were affected, come to that. So, I have to rely on the words of people that did know them, as far as any changes are concerned. For the most part though – Sexton, Father Charlesworth and a construction worker named Denton excepted, it seems that the changes were all bene-ficial. Your barmaid, Holly, is a case in point. Suddenly dropping 20 years or so off your age, and shedding 20 odd unwanted pounds, would be a very acceptable benefit to most people. Don't you agree?" Sarah dropped her stare at last. It appeared to have taken considerable energy to maintain such concentration.

"It may seem like that to you, Sir, but it's still unholy if you ask me. Nothin's free in this world. Someone always 'as to pay, and it's not always them as benefits. An' we don't know if those changes are the end of it. Or 'ow long they'll last. I'm concerned about Holly too. Since she lost all that weight, she's insistin' everyone call 'er Meg. At the time of the lightnin' strike – when we were 'avin' the ghosty parade in the bar, an' Holly was losin' all the weight – there was a student workin' in Sorry Cove. Trelaw 'is name is, Dave Trelaw. Well, 'e fell off 'is boat. Someone came runnin' to the inn to tell us they'd recovered 'is body, and Holly goes runnin' out to see 'im. By the time she got there, the doctor 'ad revived 'im an' when Trelaw opened 'is eyes an' saw Holly, 'e called 'er Meg. 'Meg,' 'e said. 'Thank God! I'm 'ome again at last.' Now, Trelaw was a regular in 'ere an' knew Holly long before this incident. Just like all the other students workin' 'ere. Holly used to serve 'em their beer. She's thinner now, o'course, an' looks younger, but Trelaw 'adn't changed that much." She paused, looking thoughtful for a few moments before continuing in a slower, somewhat puzzled manner, "Except – now I come to think of it – 'is 'air is longer than before, an' 'e 'ad a deep tan an' 'e looked tougher some'ow, more muscular. I'd forgotten that."

She resumed her former tone. "Holly – sorry, I must remember to call 'er Meg – and Dave Trelaw 'ave been livin' together ever since. 'e's in 'is early 20's and a nice young chap, an' they do make a nice couple. Holly looked about 40 years old when she first came to work 'ere. An' that was just a few months back. She was a good-looking woman an' drew the men, like flies to a jam jar, so she did. Nice personality. Now though, since that incident, she's a pretty young girl an' looks about 18. She looks younger than Trelaw since she lost that weight an' a few laughter lines. An' those two are obviously very much in love. Make me envious, they do. Never knew anythin' like that meself. That kind of love, I mean." She paused, lost in reverie for a few moments, before resuming. "Now Holly – sorry, Meg – suddenly knows more about the 'istory of Ryeport an' this inn than I do." She raised her eyebrows, creating a very surprised expression. " 'onest! I'm not jokin'. An' I've lived 'ere all me life. Father Eggleton was intrigued by all this and started lookin' up 'er family tree on 'is computer. Turns out 'er ancestors used to live right 'ere in this village, an' one of 'em actually owned this inn. Turns out, she's distantly related to my Sam. But she didn't seem very 'appy to 'ear that.

"Then there's Trelaw, a university student. Never sailed a day in 'is life before comin' 'ere. Now 'e's as good as them that 'ave been at it for a lifetime. You should see 'im with riggin' an' stuff like that. 'e mends sails an' nets, does splicin' an' all that sort of stuff, like a bloody expert. It's weird. People are sayin': It's a past-life-experience. I'd never 'eard that expression before, but now it's as commonplace as 'good mornin.'" She paused, appearing breathless from her hurried explanations.

Crowley had been soaking up her every word. "Sarah, I'm not allowed to discuss any ongoing case matters at this time, but I am free to tell you of similar happenings in Canada that are common knowledge and already reported by the media. You will remember Mr. Whitt, I imagine?"

"Oh, yes, Sir. Strange bloke, 'e was. Not a nice man, I reckon. 'ad some dayjah voo trouble when 'e first came in the 'arbour light. Some thought 'e was 'avin' some sort of fit. 'e also knew there used to be a door at the foot of the stairs, where the archway is now – right where the door appeared for that ghost to come through. That old door was chucked out about two 'undred years back. In fact, it was the same door that Sexton took to Canada for 'im. It's all too creepy. We know about the door from family stories passed down from the old days. That was before they started buildin' this addition, o' course." Crowley nodded. "Yes, Sarah. I learned all about the door when I questioned Whitt about the mock-up of the ship."

"Creepy stuff," said Sarah, giving a little shudder. 'e was scared of Sexton though, Whitt was. You could see it in 'is face. Some say 'e didn't want that door, just did what Sexton told 'im. Big bloke like that – makes ye wonder, don't it?" Crowley listened intently, hanging on Sarah's every word. "Well, Sarah, it appears that, as you say, Mr. Whitt was not a nice guy. His wife's lawyer says he used to beat her up and when she left him, Whitt did his best to make sure that she didn't get a penny of his money. She hadn't asked for anything, mind you. Just wanted him to leave her alone. After these strange events in Canada, however, he voluntarily gave her unrestricted title to the big new house he'd built, the same house where all those strange events occurred. The place is worth more than two million dollars, I'm told. I understand his wife will sell it. However, Whitt seems to be a changed man. He's suddenly become a caring human being.

"The contractor that was working on Whitt's house – his name is Smitty – had a stiff left leg. His knee had been smashed in a motor-bike accident a few years before, and the leg was held together with steel plates and screws. When Sexton died, Smitty's leg was inexplicably restored to a normal, healthy state. Medical examiners could find no evidence that it had ever been damaged, and there was no trace of the pins and plates they'd put there years before. Smitty's hair, which had been streaked with grey, was now an even dark brown. No trace of grey. No dye job either. He seems to have instantly become several years younger, and he too has a deep, healthy tan. He had to take counselling for a while, but he's okay now. He was under a lot of stress at the time and separated from his common-law wife and family. But they're back together now and very happy. Then there's Jamie of course. But I don't have to tell you about him. You are more aware than I of the changes in him.

"Oh, one other person: Smitty's helper, Robbie Denton. He's a really nasty piece of work with a prison record for assault and robbery amongst other things. This whole business has completely deranged him. Apparently, he was a mean guy and a bit strange before the incident, but now it seems he's aged about 20 years, is mentally deranged and in a psychiatric hospital under lock and key. He keeps shouting for people to cut away the rigging and that the ship is headed for the rocks. I've read the missionary's report about the wreck – the same one that Sexton read to the building crew at Whitt's new house. It seems to me that Denton is reliving the wreck of The Seahorse." Sarah listened silently, her eyes had widened, and she appeared to be in a state of shock as Crowley recounted these events. Finally, she gave a little shudder and crossed herself. "Witchcraft?" she queried. "Oh, I don't believe in such things, Sarah." He paused as if trying to find the right words. "Sarah, we've made extensive studies of every record we could find, including the logbook of The Seahorse, from her last trip. That log records that they exchanged two missionaries in Cuba. One of those returning missionaries died when the ship was wrecked here, and he is buried in your cemetery. There were also some kegs of rum on board that the captain had bought in Haiti. When our scientist analysed the rum that Sexton was using, what he called 'Caribbean Sunshine', they found it was old enough to have been that same rum. The captain also signed a black man aboard as a cook in Haiti. His name was Latour. From all those records, it would appear that Latour is a match for the man you know as Sexton. Latour actually became sexton for your church shortly after the wreck of The Seahorse.

"There are also the physical changes that have occurred to other people – in our present time – that had the effect of restoring them to the ages and physical descriptions of some people aboard The Seahorse at the time of the wreck. That's also true of Rooken because of the scar and the change in his heart condition. It might even be true of Holly. You describe her as having the physical appearance and knowledge of Meg, the innkeeper's daughter, of those earlier days. The researchers are still working on Trelaw. But my guess is that they'll say he bears an uncanny likeness to your ghostly villager: Sailmaker. Do you know that Trelaw has scars on his back that appear to be the result of a flogging? His fellow students say they weren't there before he fell overboard in Sorry Cove, and he claims he's never been flogged. Apart from that, he doesn't appear greatly changed from the student you knew. He does appear to be the same age as the man Sailmaker at the time of the wreck. You say he is more muscular now than before and his college photos seem to confirm that.

"All of those people that were changed appear to have had counterparts aboard The Seahorse, at the time of the wreck. When we found Sexton dead at Whitt's house, he appeared to be in his mid-thirties. Father Charlesworth appeared younger too, and the clothes he was wearing were a couple of sizes too large around the belly. There was also a young seaman aboard The Seahorse. His description fits the new Jamie like a glove. He was a couple of years older than the young man who left here to help deliver the door and apparently very bright." He paused, to study Sarah's anxious face. She was looking flushed and nervous, and one hand was fidgeting nervously at the base of her throat. "You're just jokin', Sir. Pullin' me leg, you are, Sir. Right?" She scanned his face nervously, hoping for a smile to relieve the nervous, creepy feeling in her belly. "No, Sarah. The records all seem to corroborate the things I've just told you. There are other strange coincidences too. One of my own officers collapsed at our station in Canada, during the time that Sexton was telling the story of The Seahorse at Whitt's house. My man, Stanton, was out cold for several seconds. He was rushed to the hospital, but the doctors could find nothing wrong. He'd had no heart attack or stroke and was in excellent physical shape. He just lost consciousness. When he recovered, he remembered nothing of his collapse and felt fine. He was released the same day, leaving the doctors scratching their heads. That same weekend, while out driving with his wife, they stopped at a local flea market. Second-hand market, or boot sale, I believe you call them here. A youngster was examining a fiddle that was for sale on a stall. The youngster tried scraping the bow over it and was obviously unsure whether or not to buy it. Sergeant Stanton pulled a face, and, telling the lad it was off tune, took the violin from him, tuned it and played a few bars of an old sea shanty before handing it back and telling the lad it was in good shape. Stanton's wife said she was dumbstruck. He'd never played an instrument in his life before and never shown any real interest in music. Since that day, however, he's bought a fiddle for himself and joined a local group that plays east coast folk music on weekends." Crowley paused, wondering if he should proceed. But Sarah seemed more composed, so he continued. "Stanton doesn't tuck the fiddle under his chin though. He couches it in the crook of his left arm somehow. That's unusual, but in the missionary's reports, they mention that the fiddler aboard The Seahorse held the violin the same way. Stanton has quite a repertoire of old sea shanties – some that aren't fit for polite company, I might add. He doesn't remember where he learned them, and more to the point, he's never had a music lesson in his life.

"Consequently, there is a theory about reincarnation running rampant at the station. So, when I discovered that Stanton's unconscious period exactly matched that of the incident at Whitt's house, I had my team investigate whether there had been any similar collapses recorded by any hospitals during the same period. First, we checked in Canada, then the States, then England and other countries, staying strictly within that same timeframe but adjusted for global time zones. My team found four similar incidents. Two here in the UK – we now consider Trelaw as number three – one in an Arizona prison, and one in Australia. When these people were questioned, they all had knowledge of seamanship relevant to the period of The Seahorse. That knowledge had not been theirs before their brief 'coma' or whatever it was that robbed them of their consciousness. And, to top it all off, they all knew the shanties that Stanton now plays. All those present at the scene back in Canada, including Whitt and young Jamie – even the poor wreck locked up in the psychiatric hospital – are also familiar with those same shanties, and when I spoke with Trelaw, I found that he knows them too. Strange, wouldn't you say? Particularly since Brannigan – the fiddler aboard The Seahorse – sang his own version of '*Farewell to you Spanish Ladies*,' and it's Brannigan's version that these men all know. Did you ever see the movie *Jaws*, Sarah?"

"Ooh! Yes, Sir. Real scary that was."

"Then you may remember the cantankerous shark hunter in that film – a part played by Robert Shaw. He sang pieces of that same shanty during the movie. His version of the first verse goes like this:

> *Farewell and adieu to you fine Spanish Ladies,*
> *Farewell and adieu all you ladies of Spain,*
> *For we've received orders to sail back to BOSTON*
> *And perhaps we shall never more see you again.*

"Now – the original wording of the third line of that shanty was: 'for we've received orders to sail back to ENGLAND – not *Boston*. The shark hunter in the film always substituted *Boston* for *England*. I imagine Boston was his home port. Well, Brannigan's home port was Bristol, and he always substituted *Bristol* for *England*. So, since The Seahorse crew always sang along with him. That's the version they all learned. 'For we've received orders to sail for old Bristol!

"All the people involved in these mysterious happenings sing Brannigan's version of 'Spanish Ladies.' Not the original words or the version that was sung in *Jaws*. The cook's journal and the missionary's letters all corroborate these facts. The journal and the letters were preserved by the cook after he survived the wreck. That man was Latour, and he became the sexton of your church. Those letters first came ashore right here in Ryeport." Sarah was looking very troubled.

Crowley pulled an envelope from his pocket, selected a photograph and passed it to Sarah. It was Sexton, his eyes closed in death but still recognisable as the man she knew so well. But he looked at least 40 years younger than when she saw him last. "That was taken the day he died," said Crowley. He handed her a folded newspaper. "What I've told you is pretty much all reported in this newspaper, Sarah. We tried to suppress all this speculation until such a time that we could confirm or disprove it, but the media managed to get their hands on most of it anyway. Then they brought in their own experts. Those 'experts' believe that the people involved in the re-enactment of the wreck are reincarnations of the original crew. It may be a lot of nonsense, but it sure sold a lot of newspapers. Reputable papers too, not the garbage rags that you see in the check-out aisle at the supermarket. The re-enactment of the wreck also took place on the anniversary of the original wreck. The 'papers' did extensive research on all those people involved. They say they were apparently restored to the same age and physical condition of their earlier counterparts at the time of the wreck. There's no way to substantiate that, of course, and never will be. But as I said: it's good for selling newspapers. And I imagine it will stir up plenty of interest in Ryeport. It should be very good for your tourism business.

"Oh, one more thing. The guy that we discovered in Australia, the one that went into a coma during the incident at Whitt's house, was eighty-seven years old and dying of lung cancer in hospital. When he awoke from his brief 'coma', he'd put on fifty pounds, appeared to be about thirty years younger than before and had a great suntan. When the doctors checked him over, there was no trace of any cancer. This guy had a lousy singing voice, but he also knew Brannigan's version of 'Spanish Ladies'. As I said before, Sarah, there is talk that they may make a movie of all this. You may get more publicity down here than you ever bargained for. It seems to me that, apart from Sexton, Father Charlesworth and Smitty's helper, Denton, everybody else came out winners."

Sarah rose from her seat, obviously shaken. She pushed the newspaper back across the table to Crowley, using a paper towel to avoid actually touching it. Then, as though to refuse processing any more of Crowley's information, she said: "We'd best be gettin' ready for Sexton's funeral, Sir. Most of the people will be walkin' to the church. There will be some cars runnin' back and forth for them as can't walk. Very few parkin' spots up there. Not enough for this affair." She started on her way back to the kitchen but paused part way and turned to face Crowley. "Some people are sayin' that Sexton ain't really dead, Sir. Some are expectin' 'im to wake up again. They say that it's 'appened before, accordin' to some letters and old diaries they've read."

"Well, Sarah, if Sexton wasn't dead before the post-mortem, I can assure you that he would have been before it was finished. But I would be most interested to see those letters and diaries. Do you think it could be arranged?" Sarah shook her head. "To tell the truth, Sir, I don't know if they really exist. There's always people who likes to talk big but claim they're sworn to secrecy or somethin' when pushed to prove what they're sayin'. Could be just a bunch of blow'ards. We've got our share o' them 'round 'ere, an' I think my ol' man's their leader."

"I suspect you're right, Sarah. Nevertheless, I would still appreciate it if you would enquire for me, discreetly of course. Just as a matter of interest, that is. Nothing official. Meantime, I must agree, it's time to get ready. Thank you again for breakfast." He rose and smiled at the troubled looking Sarah. "Thank you also for not mentioning this matter in front of Jamie, Sarah. I've learned that Sexton took Jamie 'under his wing' some time ago. The lad was very fond of him and will have a difficult enough time today without any of this business clouding the memory of his mentor."

"We all liked Jamie, Sir. Even before 'is change. We all liked Sexton too. Now it seems – if those diaries are right – the people of this village 'ave liked 'im for 'undreds of years on an' off. It's creepy really. But 'e was a good man."

CHAPTER 12

Sexton's funeral

part from some activity at The Seahorse Inn, where caterers were unloading supplies, the village appeared deserted during the funeral service. Sexton had arranged for his lawyers to rent the inn and cater for the mourners. The church and grounds were crowded. Father Eggleton had been concerned that the bizarre circumstances of Sexton's death might result in his friend's funeral being turned into a media circus. So far though, the reporters were being respectful and discreet and honouring his request that there be no cameras in the church and that they observe the boundary markers in the churchyard.

Father Eggleton was obviously distressed during the service. The fact that he was burying a close friend and mentor made things very difficult for him. He had struggled with his composure whilst Heather McDowd's father eulogised Sexton in glowing terms, giving him full credit for the recent beneficial changes in the village. McDowd's inspired eloquence was met with obvious approval, and there was hardly a dry eye in the congregation. Eventually, the last Amens were said, and the mourners dispersed, retiring to The Seahorse for refreshments. However, one very attractive, elegantly dressed, dark-skinned lady broke from the mourners to follow Father Eggleton's lonely figure as he returned to the church. She was a complete stranger to the village and obviously pregnant.

"Father!" she called, and, getting no response, called again, more loudly: "Father Eggleton! Father!" When Eggleton turned to face her, she saw that he was still struggling with his emotions. "I'm sorry, Father. My business can wait," she said and turned, intending to follow the departing crowd.

Eggleton called her back. "No! Please wait. How can I help you?"

She hesitated, seeming uncertain of how to respond. "Father, my name is Susan Latour. You wrote to my firm, Latour, Cook, and Sexton, to advise us of Sexton's death. In accordance with his instructions, I imagine." She gave a sad smile. "He was very organised. He also sent me a personal letter, advising me that you had assumed the responsibility of next-of-kin." She patted her tummy. "He wanted to spare me those duties because of my pregnancy. I should explain that Sexton and I are distantly related. But we were also close personal friends and business associates. A mutual ancestor founded our law firm nearly two hundred years ago. I'm sure you know that Latour, Cook, and Sexton have been looking after the financial and legal affairs of The Guiding Light Church ever since the founders gave us their first instructions. Those instructions were originally concerned with maintaining the oil supply for the lamps. So, although we may be strangers on a personal level, we do have a long-standing business relationship."

"Ah! I see," said Eggleton. "I must admit I know very little about those matters. It was Sexton's bailiwick, you see. What will become of those chores now?"

"Oh, no problem. Sexton has arranged continuity. The whole business of the tourist park is being managed by experts within our firm, as it has been since he conceived the idea. But we will be in touch with you and all other parties concerned to arrange a meeting and familiarise all involved with the details. However, what I really came for today has nothing to do with business. I wanted to pay my last respects and say goodbye to a dear friend. Also, to retrieve two family heirlooms, which he informally gifted to me and, which he states he left in your custody to await my collection."

"Ah, yes, of course, the ring and the crucifix. He told me before he went to Canada that when he passed on, someone would come for them. I had no idea it would be so soon. He didn't mention your name though, just said that you would present me with a letter." Susan Latour retrieved an envelope from her purse and gave it to Eggleton. There were four closely written pages in Sexton's familiar hand. Susan waited patiently until Eggleton had finished reading – and re-reading – certain parts of the letter. He kept glancing up at her with an expression of shocked disbelief. When Eggleton finally finished with the letter, he raised his head, seeming to be at a complete loss for words. He looked bewildered. It was Susan Latour that broke the silence.

"I know the contents of the letter, Father. It was in his own hand because he knew you were familiar with it and might disbelieve a typewritten copy. He also asked that I answer any questions that you have as best I can. He said a letter would never cover all of the questions it would provoke. Father Charlesworth and I were his only confidants in this matter. I also realise how this letter must conflict with your beliefs and training, even your knowledge of Sexton. But he felt that he owed you an explanation and – far-fetched though his story may seem – he knew that you already suspected that there was more than coincidence and human influence at work here. He was a good man and knew you were too. In fact, his actual words to me were: 'In Tim Eggleton, I have rediscovered an old friend. And I know that the village is safe and in good hands again.' Please don't be alarmed by the contents of the letter or concerned for the sanctity of your office or this church. You buried a good, God-fearing man here today. You need have no doubt that he belongs here in consecrated ground where he worked so tirelessly for this church and its congregation." Eggleton listened in stunned silence. Already shaken by the death of his friend and mentor, a man that he had felt inexplicably strong ties to, he had been 'blind-sided' by a totally unexpected revelation of Sexton's supernatural, and seemingly evil, connection. Eventually, with a slight shake of his head, he said: "Please come with me, Susan. The items he left for you are in his 'digs'. That's what he called his flat, here inside the church." He gently took her arm, and they walked into the church.

"Susan, this has been… a really bad day… and now this." I don't know how to handle it. Especially something… something like this," he waved the letter clenched in his fist. "But tell me, Susan: reincarnation and voodoo, do you believe in such things?" Susan just smiled. "Father, there are more things in heaven and earth…"

Once in the 'digs', Eggleton opened the centre drawer in Sexton's desk and retrieved an old leather pouch and a carved wooden crucifix. He shook his head again. "He always wore these around his neck. The villagers say he was never without them. You can imagine how surprised I was when I opened the letter he'd left for me and found that he'd left them here in his desk. It's as though he knew he'd not be coming back. Eggleton placed the crucifix on the desktop beside the leather pouch. Opening the drawstring on the pouch, he removed a gold wedding band and placed it on the pouch. Susan watched him uneasily. "Father, would you be kind enough to hand me the ring? And then, please burn the pouch." Eggleton looked up, startled. "Is this of the same substance as the letter?" he asked, looking very troubled. Susan nodded. "Yes, Father, but this is the last of it. I know the history of the pouch and have a particular loathing for it. But it can't harm anyone now. Sexton has tried to destroy that pouch many times. It wouldn't burn, and no matter how he tried to dispose of it, it always survived and was returned to him. Rather like the old door that stood outside this church for over two hundred years, it seems the pouch somehow represented evidence of Sexton's unintended pact with the demon. He was told by that demon that only after he'd fulfilled his part of their pact would it be possible for the pouch to be destroyed. It would be an indestructible link between them until then. It, and its contents, would always be returned to him. It appeared to be a communications link of sorts. There were times when, in sheer frustration, Sexton would try new ways of destroying the pouch, but he never managed it, and that always brought fast response from the demon, who made a point of returning the pouch himself. Sexton was never allowed to renege on his angry, unintentional pact. That angry, emotional expression of his was accepted as an offer to give his soul for a vengeful favour." She shrugged. "None of this would have happened but for that un-witting outburst. That pouch was the demon's contact to Latour. A tangible link that was instrumental in completing Latour's part of their so-called contract, to drown the captain in place of Sailmaker, who would then be reunited with his wife. Once the contract was completed, there would be no further need of the pouch, and it would lose its powers. Right now, my skin crawls just looking at it. I don't want to touch it, even though I'm sure that now, it really is just a dry piece of old leather."

Eggleton handed Susan the ring. She held it tightly in her hand, closing her eyes whilst she did so. She opened her eyes just in time to see Eggleton pick up the pouch and drop it into a large glass ashtray. "You shouldn't burn it here, Father. It will stink the place out." Eggleton began rummaging through the desk. "Do you have a light, Susan? I can't find a match or lighter here."

"Sorry, Father. I don't smoke. Too bad. I would love to see that thing burn. I guess it'll just have to wait. But it would be better to burn it outside. Or you could burn it in the wood stove," she nodded towards the fireplace.

"That makes sense, Susan. However, I don't know when we'll be lighting that fire again. I'll set the ashtray on the inside window ledge for now. When I find a match, I'll move the ashtray to the outside sill before I light it." He walked to the window. There were some three-ring binders on the deep window ledge. Eggleton cleared some space by stacking them on top of each other to make room for the ashtray. "Another pair of reading glasses," he said, holding them aloft for Susan to see. "These are just cheap magnifiers that you buy at the chemist's or supermarket. He would forget to carry them with him and have to buy another pair whilst he was out. He has left glasses all over the village. It seems to have been his one area of disorganisation." Eggleton placed the glasses on the top binder which, being only partially filled, had its cover sloped away from its wide spine and towards the ashtray. The spectacles started to slide down the inclined surface, and Eggleton had to catch and reset them carefully, so they didn't slide. Then he opened the casement window, saying: "A little fresh air wouldn't hurt."

Susan smiled as she offered the wedding ring back to him. "Would you please keep this safe for me, Father? As you can see, I'm pregnant. I hope you'll not think too badly of me when I tell you I'm not married. My common-law spouse, Jacob, wants us to get married. But I'm not sure yet that that is what I want. . . marriage, I mean. I'm still uncertain of how I feel about God and religion. Sexton kept encouraging me to marry. His beliefs were strong, but he got no help with this demon problem, and that caused me to lose faith in the triumph of good over evil. I abandoned any idea of a religious wedding, and I certainly don't place any value in a Registry office wedding. I don't need permission from a glorified clerk to sleep with my Jacob. To me, that is only an excuse for collecting taxes. And I'm sure you are aware how badly many marriages turn out these days. If I tie that knot, I want it to stay tied. . . and because we love each other. Not just because we signed a contract.

"However, now Sexton has been allowed to complete his cycle of life by dying, I'm hoping I might recover my faith again. According to his diaries, Sexton, aka Latour, suffered death many times but always recovered. He was never allowed to 'pass on'. I felt the demonic powers were being allowed too much control. If a good man like Sexton couldn't get God's help, what chance would a sinner like me have?" She shrugged, despairingly. "Our ancestors were missionaries, you know. There's been a strong religious thread throughout our family history, and I truly envy people the strength and courage that their faith gives them. But although I respect that in others, I can't find it for myself. However, now Sexton has been allowed to die and been buried – in consecrated ground – during a service presided over by his friend, a Christian priest, I believe his cycle of life and death might be properly restored. Perhaps now I might be able to recover the faith I was raised with and believe once more that good will triumph over evil. Then I would love to marry my Jacob. I know that would make him happy too." Eggleton was silent, standing like a lost soul before this stranger who had spent the last half hour shattering his understanding of life and death and shaking his religious beliefs. His confusion was obvious.

"Father," she continued: "if that happy day should come to pass, I would love to be married here by you, Sexton's friend, only if you could approve, of course. It would be a quiet wedding with just a few friends and family, nothing fancy. She patted her tummy. "Just not appropriate." Her confident smile had disappeared and was replaced with a look of concern as she stared anxiously into the vicar's face. Eggleton realised that this was the only time that her self-assured manner had deserted her since they'd met. There was a short silence whilst he filtered her words through his troubled mind. Eventually, he smiled and said: "When you are ready, Susan, I would be very happy to perform that ceremony. And I'm sure that Sexton would rejoice at that prospect too, knowing that the continuity established by your ancestor's wedding ring will help make your relationship a happy and enduring one. But shouldn't you try it on? It may not fit. It might possibly need some adjustment."

"Oh, no! It will fit. I know that. And I want to wear it for the first time when Jacob puts it on my finger. I would really appreciate it if you would keep it safe for me until that time. If that happy day should come to pass, perhaps you could give it to our best man just before the ceremony. It would be devastating to lose it now." Eggleton smiled, albeit rather wearily. He tucked the ring into a pocket in his wallet. "I shall lock this in my office safe until that happy day then, Susan." He then picked up the carved wooden crucifix and handed it to her. She pressed it to her cheek as she had done with other items from Sexton's desk. "This was hand-carved by Paul Latour," she said, "the man who married my missionary ancestor, Louise Gooding, in Haiti over two hundred years ago. I'll always treasure it."

The vicar could not rid himself of the fears that Sexton's letter had burdened him with. "Susan," he said, "I'm badly shaken by all that I've learned today. I don't know how to say this, except to come right out with it. Latour – Sexton –made a deal with the devil. He sold his soul for a vengeful favour. How can he possibly hope to find peace?" Susan smiled, and nodded her understanding. "Father, I felt the same way as you do until I spoke with

Sexton's friend, Father Charlesworth. He was the Catholic priest who died in Canada on that same day as Sexton. He had spent his life researching reincarnation theories, with all the resources of his church at his disposal. He believed that he too had lived past lives and that some of those might have been 'bad' lives. He also sensed that he and Sexton had shared time together in an earlier life. Why else would they have been drawn together across all those miles? It seems now that the demon set that up. However, Charlesworth strongly believed in redemption. He knew that he, himself, had lived well in the service of God and mankind and thought it was for more than just this life. He and Sexton had become close friends, more like loving brothers really. They both realised, each with their own different perspective, that despite any theatrical by-play, something momentous would happen that day. I know that Charlesworth rejected Sexton's theories regarding the outcome. And we also know that Sexton was counting on Charlesworth bringin' Jamie back to Ryeport, so he too was unaware that his friend would perish.

"It really bothered him that he didn't know which of the reincarnated souls at the building site Captain Currie was. He believed that Whitt was Currie's reincarnation because of their similar characters. Whitt really was a louse of a man. I imagine you are thinking that this is all irrelevant since Sexton has committed his soul to hell for all eternity. Am I right?" Susan searched Eggleton's troubled features. He appeared befuddled by this new, seemingly sacrilegious ground that they were covering. Susan continued, "Those were certainly my feelings, and I expressed those views to Father Charlesworth last year when he stayed with us whilst attending seminars in London. I was sure that Sexton's commitment was a done deal and totally irreversible. But Father Charlesworth told me: 'Your mistake Susan stems from believing that Sexton's soul is his to give or deal away. It isn't. It belongs to God, his Creator. If something doesn't belong to you, you can offer to give it away, but it really isn't yours to give. You have only been given the right to use it – but not the right, or power, to re-gift it. If God were to consider your soul to have no value, might He allow you to give it away? Possibly! Who knows? However, if a good soul, such as Sexton, who has apparently suffered several deaths – often in the service of others – and done only good deeds in all his time – how could his soul be considered unworthy of redemption? Remember the scripture: 'There is more joy in heaven over one sinner that repenteth'…" Susan's eyes searched Eggleton's face for some sign of agreement, but he was still analysing her comments.

"Susan. I really don't know if I can buy this reincarnation theory at all. I'm confused. And if I were to try any of these theories on my colleagues, I'm sure I'd be dumped on the bishop's scrapheap without ceremony. How could we possibly ever know if Sexton and Charlesworth were forgiven, and not condemned to hell!"

"Well, Charlesworth's soul was never part of the deal. I have no doubt that he will be reborn in the normal routine. If I might be forgiven for using the word 'routine' to describe such a miraculous event. I know Sexton was hoping to be forgiven and reborn too. It had never been his intention to strike a deal with the devil. Grabbing that pouch was just a frustrated and unwitting response to a vile and unjust situation. He had no way of knowing that the Bokor's pouch was a 'direct line' to the demon. He kept it only as a convenient and safe place for his valuables. He had long since dumped the bits and pieces that he believed to be voodoo spell casting material." She paused briefly, looking pensive. "As far as Sexton letting us know that he's okay," she shrugged. "Who can say? But knowing Sexton, I'd be surprised if he didn't find a way."

The vicar held his head in both hands. "Susan. This is too much for me to soak up. And you must be exhausted. Forgive me. I haven't even had the courtesy to offer you a chair or some refreshment. And with you carrying a baby too. I'm so sorry."

"No need to apologise, Father. I'm a strong girl, and if I'd needed a chair, I wouldn't be slow to ask for one. Now, if it's okay with you, perhaps I could drive you down to the inn. Then you could introduce me to some of the villagers. I think I could do some serious damage to the refreshments being offered there. I'm famished. By the way, I see no need to discuss our conversation with anyone else. Do you?" Eggleton shook his head as he made his way around the desk. "Even if I had the inclination, Susan, and I certainly do not, I wouldn't know where to begin."

"Father, Sexton was hoping that you would destroy his letter once you had read it."

"Certainly, Susan, I wouldn't want this to fall into anyone else's hands. I can just imagine what the press would do with it if they got hold of it. I'll burn it with the pouch." He crumpled the pages and slid them under the pouch in the ashtray. Then he took Susan's arm to lead her from the church. They had only gone a few feet when a sudden gust of wind slammed the casement window closed, startling them both. The rain was still spattering on the window, but suddenly the room brightened. The vibration had caused Sexton's reading glasses to begin sliding slowly on the inclined binder cover, and Eggleton made a move towards the window. "Excuse me, Susan, I'd better lock that window; we wouldn't want the letter or the pouch to disappear before we burn them."

Just then a bright shaft of sunlight shone through the window, brightening the room and highlighting the binders. Susan caught his arm. "Wait, Father. Please don't touch anything." They stood watching quietly as the reading glasses slid to a stop and focused a small spot of sunlight on the crumpled letter in the ashtray. "Please wait," she said, in a hushed voice. They stood silently for several seconds, and Eggleton could feel her trembling through her tense grip on his arm. They became aware of a faint smell of scorching that was soon followed by a thin wisp of smoke that rose lazily from the focused spot of light on the letter. Then that wisp of smoke became a tiny flame that suddenly erupted into a fire that engulfed the leather pouch. "It smells like a farriery in here," said Eggleton, watching the thin, dry, leather pouch collapse in a small mound of smouldering ash. "Sexton's reading glasses slid down the binder and focused the sun's rays on his letter," he said in amazement. "What possible odds could anyone attribute to that?"

Susan squeezed his hand and smiled. "Especially as the clouds parted only long enough for the sun to light the letter, and then the storm started again." They stood and looked at each other silently for a few minutes, and then Susan spoke. "I shall call you next week, Father: About our wedding, I mean."

THE END

ABOUT THE AUTHOR

Les was born in London, England in 1930. He, and his wife Joyce, immigrated to Ontario, Canada in 1965 where they raised their family in the scenic Hockley Valley.

Les was always a gifted storyteller who entertained family and friends regularly with his embellished versions of classic fairy tales and a host of made up words that he used to make every day conversation more colourful.

His first novel became a labour of love during his retirement years and was nearing completion when he suffered a serious stroke which robbed him of his wonderful communication skills. Happily with the help of his family, the original version, *The Fo'c's'le Door*, was published in 2013 and he was able to hold a copy in his hands prior to his death in 2016.

It is a long and captivating mystery involving adventures in smuggling, murder and the supernatural and met with great reviews from those who read it.

The Ryeport Redemption is a republication by his family of the original novel, with the help of a new publisher, in order to give this wonderful adventure the recognition it deserves. It is an opportunity for them to complete this part of his legacy and share their Dad's imagination and storytelling skills with the world in honour of his memory.

lescribb.com
https://www.facebook.com/AuthorLesCribb/

With every donation, a voice will be given to
the creativity that lies within the hearts of
our children living with diverse challenges.

By making this difference, children that may
not have been given the opportunity to have their
Heart Heard will have the freedom to create
beautiful works of art and musical creations.

Donate by visiting

HeartstobeHeard.com

We thank you.